Law Of Love

Lottie Moore

Law Of Love

This book is written in British English, but is set in America with American characters meaning phrases and some spellings may differ.

This book contains mature themes such as descriptions of violence and gore, murder, PTSD, trauma and assault (not between the FMC and MMC). It is intended for an 18+ audience.

Dedication

Wounds take time to heal, and that's okay.

One: Freya

My head shot up as my mother yanked the car door open, clambering in to shelter from the violent downpour outside. Her hair was sopping wet from the few seconds she had spent running to my vehicle, causing me to laugh.

"That was fast," I said, turning on the heating system. "I thought you'd be a lot longer than that."

My mom shrugged. "When you've been waiting for as long as I have to divorce your father, the papers practically sign themselves."

Gazing at her, I sighed, partly in relief but also in sorrow. It was official. My parents had been talking about divorcing for years. However, I never truly believed they'd actually do it, secretly hoping they would work out whatever was coming between them for the sake of our family. But I knew better.

They weren't happy together, and I was no longer a child. They didn't need to put me first to give me a somewhat 'normal' childhood. Although, if going to bed and hearing your parents yell at each other every night about how much they hated each other was considered 'normal', they did me a favour by staying together.

"Oh, honey, come here," she cooed, reaching over the handbrake to embrace me.

"Mom, seriously, I'm fine. I'm twenty-two years old," I reassured her, forcing a laugh as I drove. "I can handle it." There was nothing I could do to change the inevitable—even though I didn't want to accept that my family was now officially broken. "Have you heard from him? I thought he was supposed to be back by now." I briefly glanced at my phone, disappointed that my father hadn't replied to the last few texts I'd sent him—nor had he answered my calls.

My mom rolled her eyes. "You know what he's like, Freya. Working is his life. He's likely just booked a fancy hotel somewhere and is staying an extra few nights. He'll come back soon, and then he can get moving out sorted."

"Maybe." I sighed, aggravated. I constantly felt as if I was out of the loop when it came to my father. His communication skills were shoddy. He hadn't been around a lot, especially as I got older. He'd often disappear on lavish business trips with colleagues and not return for weeks at a time, forgetting to update us on his whereabouts.

I hadn't had a proper conversation with him in years, and anytime I tried to speak to him, he brushed me off like I was a major pain in his ass. His desire to spend time with us had dwindled to the point of non-existence.

"How's that new boyfriend of yours?" my mother asked once we pulled into our driveway.

My eyes widened, and I shook my head, laughing awkwardly as I waited for her to unlock the front door to the house. "Mom, he's not my boyfriend."

She held up her hands defensively before continuing to rummage around in her bag. "Where are these damn keys?"

I cocked my head, my eyebrows furrowing once I noticed that the front door was slightly ajar. I pushed it, stepping inside the house, my soggy shoes leaving brown footprints on the elegantly tiled flooring.

"Dad? Is that you?" I called out, almost jumping out of my skin, when a bald man dressed in a tight black T-shirt and smart pants stepped into the hallway. His eyebrows raised in displeasure at our arrival; his form stood tall, his chest puffed out.

"Please don't be alarmed, ladies. My name is Officer Barkle from the Virginian R.S.A," he said huskily, reaching into his pocket and pulling out a badge.

My eyes narrowed suspiciously, and my mom cleared her throat from behind me, folding her arms across her chest.

"What are you doing in my house?"

"Are you Mrs Henderson?" questioned Officer Barkle, to which my mother nodded in response.

"Excuse me, sweetheart," came a voice beside me, and I turned to see two men waddling out of the kitchen, their muscles contracting as they attempted to hold up our large silver fridge between their chests. They slipped past us and headed for the front door, causing my heart to skip a beat.

"What are you doing with all our stuff?" I asked with panic as another man in uniform strolled past me. He clutched a few pieces of our priceless artwork in his hands and offered me a pitiful smile before dropping eye contact.

"This house and everything in it is being repossessed."

My face blanched. "What do you mean, repossessed? Why?"

Reaching into his back pocket, Officer Barkle pulled out multiple pieces of paper, handing them to my mother. "These are all copies of the warning letters sent to you about paying your long outstanding debt. You can see that the latest letter was dated the twenty-ninth of October, which was four weeks ago today. It states that if nothing is paid in those four weeks, then the house and the majority of your furniture in it will be repossessed to pay your balance."

My mother's face was a mask of pure shock and despair, and she shook her head fiercely. "No, there has to be a mistake. We don't have any debt."

"I'm afraid you do, Ma'am," he responded, pointing to the letter, my mother's mouth popping open as she read over the printed words—bold and red.

"I've never seen these before."

"They were addressed to both you and your husband and were delivered to this address."

"Please, just wait!" pleaded my mother as two more men lugged out our small loveseat couch—the very one I'd fallen asleep on the other night, having spent hours talking on the phone to Zach. "Let me just call my husband, please!"

"You're more than welcome to call him, Mrs Henderson. But I'm afraid we've received no payment from you after three warning letters, so we need to proceed with the repossession."

I watched hopefully as my mother pressed her phone to her ear, her shaky hands pushing her blonde hair out of her face as she pleaded with my father to reply.

But, of course, he didn't... like usual.

"Where are we supposed to go?" she demanded, shaking her head in disbelief.

Officer Barkle shrugged. "Unfortunately, I don't get involved with that aspect, but I'm sure you have plenty of people you could call who would be kind enough to house you temporarily." He gazed around the house, gesturing to the high foyer and sparkling chandelier.

Our house wasn't massive, but it was bigger than most. My father was adamant about filling it with expensive furniture and purchasing the latest TVs and computers. He earned enough to afford it and was a materialistic person—the opposite of my mother and I.

My mom glared at the officer, muttering to herself as she began typing on her phone furiously, biting harshly on her lower lip. "I'll try and sort something out."

The next hour went by quickly. Mom and I packed our necessities and clothes in our suitcases at lightning speed, having been told that some of our belongings could remain in the house for a while—something I was thankful for, considering we didn't have the means to move everything out at such short notice.

"Why can't we just stay at Granny's?" I questioned with a frown as I pulled up beside my mother's car along the road, hopping out.

"Freya, that's almost a two-hour drive," tutted my mother, shaking her head. "How do you expect to get to college and for me to get to work every day? Besides, Jackie has been very kind in allowing us to stay until we can get this all sorted."

Jackie was a close friend of my mother's—having met many years ago at work. They'd clicked instantly and were almost inseparable at one point but had since slightly drifted apart.

"You're here!" called Jackie from her front porch, making her way down the stairs and engulfing my mother in a hug, sending me a wink.

"Jackie, we honestly can't thank you enough for allowing us to stay," muttered my mom, causing Jackie to dismiss her with a quick wave and a smile.

"Oh my goodness, look how grown up you are, Freya! You're so beautiful!"

I beamed, thanking her apprehensively before popping the trunk of my car open and dragging out my large suitcase.

Jackie ushered my mother and me inside, and I gazed around at the interior in curiosity—the walls a clean cream colour and the furniture following a neutral beige theme. It was cosy.

"Freya, are you okay with the room upstairs on the right? It's pretty bare, but I'm sure you could spruce it up with a few of your things. There's lots of closet space," Jackie told me.

"Of course, thank you." I pulled out my phone, staring at it desperately, longing for any response from my father to appear before my eyes.

Freya: Dad, where are you? Please reply. It's important.

I studied the message I'd sent mere minutes ago, looking pathetically at my other six texts, all following the same woeful thesis. My brows furrowed as I cursed under my breath.

"I've got pizza on the way."

Jackie's words caused my stomach to growl, and I took in my mom's glorious grin. She hadn't smiled that way in what seemed like forever, and I knew she was excited to have an excuse to spend more time with one of her old best friends—even if it was under dire circumstances.

My ears perked up as the doorbell sounded, and Jackie nodded at me to open the door as she hauled some plates out from the cabinet. I hesitantly pulled it open, my fingers gripping the wood tightly, my heart skipping a beat. I took in the beautiful man standing before me, his thick brows furrowed as he peered down at me in confusion.

He was one hell of a pizza delivery guy... who didn't have pizza.

My body seized up as I studied him, my throat feeling dry, and his eyes scanned my body before he huffed, our gazes locking.

His eyes were intense—a piercing grey. So grey it looked like a deadly thunderstorm was brewing in them, waves of irritation ready to pin me to the ocean's bottom.

"Are you just going to stand there, or are you going to let me into my house?" he complained, his voice husky and intimidating.

I felt Jackie's presence behind me, and I stepped aside, regaining the feeling in my feet once again.

"Kaleb?" she whispered, clearly shocked, suddenly engulfing the muscular man in a hug.

He smiled tiredly as he pushed his dark hair out of his face, scratching at the slight stubble on his chin. His eyes met mine for the second time, perplexity crowding them.

He was tall—extremely tall—probably around six foot four or five, and his broad shoulders almost reached both sides of the wooden doorframe. He gripped his bags in his spare hand—it looked like he was returning from a trip of some sort.

"Kaleb, I wasn't expecting you for another two weeks! You didn't tell me you were coming back so soon!" exclaimed Jackie, causing him to shrug and step into the house. His combat boots hit the flooring with loud thuds.

"We took Christmas break early." The overhead light fixated on the wall beamed down onto his veiny and tattooed arms, the spiralling ink detailed and intricately drawn, catching my attention.

"You look exhausted." Jackie frowned, closing the door quickly to keep the unwanted bitter evening air from entering.

"I've been driving for seven hours," the non-pizza delivery guy, Kaleb, said, his eyes still on me questionably. He dropped his bags, his eyebrows knitting together as he took in my large suitcase by the front door. It caused his jaw to flex—so sharp it could cut ice.

"Well, you must be hungry. I've got pizza arriving soon." Jackie gestured for him to sit at the table, his tall form doing so slowly. But even sitting down, Kaleb was almost as tall as me—or at least the intimidation oozing from him made it feel like he was.

"I'm sorry, you are? Staring is impolite." His attention was on me, his tone blunt as he watched me with a cocked brow, seemingly agitated by my presence.

Surely I hadn't done anything to offend him in the past thirty seconds?

"This is Sarah and her daughter, Freya. Sarah is a good friend of mine, and they ran into some trouble, so they're going to stay with us for a little while." Jackie smiled before turning to us. "This is my son, Kaleb."

"Trouble?" he repeated, narrowing his eyes and daring me to elaborate.

I shrugged, shifting my weight from foot to foot as he looked me over. I didn't appreciate his passive aggressiveness. "We're sorting it."

He leaned back in his chair, folding his arms across his chest as he hummed, giving me one last judgmental look before turning away. "Well, that sounds promising."

The sarcastic bastard.

"Kaleb, I haven't seen you since you were about eighteen." My mother laughed, trying to change the subject.

I knew Jackie had children, but I'd never met them personally. I was rather glad I hadn't, though—given Kaleb's intimidating and moody aura.

Despite that, I couldn't help but allow my eyes to study his well-structured face. He had naturally carved brows, high cheekbones, and plump lips. His skin was tanned and smooth, and his thick muscles bulged out of his black T-shirt.

I wasn't aware of the scowl that had formed on my face from his bitter comment and my lack of self-control when it came to ogling him until Kaleb cleared his throat.

"Something the matter?" he questioned huskily as he ran his tongue along the front of his teeth, his jaw taut and expression unimpressed.

I cleared my throat, feeling it tighten slightly. People didn't easily frustrate me, but for some reason, my patience felt like it was collapsing under Kaleb's blazing gaze. "I don't see see why you're–"

"So, what are you doing now, Kaleb?" my mother interrupted me, shooting me a pointed glare as Jackie made her way to the door at the sound of the doorbell, an excited intake of breath sounding from her lips at the prospect of steaming hot pizza.

"I'm a bodyguard. We work for a private company hired by the government," Kaleb stated, grabbing a bottle of whiskey from the mantelpiece, pouring himself a hefty glass, and taking a large sip. He clicked his tongue as he looked between my mother and me with indifference.

What had crawled up his asshole?

"Oh, law enforcement. Wow, that must be a lot of hard work."

Kaleb nodded once at my mom's comment, his suspicious eyes on me. They trailed down to my messy dark hair that lay over my shoulder—my collarbone slightly on show—and my body suddenly felt hot. Yanking my baggy sweatshirt back up, I dropped my gaze, not enjoying how attractive I found this man despite his ignorant attitude.

I twiddled my thumbs under the table as we all sat down, digging into the pizza. Jackie and my mother had already taken their seats, leaving the only spare chair beside Kaleb, causing my nostrils to flare. The irritation was pouring from him—so strong it was constricting.

I probably looked like an absolute mess, and I cursed at myself for choosing to dress in my old tattered sweatpants and sweatshirt—sporting the mentally exhausted look. Kaleb, however, looked put together in his clean and crease-free dark attire despite the fact that he'd been driving in a stuffy car for hours.

"I'm sorry that we're intruding, Kaleb," my mom said in between bites, flashing him a small smile. "We'll be out of your hair soon."

"Here's hoping." He held up his glass and jostled it, the corner of his lip curling upwards slightly before he took a sip. The comment was easy to pass off as a joke, but I knew it had an underlying dose of truth to it. It caused me to furrow my brows at him, unhappy with his standoffish behaviour.

I hadn't known Kaleb very long, but I didn't like him already. He was rude and obnoxious, so why the hell was he making my stomach flip? I needed to pull myself together. He was an attractive man—so what?

"Sarah, Freya, I forgot to say, spare blankets are in the cupboard at the top of the stairs if you need them before bed. I know it's supposed to be cold tonight," Jackie mentioned.

"Where are you sleeping?" asked Kaleb with interest, his eyes flicking over to the couch that was definitely not big enough for the both of us.

"Sarah's in the guest bedroom, and I thought Freya could stay in Brie's old room."

Kaleb's body tensed up at the mention of the name *Brie.* His face was a picture of animosity and fury as he remained frozen, his fingers digging into his pizza crust a little too harshly, grease dripping from it and splattering down onto the table.

"I thought we said we would leave the room untouched." He ground his teeth together, suddenly dropping his pizza on his plate, pushing his chair back and standing. The metal scraped against the wooden floor, a harsh sound filling the room.

"Kaleb, I've already—"

"I've lost my appetite." He knocked back the rest of his whisky, his knuckles white. I watched in concern as he disappeared upstairs, and Jackie released a heavy sigh as she shook her head.

I hadn't even been here an hour, but I was already dreading spending another second here with Kaleb Evans.

Two: Freya

I glared at my reflection in the mirror, unhappy with my appearance despite the effort and time I'd dedicated to making myself look presentable today. No matter how many times I redid my make-up, I still wasn't happy with it—it either seemed too much or not enough. There was no in-between.

Why was I so worked up over how I looked, anyway?

After angrily wiping it off, I combed through my freshly washed hair, grabbing my laptop and college work. Shoving them into my backpack, I muttered a string of curse words. Since the other night, I'd been in a foul mood.

Kaleb had made it clear he didn't want my mother and me here, and he was nothing if not unwelcoming. I didn't understand his problem, and it riled me up, knowing we had done nothing to warrant this behaviour. Hearing I was staying in Brie's room had been his final straw.

I felt awkward sleeping in a bed that wasn't mine, but the room was cute and cosy. The walls were painted blush pink, and the décor was minimal. Jackie had explained how she'd cleaned it out around two months ago, and although I didn't know who Brie was, I refrained from asking questions. It was clearly a touchy subject.

I made my way down the steps, not looking forward to seeing Kaleb, fully expecting him to subject me to copious snide remarks and judgemental glances. But luckily for me, he was nowhere to be seen.

"Mom, I'm leaving," I called, smiling when she popped her head around the corner from the kitchen, her arm soon following her to give me a quick wave.

After pulling my car keys out of my pocket, I unlocked my small vehicle and hopped in, turning on the ignition. However, I cringed when it made a loud cracking noise, the engine sounding like it smoked a packet a day.

"Are you kidding me?" I hissed to myself, allowing my forehead to fall forward onto the solid material of the steering wheel, defeat hitting me like a ton of bricks.

What a great way to start an already shitty day.

Shoving the key into the ignition one more time, laughing in disbelief when it made the same abominable sound, I scrambled out of my car, slamming the door shut with fury.

"Freya?" questioned Jackie as she finished her toast, grabbing her own car keys from the hook by the door. "Are you okay?"

"My car has decided it wants to test me today," I grumbled, tucking my wet hair behind my ears, my lips down-turned.

"Oh, I've got a meeting I'm already really late for, but I'm sure Kaleb could take you," suggested Jackie as she gazed up towards the stairs, raising her eyebrows at her son, who came rushing down, his face stone-cold. His hair was wet—fresh from a shower.

"I'm busy," he said, making his way past us, refusing to make eye contact, jumping into his Jeep and reversing off the driveway. His tyres screeched against the slippery gravel as he pulled out onto the road, disappearing.

Jackie stood with her hand on her hip, glaring towards where Kaleb's expensive car once was, clearly not impressed. Shaking her head, she muttered a quick *sorry* to me before her tall frame ducked through the doorway, pulling the hood of her coat up over her head.

I sighed, my eyes bulging once I noticed the time on the living room clock. I was going to be late, and my lecturer wouldn't be impressed—he'd dealt with my tardiness more than a few times this month.

"Honey, I would take you, but it's the opposite direction from my office," said my mom, offering me a small smile.

"No, don't worry," I assured her, sighing. "I can walk."

"Have a great day." She planted a quick kiss on the side of my face before walking out of the door.

Exiting the house, I huffed as the gale of wind slapped me in the face, whirling my hair around violently. I pulled out my phone as I trudged along the sidewalk in the rain, feeling anger radiate throughout my body as I read through the messages I'd sent my father.

Clicking on his name—scowling at the irritating buzzing noise as I called him again—I sighed as the seconds passed. But, just as I was about to give up, the ringing stopped, indicating that the line had been connected.

"Hello? Dad?" I exclaimed over the pounding precipitation, plugging my other ear with my finger. "Are you there?"

I sped up my pace, my heart pumping erratically as I waited for my father's response, but all that could be heard were a few laboured breaths. The line quickly went dead, leaving me staring at my phone in shock.

Had he seriously just hung up on me?

Putting it down to poor connection, I attempted to ring him again as I jogged through the storm, grunting in frustration when my bid to contact him again was sent straight to voicemail.

"You dick," I muttered, making the rest of the journey to college, sighing in relief once I stepped inside my block.

"Freya?" came a deep voice from behind me, and I turned to see Zach leaning against his locker, his face masked with sympathy as he took in my shivering form. "You missed the first half of our lecture."

"I know." I sighed, glancing at the clock.

So much for wanting to be on time this year.

"Why are you all wet?"

"My car wouldn't start. I had to walk."

"You could have asked me for a ride." He smiled at me, his dimples becoming more prominent. Zach was a beautiful man. There was no doubt about it. But a clean type of beautiful. He wasn't rugged or mysterious—just commonly handsome.

"You would have already been here by the time I asked you."

Zach and I had been getting to know each other for the past couple of weeks—his infectious smile and easy-going attitude made him straightforward to talk to. We weren't officially together and hadn't closed ourselves off to other people—yet to have that discussion.

Zach was a nice guy but enjoyed talking about himself—a lot. I'd told myself I was going to give him a chance, though. I was getting a little too good at cutting guys off to protect myself, and all it gained me was yet another evening alone with my sketchpad.

"Freya, you're soaked!" called Hannah as she turned the corner, a huge paper cup of coffee gripped between her fingers, dark bags evident under her soft hazel eyes.

"And you look like shit." I laughed.

She rolled her eyes, taking a sip of her drink, gulping loudly. "I'm running on one hour of sleep and am struggling to stay awake. This," she said, jostling her cup, "is the only thing keeping me together right now."

I rolled my eyes with a smile. It was never a dull day when my bundle of energy best friend was involved.

"Do you want to do anything tonight?" she asked, raising a brow at me. "The usual cringy romance movie marathon at yours?"

"I'm not staying at mine right now, remember?" I mumbled, causing Zach to smile sadly at me.

"Your dad will come back in the next few days and sort all this crap out," he reassured me, his hand delicately grazing my lower back. "I'm sure of it."

I tried my best to appear hopeful.

The rest of the college day dragged by, and I was grateful that I'd only received a few choice words from my lecturer. Although, by the time the day was over and Zach offered me a ride home, my clothes were still soggy, my bones shivering.

"Thanks for driving me."

"Can't let a girl like you walk home in this weather." As Zach parked outside Jackie's house, he turned to me, his large hand swarming my thigh, clutching it seductively. "Maybe I could come inside for a bit?"

My legs clenched together at the question, and my stomach twisted at how forward Zach was being. Our relationship hadn't stretched as far as being overly intimate yet, and my mind ran back to last week when a few girls in my class claimed Zach was a horny bastard. I wasn't a fan of meaningless sex. I'd done it in the past, and it just didn't benefit me.

"It's not my house," I said, shrugging.

"It's two o'clock. Will anyone be home?" Zach pushed, his hand moving higher up my leg, tracing dainty patterns.

"I don't know Jackie's working schedule," I lied. She actually worked nine-to-five, five days a week, but Zach was pissing me off, his persistent push to be more intimate over the past week irking me deeply. The fact that he was so eager for it to happen made me want to delay it further.

"Okay, fine." He sighed, dropping his hand and offering me a deflated smile.

I thanked him, quickly entering the house, and my stomach lurched at the idea that he only wanted me for one thing. He claimed he loved how bubbly and self-assured I was, but was it all a lie just to get in my pants?

"Fuck," I muttered to myself, closing my eyes, leaning my head back against the front door.

"Didn't put you as one to use that sort of language."

I gasped at the voice, snapping my eyes open to see Kaleb standing before me with his arms folded. He was dressed in a black long-sleeved workout top and pants, the tight-fitting material causing my throat to bob. Every muscle was visible.

"How would you know? We've been in each other's presence for a total of five minutes." I narrowed my eyes at him, causing him to huff. Technically, that wasn't true, but it sure as hell felt like it with the little amount we'd conversed.

"Five minutes too long," he responded. His eyes were resentful, but my snappy response had caused his lip to twitch upwards slightly, the small action making me tilt my head. "Why are you soaking wet?"

His question left me gesturing towards the rain-splattered window. "Because it's pouring outside? My car is broken, so I had to walk to college."

Kaleb nodded once before he pulled out his phone and began typing furiously, scowling at the screen in annoyance. "What do you take?"

"What?" I asked in confusion, and he shook his head at me.

"College. What do you take?" he repeated crabbily.

"Oh, umm, Fine Art."

Kaleb cocked his head at me and hummed. "Right, so you want to be what? A painter? A designer?"

I felt sheepish. I hated answering this question because I actually didn't know what I wanted to do yet. Art was something I loved, and I wasn't half-bad at it. The art world was where I belonged, but it was pinpointing where that was the tricky part. There were so many routes to take and I felt like I was floating along without a clear path to take. Art was my calling, but failure frightened me. I often felt like I was the only person in the world without a foolproof plan. "At the moment, I teach children art once a week, but it's not what I want to do long-term. I mean, I would love any career involving creativity. It just depends on what comes my way."

"Comes your way?" Kaleb raised a brow. "Life doesn't work like that."

"It's just a saying, but thanks for the tip, Mr Sunshine."

"So, you like kids?"

I dipped my chin. "Yeah, I do. They can be a handful, but I enjoy it."

Kaleb's opened his mouth to speak but growled as his phone rang. "What?" he snapped to the person on the other end of the line, cursing to himself as they spoke. "No, I told you I don't want anyone in my house."

I raised my eyebrows questionably, his voice like gravel, and I moved past him to head for the stairs. I needed a warm shower. That, and being under Kaleb's intense gaze was making me unsteady on my feet. How could somebody's eyes hold so much emotion?

"Fuck. Fine, but I swear to God, Brent, keep it small," Kaleb muttered. "I want everyone gone by eleven."

I craned my neck to look at him. He'd ended the call and was studying me. "We have the house to ourselves tonight, and *apparently*, I'm having people over." He huffed. "If you're going to come down, try not to do or say anything to embarrass yourself."

I mentally cringed, my nostrils flaring.

Ouch.

Three: Kaleb

The house was silent. I'd expected Freya to be louder, but I could barely tell that she was upstairs besides occasionally hearing her hum or patter around inside Brie's bedroom.

My fists clenched at the thought.

My mother had lied to me. She'd told me we were going to leave Brie's room as it was, and instead of sticking to her word, she'd moved all of her belongings out and stowed them away in the attic like they were junk. Not only that, but some unknown girl was staying in there—sleeping in Brie's old bed. Folding her clothes away in *her* chest of drawers. Using *her* mirror.

Freya Henderson.

The five foot five dark-haired beauty that had infiltrated my home. She was too attractive for her own good, and the heated blush on her cheeks when her eyes met mine for the first time was branded into my brain.

I'd picked up on even the smallest of details about her. Her purple-painted nails that were slightly chipped. The small line of freckles dotted over the top of her nose. The tiny scar that ran through the end of her eyebrow—looking like a childhood injury of some sort.

She was a hell of a nuisance, though. A royal pain in my ass.

My mother didn't go into much detail about why Freya and her mom were here, letting me know there was a mix-up with some debt and that it would be sorted soon. The last thing we needed in this house were people who had issues with money, though. My father had been a gambler, and it hadn't got him very far in life. He was a loser, a nobody, a waste of space.

The sound of the doorbell dragged me from my daydream, and I yanked the door open with a scowl to see Brent wearing a cheesy grin—multiple people behind him. Stepping aside with a grimace, I clutched Brent's shirt and dragged him to the side as people filed in.

"You call this small?" I demanded. "Why the fuck is Maggie here?"

I glared at the tall brunette as she settled on my couch, stealing curious glances at me every few seconds.

Brent shrugged. "You slept with her years ago, Kaleb, and she's good friends with everyone here. I didn't think it would be an issue."

"Well, you thought wrong." I pushed past him and entered the kitchen, pulling myself a beer from the fridge.

Maggie wasn't somebody I wanted to see again. Nor was she someone I thought I would. We were nothing—simply just a one-night stand, but she hadn't left me alone for months after.

Music filled the room, and I mentally groaned, turning around to glare at the people who stood in my kitchen. I knew everyone here, but I hadn't spoken to most of them since leaving to join my bodyguard organisation.

Parties had never been my thing, but after entering the law enforcement profession, discipline and self-restraint had become second nature to me. I didn't take part in anything that didn't benefit me.

And parties definitely didn't.

"Kaleb."

I gazed at Maggie over the top of my beer bottle, arching an eyebrow at her as she smiled up at me.

"How've you been? I haven't heard from you in a while." Her tone was flirtatious. Seductive. Needy.

"Fine." I looked away from her, leaning back against the wall. Not only was Maggie a possessive lunatic, but she was also a nasty piece of work. I'd seen the way she treated other girls, and frankly, she was a bitch.

A pretty bitch, but still a bitch.

"You didn't tell me you were coming back," she continued, and I resisted the urge to tell her to get the hell out of my house. This was her circle, though, and it had been mine once too. But not anymore. What was the point of getting drunk every weekend? It was all these people knew how to do—besides Brent, who actually possessed this handy little thing called self-control.

"There's a reason for that," I responded coldly, turning away from her and heading into the living room.

I was going to kill Brent.

Four: Freya

The music's thumping vibrated the bedroom floor, aggravating me and making it extremely hard to concentrate on my work. Kaleb didn't have that many people over—probably only around eight or nine—but they were so loud that it sounded like he was having a full-blown party downstairs.

I was attempting to finish a sketch I had spent the past few weeks on, continuously deciding I hated it and starting again. However, this time, I was happy with the shading and detailed lines I'd faintly drawn, and I got to work slowly, worried I was going to ruin my efforts for the fourth time.

My pencil glided across the page effortlessly, the stress of everything melting away as I was utterly consumed in my own world.

But it didn't last long.

A symphony of laughing outside the bedroom caused my fingers to falter, and I dropped my pad and pencil. Pulling open the door, I saw three girls standing behind it with confused expressions.

"Oh, sorry," one of them said, causing her tipsy friends to laugh.

"We were just looking for a bathroom to do this in," said the girl to my right, pulling out a small bag filled with white powder from her bra.

I paused for a few seconds, shaking my head and releasing a deep breath. "The bathroom is down the hall and to the right."

Who was I to tell them not to? There was no way they'd listen.

Curiosity got the best of me, and I took a few steps forward, peeking over the landing to see Kaleb splayed out on the couch with a few other guys, all chatting loudly. He wore the same grumpy, bitter expression he usually did, listening to his drunk friends babble on, looking eager for them to leave.

One girl looked me up and down, pursing her lips. "You don't need to do that. Kaleb doesn't care."

"I wasn't—"

"Who are you anyway? Are you even allowed up here?"

I blinked at the blunt question, furrowing my brows. "Yes, I *am* allowed up here, actually."

"Kaleb specifically told everyone to stay downstairs," jeered the tallest girl, her frame feeling feet above mine. She arched her eyebrows, a fake smile playing on her lips.

I scoffed as she yelled down at Kaleb, waving him upstairs, which he reluctantly adhered to after a few seconds of complaining.

He gazed at the girls questionably. "What, Maggie?"

"Who is this girl? She's up here in a bedroom."

I gazed up at Kaleb, raising a brow, silently asking him to take care of his friends. They were more than annoying, and I didn't want any part in their game. They were looking for trouble.

"Maggie." Kaleb sighed, running a hand down the side of his face, scratching at his stubble in irritation. "Jesus Christ. Just leave her and go downstairs."

She brushed her long, dark hair behind her shoulder, groaning as Kaleb stepped aside, making room for the girls to shuffle past him and head downstairs. However, she didn't follow, glaring at me instead. "What are you staring at?"

"Are you just looking for a fight?" I laughed, shaking my head in disbelief. She was definitely an aggressive drunk, and people like that baffled me. What was the point in ruining everyone's fun to feed your ego? It didn't impress anybody.

"Do you *want* a fight?" threatened Maggie, taking a step forward, her face inches from mine.

I laughed. "Oh, please. You're so drunk I could push you over with my middle toe."

Her eyes blazed. "Why don't you just—"

"That's enough, Maggie." Kaleb slid his hand between our bodies, gently nudging her backwards.

"God, some people are just so boring," she jeered at me as Kaleb ushered her away.

He raised a brow at me, a frown masking his face. "What did you say to her?"

"Nothing," I told him, scoffing.

An awkward silence settled upon us.

"Maggie and her friends are bad drunks." Kaleb's jaw twitched. "Or more like bad people."

I nodded, dragging my bottom lip into my mouth. As much as I never let words get to me, Maggie's *boring* comment had wriggled its way under my skin. I was never usually one to turn down an opportunity to socialise. However, since receiving my disappointing college grades a year ago, I'd decided it was time to knuckle down and actually begin trying. I couldn't float along anymore.

"Well, I'll let you get on with whatever you were doing." Kaleb turned to leave, but before he could take another step, I closed my bedroom door, making my way past him.

I would show Maggie just how *boring* I could be.

There was nothing wrong with taking a brief break, and it was also impossible to concentrate with the noise, anyway. That was the excuse I was going with.

Kaleb released what sounded like a small chuckle from behind me, but I refused to look at him, moving past a few people who were too engrossed in their conversations to move out of the way.

Grabbing the first drink I could find once I entered the kitchen, I poured myself a shot, downing it and releasing a strangled hiss. Drinking on an empty stomach was definitely not a good idea. However, I was too frustrated to care.

My father had answered my call but hadn't said anything. I'd come to the conclusion that he'd probably listened before realising he didn't care for my pleas. Maybe he'd finally left for good. It made sense. He'd hidden the debt from us, and now he didn't want to face the consequences—the coward.

Not only that, but I had a bunch of bitchy girls acting as if they owned Kaleb's house, berating me for simply trying to mind my own business.

"Woah," came an amused voice from behind me, making me turn. A tall, attractive man stood in the kitchen's doorway, a smirk playing on his lips. "Take it easy there, sweetheart."

I rolled my eyes, throwing back another shot, dropping the plastic cup on the counter.

"Tough day?" he asked, pouring himself a shot and downing it, keeping intense eye contact with me as he did so. He drank it as if it were water, a few droplets of liquid escaping, seeping out of the corners of his mouth. His hand moved to run over his buzz-cut head, and he leaned back against the kitchen counter, crossing his arms over his chest. He was good-looking, for sure, but not really my type.

"I guess you could say that," I replied, giving up on the shot glass and grabbing the bottle of tequila, taking a large swig of it, and attempting to swallow it without a reaction—just like he had. However, I was sure that my display was less convincing.

"I'm Brent," he said, holding his large hand out for me to shake.

"Freya."

"So, how do you know Kaleb? I haven't seen you around."

"My mom and I are staying here for a while. She's good friends with Jackie." I gestured to the surrounding space. "Is there a special occasion I'm missing here?"

"It's Kaleb's 'welcome home' celebration. He hasn't seen most of these people for over three years. He doesn't visit often."

It made sense. Kaleb didn't look like he was a fan of most of these people.

"You'd think he'd be a little more inclined to relax at age twenty-six, but the guy's a bit of a workaholic." Brent rolled his eyes.

"How do *you* know Kaleb?"

"We're both based at the same bodyguard base, but we've been friends since we were young."

"Did you guys come back together?" I asked, genuinely curious.

Brent nodded, pulling open the fridge, grabbing a beer, and popping it open with his teeth. "Yeah, we followed the same career path. We share a house near base, but when I told him I was coming down early for Christmas, he did the same."

"Right, so what does being a bodyguard involve?" I'd been interested in querying Kaleb on the subject, but I knew I'd probably receive a scoff or a glare as my answer.

Brent shrugged. "It's kind of a mix of everything since it's a private company, but we just use the term bodyguard because it's easier. We're trained to do raids, too, as well as guard people who need protection. We work alongside the police since they're so understaffed."

My eyes travelled down to Brent's waistband, a bulky object strapped to it, and they widened once I realised what it was.

He laughed, pulling the small handgun from its holster and holding it up. "We carry them everywhere."

"Does Kaleb have one?" I asked, gulping and touching the cool black metal of the gun, having never seen one before in real life.

Brent nodded.

The thought of Kaleb being involved with raids and handling deadly weapons made me even more intimidated by him, knowing he was trained to fight and, most likely, kill if necessary. It caused me to shiver, and I wondered if he had ever actually taken anybody's life.

"We're about to play a game. Do you want to join?" asked Brent, holding his hand out for me to take.

I hesitated for a brief second, humming. *What did I have to lose?*

I grabbed Brent's hand, allowing him to pull me through the kitchen doorway, stopping behind the couch that Kaleb was sitting opposite. He narrowed his eyes slightly when he noticed Brent's hand intertwined with mine, his questionable gaze lingering on his friend a little longer than necessary.

I attempted to gaze down at his waistband for any sign of a gun, but his shirt was covering too much, and I didn't want to get caught looking. The last thing I needed was for Kaleb to think I was checking him out.

"Okay, let's play," said Brent, pulling me towards the couch, ushering everyone to move up so there was room for me to perch on the end, facing Kaleb and his watchful gaze.

Five: Freya

I glanced down at the cup in the middle of the coffee table, a multitude of cards splayed around it. It was filled with a brownish, foamy liquid, and I was pretty confident it was a mixture of a few alcohols that definitely didn't belong together.

"Pick a card," encouraged Brent, nodding at me, and I snuck a glance at Kaleb. He swung his muscular arm over the back of the couch, getting himself comfy as he watched me. Sweat coated the back of my neck like a white-hot spotlight was shining on me from above, raising my temperature by what felt like fifty degrees.

"It's a three of clubs," I stated after I picked one and turned it over, looking around at everybody, unsure of what I was supposed to do next.

"Clubs means you have to take a shot," cheered a red-haired girl from beside Brent, casually pouring me a small cup of vodka and thrusting it in my direction. She wiggled an eyebrow at me as I shot it back, the liquid burning my throat, but I held back my gag.

"Brent, it's your turn," said the redhead, giggling as he picked up a card and turned it over to reveal nine of hearts. A smile made its way onto his face as he glanced at me.

"What?" I questioned.

"Hearts means I get to choose someone to kiss." He raised a brow at me questionably.

I looked out at everyone, their eyes boring into my own, causing me to gulp. Kaleb sat with an intrigued expression while Maggie sat next to him, her judgemental gaze piercing through my soul, making me overly frustrated and annoyed.

What the hell was her problem? What was the point of being a bitch just for the sake of being a bitch?

With alcohol flowing through my system, I closed my eyes as Brent leaned forward, pressing his lips to mine and kissing me softly. It was a simple peck—I'd made sure of it—but I couldn't help but feel guilty. I thought of Zach, but I reminded myself of how he'd expressed himself that getting to know somebody didn't mean that you couldn't get with other people.

Multiple other people had their turns, taking shots and completing dares. However, when it reached Kaleb, I was nervous, worried he would be given a dare involving me. I didn't want to kiss him, even if he was ridiculously attractive. The thought caused my heart to palpitate, and I pushed the image from my brain, scowling at the ground.

I didn't want that. Definitely not.

"Four of hearts," said Kaleb with a huff, and Maggie placed her hands on his thighs, pushing herself closer to him. He gazed at her with dark eyes, her own pleading ones widening once he took hold of her hands and pushed them away. "I'm skipping my turn."

She huffed, opening her mouth to speak, but when she received a blazing glower from Kaleb, she clamped it shut.

Once it was my turn again, I picked a card, and everyone laughed and hissed when I turned it around, revealing a joker.

"Ooh, tough luck, Freya," mumbled Brent, looking at me apologetically.

"What does a joker mean?" Judging by everyone's reactions, I didn't want to know.

"See that?" chirped Maggie, snickering while pointing at the cup full of disgusting liquid. "You have to drink all of it."

I grimaced, looking over at Kaleb to see his jaw stiffen, his eyes flicking between the cup and me with concern.

"Do you need me to do it for you?" Maggie asked, standing up to lean across the coffee table and grab the drink, raising a brow at me before she did so. Her hands hovered over it before picking it up gently, looking frustrated by my hesitation, toying with it in her palms, causing me to scowl.

A sigh escaped my lips, and I took the cup from her and brought it to my lips, guzzling down as much of the liquid as I could. My eyes watered as I swallowed, and I had to stop to take a breath, wiping at my mouth. Looking down into the cup, I frowned, disappointed that I'd only finished just over half of it.

"You don't have to do the rest," said Kaleb with furrowed eyebrows, watching my nervous face. However, after seeing Maggie giggle with the other girls, I regretfully allowed my pride to cloud my judgment and tilted the cup towards my mouth again.

"You better pace yourself." Brent chuckled from beside me, and a small gasp fell from my lips when the cup was taken from my hands.

I gazed up with wide eyes.

Kaleb was shaking his head with the cup in his hands, and he placed it back down on the coffee table, his face glum. "Don't make a decision you're going to regret."

I furrowed my brows, and once Kaleb noticed my heavy limbs and hazy eyes, his mouth downturned into a frown. He ran his tongue along the front of his teeth in angst, taking a seat.

The rest of the game went by quickly, and I was grateful that I picked no more horrendous cards, laughing when Brent was made to do three shots in a row, his face scrunching up after the third one.

However, I felt groggy, my vision was blurry, and my skin was tingling despite feeling completely numb at the same time. I had nothing but alcohol inside of me, though, so I narrowed the nausea down to that.

I stood up along with some of the other players—some grabbing their empty cups to refill them, some heading to the bathroom—but I didn't have any time to even think about making my way to the fridge to grab a snack before Maggie stopped me. She eyed me up, a smile gracing her devilish lips.

"Would now be a bad time to tell you I added my own special ingredient to that drink?" She pulled the small bag from earlier out of her bra. The white powder was fucking gone.

My eyes rounded, and my heart dropped into my stomach, my blood suddenly feeling fiery. Had she seriously just said that? Or was I imagining things?

"What the fuck did you just say?" growled Kaleb in a low voice from the couch. His expression was deadly as he stood to his feet, stalking towards Maggie, whose expression quickly turned from humorous to uneasy.

"Maggie, are you kidding me?" spat Brent, taking my hand and attempting to gain my attention. However, I couldn't focus on him. The world around me was spinning.

"You're a fucking bitch." I clamped my eyes shut briefly, my head pounding. "What did that gain you? Seriously?" I was furious.

"You think drugging somebody is funny? Get. The. Fuck. Out of my house," ordered Kaleb, his form towering above Maggie's, making her look like a puny mouse compared to him—although she was on the taller side for a woman.

She scoffed, rolling her eyes. "Are you serious? Wow, Kaleb, so you disappear to become a cop and come back up your ass?"

"What did I just say, Maggie? Leave. Before I make you."

"Fuck you," she grunted, shouting a string of ugly words at him as she slammed the front door shut behind her.

I was left standing with Brent by my side and Kaleb in front of me, their faces perturbed.

"Freya? Do you feel okay?" Brent held his hands out to steady me, noticing my swaying stance.

The mix of alcohol I'd drunk in a short space of time and the drug Maggie had spiked me with was hitting me full force.

"Okay," Kaleb muttered, sighing, pinching the bridge of his nose, and slowly approaching me. He attempted to have me focus on him. However, he was bleary. "Let's go upstairs where it's quieter."

"I'll get her some water," said Brent, quickly disappearing.

I tried to take a step but ended up ramming my shin against the side of the coffee table, the jagged wood digging into my skin. It caused a few cups to topple, liquid spilling over the living room carpet, staining the cream-coloured rug.

"Shit," I mumbled, becoming sweaty, droplets forming on my upper lip. My clammy hands were shaking, and anxiety was coursing through my veins. I couldn't tell what was worse—the feeling of actually having drugs in my system or the paranoia that the drugs were going to wreak havoc on my body and cause permanent damage.

How much had Maggie put in that cup? Surely not all of it?

Kaleb took hold of my wrist, his fingers grazing against mine as he pulled me away from the couch towards the steps. However, when I reached the bottom, he noticed my futile expression, each step looking daunting. Sensing my reluctance, he tucked himself behind me, nudging me forward and hovering behind my lower back in case I fell.

Brent quickly appeared behind us, clutching a glass of water. His mouth was down-turned, but I refocused my attention away from him to concentrate on moving my feet.

I felt even more off balance once we reached the landing, and Kaleb gripped me, guiding me to the nearest room.

His room.

The clean and musky scent of him wafted up my nostrils and filled my sinuses, and I cocked my head at the sight of his perfectly tidy bedroom. I hadn't expected Kaleb's room to be a state, to be honest, though. He was organised and orderly, and it looked like he preferred to match his surroundings to his character.

"Drink this." Brent thrust the glass of water in my direction as I seated myself down on the edge of Kaleb's bed, the duvet plush beneath me. I took a sip, which only made me feel even more nauseous, and I handed back the glass, resting my head on my knees.

My heart was racing.

"Freya, listen to me," said Kaleb quietly, kneeling in front of me, tapping at my leg to gain my attention, and I gazed out from my knees to look at him. "When's the last time you ate?"

I furrowed my brows, unsure of the answer. I was running too late for college to have breakfast, and I'd spent my lunch trying to catch up on the work I'd missed. Food had been at the back of my mind, and even when I'd got home with a growling stomach, I'd headed straight upstairs to shower and work on my sketch.

"I… don't remember," I admitted, pushing the hair that had come loose from my claw clip out of my face.

"She's got nothing but alcohol and drugs in her system," Kaleb breathed out, standing up, his form stiff and eyebrows pinched.

"She needs to throw it all up," suggested Brent, nodding his head towards the bathroom, his mouth set in a firm line.

Suddenly, as if it were an order, I clutched at my stomach and rushed into Kaleb's en-suite, kicking the door shut behind me and throwing up the contents of my stomach. It burned my throat, and I cursed under my breath, flushing the toilet and slumping back against the wall.

"She drank the drugs towards the end of the game, so they wouldn't have affected her body much. I think she'll be fine," Brent said from the other side of the door.

"Just thinking isn't really good enough, though, is it?" Kaleb grumbled.

Their bickering was slicing right through my skull, but I did feel a hell of a lot better for vomiting.

"Just get everyone out. I'm done with their childish shit," Kaleb ordered his friend, peeking open the bathroom door to step in, checking me over. I ran my hands down my face, trying to block my vision of his conflicted expression, and he narrowed his eyes. He leaned against the bathroom wall, his tongue skating along the front of his teeth once again as he watched me like a hawk.

Six: Freya

I rubbed my eyes as I awoke, my head pounding, my stomach bubbling with a strange combination of queasiness and dread. Sitting up, I gazed around the room, Brie's pale pink walls nowhere to be found. Instead, I was surrounded by a dingy navy cream colour, the accents pretty uninspiring.

This wasn't my room.

"Oh, fuck," I groaned to myself. I knew whose room this was, the drama that had unfolded last night coming back to me and playing vividly in my mind like a movie scene. I shouldn't have allowed Maggie's words and the fact that my father wasn't replying to get to me. However, I had given in and joined the party as a distraction when I should have been finishing my college work. I was going to need to keep my head down and focus this weekend.

Swinging my legs over the side of Kaleb's double bed, testing how my feet felt against the cold wood, I tested my balance. Apart from feeling a little unsteady, I was fine, and I headed towards the landing railing, peering over it.

A very fed-up-looking Brent was splayed out across the couch downstairs, his head hung over the back, eyes barely open. A toxic-looking energy drink was clutched in one of his hands, and after listening for a few seconds, I picked up on the soft snore emitting from him.

Someone was hungover.

After a shower, I padded downstairs hesitantly, gaining Brent's attention, his mouth curling upwards once he took in my state.

"You look like shit, girlie." He chuckled, taking a final swig of his drink and setting it on the coffee table.

"Thanks. That's exactly what I wanted to hear," I mumbled sarcastically, looking around the room in astonishment.

There wasn't a hair out of place. It looked spotless.

Brent laughed. "Kaleb may be a guy, but he's not a slob."

"That makes one of us." Kaleb scowled, coming from the kitchen to glare at Brent, snatching his empty can up. He turned to me. "So, how are you feeling?"

I shook my head, raking my hand through my wet hair. "My head hurts, but other than that, I'm okay," I replied, my mouth set in a firm line, gulping as I took in his attire. It had to be illegal for someone to look *that* good in just grey sweatpants.

"You fell asleep by the toilet last night, so I kept you in my room so you had easy access to a bathroom."

"And you slept...?"

"I slept on the couch. No need to panic." Kaleb's mouth curved upward, my heart hammering against my ribs in sudden relief. He clearly enjoyed my reaction.

The thought of Kaleb and me in the same bed together pushed its way to the forefront of my mind, and I shivered as goosebumps arose across my arms, imagining his warm body so close to mine.

Was he a pyjama kind of guy? Or did he sleep in just his boxers? Perhaps he even—

"Don't worry, Kaleb's already dealt with Maggie." Brent's loud voice yanked me from my wildly unrealistic fantasy.

"What do you mean, he dealt with her?" I questioned.

Brent paused. "He went over to her house and—"

"Get off the couch," Kaleb said huskily, kicking at his friend's feet and nodding towards the front door. "We're late."

This caused him to groan, but he shot me a cheesy grin, looking like a fantastic idea had just popped into his head. "Freya, do you want to join us?"

"No." Kaleb jostled his keys between his fingers, his jaw taut. "Don't be an idiot, Brent."

"Kaleb, the girl got drugged by one of our friends. The least we could do is invite her to join us so she isn't sitting here alone all day."

"Maggie isn't my friend. Most of those people last night weren't my friends. Use your brain, Brent." Kaleb's tone was harsh.

Frustration flashed behind Brent's eyes, and he stepped closer to his friend. "Come on, Kaleb. What's the harm in bringing a friend along? Think about it. It'll look nothing but normal. Plus, Freya looks like she needs some fun."

Brent put the emphasis on the *normal.*

I pinched my eyebrows together. What the hell did that mean?

Kaleb ran his tongue along the front of his teeth before he glared at Brent with intense eyes, cursing under his breath. His gaze flickered between us, and he shook his head in defeat. "Fine, but I don't want her getting in the way. We had enough drama last night."

A grin broke out on Brent's freckled face as he addressed me. "Come on. No point staying indoors all day."

My interest got the better of me as I watched Kaleb stalk towards his large black Jeep and hop in. The engine roared, my body shuddering. There was something about him that felt so dangerous and mysterious, and although I knew it was supposed to drive me away, it didn't. I wanted to dig a little deeper.

I also didn't like that he disliked me. If we were going to be living under the same roof, we needed to learn to get along. I wasn't sure when my father was going to be back, and I knew it could be another couple of weeks before he returned our texts and calls and sorted the debt out.

I followed Brent toward the car, sitting in the back, my eyes travelling down to Kaleb's waist. I spotted his hefty handgun—the one that I'd been searching for last night—and gulped at the thought that he could kill anyone he wanted to with the flick of his wrist.

"Where are we going?" I asked after a minute of silence, the thick air feeling tense and almost suffocating.

"To a shooting range," Kaleb responded, glancing at me through his rear-view mirror, a smirk playing on his lips. "We can turn around if that's too much for you. I have no problem dropping you back home."

A huff escaped my lips, and I shook my head at him before resting my forehead against the cold window. Concentrating on college work was unfathomable with a pounding headache anyway. I rubbed at my temples, the quick movements of the car making me feel slightly dizzy and nauseous, and when we finally reached our destination, I all but leapt out of the vehicle.

"Whatever you do, don't mention anything about our jobs," Kaleb warned me quietly. I opened my mouth to question him, but a loud voice cut me off.

"Kaleb, Brent! Who have we got here?"

We all turned to see a tall, middle-aged man with slicked-back hair stalking towards us. He grinned at the boys, gazing down at me with confusion, raising his brow.

"Will, this is Freya," Brent said, and I smiled. "Freya, this is Will Sheffield. He owns this place."

Will gazed at me through dark brown eyes—red and bloodshot. He clutched onto a cigarette with stubby fingers and took a puff as he grinned. "Nice to meet you. How long have you been shooting for?"

"Oh, I don't—"

"She's a great shooter," Kaleb interrupted, playing with his gun in his hands and stalking toward the entrance to the shooting range, beckoning us with a nod of his head.

I'd never picked up a gun in my life. Why lie?

The sound of gunfire immediately ricocheted off the metal walls and hit my eardrums piercingly, my headache becoming even more intense. There were only a few other small groups here, and Will took us over to a spot in the corner before leaving us to it, a target having been placed at the end of a long stretch.

Thin metal walls separated every group of shooters, and the sound of limbs coming into contact with tin travelled through the air as a few men kicked at them in frustration after missing their shots.

Kaleb immediately pulled his gun out, aiming it and shooting, the bullet flying through the air and hitting the target bang in the middle. He wasn't wearing eye or ear protection, and it made me realise how rundown and shady this place actually looked.

People were milling about casually, laughing and joking with each other as they strutted through the building with their loaded guns hanging from their waists—most of them heavily tattooed and eerie-looking. It didn't look like anyone was without an alcoholic drink, either. Was drinking and shooting really a good combination?

Brent pulled his gun from his jeans and aimed, his bullet soaring through the air and hitting the target also—his a little too far to the right.

"How do you never miss?" Brent grumbled, shaking his head as Kaleb took another shot, the gun recoiling back slightly in his large hands.

"I practise when you piss me off," he muttered casually, his lips threatening to curve upward.

Had Mr Grumpy just made a joke?

Brent held his gun out to me, causing my eyes to widen, and I shook my head, shifting my weight from one foot to the other. I'd never held a gun before—let alone shot one.

Kaleb leaned back against the wall with folded arms, eyeing me up as I stared between the gun I was being offered and Brent's cheesy grin.

"She'll kill someone," Kaleb stated, shaking his head. His throat bobbed up and down as he released a slight chuckle, his prominent Adam's apple causing my throat to tighten.

"Not if we show her how to do it," Brent argued, pressing the gun into my grip and encouraging me to step up to the shooting pass. I did so with sweaty palms, the gun feeling as if it was about to slide right out of my hand.

"No, no," Kaleb groaned, moving closer to me and scowling down at my grip on the gun. "Your middle finger should go here." He manoeuvred it upwards slightly before holding onto my arm to adjust my entire grasp, nodding at me once satisfied.

I gulped. I hadn't expected him to touch me, and for some pathetic reason, it sent shivers down my spine. The scent of his cologne wafted up my nostrils, and I breathed it in greedily before I composed myself. This guy was hot, but he was also an ass. I needed to remind myself of that.

"Okay, now just aim and shoot," Brent encouraged.

"You say that like it's easy." My heart palpitated as I raised the gun just a little more, attempting to hold it steady. I took a deep breath, feeling a droplet of sweat dribble down the back of my neck as I pulled the trigger, the gun almost flying out of my hand as the bullet barrelled down the narrow stretch. It hit the wall above the target, bouncing off it and landing on the floor with a loud *clink*, slowly rolling to a stop.

What a pathetic attempt.

"Well," Kaleb mumbled, taking a few slow steps towards me, placing his hand on the gun, lowering it, and taking it from me, "you didn't shoot a hole through your own head, so congratulations."

"Nice job, Freya. You're a natural. I'll go and grab us some more bullets." Brent headed towards the entrance, leaving me alone with Kaleb, his stormy eyes on me.

I cleared my throat awkwardly, kicking at the dusty ground. "What did Brent mean when he said you dealt with Maggie?"

He clicked his tongue, grinding his teeth together. "Will you refuse to drop it if I don't answer?"

I raised my eyebrows, waiting for him to continue, causing him to grumble.

"I went over to her house, and I told her that if she ever drugged anybody again, I'd make sure she regretted it."

"What does that mean?"

Kaleb huffed. "It means what I just said, Freya."

I pursed my lips. He clearly didn't want to discuss it, and I didn't want to frustrate him further. The fact that we were here together, partaking in a recreational activity, was a miracle. There was no point in pushing it.

"I don't think drugs and I mix very well." It was supposed to be a light-hearted joke, but I realised as soon as I'd said it just how unfunny it was. Kaleb and I had settled into an awkward silence, and I'd said the first thing that had popped into my head to break it.

He hummed in response as he played with his gun, his brows collapsing in on one another.

Feeling awkward, I pulled my phone from my pocket, checking for any messages from my dad.

I frowned as I stared at the screen.

Nothing—not even after I'd sent him a message asking why he'd answered my call and then hung up.

I'd really been blessed with a loving father, hadn't I?

The tension was cut once Brent reappeared and handed Kaleb a fresh set of bullets. They continued to shoot, and I stood behind them with my back against the wall, scanning the room, taking in how boisterous everyone was. My brain throbbed from inside my skull.

I sighed. This wasn't my scene.

Feeling my phone vibrate in my pocket, I snatched it from the fabric with hope, but my face fell when Zach's name popped up.

Zach*:* Hey, Freya, did you want to do something? We could grab some food?

I hesitated, biting down harshly on my lip. I was starving and needed an excuse to leave this creepy shooting range.

Freya*:* Sure, I'll meet you at Lenny's diner in twenty minutes if that works?

Zach: Sounds good.

"Okay, I think I'm going to go," I said, causing both men to turn to me, a slight smirk gracing Kaleb's lips.

Asshole.

"It's not for everyone," he replied. "See you at home."

"Yep," I muttered with hard eyes, waving a quick *goodbye* to Brent before I rushed out of the building, the smell of iron and alcohol filling my nostrils as I raced through the hallway. Will caught my attention as I reached the front door, though, another half-smoked cigarette in his mouth.

"Leaving already?" he asked, puffing out a cloud of smoke to the side.

"Yeah," I responded. "I've got some things I need to do."

"It isn't often Kaleb and Brent bring people here when they come back to town, but it was good to meet you, Freya...?"

"Um, Henderson," I said, nodding once, my body stiff.

"Henderson?" Will repeated, taking another puff of his cigarette as he looked at me strangely, nodding to himself as he attempted to lower his questionable brows. "Well, I hope to see your face around here more often, Freya Henderson."

"We'll see." I smiled awkwardly and headed out of the complex and toward the road, gulping as Will stepped out of the building and studied me from afar. He narrowed his eyes as he watched me disappear around the corner, his intense stare making me shiver, uneasiness filling my bloodstream.

Seven: Kaleb

Brent was an idiot for inviting Freya along with us. The shooting range wasn't the place for people like her.

Innocent.

Guiltless.

Good.

She'd been way out of her depth last night, too, and the memory of Maggie drugging her made my jaw twitch. Maggie was a psychotic wench, but I never put her down as the type of person to do that to somebody. She'd crossed every boundary. Every line.

Her face was a picture when I'd shown up at her house and threatened her, her tanned skin paling and her bottom lip trembling slightly before she plastered a scowl onto her face. She'd shouted her usual profanities at me, but I paid it no mind. I wanted to get my point across, and I definitely had.

"Next time, leave Freya out of this," I muttered to Brent as he took another shot, cursing to himself when he missed the target completely, turning to me with a glare.

"She was fine. Nobody's going to get hurt."

I wasn't so sure of that.

"When is she moving out anyway?" Brent questioned, taking a sip of the beer that the female bartender had brought over. She had a soft spot for my friend, and although she'd tried chatting me up more than once, my chilly reception meant she'd laid off.

I shrugged. "Soon. Hopefully."

Freya was getting in the way, and even though the way she had marched right downstairs after Maggie had called her *boring* made me smirk, I knew she wasn't as invincible as she believed.

Brent was determined for her to come today. I knew why, but I still didn't like it. It wasn't right.

I scanned the area for what felt like the hundredth time this afternoon, meeting the eyes of a few beefy men who couldn't shoot for shit. It made me laugh.

Because of our jobs, we were often put in dangerous situations, which immediately made our families targets. I spent as little time down here as possible for that reason—just in case anybody was keeping tabs on me—but this was unavoidable.

Freya didn't belong in this world, and we needed to remember that.

Eight: Freya

My head was still pounding as I made my way through the spitting rain. I had to use my phone to get directions since we were so far out—the shooting range was in a desolate and down-trodden part of town.

When I eventually reached Lenny's diner, my hair was soggy, and my skin chilled.

"You call that twenty minutes?" Zach chuckled after I pushed the door open, the bell ringing as I practically flung myself inside.

"Sorry. It took a lot longer to get here than I thought it would."

"What were you doing last night? I tried calling you, but you didn't pick up."

I glanced down at my phone, realising that I did indeed have some missed call notifications—one from my mom and three from Zach. Last night had been a blur, and I hadn't had the time to go through my phone and check them.

"Sorry," I said sheepishly.

Zach smiled, grinding his teeth together, looking slightly agitated. "So, what were you doing then? Did you fall asleep early or something?"

I cocked my head at him. "Um, no, I was just busy studying. I really don't want to fall behind."

Zach hummed, opening his mouth to say something else, but our server interrupted him. I wasn't the best liar, and I was concerned that Zach would see straight through me, but if he suspected me of fibbing, he didn't say anything. However, suspicion pooled in his dazzling eyes.

"Any update on your dad?" he questioned, and I shrugged, sighing, my breath hitching when I felt him touch my thigh from under the table. I could tell he was trying to comfort me, but his gaze held a glint of something else that made me want to push him away. What had got into him lately?

He'd been so sweet when we first met, but something had changed. It seemed he only ever wanted to see me when he wanted some.

"No, I haven't spoken to my mom since yesterday morning, so I don't know if she's had a response from him. She's been away with work."

"Do you know where he went?"

I bit down on my lip. I actually didn't. He travelled so much that it was hard to keep track of when he was in and out of the state—or country. "I know he visits New York often, but I don't know where he went this time."

Our food came quickly, and we talked about a few things related to college, but like most of our conversations, it was all surface-level.

A part of me wondered if I was obligated to tell Zach about the small kiss Brent and I had shared. It had only been part of a game, but I couldn't help but worry that he would find out and accuse me of messing him around. He'd been the one to tell me we weren't tied down to each other, though, and the more I thought about it, the more I realised Zach was morphing into a bright red flag kind of shade.

"Freya, are you alright?" he asked as he finished his food. "You haven't eaten much."

I'd been drifting in and out of my daydreams and hadn't even realised how little I'd eaten. "Yeah. I'm just not overly hungry."

We finished quickly, and Zach slipped his cash out of his wallet, holding his hand out to stop me from doing the same. "Nope, I asked you out, so I pay."

"Are you sure?"

"Of course. Do you need a ride home? Or we can go back to mine? My mom isn't home."

There it was.

We exited the diner, the rain still trickling from the cloudy sky.

I knew what Zach was suggesting, and I cleared my throat. "I have a lot of college work to do. Would it be okay to drop me at Jackie's house?"

I wasn't opposed to sleeping with him. Girls had needs, too, but there was something inside of me that screamed at me not to. If that wasn't a sign that this wasn't going to work out, I didn't know what was.

Zach kicked at the ground, shoved his hands into his pockets, and nodded after a long pause. His frustration was evident as he hopped into the car.

I directed him to Jackie's house, picking at my cuticles as he pulled to a stop. "Thank you for today. It was a good distraction from everything." I smiled as I clambered out of the car, Zach following the action.

"So I'm just a distraction?" he teased, laughing as he placed his hands on my waist, moving his face closer to mine. We'd kissed several times, but they were never long or meaningful and were usually followed by Zach suggesting we head somewhere 'quieter'. It appeared he had some kind of strange fantasy to fuck in the college locker rooms.

"No, obviously not." My breath hitched as he suddenly pressed his lips to mine, but once he tried to deepen it, I dropped my head.

"I guess you're not going to invite me in?" he wondered aloud, knitting his eyebrows together as he stared at my lips, his hands wandering a little lower than my waist. "That's usually what people do on dates."

I stepped away from him. "Thank you for the food, Zach. I'll see you on Monday."

Kicking the front door shut behind me, I ran a hand down my face. I was having serious doubts about where things were going with Zach and me, and I knew I was going to have to let him know I didn't see us working out. I wasn't sure he'd take it too well, though.

My eyes wandered to the living room coffee table, and they widened when I spotted a black handgun sitting on top of it, the metal shiny and inviting.

I hadn't enjoyed shooting, but it had been a rush, causing my adrenaline to spike. I'd never considered myself to be an adrenaline junkie, but perhaps this was my awakening. Kaleb had watched me so intently. There was something about his eyes. They drew me in, and I found myself continuously drowning in them.

Without thinking, I made my way over to the gun and picked it up. I turned it around, thinking back to how Kaleb's hands had felt on mine when he'd been adjusting my grip. I tried to remember how he'd manoeuvred my fingers into the correct form, lifting my arm to aim as if I were going to shoot.

"What the hell are you doing?" demanded Kaleb loudly as he entered the living room, his eyebrows collapsing in on one another as he moved over to me and snatched the gun from my hands. "This thing is loaded, Freya. You'll kill yourself. Don't fucking touch it."

I gulped, blinking multiple times to bring myself back to reality. "It's loaded?"

"It's always loaded." Kaleb shoved the gun into the waistband of his jeans, the action causing his shirt to lift briefly, giving me a flash of his chiselled abs. He looked like he'd been carved from the gods—it must have been a mistake that he was placed on this earth with the rest of us. Too bad he was such an ass.

He sighed, having caught me gawking. "Seriously, Freya. Just because you fired a gun at the shooting range once doesn't mean you should handle them alone."

"Well, don't leave it around then," I snapped back, and he glared at me before chuckling with disbelief, shaking his head as he ran a hand down his face.

"Jesus Christ."

The air was thick with tension, and we glared at each other, my teeth drawing my bottom lip into my mouth.

"Was that your boyfriend?" Kaleb asked me, nodding towards the front door.

I cocked my head. "Zach? No, he's not."

"That was a quick 'no'." Kaleb was teasing me, and even though it frustrated me, I couldn't help but enjoy it a little.

I shrugged. "Because he's not." I wanted to change the subject. Zach was not who I wanted to be talking about. "I'm not going to say anything to my mom about last night, by the way—just in case you were worried. She's already got enough on her plate, and I don't want to add that to the mix."

Kaleb arched his brow, silently asking me to elaborate.

I sighed. I was staying at his house, so he deserved to know why. "My dad was supposed to be back from a business trip days ago—but nobody's heard from him—and we got evicted from our house because we hadn't paid our debt. My mom and I knew nothing about it, so we're waiting for my dad to come home and clear all of this up." I said hastily, unsure if Kaleb had made sense of the jumbled mess of words.

"So, he's running away from his problems?" Kaleb asked, and I scowled, crossing my arms over my chest.

"My mom and I aren't problems."

Kaleb laughed, but it was one of *his* laughs. It wasn't genuine. "I didn't say you were." He settled on the couch, resting his elbows on his knees and lacing his fingers together. "But if you see my gun lying around, don't touch it. Don't even look at it. I don't trust you not to shoot a hole through the television."

I couldn't tell whether it was supposed to be a joke or not, but I decided against laughing. Kaleb was an easily riled-up man, and I didn't want to put his limits to the test. *Today, at least.*

I turned towards the mirror, huffing at my appearance and pulling my soggy hair back into a bun. We settled into an awkward silence, and it caused my skin to crawl. "What's up with that Will guy, by the way? He was kind of creepy."

Kaleb paused, his jaw taut as his face morphed into a frown. "Why? What did he say to you?"

"He just asked for my full name. He didn't say much, but he was just... strange."

Kaleb cursed. "Brent was an idiot for suggesting you come with us. If you ever see Will again, don't speak to him."

His comment caused my eyebrows to furrow. Kaleb shot at his shooting range, so why would he be opposed to me speaking to Will? I was under the impression that they were friendly.

"I wasn't planning on it." I didn't see myself revisiting the shooting range anytime soon, despite how much of a rush it was to fire a gun. I wasn't cut out for it, and I didn't fancy being eaten alive.

Kaleb hummed, briefly looking me up and down before standing and turning to walk out of the room. But as he did, he craned his neck to glance back at me, smirking. "It's probably best that Zach guy isn't your boyfriend," he chortled, "because that kiss looked awkward as hell."

I scoffed, clenching my fists as I glared at Kaleb's back.

Dick.

Nine: Freya

It had been almost two weeks. Almost two weeks of radio silence at my father's end despite our attempts to reach out. My mother was becoming increasingly frustrated—especially since I'd informed her of how he'd picked up the phone for a few seconds before ending the call—and she continued to apologise to Jackie about how much of an inconvenience we were.

Obviously, Jackie responded by telling us we were welcome as long as we liked.

I hadn't seen too much of Kaleb. I was either spending my time with Hannah, studying, or working at my once-a-week job teaching art to kids, and he was at the shooting range—or doing whatever Kaleb Evans enjoyed doing.

We'd spent a few awkward dinners sitting next to each other while our moms blabbered about work, but he'd spent most of his time on his phone, purposely avoiding eye contact with me. I'd even refrained from adding salt to my meals since I needed to ask him to pass it.

However, his presence altered my brain chemistry, and I didn't know why. My stomach twisted, and my heart faltered. I needed to remind myself that he was a cocky jerk who I would probably never see again after I moved out, though. Our worlds were light years apart, and mixing would cause another big bang to occur—the kind that destroyed things instead of creating them.

Peeling myself out of the sheets I'd been rotting in all day, I made my way downstairs, spotting Jackie laying the table. My mother followed closely behind her, holding what appeared to be some steaming pasta dish.

"Oh, Freya," Jackie exclaimed. "You're awake."

"I was napping," I answered sheepishly. I'd spent most of last night sketching, the perfectionist in me forcing my hands to crumple up each piece and toss it aside before beginning a new one that I was determined to get right.

Jackie and my mother took their seats at the dinner table, yet again leaving the only empty chair right next to Kaleb. I shuffled it sideways slightly, which gained his attention, and he rolled his eyes and shook his head.

"I'm guessing you haven't heard anything from dad?" I asked my mother once I noticed Jackie and Kaleb were engaged in conversation.

"Nothing yet, I'm afraid, honey, but I'm going to try to get a contact number for his work to find out where he is," she responded.

I felt my stomach lurch. Each passing day he was gone solidified my theory that he was planning on not coming back. The rejection was a stab to the heart, and even though my father and I had never been that close, I hadn't expected him to pack up and leave when things got tough.

I hadn't even realised I'd been aimlessly swirling my food around on my plate until Jackie cleared her throat to get my attention. Kaleb stood beside me with his hand out, arching his brow.

I gazed at him, confused. "What?"

"I said, are you finished playing with your food like a child so I can take the plates out?"

I blinked, passing him my plate and thanking him quietly. My mom and Kaleb made their way into the kitchen to wash up, and just as I was about to follow, Jackie called me over, seating herself on the couch.

"Freya, I just wanted to check in with you to make sure you're doing alright?" She kept her voice hushed. "You've been napping a lot during the day, and I know for some people that's common, but sometimes that sort of thing is brought on by stress."

A small smile graced my lips. "Thank you, Jackie. I think the whole situation with my dad is freaking me out a little." My throat tightened. "It's just hard not knowing where he is and if he's even coming back. A part of me wonders if he's gone for good."

She clicked her tongue. "Well, if that's the case, then he's a piece of crap. You'll have to excuse my language. Kaleb and Brie's father did that just after Brie was born. He found another woman and left and hasn't called since."

I pulled my eyebrows together. "I didn't know that."

Brie was Kaleb's sister—I'd put that much together.

"I don't believe your father would do something like that, though. Like your mom said, he's most likely living it up somewhere on vacation. Maybe he met a lady out there, you know? He'll get back to the both of you soon, and this situation will be dealt with."

I forced a smile. My father had never been much of a ladies' man. He never appeared interested in other women—even when my mother and he finally ended their relationship for good. Although, admittedly, I hadn't seen him much recently. Perhaps he *had* met someone out of state.

Jackie gazed off into the distance, her eyes settling on a photo hung on the wall in the room's corner, a high leafy plant half-covering it. It was of Kaleb and Jackie, with a young brown-haired girl at their feet, clinging onto Kaleb's legs as she beamed. She appeared to be around eleven or twelve, and a younger-looking Kaleb was actually showing an emotion other than irritation—joy. He was smiling, and it was a *real* smile.

"Brie's your daughter?"

Jackie nodded, releasing a sigh. "That's my Brie."

"Where is she now?"

She gazed at me, gulping. "She was thirteen when she was killed."

I froze, my blood turning to ice, thick inside my veins.

"We'd been out at a Christmas market, and on the walk home, we found ourselves in the middle of a fight between members of a gang. We couldn't move out of the way quickly enough, and Brie was caught in the crossfire. She died in the hospital a couple of hours later from gunshot wounds to the chest and head."

My face paled. I'd had no idea that Jackie's youngest child had been murdered. "I'm so sorry, Jackie. I didn't know."

"It's coming up to the five-year anniversary, and it's always hard." She took a big breath. "We kept her room just how she had left it that night, and we hadn't touched it since, but when Kaleb was away at base again, I decided we all needed closure. I knew we couldn't leave her room like that forever, and I cleared it out and put all of her stuff in the attic." Guilt swarmed her tired eyes, and she moved over to the photo. "I should have told Kaleb about it, but I didn't want him to come home and take time off work. He would've wanted to keep it the way it was, but it was stopping both of us from moving on."

It made sense why Kaleb had been so upset about me moving into Brie's room. I felt awful. "No one should have to go through losing a child." I stood up to inspect the photo, cocking my head as I studied it.

Brie looked so much like Kaleb. Piercing grey eyes. Dark hair. Tanned skin. Gorgeous.

"She was the most beautiful young girl." Jackie laughed. "Her smile was infectious. She wanted to be a singer and refused to talk most of the time—she'd sing instead."

"I bet her voice was amazing."

"I mean, I was always a bit biased, but yes, it was. She won her school's talent competition two years in a row. She'd been preparing for the third year but never got to attend. Sometimes, I play the recordings of her singing at night when I can't sleep."

"I'm happy Kaleb is back. It must be lonely here by yourself."

"It is, but I understand my son has a career he's passionate about and wants to pursue. I don't want to be selfish and ask him to stay." Jackie's eyes watered, but she scowled, willing the tears away. "It's why your mother and I aren't as close as we once were. When Brie died, I isolated myself, and although she tried with me, I wouldn't speak to anybody. Kaleb had to look after me because I was bedridden. I just don't want him worrying about me spiralling again. He's already given up so much."

Kaleb had a tough outer shell, and it made sense why. I'd assumed he was just an arrogant and moody dickhead, but he'd been through a hell of a lot. His father had abandoned him, his little sister had been murdered, and then his mom had completely shut herself off, and he'd had to care for her—all while being young himself.

"I'm coping much better now, though," Jackie said. "I just still have my moments."

"Of course, that's normal. Nobody expects you never to be sad again."

I felt guilty for mentioning my father and our debt. My situation didn't even compare to Jackie's. I was certain she'd take on millions of dollars of debt just to spend one more day with her daughter.

"I know you and Kaleb don't know each other well, but you aren't far off his age, and I wonder if he needs someone younger than me to ask if he's okay. He won't speak to me. He claims the anniversary doesn't affect him much and that he's fine, but I know he's hurt."

I understood Jackie wanted me to converse with Kaleb to see how he was coping, but he was a closed book. There was no way that he would open up—especially to me, of all people.

"Kaleb has Brent," I said, smiling. "I know he's a good friend of his. Don't worry, he's not alone."

Jackie turned to laugh at my mother as she rushed past us with her phone to her ear, mumbling about how work never left her alone. "Thank you, Freya."

"I'll finish drying the dishes," I said, and Jackie engulfed me in a tight hug before I made my way into the kitchen, gazing at Kaleb with curiosity. I opened my mouth to speak, but he furrowed his brows, running his tongue along the front of his teeth as he scrubbed at a plate in the foamy basin.

"I know what you and my mother were talking about," he muttered, his jaw muscle flexing. "Don't even go there."

Ten: Freya

The house was quiet, apart from the sound of the shower upstairs. Kaleb had been in there forever, and I knew that because I had spent the past twenty-five minutes imagining what he looked like under the hot jet of water. Broad shoulders melting into defined pectorals, with hard chiselled abs leading to...

My phone buzzed, and I glanced from my laptop screen to glare at it, Zach's name popping up again for what felt like the thousandth time this morning. I hadn't responded to him for a few days, and although I'd been dropping subtle hints that I wasn't feeling it anymore, he still wasn't getting it. He was going to need to be told straight up. He clearly wasn't the sharpest tool in the shed.

"Skipping class?" Kaleb asked as he appeared beside me, his hair wet, small droplets of water trickling down his neck. I couldn't help but admire him, and I was sure that he was clocking on to the fact that I liked how he looked when freshly washed.

"No, it was cancelled." I put my laptop back on the coffee table in front of the TV, sulking. My brain wasn't working today, and I couldn't find the motivation to continue my essay. We were covering a particularly dull topic, and even Hannah—the biggest art nerd of us all—was finding it dry.

Kaleb hummed as he tilted his head at my sketch pad on the floor, moving closer to pick it up.

"No, don't," I complained, but he was already gripping it in his large hands—the size of it compared to them making the pad look like a child's toy. It wasn't a piece I was proud of, the colour theory clashing and my pencil strokes sloppy.

"You drew this?" Kaleb questioned, holding it up to me. His eyebrows raised as he pointed at the large, intricate drawing of an elephant drinking from a watering hole, a colourful woven blanket resting over its back.

I bit down on my bottom lip, shrugging. "Yeah, last night when everyone was in bed. Give it back."

"Don't get your panties in a twist."

"My panties are perfectly untwisted, thank you very much."

Oh God. I was talking to Kaleb about my panties. Absolutely not.

I took the pad from him, closing it so he couldn't sift through and view my other sketches.

"Are you going to shoot today?" I asked, trying to fill the silence as I stared at my laptop screen, angry that the words weren't typing themselves.

Kaleb and I were now able to have surface-level conversations, and to me, that was a win. As long as we were under the same roof, we needed to learn to get along.

He fiddled with the gun attached to his belt. "Brent's busy this morning."

"Is he your only friend?" I questioned, the words coming out harsher and ruder than I intended them to be. I had meant it as a genuine question.

"Is your sketch pad yours?" Kaleb snapped back, narrowing his eyes at me and entering the kitchen, leaving me with my arms crossed.

Deciding I could no longer attempt to work on my essay, I brought up the search engine on my laptop, tapping my pen against the mahogany coffee table with boredom.

Remembering what my mom had said at the dinner table about my father, an idea popped into my head. There was no harm in researching his company and possibly getting a contact number for my mom to use. It saved her doing it.

Namalix.

That was the company my dad worked for. Who the hell had named it that? I hoped they'd been fired.

Sifting through the results, I knitted my brows together. None of them were what I was looking for. I tried spelling it differently, but no company appeared in America under the name.

"What the hell?" I mumbled to myself as I clicked on a result. The link took me to a company based in Singapore—one in the interior design field, which was far from what my dad claimed his company did.

"You're going to wrinkle early if you keep making that horrible face," Kaleb told me as he chewed on his cereal bar in the doorway to the kitchen, his eyebrows raising once I didn't react. I was too focused on the screen.

"Russia?" I mumbled to myself. "No, it's not in Russia. America. Give me results in America, or I'll punch a hole through you."

"Why are you threatening an inanimate object?" Kaleb perched himself on the couch behind me. He was chatty this morning. "Namalix?"

I turned to him. "Are you done being nosy?"

"No," he muttered, deadpanning me. "What are you trying to find?"

Pushing my laptop away from me, I huffed in defeat. "I was trying to get a contact number for my dad's company so we could ask them if they know where he's gone, but I can't find the website."

Kaleb hummed, scrunching up his cereal bar wrapper and throwing it onto the table, the plastic landing in my cold mug of coffee. "What does the company do?"

"They design and create the bottles used for medicines for a few different pharmaceutical companies. Apparently, it's a big business," I told him, giving up.

"Well, a company like that is sure to be easy to find," Kaleb said, shrugging as he flicked on the TV, causing me to arch my brow at him. His musky cologne wafted up my nose, and I forced myself to ignore how close he was. I could practically feel the heat radiating off him, and although my mood was icy this morning, Kaleb was helping to thaw it—which only confused me.

"It's only coming up with results in other countries. There's no mention of a company named Namalix in America."

"There's got to be something." Kaleb kept his eyes glued to the TV.

I shrugged, pulled out my phone, and searched again. I wasn't sure why I thought looking it up on a different device would alter the results, but yet again, I found nothing of use. My phone lit up with a text, and I huffed at it, causing Kaleb to peer over my shoulder, clicking his tongue as he eyed up my screen.

Zach: Freya, why are you ignoring me? You haven't seemed yourself lately. All I'm asking for is a response. Come on.

"Lover boy sounds like a marshmallow." Kaleb chuckled, shaking his head and crossing his arms over his chest as he turned his attention back to the screen in front of him.

I moved my phone away from his line of sight, swiping up on Zach's message. He was persistent, and I knew he wasn't going to stop until he got a response.

"He's... interesting."

Marshmallows brought joy and deliciousness—something Zach was lacking in.

I shot a quick text back.

Freya: Zach, I've been trying to do this subtly, but I'm just going to come out and say that I just don't see us working out. If you want to have this conversation at college, then we can do that.

He responded almost immediately.

Zach: So I buy you lunch, give you rides home, and you then decide you don't need me anymore? Wow…

I scoffed at the message, rolling my eyes and shaking my head. I hadn't asked him to pay for my meal at the diner. He'd insisted.

Freya: It's not like that. If you want me to send over some money, I will.

Zach: Don't bother, Freya.

"I can't find any company named Namalix based in America," Kaleb muttered, turning his phone around to show me the results, the spreadsheet on it confusing me.

I scanned the page. "What is that?"

"It's a public site that shows all registered companies within the country. There isn't a Namalix on here, Freya." He passed his phone to me, causing me to gulp.

My throat felt tight, and I began to sweat, my heart slamming against my ribs harshly.

The company my father claimed to work for didn't exist.

Eleven: Freya

"I'm not ready yet," Kaleb mumbled into his phone in a frustrated tone. "Just come in for five minutes." He flung the front door open, revealing a chuckling Brent who watched his friend with amusement as he disappeared upstairs to get dressed in his shooting attire—a tight black long-sleeved top and cargo pants. It was my favourite outfit of his.

"Hey, Freya," Brent greeted me, his smile reaching his ears.

"Hey. Both heading out?" I locked my phone, my eyes feeling square after staring at it aimlessly for what felt like hours. I'd been scouring the internet for more information on my dad's company but had come up empty-handed.

Brent moved over to the couch, settling down next to me. "Yeah. You're not at college today?"

"Class was cancelled."

"So, what have you been doing all day? You look tired."

"You are charming, Brent. Thank you." I shook my head and laughed. "I've just been doing college work, but I haven't been able to concentrate. My mind isn't with it."

"Well, you know what the best thing to do is when you feel like your mind isn't doing what you want it to?" He paused for dramatic effect. "Shoot."

I rolled my eyes.

"Oh, come on," he encouraged, shrugging. "For your first time shooting, you actually weren't half-bad, and it's always nice to have some company that isn't a grouchy Kaleb. He cramps my style."

"Thank you for the invite, but I definitely don't fit in there. I stuck out like a sore thumb."

"Maybe next time, then," Brent said with a tilt of the head, both of us gazing up as Kaleb made his way down the steps.

Why did he have to have the face of an angel? It made it so much harder to dislike him.

"Brent, stop flirting. Let's go." He pulled his keys from his pocket.

"I was just asking Freya if she wanted to join."

Kaleb's jaw tensed, and he narrowed his eyes at his friend. "No. Freya isn't coming. Don't be an idiot. You were already stupid enough to invite her once."

"Relax, man. It was just a simple question. I wasn't pushing or anything."

Kaleb took a step closer to Brent, lowering his voice. "If you're not going to take this seriously, then—"

Brent's eyes widened, his worrisome gaze flickering to me for a split second. "I am. Let's just go, alright?"

Kaleb nodded, glancing at me briefly before they both ducked out the door.

What was that about?

My phone buzzed, and I debated strangling it, expecting Zach to appear on my screen again.

Hannah: Josh has invited me to his house for a party, and I need someone to go with. Meet me at mine at eight and we can walk together?

I tapped my fingers against the screen. Hannah and Josh were slowly becoming an item, and I knew that going to this party would allow her to make her move. What kind of friend would I be if I refused to wing woman her?

Freya: Fine, I don't see why not. See you then.

Laying back down on the couch, I switched on the TV, losing myself in some cringy and barf-worthy reality show. I enjoyed watching other people try to manoeuvre their way through their messed-up lives. It made me feel better about mine, although the people on TV were getting paid to do it. I was doing it for free.

What felt like an hour or two passed quickly, and the sound of a car pulling up outside sparked my interest. I waited for the joyous melody of Kaleb and Brent's usual bickering. But I heard nothing.

Snooping, I poked my head up to peek out of the window, my heart skipping a beat when I spotted Zach's car parked outside.

Shit.

I panicked, ducking down so I couldn't be seen. The top of Zach's head bobbed up and down as he climbed out of the front seat, leaning back against the hood.

My phone vibrated from next to me.

Zach: I'm outside. Can we talk? There's been a huge misunderstanding, and I think you're just really stressed about everything and have acted impulsively. Let me in so we can talk. We need to sort this out.

Showing up at my house was a crazy move. He was acting deluded.

Freya: Zach, please just go home. I'm trying to work. I meant what I said earlier, but we can talk about it tomorrow before class. Now isn't the right time. This isn't even my house.

Zach: I'll wait here until you change your mind, then. Don't be a coward, Freya. Come and say it to my face.

Was this boy for real? I was more than happy to say it to his face, but I really wasn't in the mood for his shit.

A gasp escaped my lips when I heard a knock at the door, and I yanked the curtain shut, but after a couple of minutes of incessant knocking, it was apparent that Zach wasn't going to give up.

"Freya, come on!" he yelled from the other side of the door, the wood creaking as he—what I assumed was—kicked it. "You're just embarrassing me now!"

"*I'm* embarrassing *you*?" I growled, grinding my jaw in frustration. Zach had flipped. He'd never acted this way before, but it appeared he believed he had some creepy claim over me.

I flung the door open, adrenaline pumping through my body, making me see red. "What the fuck are you doing? You're acting like a madman!"

Zach's eyes blazed, and he jutted his foot out so I couldn't shut the door before getting in my face.

"What are you going to do, Zach?" I seethed. "Force your way in here and demand I explain my reasoning for cutting things off with you? Do you actually believe this is salvageable after you've reacted this way?"

He simmered, and I could've sworn I saw steam puff out from his ears. He grabbed me by the biceps, yanking me into the kitchen with him, his long fingers digging into my skin painfully.

"Zach, let me go! What the hell is wrong with you?!"

"You want to treat me like shit for no reason? Why? What did I do to you? I've been nothing but a gentleman," Zach complained loudly, backing me up against the kitchen counter and trapping me.

"Get out, or I'm going to call the police," I spat with as much confidence as I could muster. I shoved at his chest, and although he grunted at my harsh *whack*, he didn't budge.

Zach snatched my phone from my hand and lobbed it to the other side of the room, the device clattering to the ground.

"You're fucking paying for that if you've broken it."

"You're just one of those girls who enjoys playing with men," he snapped. "You used me as a prize. I bet you loved waltzing around campus with a hot guy on your arm, but what did I gain from it? I wasted so much time on you, you know that?"

"Get the fuck off me!" I yelled as he pressed his chest to mine, his eyes smouldering. Gazing to my left, I thanked my lucky stars that the cap to the cooking oil wasn't on, and I grabbed it and threw it into Zach's face, profanities escaping his mouth as he frantically wiped at his eyes. It was just a shame the oil hadn't been hot.

He growled in my face, the liquid dripping from his chin. "What was the point in me treating you so well when you didn't appreciate it? Do you know how many girls want me?"

I drove my knee upwards towards his balls, but he angled his body to the side, so I ended up jabbing his inner thigh instead, and I took the opportunity from his slight movement to slip past him and launch myself toward the front door.

However, it was shoved open before I could get to it, and my wide eyes landed on a frantic-looking Kaleb—Brent close behind him. Both of them held their guns high.

They moved towards us quickly, and Zach was shoved to the ground in a split second. Kaleb clambered on top of him and launched a punch to his face while Brent checked me over for injuries, but I couldn't help but cringe as Kaleb continued to sock Zach in the face, the sound sickening.

"You want to touch a woman against her will, hmm? I'll rip your hands off your body so you can never use them again," Kaleb taunted with a surprisingly calm tone, continuing to assault Zach until his nose was spurting blood. I shot Brent a wide-eyed look, causing him to yank Zach up by the collar and pull him away, shoving him against the frame of the doorway.

"What happened? Did he hurt you?" Kaleb asked me, swallowing harshly. The side of his face was smeared with Zach's blood, and after noticing my eyes continue to flicker to the spatter, he wiped at it with his sleeve. Pinching the bridge of his nose, he gazed over at Brent, who kept Zach pinned against the wood. "Do you want to press charges?"

"Although Kaleb will get in shit for beating the fuck out of him," Brent added loudly, but Kaleb scowled, silencing him.

Zach groaned in response, his head lolling back as he regained his senses.

I shook my head. "I think he got what he deserved."

"Barely." Brent scoffed before dragging Zach out of the house, throwing him to the ground, and marching back after warning him never to come anywhere near the house again.

I settled down on a dining room chair.

"We heard you yelling from outside," Brent said, clicking his gun back into its holster.

"He just showed up and barged his way in."

Kaleb cursed, pulling up a chair and sitting opposite me. "What's his name?"

"Zach."

"I know that." A sigh escaped his lips. "His full name, Freya."

I twiddled my thumbs on my lap.

Kaleb raised his thick brows. "I'll find out whether you tell me or not. You'll just be saving me time."

Dragging my bottom lip into my mouth, I focused on how Kaleb's tongue scraped against the front of his teeth. It was something he always did when he was upset or uncomfortable—a telltale sign he wasn't thrilled right now. "Zach Peters." I attempted to catch my breath, but my throat felt like it was closing. I was a pretty tough cookie, but what had just happened had thrown me into a state of shock.

"Freya, you're fine," Kaleb said, kneeling down on the floor before me after noticing my shaking hands. He placed his palm on the back of my head, guiding it down. "Put your head between your knees and close your eyes. Try to breathe slowly."

I did as he said, my pulse rapid and my skin clammy. The room was primarily silent as I tried to calm down, and I focused on anything but my elevated breathing rate, counting the number of cracks in the wood beneath me and the small individual splatters of mud on the laces of my tennis shoes.

After a couple of minutes, my chest loosened up.

"Better?"

"Yeah," I mumbled, lifting my head slowly to avoid any dizziness.

"Okay." Kaleb's jaw was taut, and his eyes were heated, his pupils blown out. "I'm getting the house security cameras in case that asshole comes back."

Twelve: Kaleb

It had been hours since Brent and I had found Zach in the house with Freya, and I was raging. I could still feel my fury flowing through my veins and seeping out of my pores, coating me and making my skin itch.

My gun hadn't left my hands, and I squeezed the cool metal barrel, imagining myself firing a bullet straight through Zach's cold heart. The world would be better off without him.

"Do you think she's asleep?" Brent asked me from the other side of the couch, and I shrugged, keeping my gaze on the cream-coloured carpet.

I'd made Brent stay because I knew that if I was left alone, I was going to hunt Zach down and subject him to copious amounts of pain before burying him six feet under. It was what he deserved—he'd got off easy. A broken nose was nothing compared to what I *wanted* to do to him.

Freya had gone upstairs to shower, but we hadn't heard her make a sound for hours. She needed the rest, so we tried to remain as quiet as we could downstairs.

I didn't really have an opinion on whether or not Freya pressed charges because I knew what the system was like. There was a high chance that Zach wouldn't be punished at all because of insufficient evidence or some similar crap, and that was the reason more people didn't speak up about assaults and abuse. It was absolute bullshit. The system continued to fail people.

I was going to ensure that Zach went nowhere near Freya again, though. I'd called up one of the guys from the organisation and he'd sent me some information on him. It turned out he wasn't so perfect after all and had been in trouble with the law for possession of Class B drugs and driving under the influence.

The most recent offence was four months ago, and I was going to make sure that the college knew about it—somehow, it had gone under the radar. I assumed it involved a bribe from Zach's very wealthy father, but he wouldn't be a student there much longer.

My head jerked up at the sound of shuffling, and Freya padded down the stairs. She didn't look as disturbed as I thought she'd be—with her hair slicked back into a sleek ponytail and her face lightly dusted with makeup. Something in my gut twisted at the sight of her. She didn't even need the makeup. She was naturally beautiful. Plump lips. A slender face with a pointed chin. A slight dotting of freckles over her nose. Eyes that spoke to me while her mouth said nothing at all. *Fuck.*

"Where are you going?" I asked, inhaling deeply. Why did she always have to smell like vanilla and cherries? It made it extremely hard to dislike being in her presence.

Freya sighed. "A party. I gathered it was better to go to that than lay in my bed feeling sorry for myself."

"Is that really a good idea?" I stood up.

"I guess I won't know until I get there."

Alcohol and high emotions didn't mix, and I wanted to tell Freya to stay home and watch a film with us instead, but I knew that wouldn't go down well. She didn't like being told what to do, and deep down, it was something that I liked about her.

"Is Zach going to be there?" Brent queried, looking unnerved.

My jaw twitched at the question, and Freya shrugged. "Probably not. He's not friends with Josh, and I can't imagine his face looks too pretty right now."

I arched my brow. "Who's Josh?" Brent chuckled softly from beside me.

"Hannah's half fuck-buddy, half boyfriend. It's his house."

"Right," I said. "We'll come. I don't trust Zach not to make a reappearance."

Brent groaned from beside me, tilting his head back and cursing up at the ceiling. "I don't want to go to a college party."

I took in Freya's perplexed expression, and she chewed on the inside of her cheek as she studied me. "You guys don't have to come. I'm sure it'll be fine."

I grabbed my car keys from the hook, shrugging, gesturing towards the door, but Freya shook her head.

"You can't show up with that hanging from your waist." She pointed at my gun I'd clipped back into its holster. "People will freak out."

"Right." I clicked my tongue, grabbing my leather jacket that hung over a dining room chair, the end of it just about hiding my weapon. "Let's go."

The journey didn't take long, although Freya had to direct me the entire way, and because she wasn't the queen of instruction giving, we took more than a few wrong turns. I hoped it would give her enough time to change her mind, but she seemed set on attending the party, and I wasn't about to argue with her.

"That looks feral," Brent muttered in disgust as we approached the house. People practically spilt out of the windows, and the flashing lights inside were blinding. The music vibrated the road outside, and college students cheered and sang while they sloshed their overfilled cups around.

"Still time to back out?" I cocked my head at Freya, hoping that the carnage would be enough to deter her, but although I could tell she was slightly hesitant, she huffed and strolled into the house.

I gazed around the room with aversion, muttering a string of curse words as I scanned the large living area for any sign of Zach. *Nope.* No dickhead fuck-face with a bruised and swollen nose here. It didn't mean he wasn't upstairs or outside, though—the party appeared to stretch out into all areas of the house.

How many people were even here? Who had this many friends?

"How old is everyone?" I questioned out of curiosity, eyeing the empty bottles of beer and vodka scattered on the hardwood flooring.

"I don't know," Freya said, shrugging. "But this isn't the time to go all cop mode."

I hummed. I was always in cop mode. Not that underage drinking bothered me. I had more important things to worry about.

Suddenly, a squealing, mousy brown-haired girl rushed up to Freya, wrapping her arms around her tightly, causing a small laugh to bubble up her throat.

"Hannah, you're crushing me."

"You're late, you bitch. I had to walk here all by myself. I called you a thousand times."

Freya apologised sheepishly, explaining that she'd fallen asleep, but her friend didn't seem too concerned and thrust a red cup in her direction. However, Freya shook her head.

"I don't think I'm going to drink tonight," she stated, surprising me.

Her friend gazed up at me, her bold eyes widening before she sent Freya a look, smirking.

Brent and I stood in the middle of the crowded room awkwardly—stiff as boards—and I turned my head to see him being approached by a small group of girls. They all gawked at him flirtatiously, causing my eyes to roll.

Freya stiffened beside me, her gaze trailing down Brent's body, and she looked up at me with perplexed eyes. I couldn't understand what she was silently trying to tell me, though, and I cocked my head at her as she attempted to gain Brent's attention.

You're showing, she mouthed to my friend, and his eyes darkened, his hand immediately flying to his crotch with confusion.

"No," I mumbled with a chuckle, pushing my leather jacket back the tiniest bit, showing just the tip of my gun, and Brent nodded in realisation, yanking his own jacket down slightly to cover his weapon that had dislodged itself from its holster. He politely smiled at the small group of girls and excused himself so he could subtly adjust the positioning of his gun.

"Let's dance," Hannah ordered, clutching onto Freya's hand.

"Do you want to come?" Freya's question took me off guard, and I narrowed my eyes at her, continuing to scan the crowd.

"I don't dance."

She hummed before they sifted through the mess of people, and I made my way to the corner of the room so I had a view of everyone. There was no way I was going to let Zach slip through my fingertips. If he was here and went anywhere near Freya, I was going to hang him from the wall and use him as my own personal live shooting target.

The corner of my lip flicked upwards at the thought, but I was snapped from my vulgar mind as someone stumbled over my foot, and the short guy wearing glasses turned around to apologise, frowning at the liquid he'd spilt over my shoes.

I huffed.

God, I hated college parties.

Thirteen: Freya

The party was chaotic, and I didn't feel much better being here. It was a distraction, sure, but after an hour, I was about ready to leave. There was no sign of Zach, but I found myself paranoid. Any tall, brunette man that moved past me caused me to jump, and they looked at me as if I was crazy as I smiled awkwardly and shuffled aside.

I wondered if Kaleb and Brent were about ready to go, too.

Turning around, I caught sight of Kaleb in the far corner of the room. He was leaning against a wall talking to a beautiful blonde, her wavy hair cascading down her back and her slim figure standing closer to him than necessary. He ground his teeth together as she spoke, his arms crossed.

I couldn't help the pang of displeasure that rocketed through me, especially since she was absolutely stunning. It was stupid of me, though. Kaleb and I barely even tolerated each other.

I stood in the middle of the crowd, watching them both, my eyebrows raising when she took a step towards him, reaching out and placing her hand on his arm. He noticeably stiffened, his jaw tense as he looked past the blonde, scanning the crowd again.

I couldn't help myself as my legs moved on their own accord towards the pair, and I cleared my throat awkwardly to catch their attention. Kaleb glanced down at me with questionable brows, and the blonde looked pissed off—rightfully so—but I paid her no mind as I stared into Kaleb's concerned eyes.

"Freya?" he questioned, cocking his head, waiting for me to speak. "You okay?"

"Umm, yeah, I've lost Hannah."

Big. Fat. Lie.

"Right, excuse me." Kaleb brushed past the beauty, her eyebrows scrunching together in irritation as she watched him and me move away from her. "Freya, she's right there. At the table. Where you were." Kaleb pointed over to the drinks table where I'd just come from, gesturing to Hannah, who had her arms wrapped around Josh's neck.

I nodded, swallowing, and he dipped his chin, flashing his straight teeth as he chuckled to himself.

"If you wanted to get me away from her, all you had to do was say that, Freya."

My face turned as red as a tomato, and I gazed up at Kaleb with round eyes, my heart feeling as if it was going to fall out of my ass. "I didn't..." There was no point in me even finishing the sentence. We both knew it.

Kaleb didn't speak. Instead, he allowed me to wallow in my embarrassment, and it was clear he found it entertaining. "If you'd rather I stay and talk to you instead, I'm happy to keep you company."

"No," I replied, my voice quiet. "No, I can see Hannah now, so don't let me cockblock you." Regret flooded my system.

Kaleb shrugged, taking a backwards glance at the blonde. "She's not really my type."

Oh, I mouthed, twiddling my fingers, resisting the urge to chew my nails off. "So, then, what is your type?"

Kaleb hummed, his eyes travelling up and down my body briefly before he clicked his tongue. "I prefer brunettes. I like women who can stand their own ground. Some call them bossy, but I prefer the word self-assured. Or fiery. I like when they can keep me on my toes, and I could tell after just one minute of talking to that girl that she was none of those things."

A chill ran down my spine at his confession, and I nodded casually as he smirked down at me.

"I would ask you your type, but I have a feeling I already know." He continued to scan the room, glaring at a couple next to us who almost bumped into me as they danced. One look from Kaleb had them backing up immediately.

"What do you mean?" I questioned. "You don't know my type." Zach hadn't been a good representation.

"Judging by how you're always staring at me, I do."

My breath hitched.

What on earth was I supposed to respond to that? Was denying it the best route to take? Or was laughing and shrugging it off going to come across as more believable? Frankly, I wasn't about to admit to Kaleb that he'd hit the nail on the head. He was exactly my type, but then again, I didn't see how he couldn't be. He was drop-dead gorgeous.

"I don't know what you're talking about," I said before I even had time to think. Denying it, it was.

"Freya, I didn't say I minded."

My stomach suddenly decided it wanted to take up gymnastics as a new hobby, flipping and tumbling, and I awkwardly cleared my throat. I was usually a pretty confident person, but there was something about Kaleb that made me flounder.

“If it makes you feel any better,” Kaleb continued, “I feel like I'm going to need to punch about ten different guys right now for looking at you like you're a meal. You're the most attractive woman here by far, and they're not being subtle about it."

I craned my neck, spotting a few men gazing at me suggestively, some just outwardly staring at my breasts with no shame. *Creeps.*

The guys weren't the only ones, though. It looked like the majority of the women in here were eyeing up Kaleb, and I couldn't blame them. He stuck out like a sore thumb with his impressive height and large muscles, oozing an intimidating and unbothered aura. Many women were drawn to that kind of personality—including me.

I hadn't noticed how hot it was until I felt perspiration collect on the nape of my neck, and I fanned myself with my hand, which earned me a concerned look from Kaleb.

“Let's go outside,” he said, turning, and I furrowed my brows at the way the crowd parted for him—as if he were Moses and they were the Red Sea.

The cool air calmed me immediately, and Kaleb and I leaned up against the side of the house. A few people were lingering around outside—some smoking and some chatting and laughing—but they took no notice of us.

He took a deep breath, tilting his head back and gazing up at the stars, looking fed up. He dragged his phone from his pocket, and his lock screen caught my attention. He, with a young Brie, sat on his lap—his little sister mid-giggle as she pinched his cheeks, attempting to get him to smile for the camera. A sigh left his lips once he noticed my interest, gazing down at the photo before locking the device.

"Your mom told me what happened," I said quietly, kicking at the ground. I wanted to apologise for sleeping in her room. I understood how much it upset Kaleb; it seemed to be the elephant in the room whenever I'd head to bed. His eyebrows would knit together, and his mouth would turn downwards every evening, and I often waited for him to call it a night before me so I could avoid his reaction.

Kaleb hummed in response, his Adam's apple bobbing up and down as he swallowed, refusing to look at me.

"I just wanted to say how sorry I am for staying in her room. If I'd known about it when I first arrived, I would have offered to stay on the couch. I still can if—"

"It doesn't matter," Kaleb responded, running his tongue along the front of his teeth. Jackie was right when she said he refused to talk about it and acted as if everything was fine. He was bottling it all up, and it was clearly affecting him.

"It does," I muttered. "I know how hard it is for you."

Something inside Kaleb snapped, and he turned to me with a scowl. His anger wasn't directed at me, but I could see the hurt lingering in his coal-like eyes. "I don't think you know what it feels like to have somebody die because of you, Freya."

"Brie didn't die because of you, Kaleb. Your mom said—"

"She doesn't know the full story," he interrupted me, taking a deep breath.

My mouth parted slightly, and I knitted my brows together. An awkward silence filled the air between us—thick and uncomfortable. I felt like I was choking on it, and after a few minutes, Kaleb gazed at my conflicted expression and cursed to himself.

"The people who shot Brie were really aiming for me," he mumbled, running his hands through his hair. "I pissed them off, and they followed me. Three people died that night—one of them being my little sister, who was completely innocent."

My face blanched.

"My mom thinks I got into this line of work because that incident made me realise I wanted to protect people. She doesn't know it actually stems from a place of guilt."

"You never told her?"

"Brent is the only person who knows."

"You didn't pull the trigger, Kaleb." I took a step closer to him. "It isn't your fault that Brie isn't here anymore."

Kaleb scowled, his mouth down-turned. "Yes, Freya, it is. Just because I didn't actively shoot her doesn't mean it isn't my fault. If it weren't for me fucking with them, those guys wouldn't have had a reason to try to kill me. I knew they hated me, and I pushed, thinking it was funny. It should have been me that night. Not Brie."

I gulped, chewing on the inside of my cheek.

"I shouldn't be telling you this." Kaleb ground his teeth together, leaning his head against the house and shutting his eyes. "I'm going to the shooting range, so I'll take you home."

"Is it open at this time?"

"It's always open."

"Right," I said. "I'll go with you."

He arched a brow, dragging his bottom lip into his mouth as he deliberated. "I don't think—"

"Zach could have hurt me earlier. I think we could both benefit from a way to release some pent-up anger, don't you think?"

The innuendo left my mouth before I realised its double meaning, and Kaleb raised his chin, humour sparking in his eyes.

"Will never stays later than eight, but don't speak to anybody inside. I'll message Brent to let him know we'll be back soon."

I nodded. Hopefully, my shooting skills had magically improved since the last time, but I had little hope.

By the time we reached the shooting range, adrenaline was soaring through my veins, making me feel buzzed with anxiety and excitement.

Hearing that Kaleb tortured himself on the daily regarding Brie's death caused my heart to ache. He'd messed with some guys, but I knew if he'd known that there was even the slightest chance that Brie would get hurt because of it, he wouldn't have taunted them.

His hands were tight on the wheel, the metal groaning underneath the force, his veins pulsating. Once stopped, he gripped his gun, beckoning me to follow him inside with his head.

The shooting range looked eerie at night, the few smashed windows at the front reflecting the moonlight, the wind whistling through them. So *that* was the reason it was so cold inside.

"You're sure Will won't be here?" I asked, cocking my head. I wasn't going to suggest turning back if he was, but I *did* want to prepare myself to be creeped out. He emitted strange energy, and it was clear I wasn't the only one who thought so, judging by how Kaleb didn't want me speaking to him.

"He doesn't like spending his evenings here."

The scent of cigarettes and sweat wafted up my nostrils as we entered the building, causing them to burn. I scrunched up my face, and Kaleb twisted his head from side to side as he scanned the room. "It's practically empty."

He was right. I'd expected it to be busy late at night, but it seemed the shiftiest of people preferred to do their shooting at midday. There were two men in the far corner, but they didn't pay us any mind as they continued to shoot and laugh, the sound of their guns firing bouncing off the metal walls and making my ears ring.

Kaleb claimed the furthest spot away from them, the side of his lip curling upward. "Ladies first." He chuckled as he passed me his gun, leaning back against the wall with his arms crossed.

"Right." I sighed, clasping the weapon between tentative fingers, the memory of how to grasp it having fizzled from my mind. I took a deep breath and shut my eyes momentarily before opening them and pressing down on the trigger. The bullet went flying, hitting the corner of the target and bouncing off in another direction, making me yelp, afraid it was going to hit us.

Kaleb hummed, taking the gun from me, his tall form towering over me intimidatingly. "Well, that was significantly better than last time."

He wasn't lying. I'd actually hit the target this time.

Kaleb shot with ease—not even looking for the last one, his curious gaze settling on me. I couldn't stop thinking about what he'd said back at the party, though. It was clear I'd been trying to get him away from the blonde, and he felt no shame in letting me know he was aware of the fact. Not only that, but he'd admitted that he found me attractive.

The feeling was mutual.

But he already knew that.

It had been about forty-five minutes, and my eyes were beginning to droop. I'd shot a few more times—all of them even more terrible than the last—and eventually, I left Kaleb to it while I watched. The young lady working the bar had brought over two shots for us before she left, and after a bit of reluctance, I managed to make Kaleb cheers to having a shitty day before we swallowed the fiery liquid.

The two men on the other side of the room had also called it a night, leaving Kaleb and me alone, the quiet folk music playing in the background suddenly sounding overly loud as it filled the silence. My head was thumping with every guitar string, a headache having set in. However, even with my skull pulsating, there was one thing on my mind that, for some stupid reason, I couldn't let go.

"What you said at the party..." I began, the words tumbling out of my mouth before I could stop them.

"What?" Kaleb asked, taking another shot at the target. "About you being the most attractive woman at the party?" A low chuckle sounded from his chest. "I'm not blind, Freya."

I had to refrain from blushing, feeling my face become hotter and hotter, and I could tell that the tip of my ears had tinged pink.

Kaleb Evans said I was attractive. So what? Not a big deal.

"Does that surprise you?"

"What?" I picked at my cuticles—a nervous habit I'd possessed since childhood.

"That I find you attractive? Does that surprise you?"

"I guess I've never thought about it before."

I was full of fibs today.

This caused Kaleb to nod. "I'm sure you haven't," he said sarcastically, and I heatedly took a step closer to him, shaking my head.

"Enough with the teasing," I ordered him. "I don't like it."

He took notice of our proximity, his eyes darting to my lips briefly before he nodded, smiling. "Noted. Would you prefer it if I were to follow through with my flirting?"

I froze. I was dizzy. So very dizzy. "I... I don't know," I muttered, unsure how to respond.

"That's not a no," Kaleb commented, taking a step closer to me, his jaw flexing as he swallowed, his eyes intense.

"No," I said breathlessly. "It's not." My mouth suddenly felt as dry as the Sahara desert as I glanced at Kaleb's lips. His eyes followed my own actions.

I hadn't realised my back had touched the wall behind me until I felt the icy metal sting my skin, and I gasped as Kaleb shuffled closer.

"Just tell me if you want me to stop, Freya."

There wasn't a cell in me that wanted him to stop. I was glued to the ground, my heart slamming against my ribcage forcefully, causing them to ache. An ache I adored, though. An ache I never wanted to come to an end.

Hooking his finger under my chin, Kaleb studied me for a few seconds, releasing a pent-up breath. "Fuck it." Suddenly, he crushed his lips to mine. I immediately responded, wrapping my arms around his neck and digging my nails into his skin. As we kissed, our flaming bodies pressed against one another—Kaleb tasting like mint and sarcasm—my new favourite flavour.

He released a throaty groan, and the sound caused me to tighten my grip on him, sliding my hands from his neck to his chest. I fisted his leather jacket, shrugging it off him and pressing my palms to his toned chest. I'd imagined myself doing this a hundred times, and it was even better than I'd expected.

My peaked nipples grazed against him, and the friction caused me to moan, tilting my head back so Kaleb could press harsh kisses down the column of my throat, ending up at the base. The warmth of his body radiated onto my own, making me sweat, and he greedily brought his lips back to mine, smothering me in one thousand tonnes of bliss and tranquillity.

But the sound of Kaleb's gun dropping from its holster and clattering to the floor caused me to jump, and he stepped away from me with dark eyes. His nostrils flared, and he breathed heavily, taking in my lust-filled state before he frowned. "Shit," he muttered, running his hand through his hair.

We'd just made out, and it was the single best feeling I'd ever had the pleasure of experiencing. However, I knew that the bubble of ignorance we were surrounded with was soon to burst.

"Shit," he repeated, turning away from me. "We shouldn't have done that."

I furrowed my brows at him, my stomach twisting painfully.

Kaleb sighed, running his hand down his face. "We shouldn't have done that, Freya."

"Really?" My blood turned hot, and a glower etched itself onto my face as I tilted my head questionably, silently asking Kaleb if he was serious. His face told me all I needed to know, though, and I grabbed my coat and rushed past him toward the exit. Embarrassment coursed through my veins, spilling over and taking hold of my body, sending my brain into a frantic mess.

Kaleb called after me, but I couldn't hear anything other than my inner monologue cackling at me for giving in to the temptation.

Fourteen: Kaleb

Shit. Fuck. A thousand fucks.

I wasn't supposed to kiss Freya. It wasn't meant to happen, but in my desire-driven state, I had. The worst part was that it felt good—more than good. There wasn't a word to describe it. It was nothing but pure ecstasy.

I wanted my chest flush against hers again. Her delicate hands pressed to my chest while my own snaked around her waist. *Fuck, what was wrong with me?*

Did I regret it? Yes and no. I wanted it to happen again and again, but I couldn't allow it to. Freya and I were living in two completely different worlds. She was innocent, and I was far from it.

I had killed. I had taken people's lives and thought nothing of it. She had a promising future ahead of her—a future where she could be safe. Anyone mixed up in my world was a target; she didn't deserve to be subjected to that.

Many crime organisations knew of us—which was why we had to stay under the radar. A few years ago, one of the guys in my team had his name leaked, and a gang attempted to assassinate his son. They'd almost got away with it.

There was something about Freya that intrigued me, though. She snapped back. She always had an opinion, and I liked it, even if what she was saying *was* laced with a moody and catty undertone.

When I'd first met her, I'd convinced myself she was the most annoying person to walk the planet. She'd invaded my personal space, but I'd started to see past our differences. I craved being around her. When I'd come home, and she wasn't in, I'd be somewhat disappointed. I'd never felt these kinds of emotions before, and frankly, they were frightening the fuck out of me.

Not to mention she was the most beautiful women I'd ever laid eyes on. She had dark features—my weakness—and had a body to die for. When she smiled... fuck, it did something to me.

By the time I'd raced outside to reason with her after our kiss, she was gone. I had no choice but to drive home and hope that she'd made it back safely, but I kept an eye out for her the entire journey, driving slowly in case I came across her.

It was just turning twelve when I reached the house, and it was evident that everybody was asleep—all the lights off and the house deathly silent. Brent had tried calling me a few times, but I'd ignored him, and I groaned as his name flashed up on my screen yet again.

The party was probably wrapping up, and he was most likely wondering where I was and if I was coming back to pick him up.

Kaleb: Get a cab home for me, will you? I'll send you some cash for it. See you tomorrow.

My thumbs felt heavy as I typed out the message, moving up the stairs and stopping outside of Freya's room, listening for any sound of her. I needed to see her in the flesh to convince myself she was home and safe.

Knocking on the wood gently, I waited, tapping my foot impatiently against the carpeted floor. The last thing I'd wanted to do was upset her, but my words had wounded her—that much was obvious.

I couldn't allow myself to lose control around her again. It wasn't fair on her—especially because after Christmas, I would be heading back to base, which was hours away, and there was no guarantee I would be stationed there long-term. There were plenty of other bases states away that I could be moved to.

Freya was sensitive and sweet and deserved more than just a Christmas fling. She deserved someone better. More reliable. I was a loose end, and trouble seemed to follow me around like the Grim Reaper. It wasn't right to get her wrapped up in my life issues.

I didn't enjoy invading people's privacy, but I couldn't wait for a response any longer, so I pushed the bedroom door open slightly, peering in to see Freya snuggled up in bed—I assumed she'd caught a cab home. She appeared asleep, although I wasn't sure if she was pretending to avoid talking to me.

Being a sensitive guy had never been a characteristic I possessed, but Freya made me feel things that had been dormant for years. It was as if she was unlocking a vault within me that I didn't want to be opened, and even though I hated the idea, I couldn't resist handing over the combination. It was endearing just as much as it was frustrating.

Throwing myself into my room and shutting my door a little too loudly, I clamped my eyes shut. I was still buzzed from the kiss, and there was no way I was going to be able to fall asleep.

Tonight was going to be a long night.

I awoke to the sound of my phone vibrating by my ear, and I groaned as I rubbed a hand down my face.

I hadn't drunk anything last night but a small shot of tequila, but for some fucking reason, I felt as if I was battling a horrid hangover. My limbs were achy. My head was throbbing. And my mind was fuzzy. I'd spent the majority of the night stressing about my kiss with Freya. *God, what the hell was she doing to me?*

I brought the phone to my ear, readying myself for Brent's cranky attitude.

"You're late," he muttered, sighing down the line. "I'm at the shooting range at the time you requested, but *you* aren't."

I was usually the one having to remind Brent to be more professional, and I didn't enjoy being scolded like a teenage boy.

"Yeah, I know." I quietly dragged myself out of bed so he didn't hear the creak through the phone. "I'm literally leaving the house now."

Brent hummed in response, mumbling a quick *hurry up* before ending the call.

Knowing I probably smelled of displeasure and regret, I hopped in the shower. It was nine-thirty, and Freya had most likely already left for class.

I didn't know what we were both going to do now. There were two options: go back to how we were when she'd first arrived or pretend that the kiss never happened and continue to be somewhat friendly. I didn't particularly like the sound of either of them. I just wanted what was best for her.

As I'd promised myself, one anonymous email to the school with evidence of Zach's arrests had been sent. I didn't get a response, which was expected, but I'd slipped the bait and just needed to wait for the school to bite. He deserved to be rotting in a jail cell for forcing his way into the house and assaulting Freya. Even just thinking about it caused my blood to boil and my skin to crawl.

I reached the shooting range twenty minutes later—met with a very unimpressed-looking Brent. He crossed his arms over his chest as he glared at me.

"I got here early because you told me I couldn't be late one more time, and now you show up looking like absolute shit," he said, a hint of humour lacing his tone. It seemed he wasn't as angry as he was trying to come across. It took a lot to get him riled up because, for the most part, Brent was a cheerful guy.

I waved his concern away, shaking my head. Even just his voice was intensifying my pounding headache. "I'm not one for apologies, so let's go inside. You got home fine in the end, and I sent you money for the ride."

Brent shrugged. "I mean, it wasn't too much of an issue for me. I went back to some girl's house and—"

Holding my hand up to stop him, I headed towards the entrance of the shooting range. "I don't want to hear about it. I really don't."

"Well, at least tell me about your night, then." Brent nodded at the young receptionist as we entered. The place was busy today. "You said you and Freya went somewhere? But then you never came back. Sounds like an interesting night to me."

"Shut up before I shoot you instead of the target." I gripped at my waistband for my gun and delved into my pocket to grab my bullets, but I came up empty-handed, and I furrowed my thick brows. I'd forgotten my extra bullets, and that was something I never did. Ever. It dawned on me that this was the effect that Freya had on my way of thinking. She was muddling my mind. I was mind muddled.

"I forgot my bullets," I croaked, my voice hoarse. Being here without an extra stash was far too risky. "I'll be right back."

Heading towards the reception, I greeted the worker behind the desk, her eyes darting up and down my body quickly before she composed herself. "Need anything?" she asked with a smile, leaning forward over the counter a little too much, revealing her cleavage suggestively.

"I need some bullets," I muttered, ignoring her advance. I wasn't interested in the slightest. "Can you help me out with that?"

"Sure we can," said a familiar voice from behind me, and I rolled my eyes as I turned to see Will smoking his usual cigarette, looking mighty tired. Did the guy ever sleep? "Usually, we'd ask people to pay a small charge, but there's no need for you to do that, Kaleb."

I nodded, taking the pack of bullets from the woman behind the desk, and Will glanced directly at her breasts, licking his lips and humming.

Vile.

"Where's your pretty brunette friend?" he questioned me as I re-entered the main building, holding in the irritated sigh I wanted to release. Why was he so nosy? I wasn't telling him shit about Freya.

"I don't think she'll be coming back here," I replied, wanting to give off the impression that she wasn't anything special to stop Will from hounding me. I was surprised his nose wasn't red raw from the amount he stuck it into people's business.

He hummed, dipping his chin at Brent as a greeting, watching him shoot, smiling as he hit the centre of the target. "That's a shame. She was a beauty, wasn't she? But I suppose going back for seconds gives them the wrong message."

Who the hell was he talking about? He was a married man. I cleared my throat, ignoring Will's comment, hating how he referred to Freya as a *beauty*, but as much as I wanted to punch him square in the face, I couldn't.

I couldn't get on his bad side.

It was imperative.

Fifteen: Freya

I'd been shamefully avoiding Kaleb since our kiss. We still saw each other—we lived together, so it was inevitable—but I made sure I was never alone with him. If both my mom and Jackie were out, then so was I. Kaleb's lingering glances were off-putting, and we both felt the thick, choking tension in the air between us. We couldn't go without oxygen for too long, though. Soon enough, we were both going to have to come up for air and discuss what had happened.

There was just something about Kaleb that drew me in—I couldn't put my finger on it—but perhaps that was because I didn't want to know what it was. If I did, I'd be able to ignore it purposely. I felt safe with him. I'd managed to un-peel the many solid layers he wrapped himself in, and even he'd admitted Brent was the only person he'd been semi-vulnerable with.

I was walking back from college, relief spreading through me that I hadn't bumped into Zach again. He hadn't been to class once since the incident, but it didn't take a genius to work out why. He definitely had a hell of a shiner, and being seen in public with it would undoubtedly aggravate his ego.

My phone buzzed in my hand—luckily, Zach hadn't broken it—and a shred of anxiety mixed with hope hit me. Was my dad finally answering my texts?

Mom: Jackie received a promotion today at work. We're all going out for a meal tonight to celebrate. Get home as soon as you can.

My eyes widened as I stopped on the sidewalk, apologising to a runner as they almost slammed into the back of me because of my sudden cease of movement.

I couldn't tell my mom I didn't want to come because things were awkward between Kaleb and me since we'd made out at some creepy shooting range. Jackie would be disappointed that I'd hooked up with her son while she was kindly allowing me to stay at her house—in her deceased daughter's room, for that matter.

Freya: Looking forward to it.

Far from it—I was going to have to put on a smile while sitting across from a guy who was confusing the heck out of me, and that didn't sound appealing at all. The kiss shouldn't have happened—no matter how right it felt. How right it felt to have Kaleb's body flush against mine. How right it felt to have his large, calloused hands digging into my side, squeezing me possessively. How right it felt to have him peppering urgent kisses down my throat while I sighed in bliss. *Shit.*

I walked back to the house as quickly as I could, my mind wandering once again to the fact that my dad's company didn't exist. I hadn't had the guts to tell my mom about it yet, but I was becoming antsy. Judging by the fact that she hadn't informed me she hadn't been able to find any contact information, I gathered she hadn't researched it yet. Work was running her into the dirt, apparently.

Dropping my bag by the door, I peered into the house, trying to be as quiet as possible. The thought of facing Kaleb was nauseating. I didn't know what I wanted to say to him, and I knew hearing him admit he had no interest in me romantically would hurt like a bitch. It was a conversation that needed to be had, though. I'd been avoiding it too long.

"Oh, good!" My mom rounded the corner from the kitchen—still in her work attire—her heels clacking against the floor. "I was worried that you wouldn't get home in time."

"So, where are we going?" I questioned, glancing up at the landing once I heard a door open, spotting a beaming Jackie.

"To a fancy little restaurant on the outskirts of town," she responded excitedly. "It's one of my favourites."

By the way and Jackie and my mother were giggling, it was evident they'd already been on the wine. My mom was a bad drunk, so I was going to have to look after her tonight.

"Is Kaleb coming?" I asked hesitantly, brushing my sweaty palms down my pant legs, dusting them off.

"He's in the car." Jackie nodded through the open door, and I peered out to see him inside his black Jeep, typing away furiously with the same scowl he always wore. Why did that stupid scowl have to look so good on him, though? His eyes instantly found mine through the rear-view mirror as we hopped into the car, and we gazed at each other for a good few seconds before his phone buzzed on his lap.

"A few guys will be over to install the security cameras by the front and back doors tomorrow," he said to his mother, shoving his phone into his pocket and starting the car.

"I don't know why you suddenly insist we get them, Kaleb."

He merely hummed in response, focusing on the road before him as he drove.

"What's happened recently that's made you want to have them installed?" Jackie pressed, seeming slightly worried about her son's pushiness on the subject. Even though she claimed they didn't need them, he was insistent that he paid for them and had them installed as soon as possible.

My breathing hitched, and I panicked, worried he was going to admit to Zach barging his way into the house and attacking me.

Kaleb glanced at me again. His hurricane-like eyes clung to mine for a few more seconds before he averted them, shrugging at his mother's question. "No reason. It's just safer."

Thank God.

The drive took around fifteen minutes, and once Kaleb had parked in the middle of what looked like nowhere, we made our way around the corner to a small Thai restaurant. Jackie gazed up at it with what appeared to be a mix of sorrow and excitement, and I smiled at her with questionable brows.

"This was Brie's favourite restaurant," my mom whispered to me as we hung back slightly, noticing my confused expression. "I don't think they've been here since she passed."

I nodded in understanding, picking at my cuticles, and my mom sighed after noticing my sombre expression.

"Honey, I was going to tell you but didn't have the time. I contacted the police the other day about your father, but they didn't take my claim seriously. They said since this doesn't seem too out of character for him, they aren't overly worried, and I need to contact them again if he's not back by next week."

I arched my brows, shaking my head. "How could the police not be worried? He's a missing person." I'd spoken louder than intended, gaining a couple's attention nearby.

Jackie and Kaleb were glancing at us from the restaurant table with strange expressions, and my mom cleared her throat, nodding to them. "We can finish this conversation later. Right now, let's celebrate with Jackie. She's worked very hard."

Tightening my jaw, I sat down next to Kaleb. Our legs brushed as I got comfortable, and he stiffened from beside me, his throat bobbing up and down as he swallowed.

"Welcome, guys. Can I get you all something to drink?"

I recognised that voice. Gazing up at the server, I narrowed my eyes. "Ty?"

"Oh, my God." He chuckled. "Freya? It's been ages!"

I beamed, standing up to hug him, his arms wrapping around me tightly. "I know. How have you been? We haven't spoken since high school."

"I'm good, I'm good. I'm playing ice hockey for Richmond now. Coach wants us to remain humble, and his plan is to get us to work once a week to stop us from getting too cocky, as he thinks it affects the way we play, hence this side hustle. Plus, with the name Ty, it's kind of fitting to work here." He laughed, gesturing down to his server's apron. "How's college?"

"It's good. I'm studying art."

"Of course you are. You always had a talent for drawing. I expect to see your artwork hanging at the Louvre soon." His words caused my mom to chuckle, and they exchanged a quick *hello*. "Look, I'd love to catch up, but I've got a heap of orders to take, so could I just grab your drink orders, and maybe we can chat later?"

As Ty walked away with our order in hand, I glanced at Kaleb, noticing his blazing eyes locked in on my old friend. His eyebrows were pulled together, and his jaw flexed. He was looking at him as if he was a meal.

The evening mainly consisted of Jackie and my mother giggling, and Kaleb pulled out his phone every couple of minutes to type while I attempted to keep my focus away from his fast-moving fingers. He seemed to always be in the middle of an important and heated conversation with someone.

"So, Christmas is coming up soon." Jackie laughed—now on her third glass of red wine. "Do either of you have anything planned for it?"

I hadn't really thought about Christmas, but I hadn't imagined that we'd spend it anywhere other than my house. The way things were going, though, it looked like my mother and I would be staying with Jackie and Kaleb a little longer than we'd first expected.

"I think—"

My mother cut me off with a loud curse, and Jackie stared wide-eyed at the wineglass she'd just smacked onto my mother's lap, red wine coating her black pencil skirt and white, knitted sweater.

"I'm so sorry!" she complained, reaching for some napkins.

"That's my fault for insisting we drink red tonight," my mom cackled. "I'm just going to head to the bathroom. Wine stains."

"I'll come." Jackie worriedly knitted her brows together at Kaleb and me as she followed my mother around the corner.

I cleared my throat, continued to chew on my chicken curry, and stared at the plate as if it were the most interesting thing in the restaurant. It was far from it—the most interesting thing was sitting right next to me.

"We should talk about what happened," I blurted out. It had to be done. I needed to stop chickening out.

Kaleb sighed, biting the inside of his cheek as he studied me. "Freya."

Why did he have to look so gorgeous when he was trying to let me down?

"You don't have to say it. It was just a kiss. Friends, it is."

At my comment, Kaleb's eye twitched, and the corner of his mouth curved downwards as he ran his hands through his dark hair. As usual, his tongue caressed his front teeth. "I—"

"Hey, I brought over some extra napkins," said Ty cheerily from behind me, placing them on the table, his hand on my shoulder.

"Oh, thanks." I reached over the table, wiping up the spillage. "I'm sorry about the mess."

Ty waved my worries away, flashing his perfect white teeth again. "No, don't even sweat it. Oh hey," he suddenly said, turning his attention to Kaleb, holding his hand out. "I'm sorry. That's rude of me. I'm Ty. You must be Freya's boyfriend."

"Oh, he's—" I began, but Kaleb cut me off, taking Ty's hand and shaking it firmly.

"Yeah, that's me."

Sixteen: Kaleb

I wasn't sure what came over me. *Yeah, that's me.*

Shit.

I couldn't help it, though. The way he'd put his hand on Freya's shoulder and the way she'd smiled up at him—it pissed me off. It shouldn't have, but it did, and I knew how big of a problem that was.

Freya all but choked on her curry as I half-smiled at Ty, looking him up and down. He was a good-looking guy—tall and muscular. There was no doubt in my mind that any woman would find him attractive, and that only bothered me further.

"Kaleb," I introduced myself, pulling my hand away from his. I didn't care if he didn't see Freya romantically. He genuinely seemed like a nice guy, but sometimes, they were the worst type of people. They could get away with anything because everyone around them saw them as so *nice*. I'd learned not to trust anyone until they proved otherwise.

Ty's eyes scraped over my heavily tattooed forearms with a curious expression, causing me to raise my eyebrows at him, and he excused himself to take another table's order.

"What the hell was that?" Freya spluttered, taking a sip of her water.

I shrugged. "I was saving you. He was going to ask you out."

Freya cocked her brow, crossing her arms over her chest as she glared at me. "Ty? We've known each other since we were fourteen. We're platonic."

I hummed in response, nodding at her with a sarcastic *I believe you* kind of look.

"You're the one who said we shouldn't have kissed." Her tone was sharp. She thought that I completely regretted it. I didn't—far from it—but I knew she and I would never work.

Tongues of flames lapped at me, furious at my inner monologue. I'd never been so confused in my life. It was a foreign feeling for me. I was always sure—always prepared—but Freya was changing that. It ignited something inside of me, and I absolutely loved it and hated it at the same time.

"It's best if we just forget it happened."

Freya's expression gave little away, and she held her chin high as she nodded. "I agree."

My jaw twitched. It was what was best, but hearing her say it? Fuck, it didn't feel good.

The rest of the meal went smoothly, with Ty coming over to say a quick *goodbye*, laughing with Freya's mother about the substantial purple stain spattered onto her knitted sweater.

I drove home quickly, my eyes continuing to catch Freya's. She looked beautiful tonight in her smart black pants and high-neck top, perfectly sculpting her hips and breasts. I'd caught myself staring on more than a few occasions, and I was going to have to get that under control. It just felt impossible to stop.

It was late by the time we arrived home, and I hadn't actually realised how long we'd been at the restaurant. After my mother had suggested dining there to celebrate, my throat had closed up and my stomach had tightened, remembering how much Brie loved the khao soi and the tiny after-dinner chocolates they gave us at the end of every meal. We hadn't visited since her death, but my mom was adamant that she would have wanted us to keep going and enjoying it. It was weird but somewhat comforting—as if Brie was there in the building with us. Bittersweet.

"Well, I'm drunk, and I have work tomorrow," mumbled Sarah, pinching the bridge of her nose, causing my mom to agree. They both headed up the stairs, giggling together, leaving Freya and I eyeballing each other awkwardly.

"Do you have college tomorrow?" I questioned, trying to make conversation. *That was the kind of thing a friend would ask a fellow friend, right?* Because that was what we had to be. Friends.

"I do. First thing."

"Have you seen Zach lately?"

"No, I don't think he wants to show up looking like he's been trampled by rhinos." Freya's lip held a hint of a smile.

Or maybe it had something to do with the fact that the college had been tipped off about his illegal extracurricular activities, but who was I to tell her that?

"You should get some sleep," I told her as she yawned, and I watched with a frown as she reluctantly disappeared upstairs.

I got myself into bed a few minutes after her, stripping off and staring up at my ceiling. My body vibrated, my head refusing to settle down. I didn't know what it was, but it appeared to be a mixture of work, Freya and I agreeing that we needed to forget about our kiss, and the memory of Brie that was stopping me from falling asleep soundly.

My phone buzzed.

Brent: Invitations for the bodyguard ball have been emailed out. Who are you bringing?

I scrunched up my nose. The bodyguard ball was a celebration my organisation did every year to thank everyone for their hard work and service. I'd skipped the last one, coming up with a bunch of excuses why I couldn't make it, and my chief was less than impressed with my absence. I knew I had to attend this year.

Kaleb: I'm not bringing anyone. I just want to get it over with.

Brent: Other guys are bringing plus ones. I'm gonna bring the girl I met the other night at the party. Don't be that guy that shows up without a date, Kaleb.

Kaleb: I'm not obligated to bring a date.

The ball was held in the same hotel every year. It was exquisite and flashy—a little too much for my taste—but my organisation claimed they wanted to provide us with only the best. It was at least a five-hour drive from here, and most people were put in the hotel for free since we were all coming from different places.

I didn't socialise much with people on my team—besides Brent—and the thought of doing so pissed me off. I didn't see the point. We were all there to do our jobs. Why chat meaningless shit for hours over delicate glasses of overpriced champagne? It was a waste of time.

I was tossing and turning in bed all night, getting tangled in the sheets and unable to sleep. A curse fell from my lips after I turned to look at my bedside table clock. *Three in the fucking morning.*

Pushing the covers off of me, I slowly and quietly made my way downstairs. When I couldn't sleep, I'd often head down to crash on the couch. I'd fall asleep pretty quickly, and I believed it had something to do with Brie's photos surrounding me—like a guardian angel.

Huffing, I pulled out a blanket from the cabinet, fumbling around in the dark for a cushion, resting my head on it as I squeezed myself onto the small couch. I barely fit, but it wasn't as suffocating down here as my room felt.

I was almost asleep when I heard a door open, and I peered up towards the landing to see Freya, her form padding down the stairs. I remained completely still as I watched her, clutching an empty glass in her hands, heading for the kitchen to refill it.

My eyes could do nothing but linger on her. She was wearing the skimpiest little pyjama shorts—her ass peeking out the bottom of them. Her midriff was on show, revealing her flat and toned stomach, and she wore a tiny grey crop top, her breasts spilling out of the top of it. Her nipples were hard due to the sudden temperature change, and it caused a shudder to rattle my bones.

I wanted to say something—to alert her to my presence—but I didn't want to embarrass her for being caught in her tiny sleepwear.

Instead, I remained still and quiet on the couch, averting my eyes as she entered the kitchen, only to reappear a minute later with a full glass of water. As she ascended the stairs, I focused on the fraying cushion below me, hearing the click of her bedroom door closing. I pushed the blanket off me, suddenly extremely hot and bothered, my body tingling. After telling myself we would remain neutral, that outfit was the last thing I needed to see Freya in.

My frustration was boiling over, spilling out of my pores and tarnishing the couch I was lying on. *Why the hell was it so hot?* It felt like I was resting on a bed of hot coal, my skin slowly singeing. In displeasure, I tapped my fingers against the soft couch, my body twitchy and on edge,

Why couldn't I get her out of my head?

Damn it.

I wasn't a weak man, but when it came to Freya, I was fucking powerless.

"Back again, boys?"

I cringed at the usual huskiness of Will's voice, his smoker's lungs struggling with every word.

Brent grinned at him. "You know this is our favourite shooting spot in town."

"It's the *only* shooting spot in town. The next one is seven miles away." Will chuckled, the sound grating. Brent took another shot, and Will watched him with dubious eyes before he turned his attention to me.

"He's a good shooter," he murmured, leaning up against the metal wall that separated us from another two men. "But not nearly as good as you."

"I've had more practice."

"Was bringing Freya here just a one-time thing, then?"

The question caused my nostrils to flare. *He was using her name now?*

Brent eyed us up at the mention of Freya, and I wanted to do nothing more than turn around and wrap my hand around Will's throat for muttering it, but I took a deep breath to compose myself.

"She's not really relevant," I responded, trying to keep my tone neutral, but Will chuckled.

"Seems like someone has a crush." He lit up another cigarette. "Nothing wrong with that."

I remained silent, sipping on my drink.

"She was beautiful, Kaleb." Will shrugged. "I can't blame you."

God, I'd pay good money to get him to shut the hell up. I despised the way he spoke about her.

He snickered, toying with his own gun that hung from his waistband. "That's clearly a sensitive topic, so let's change it." He shot me a toothy grin. "When are you boys planning on leaving town again? I hope not anytime soon. It's always quiet around here without you."

I smiled—a very, very fake smile. "Still undecided. We've got some business to take care of, but we want to stick around for as long as possible."

"Good. You fit in here."

I mentally chuckled.

Not for long.

Seventeen: Freya

I had a feeling that my mom had been avoiding me. I wanted to talk to her regarding Dad's disappearance and the fact that I couldn't find his company online, but she had been leaving for work early and getting back late, claiming she was in the middle of a big project and had important deadlines to meet.

I just couldn't wrap my head around the fact that the police didn't seem to care about my father's disappearance, though. It was as if it was some kind of inconvenience to them, and his case had been tossed into a pile with others to rot away in a dark room where no one ventured.

"Everyone is asking me if I know where Zach is," muttered Hannah, turning to me with a cocked brow. I'd told her briefly about what had gone on between Zach and me, but I'd utterly dulled down the intensity of the situation, leaving out the part where he'd practically assaulted me and Kaleb had beaten the shit out of him.

"I know. People have been asking me too. I guess he just needs some time to himself after what happened between us," I responded, glancing over at Josh, who flung his arm over Hannah's shoulder, pecking at her cheek. The two of them looked pretty loved up.

Was I jealous? No comment.

"He took it that bad, huh?" Josh questioned as he leaned against the college lockers, and I shrugged, picking at my cuticles.

"I need to go, but I'll see you both tomorrow." I rushed out of the building, glancing at the sky, thankful it wasn't raining. It'd been pouring all week, and since my car still wasn't running, I had been having to walk to and from college—resulting in me getting drenched. The bus services around here were shocking, and I didn't have the money to take my car to a garage right now.

Once I got home, I narrowed my eyes at the camera staring at me as I unlocked the front door. The way it buzzed as it moved to follow my movements creeped me out, and I tilted my head at it as if we were competing in a staring contest and I was going to win.

My eyes widened after I spotted my mom, and I dropped my things and sighed. It didn't look like anybody else was around, and this was the perfect opportunity to talk to her about Dad. "Mom, can we please talk?"

She paled, nodding and settling down at the dining room table after a few seconds, lacing her fingers together. "I'm sorry. I've been swamped at work."

It was a lie. I knew it was. My mother had never been the confrontational type. She preferred to push things to the back of her mind and leave them for a later time, and then things would come crashing down around her all at once, and she would spiral.

I was used to her awful coping strategy. It was why it had taken her and my father so long to divorce. She never wanted to address their arguments.

"Tell me what's happened again. You reported Dad missing to the police?" I needed answers.

"They said to contact them again if he's still missing by next week. I'm not sure what the next step is after that. They might want to interview us, but overall, they didn't seem too concerned since he's in and out of the state so often."

I huffed, running a hand down my face. "You and he just divorced, and he was hiding a shit tonne of debt from us. How is that not concerning in the slightest?"

"I really don't know." She sighed heavily.

Taking my phone out, I searched for the website Kaleb had shown me. "His company isn't registered, Mom. It technically doesn't exist."

She hummed in disapproval, swiping up and down on my phone and pushing her glasses higher onto her nose, squinting at my screen. "I'm at a loss. I'm guessing if his company isn't registered, then there isn't a way we can get in contact with any of his colleagues. It's all a mess."

"I'm worried." I gulped, the gloomy thought weaving its way into my head and causing my insides to tighten. It'd been invading my thoughts for the past few days, and it terrified me. "What if he's...?"

"No, Freya," muttered my mom, shaking her head and moving around the table to take my hand. "Your father wouldn't do that to us. We may have issues, but he would never take his own life."

I breathed in a shaky breath. My dad had never seemed down or depressed, but then again, I hadn't spent too much time with him over the years. He just didn't seem like the type of person to consider suicide, though—being a straightforward and blunt individual. He loved his vacations and enjoyed the finer things in life. I didn't see it as an option for him.

My mom and I both jumped as Kaleb burst through the door. He didn't say anything, his eyes raking over me before he made his way up the stairs and into his room, causing me to stiffen. He was dressed in a black workout top and dark jeans, his combat boots pounding against the floor as he marched. His hair was tousled, and his eyes were as piercing as ever.

"He didn't look very happy," my mom commented, cocking her head at me and humming, moving away, towards the kitchen.

Our conversation was over, then. *Very on brand.*

She was right, though. Kaleb hadn't looked happy.

He and Brent had been together every day for the past four days, and I hadn't seen much of him. I'd often overhear him telling his mom he was heading out to the shooting range, and he would usually be gone almost all day. He *really* loved shooting.

Grabbing my backpack, taking out my most recent sketch—ready to fix the atrocity—I ascended the stairs, leaping out of my skin when Kaleb flung his door open. He stared at me, and I froze.

Say hi. It's what friends do.

"Um, hi."

Kaleb chuckled, clearly amused by how flustered I was, and the corner of his lips twitched upwards. I should have continued walking to my room, but for some stupid reason, I didn't. My feet were super glued to the ground.

He eyed up my sketch pad, holding his hand out to me, his eyebrows raised.

I widened my eyes, shaking my head. "Why? I need to start it again."

"Just show me the damn sketch pad, Freya." He sighed, and I eventually gave in, slowly handing it to him and focusing on the carpet beneath my feet.

It needed vacuuming.

"This is good," he muttered, cocking his head at my half-finished sketch of a bluebird soaring through the air with its beak to the sky, the wind rushing through its feathers and causing them to appear ruffled. "Maybe your little waiter friend was right. Your work might be hanging in the Louvre one day."

"Thanks," I said awkwardly, clearing my throat and taking my pad back. "How come you looked in an even worse mood than usual when you came in?"

"Tough day working." Kaleb leaned against the doorframe, his biceps bulging, making it extremely difficult to focus anywhere else.

"Working? I thought you went shooting."

He didn't speak for a second, pinching his eyebrows together, his tongue skating along his teeth.

He was stressed.

"Yeah, shooting is working for me. It's practice. I can't let my skill level drop over Christmas break."

"Oh right, yeah."

"Any more on your dad?"

"Mom reported him missing to the police," I said hopelessly.

"And...?"

"They don't seem interested. They don't believe it's out of character for him, so they want us to give it a bit more time."

Kaleb appeared a little taken aback. "That's kind of unusual. It's not the procedure usually followed."

That was interesting to know.

His eyes wandered briefly, honing in on my lips, and he opened up his mouth to speak.

"I'm home!" announced Jackie as she rushed into the house, pushing her long hair away from her face, huffing as she dropped her bags of groceries onto the floor. It caused Kaleb's eyes to round, and he quickly made his way downstairs to help her carry them to the kitchen.

"How was your day?" I asked, following them.

Jackie shrugged. "Besides a boss who won't get off my back now that I've got my promotion? Great." She laughed. "Hey, you finally got your car fixed, Freya; that's good."

My eyebrows dropped, and Kaleb faltered for a second as he dug deeper into the grocery bag for a sack of potatoes. "I—I didn't..." I muttered, confused.

Jackie glanced at me curiously. "Well, it was parked up on the road instead of in the driveway, so it's been moved. I assumed you'd fixed it? Looks like it's been cleaned, too." She finished unloading her grocery bag, yanked off her work heels and groaned with relief as she sauntered out of the room.

The cogs in my brain were working overdrive as I bit down on my lower lip. I hadn't noticed my car had been moved. *God, I really needed to start paying attention.*

"Here," mumbled Kaleb as he threw me a set of keys, and I caught them with a small yelp, glancing down to see my lilac heart-shaped keychain hanging from the metal.

"You—you fixed my car?" I asked in disbelief, causing him to shrug like it was no big deal, packing away a box of pasta.

"Don't say I never do anything for you."

"Why?" I asked, squeezing my keys between my hands. That must have cost him a fortune. Or had he done it himself? The thought of Kaleb all sweaty and covered in car grease made me gulp.

I didn't have the money to pay him back right now—the amount I made from my once-a-week job wouldn't cut it—and guilt hit me like a tsunami.

"You were walking to college in the rain," Kaleb responded, tucking the empty shopping bags away in a drawer, studying me.

"Thank you." I smiled. "But an umbrella would have sufficed."

He stepped closer to me, smirking. "I'm not really the bare minimum kind of guy." A chuckle escaped his lips, and he stepped past me into the doorway. "Plus, I like women only one type of wet."

My breath hitched, and sudden arousal flowed through my body, my mouth popping open. I stood motionless, welded to the kitchen floor with, my heart beating so fast I thought it was going to fall out of my ass.

Eighteen: Freya

Kaleb had enjoyed my floundering after his *little* comment, but it confused me even more. He'd made it clear that despite his attraction to me, we couldn't be anything. I'd believed we would be friendly with each other, but then Kaleb came out with *that*.

I had to brush off the comment, though. It was teasing. He wanted a reaction. It didn't mean as much as I thought it did.

He refused to tell me how much fixing my car had cost him. I still wasn't sure if he'd done it himself or paid someone else to fix it, but I accepted I wouldn't get an answer to that query, either.

My mom and I hadn't spoken much about the issue regarding my father. His company didn't actually exist, and there was nothing we could do about it until the police showed a sliver of interest. I'd given up texting and calling him—as had my mother. We knew we wouldn't get a response.

I was sitting in Hannah's bedroom, staring off into the distance as I reminisced how Kaleb's lips had felt when so close to my ear five days ago in the kitchen.

I like women only one type of wet.

I shivered.

"Are you writing any of this down?" Hannah said, yanking me from my delicious daydream. My eyes rounded, and I gazed down at the empty sheet of paper in front of me, my ballpoint pen hanging limply from my fingers. She laughed, shaking her head. "This project is due in one week, Freya, and we've done nothing."

I pulled my hair back into a ponytail, grinding my teeth and shaking my head, attempting to rid Kaleb from my brain. "Right, I'm sorry. Let's do this."

The topic we'd been given didn't interest me—the history of Fine Art. However, it was a crucial part of the course and had to be done if we wanted a good grade. It was our final year.

"What are you thinking about?" Hannah teased, cocking her head at me as she sat up in her bed. "Your hot bodyguard lover?"

"He's not my lover, Hannah."

She rolled her eyes. "Yeah, that's what they all say. You kissed and expect me to believe you aren't thinking about him?"

"Well, don't get your hopes up. He's leaving in early January, and I don't know if I'll see him again after that." My own words caused my insides to crawl, and I sighed. The thought of never seeing Kaleb again—I didn't like it.

"Freya." She chuckled, shaking her head. "He fixed your car for you—free of charge! Guys don't just do that for any girl. Listen to me when I tell you that you *will* be seeing him again. You want to hear my advice?" She beamed at me—a kind of smile that held an evil undercurrent to it—and I mentally cringed. She could be sneaky and manipulative when she wanted to be, but I kind of loved it—when it didn't involve me.

"Not really. You scare me sometimes."

"Shush. He says you need to forget about the kiss, but then he flirts with you. He clearly has feelings for you he can't suppress, but is denying it because he knows he can't take back what he said about not taking it further. If he wants to flirt, then you flirt too, but better."

I arched my brow. "Better?"

"Better," Hannah confirmed. "The best part about being a woman is that we can use our body to our advantage." She smiled that same wicked smirk.

I shook my head frantically. "I don't know if I want to play any games, Hannah."

"Kaleb started it. You'd be rude not to join in. He can't flirt and then expect you to think nothing of it. See it as a challenge, and last time I checked, Freya Henderson doesn't back down from a challenge."

She had a point.

"Are you trying to manipulate me?" I laughed.

"Yes, but for the right reasons."

I grinned. Kaleb wanted to see me squirm? Well, I was going to make him sweat. Buckets. He wanted to tease me like it was nothing and then leave early January? Fine, but I wasn't going to make it easy for him.

"Tell me what I need to do."

Hannah tilted her water bottle as it hovered above my head, allowing its contents to trickle down my face. I laughed, smearing as much of it as possible over my neck and chest. My hair was pulled back into a tight, high ponytail, and I was dressed in one of Hannah's tiny sports bras and a pair of spandex blue running shorts. They were short. A little too short.

“I think I need a bigger size,” I said as I tried shoving my breasts back into the sports bra, grunting as they continued to spill out from the top.

“No, it's perfect.” Hannah laughed, fiddling with her own workout gear. Although, she had leaned towards a more modest look, insisting she wanted all the attention on me.

“Okay, do I look sweaty enough?” I gestured to myself as we hung around on the corner from Kaleb’s house.

God, I hoped he was home. Otherwise, this would be a complete waste of time.

Hannah shot me a thumbs up, and I began the jog down the sidewalk, panting as if I'd just run a mile. I pushed open the front door, exhaling heavily.

Kaleb and Brent immediately caught my attention, and I mentally thanked whoever was watching me up above. Somebody had my back. Bracing my hands on my knees and pretending to catch my breath, Hannah followed in after me, wiping at her 'sweaty' forehead and pulling her headphones out of her ears. I was willing to bet money that they weren’t even playing any music.

“That was our best time yet,” Hannah said with pride as she checked her phone, nodding to herself.

“Good.” I smiled, ensuring that I was leaning over enough, my ass facing Kaleb. Hannah subtly widened her eyes at me, signalling that we had caught the boys' attention, and I turned with fake surprise, smiling at both of them. "Oh, hi."

"Freya," Brent greeted me, his eyes raking over my body for a split second before he composed himself, taking a deep breath, appearing embarrassed. "You guys been running?"

Hannah nodded, leaning against the wall and throwing me her water bottle. I took a few tentative sips, pulling my hair from its ponytail and flirtatiously shaking it out. I made my way over to the guys, settling down on the couch close to Kaleb. He was looking down at me with a taut jaw, his brows scrunched together and his body rigid. I crossed my arms over my chest, causing my breasts to spill out of my bra even more, and his eyes snapped to them for a split second before he cleared his throat, dropping his gaze.

"What have you two done today?" I questioned as I focused on the boring TV show they'd been watching.

"We just got back from shooting," Kaleb said huskily, twisting the rings he was wearing around his fingers to distract himself.

God, I loved a man who wore jewellery.

"Oh, yeah? How was it?"

"He kept missing," Brent interjected, causing Kaleb to shoot his friend a sharp glare. "He was distracted as hell today."

"What was distracting you?" I stood up again and kept my eyes on him, moving over to grab the TV remote to change the channel, although I was really just using it as an excuse to stand up again. I wanted Kaleb to know that if he was going to flirt with me, then this was what he was going to face as a repercussion. I would parade around in skimpy outfits, and he would have to act like it didn't bother him—just like I did when he teased me.

His penetrating grey eyes raked over my body, and he inhaled deeply, his tongue swiping along the front of his teeth.

Somebody wasn't happy.

"Oh, Freya," Hannah said from across the room, holding her phone up. "I was texting Ty, and he asked when you were free for dinner?"

The big finale.

Kaleb's eyes narrowed, and he tilted his head towards me, his glare holding an emotion I couldn't quite pinpoint.

I pretended to think, placing my hand on my hip. "Um, let him know that I'll give him a text."

"The waiter?" Kaleb's voice was slightly husky.

I smiled at the TV.

Hook, line, and sinker.

I turned towards him, raising my brows. He was now standing, his form tall and tense. He wasn't standoffish or demanding, but there was an underlying hint of resentment to his words.

"I mean, he thinks I have a boyfriend, remember?" I smiled, nodding towards him with crossed arms. "But I could just tell him we broke up."

Kaleb hummed, and Brent coughed, sensing the awkwardness in the room. "Kaylee is expecting me," he mumbled. "I'm going to go."

Hannah also took the hint and smiled, ducking out of the house.

Perching back down on the couch with a sigh, Kaleb turned his attention to the television, grinding his teeth together as he tried to hide his displeasure.

This was the last part of Hannah's plan. I didn't want to do it, and I was going to be embarrassed as shit, but she'd insisted that this was a crucial step. "You didn't answer me about what had you so distracted from your shooting. I thought you never missed?"

Kaleb shrugged, his eyes lingering on me. "Just this and that. My mind's busy."

Well, that was vague.

Opening up my mouth to speak, I took a step, pretending to trip, tumbling forward and bracing my hands on Kaleb's thick thighs. He caught me, his huge hands latching onto my hips, his fingers digging into my flesh.

I gulped. Having him so close made my logic soar, and it was clear I wasn't the only one. Kaleb's nostrils were flared, and he swallowed, appearing to be holding his breath.

I needed to step away, but it was as if I was rooted to him—our cells intertwined and impossible to separate.

His thighs tensed under my touch, and the pair of dark jeans he was wearing suddenly became an enemy to me. They were the only thing between the palms of my hands and his muscles. I wanted them gone.

After allowing myself to enjoy the moment for another second, I cleared my throat, pulling back. "Sorry, I tripped," I said, trying to brush it off, offering him an innocent smile. "I'm going upstairs. I'm in need of a shower."

I turned and walked away without another word, hearing Kaleb inhale sharply from behind me, causing a grin to appear on my lips.

Hannah, you genius.

Nineteen: Freya

I was smug, to say the least. The look on Kaleb's face when he'd caught sight of me in Hannah's short shorts was priceless. She was insistent that I also pretended to be going on a date with my old friend Ty, and as Hannah had expected, Kaleb hadn't been overly thrilled by the idea.

Two could play at his little flirtatious game.

And so far, it looked like I was winning.

I tapped my pencil against my lips as I stared down at my artwork, finally happy with a piece I had drawn. Dragons twirled around each other in some kind of strange amorous mating dance, their sparkling scales scraping against one another as they roared. It was cliché and nowhere near good enough to use as a submission for my assessment, but I was getting somewhere.

I heard mumbling downstairs—the person sounding panicked—and I dropped my pad on my bed and gazed over the landing railing. Jackie was in the living room, muttering away on her phone.

Her eyebrows were collapsing in on each other as she paced from one side of the room to the other.

Padding down the stairs, I cocked my head at her. "Jackie, are you alright?"

"Freya, you scared me." She chuckled after releasing a small yelp, clutching at her chest. "It's awards night at work, and Kaleb said he would come with me. We need to leave soon, and he's still not back. I've left two messages, but I'll have to go alone if he doesn't show up." I sensed the disappointment in her voice, and it caused my heart to pang.

"I'm not doing anything right now," I said, shrugging and slipping on my shoes and coat. "I'll find him for you. I have a feeling I know where he'll be."

Hopping into my car, noticing again how much smoother it ran, I headed off toward the shooting range. The likelihood of Kaleb being there was high.

I parked outside the shifty-looking building, shivering as I stepped out of the car, the wind gusting through me. The area was pretty bare, so there was nothing to shield me from the blast.

I rushed in, the young red-haired receptionist peering in my direction briefly before dropping her gaze. She was leaning back in her chair, chewing on her gum loudly, my presence having not bothered her one bit.

How did this place even stay open if they charged no one to shoot? Did they really make all their money from selling alcohol at the bar? It didn't seem likely.

The usual sound of guns blasting reached my ears, and I hurried down the narrow corridor to push open the door to the main hall. It was busy today, and I gulped, taking in the sheer amount of beefed-up men sporting tattoos and bald heads.

Beer coated the floor, making it sticky, and men laughed in every corner as they talked over each other, desperate to be the centre of attention and assert their dominance.

I wandered around the room, noticing a few older men turn and tap their friends to draw their attention to me. I didn't belong here, and I looked like a deer in the headlights as I tried my best to weave in and out of people without being spotted.

It didn't surprise me I was being stared at, though. I was dressed in an old T-shirt two sizes too small without a bra—having not even thought about it before I left the house.

Yanking my coat over my chest to cover myself, I stopped in my tracks when a bearded man stepped out in front of me, clutching onto a large handgun. He waved it around, wiggling his eyebrows at me.

"What's a pretty lady like you doing here?" he said, his words merging to form one almost incoherent sentence. *Obviously drunk.* "We don't get too many of those. The women here usually look like men themselves."

All his friends laughed from behind him, and I crossed my arms over my chest. "Yeah, alright. Excuse me, I'm looking for someone." I attempted to move past him, but he chuckled, blocking my path.

"Woah, woah, hold up. I just want to talk. There's no need to be rude."

I narrowed my eyes into slits. "Actually, there is because you're in my way."

The bearded man cursed, his eyes turning dark. "Well, you're—"

"Watch your mouth, Brush. She's Kaleb's girl."

Will.

I wasn't, but I wasn't about to correct him on that. The bearded man—named Brush—took a few steps back to his group of friends, and Will moved closer to me, smiling. I instinctively backed up.

"Speaking of Kaleb. Have you seen him?" I questioned, and Will nodded towards the exit.

"You just missed him. He left in a rush, saying he was late for something." He gestured for me to follow him, and I did, but only because I was heading towards the exit myself. "I assumed he was heading somewhere to meet you."

I shook my head, clearing my throat awkwardly. There was something about Will that put me on edge me. Perhaps it had something to do with the fact that he was almost six foot four—just shy of Kaleb's stature. His voice was gravelly, and his eyes were icy. They drew you in and held you captive, but not in a good way. It froze people in fear, and he knew it. He thrived off it.

"Kaleb tells me he and Brent run their own distillery down where they live," Will suddenly said once he noticed I was moving closer and closer to the exit. "As well as a few other businesses. They never go into great detail, though."

I arched my brow. Kaleb and Brent ran a distillery? That was the first I'd ever heard of it, but I honed in on how Will leaned against the wall, a smirk playing at his lips. He was phishing for information. *The nosy fuck.*

Kaleb had instructed me not to say anything about his and Brent's line of work before I entered the building for the first time, and I gathered that telling the owner of a shady shooting range that you were a cop wasn't the best idea. It did make me wonder why Kaleb and Brent shot here, anyway. As people involved in law enforcement, why would they want to spend their time at a place like this?

"I haven't spoken to Kaleb about his occupation much."

Will raised his eyebrows, pushing himself off the wall and taking another puff of his barely lit cigarette. "Much? Meaning you have spoken about it at least somewhat?"

My heart thumped in my chest, causing me to shift uncomfortably.

I didn't know what to say. I didn't want to confirm the distillery in case he was bluffing and trying to catch me out. Was he suspicious of what Kaleb and Brent were? They definitely wouldn't be welcome if so.

Remaining casual, I smiled at Will, attempting to appear innocent. "I mean, yeah, it's come up here and there, but I've never asked much about it."

"Why's that? Is it because he's so secretive? Because that's what I've found. He's vague. About everything. Vague usually screams guilty."

The heat was ramping up, and I backed up against the wall, glancing sideways towards the exit. Running was an option, but that would make Kaleb and Brent look extremely fishy. I had to play this off. "Guilty?" I chuckled. "He's a private guy. It's hard to get him to open up."

Taking a step back, Will laughed, holding his hands up defensively. "You look like you're worried I'm about to tie you up and throw you into my back office. I was just simply asking you some questions, Freya. No harm done."

I hated the way he used my name. It felt slimy.

"I know," I said, faking my confidence, a bead of sweat trickling down the back of my neck. "I *do* need to go, though."

Will watched me with curious eyes as I turned to leave but cleared his throat close from behind me. I stilled. "I am curious about you, Freya." His voice was almost demanding. "What do you do?"

I rolled my eyes before I turned to him again. "I'm an aspiring author." There was no way I was going to give this man any information about myself.

"And what about your parents? You mentioned your last name was Henderson, correct?"

I cursed at myself for having told him my full name, but it was during our first meeting, and I hadn't expected to see him again. "Why?"

"No reason. Just trying to get to know Kaleb's girl a little better."

I nodded. "My mom is expecting me home, so I need to go."

Will smiled, holding the door open for me as I tried my best not to scurry out. "See you soon, Freya."

I took deep breaths as I wiped down my clothes inside my car, trying to rid myself of the scent of beer and cigarettes. It was all that surrounded me, though, and I shook off my coat, launching it into the backseat. I drove home as quickly as possible, pulling up outside Kaleb's house and laying my head on the steering wheel with a harsh *thud*.

Jumping out of my skin at the sound of someone knocking on my car window, I stared up wide-eyed at Kaleb, his own filled with worry. Sighing, I pushed open my door.

"Are you okay?" he asked, his eyes raking up and down my body quickly as he searched for a reason as to why I looked so on edge. "My mom said you went out looking for me."

"Yeah, she was freaking out about her awards night, so I went to the shooting range and—"

"What?" he interrupted me, his body rigid and his tone frosty. "Freya, please tell me you didn't go inside."

The tension was so cold it could freeze water. It was as if the Ice Age had just reoccurred, trapping me in a giant block of ice and rendering me motionless.

"Only for a few minutes."

Kaleb clamped his eyes shut and tilted his head back, cursing up at the clouds. "Freya. I told you it was too dangerous. You shouldn't be in there alone."

I shrugged. "You never actually said it was too dangerous—just not to talk to Will again."

"And did you?"

"He told me you'd just left."

His gaze held nothing but raw emotion. Concern. Dread. Panic. He shut my car door for me, and we settled on the couch inside, his jaw clenching.

"Okay, tell me what Will said to you," he demanded, pulling up a dining chair, lifting his leg over it, and sitting on it backwards. He crossed his arms over it as he watched me, but I couldn't focus on anything other than his muscular thighs and veiny forearms. "Freya, come on, sweetheart. You can ogle me later. What did Will say to you?"

Sweetheart.

My face reddened. "Um, he was asking about you. Questioning what you and Brent did for work, and wanted to see if I knew anything about the distillery you said you owned."

Kaleb huffed, dropping his head down onto his arms, groaning. "Fuck, okay. Anything else?"

"Um, he was asking me about my parents. He said he wanted to get to know me."

He snapped his head up, biting his bottom lip harshly, gazing off into the distance, his tongue grating across his teeth. A thunderstorm brewed in his eyes, and I swear I felt the jolt of a lightning bolt driving through me as I glanced into them.

"Will will retaliate if he knows what Brent and I are." Kaleb dug his nails into his tattooed forearms. I couldn't help but follow his movements, and I felt a sudden urge to make my way over to him and comfort him, but now wasn't the time to test our boundaries.

"What's the worst he can do, though?" I asked. "Tell you guys to leave and not come back? You can find another shooting spot."

Kaleb narrowed his eyes at me, sighing. "I don't think you understand this guy, Freya."

"What do you mean? Besides the obvious."

He looked to be debating with himself on whether to talk. "I'm meeting my mom at her awards evening, so I need to go."

I raised my eyebrows. "Why are you getting so stressed about Will? You said that you and Brent have been shooting there for years. What's suddenly made him suspicious of you two?" I dragged my bottom lip into my mouth, and just as Kaleb opened his own to speak again, the doorbell rang.

"Do you ever hang out at your own place?" he grumbled as he flung the door open to reveal Brent, and he plopped himself down on the couch next to me, swinging his arm over the back of it and shooting me a wink.

"I just came back from the shooting range," I told Brent, causing Kaleb to curse and slump against the wall. "I bumped into Will, and he was rather intrigued to hear about this distillery you guys own." I waited for Brent to elaborate.

"Um, yeah, obviously we don't." He chuckled, shrugging, releasing a stressed sigh a few seconds later.

"She knows that, Brent," Kaleb snapped. "Will is getting suspicious."

I huffed, pushing myself onto my feet and smiling falsely. "Well, you guys must love this shooting range a hell of a lot judging by the way you're so worried about Will finding out what you both really do for work, but since you're talking so cryptically and I have no idea what's going on, I'm going to excuse myself and work on my project upstairs."

Brent watched me with curious eyes as I began to walk away, and he groaned. "Kaleb, man, why don't we just tell her? Will knows who she is now, and it's in her best interest."

“Yeah, and that’s your fault,” Kaleb muttered, his eyes blazing, beckoning me with his head and sighing as I sat back down. He pinched the bridge of his nose. “Right, so you’re aware that Brent and I took Christmas break early, and that's why we're back in town?”

“That's what you said when you first arrived.”

Brent chuckled. “Well, that's not true. We're still working.”

“What do you mean?”

Kaleb was so tense he resembled a stone statue rather than a living human being, and I was concerned that all the stress was going to cause him to crumble into a pile of dust on the floor.

“Freya, what we are about to tell you has to remain confidential. It's crucial. The reason I'm telling you this is for your own safety, but this whole thing could be fucked if anyone finds out.” I’d never heard Kaleb so serious.

My stomach lurched. “Okay.”

He clicked his knuckles. “Our organisation has been building a case against Will for years. Since Brent and I were already from the area, we were assigned to the case. We come back throughout our breaks to continue working on it, but evidence has always been scarce. We received some intel that he's ramping up the intensity of his crimes, so we came to watch him.”

So that was why they were always at the shooting range? They were spying on Will.

“He's involved in a big illegal drug ring, and he's the brains behind the operation,” Brent chimed in. “We’re hoping to have him arrested by the end of the year.”

I gulped. I’d been inside the shooting range with a criminal, and anger bubbled up inside me that I'd been put at risk. “You took me there.”

Kaleb glared at Brent. “That was this idiot's fault.”

Brent shrugged. “We have to look like normal guys. Normal guys hang out with hot women. Having you join us was good for us, and we knew you weren't going to be in harm's way. Will *does* run it as a shooting range with a bar to cover up the money he makes from his crimes, and he wouldn't act out with other people there. He does it all under the radar. Most of the people who shoot there don't know what's really going on.”

“It was still too dangerous for her,” Kaleb complained. “I could call the chief and get you fired for it.”

Brent smirked at his friend. “But you won’t.”

“When you say Will is ramping up the intensity of his crimes, what do you mean?” I was deathly curious.

Brent and Kaleb gazed at each other, and Kaleb sighed. “We really can't go into—“

“We found out he's linked to some murders, but the evidence isn't strong enough yet,” Brent responded casually.

“You’re putting her at risk by telling her every detail Brent.”

“Ignorance is putting her at risk. Will's been questioning her. Besides, look at her—as if she's going to tell anyone. She doesn't have *that* many friends.” Brent turned to me, shooting me another wink. “No offence, darling.”

I shook my head. “How did you find out he—“

Kaleb’s phone blasted, and he huffed as he glanced down at his screen. “I’m late. Brent, keep your mouth shut until I get back.” His eyes immediately softened as they settled on me, and he swallowed before ducking out of the house.

“Well, now that it's just you and me, baby girl,” teased Brent as he pretended to lean in for a kiss, and I grabbed the cushion from beside me and smacked him in the face with it, causing him to chuckle.

"I won't say anything to anyone about what you guys told me," I promised him.

Brent hummed, nodding. "Nah, I trust you. Kaleb is paranoid. He wanted to keep you out of it."

I was desperate to ask more but didn't want to get Brent in trouble with Kaleb, so I opted to change the subject. "So, who's Kaylee?" I wiggled my eyebrows.

"I met her at that party we went to, where you and Kaleb ditched me." He fake glared at me. "She's really great. I actually like her a lot."

I nudged him. "You mean you *like* her?"

"I mean, yeah, she's great, but it doesn't matter much. Nothing will come of it."

"Why do you say that?"

Brent shrugged at me like it was obvious, his attention on the TV program I had switched on. "My line of work isn't overly compatible with having a relationship. The others who do what Kaleb and I do are pretty much all single. It's the people who are stationed in places permanently that find it easier to settle down. After this case is closed, we'll be moved to a different base since we're currently stationed at the nearest one to here. It could be halfway across the country or even abroad."

My stomach twisted painfully.

Kaleb. In an entirely different country. That was going to be a kick in the teeth.

"I can understand why people don't fancy having to move just to follow their significant other around, especially since they don't even know if they'll be coming back from work every night. Some of the stuff we do is dangerous, and dying isn't unheard of."

My heart skipped a beat. "Really?"

"Yeah," Brent replied, chomping on a chocolate bar he'd just pulled from his pocket, his mouth full. "A few months ago, we were doing a raid and one of our guys got shot in the leg. There was blood everywhere, and he couldn't get to cover. We had to drag him behind a storage unit, but he didn't make it." He spoke so casually about the subject, his voice holding little emotion, and it was evident that he'd become desensitised to the gruesome side of his line of work.

Gulping, I began abusing my cuticles. Just the thought of going to work and not knowing if you were going to make it home alive was terrifying. Was that how Kaleb felt every time he left the house?

My phone buzzed in my pocket, and I pulled it out to see Hannah had sent me a few messages about our project. I replied quickly, my finger subconsciously lingering on my father's number a few messages down. Frowning, I clicked on his name, grinding my teeth as I allowed the call to go through, moving my way into the kitchen away from an unbothered Brent, who was gawking at the TV.

Hearing about how life was never guaranteed had hit a nerve—because the thought that there was a chance that I'd never see my dad again was pulled to the forefront of my mind.

I was going to give it one more shot.

My phone made a strange beeping sound, and I listened to the automated woman's voice on the other end.

This number is no longer in service. Please contact your provider if this issue is believed to be an error.

Staring at my phone in shock, I shook my head, my mouth becoming dry and my heart banging against my chest as if it were eager to escape.

What the fuck? My father had changed his number.

Twenty: Freya

I felt awful. Hannah had trusted me to complete my part of the project, and instead of doing so, I'd spent the evening in bed staring aimlessly at my sketchpad. Drawing always made me feel better, but it hadn't this time.

We were now way behind schedule, and like my father, I was leaving others to pick up the pieces. It wasn't like me.

"You okay?" she asked me once we left our lecture, turning to me with a frown. "You didn't send over your part of the project."

I gulped. "I know, I'm so sorry. I'm going to do it tonight."

Cocking her head, my friend furrowed her eyebrows. "Freya, are you sure you're okay? You look, and no offence, like crap."

"I was restless last night. My dad changed his number."

Hannah's mouth fell open, and she gawked at me, her hazel eyes like saucers. "What the fuck! What an asshole!"

I didn't want to think about it. I'd wasted so much of my time worrying about him and his well-being when, actually, he'd left us for good.

"Get your part of the project over to me when you can." Hannah sighed. "There's no pressure to do it tonight if you need some alone time."

Giving her a good squeeze, we both made our way out towards the parking lot, but a small gasp left my friend's lips, and she gripped my bicep tightly.

"Ow," I complained. "What?"

I followed her gaze to see Zach making his way out of his car. Both of his eyes were encased in painful-looking purple bruises, with a tinge of green at the corners. He hadn't been back to college, and this was the first time I'd seen him since he'd barged into Kaleb's house.

Spotting me, he narrowed his eyes, clutching his files and lanyard tightly, hurrying into the building after slamming his car door harder than necessary. He turned an immediate left—heading for the office.

"I thought he'd dropped out already, to be honest," Hannah muttered. "It looked like he was handing his stuff in."

I hummed in response. The thought of never seeing Zach again was a relieving one, but I didn't understand why he'd just drop out of college. Surely not because he'd been beaten up?

Dropping Hannah home, I sped to Jackie and Kaleb's house. I hadn't seen him this morning—my guess being that he had gone to the shooting range with Brent. I hoped they hadn't. Will was suspicious of them, and after finding out he was most likely responsible for more than one murder, I felt uncomfortable with them being in his presence.

I entered the house to see Kaleb splayed out on the couch, watching the TV at an excessive volume, his gun on his chest, the cold metal sitting right in between his pectoral muscles. He was playing with it, seeming to have not noticed me, and I crept towards him with my eyebrows raised. "What are you watching?"

He hopped up from the couch at lightning speed, clutching his gun and pointing it straight at me, his eyebrows pulled together.

I yelped, taking a few steps back, only for him to drop his gun and run his hand down his face. "Fuck, Freya. You know better than to sneak up on a cop who has someone out to get him."

He looked as if he hadn't slept. The Will situation was definitely getting to him.

"Sorry," I said, holding my hands up. "Maybe that's a lesson to turn the volume down so you don't burst your eardrums."

Kaleb sighed, flopping back down on the couch. "How was class?"

I chewed on the inside of my cheek. I couldn't actually remember anything the lecturer had said. I was supposed to have been making notes, but the neurons connecting my hand to my brain weren't working properly today.

I shrugged, settling down on the couch beside him, ensuring I left a gap. Just because we flirted didn't mean we could overstep the boundary into deeper water.

Kaleb cocked his head at me, the light streaming in from the living room window catching his sharp jawline. "Are you okay? You don't look so good."

I scowled at him.

"Not like that, but you just look tired today. Didn't get much sleep?"

I shook my head. "No, not really. I just… I don't know."

I didn't want to have to tell everyone that my father had decided I wasn't worth having in his life. It was playing with my insecurities and making me doubt myself, and I also didn't want the pity. Being babied wasn't something I enjoyed.

"Brent and I spent most of the night working out how to deal with Will," Kaleb told me. "He's on his way over now. He says he has an idea."

He was wearing a T-shirt I'd never seen him in before, and I knew that because I always found myself staring at his pectorals through the fabric. It hugged his biceps perfectly, and I studied his tattooed arms, narrowing my eyes at a few dates inscribed into his flesh.

Kaleb took notice of my staring and turned his arm over to give me a better view of the ink. "It's Brie's birthday."

I offered him a warm smile. "What's that one?" I pointed at the tattoo further down his arm. The snakes on his flesh glared at me, looking like they wanted to pounce.

"They're cobras—my mom's favourite." He released a chuckle. "Don't ask me why. She's fascinated by them—likes how they can survive months without eating."

It made sense. There were many snake-themed things around the house—including paintings and sculptures. The small wooden statue in the middle of the dining room table was rather off-putting, though, and my mother had to move it aside every time we ate. Snakes were her worst nightmare. No wonder they were friends. Opposites really *did* attract.

Kaleb had moved closer to me, having shuffled further along the couch to give me better access to his arms, and the only thing that separated us was his handgun.

The sound of a fist knocking against the front door caught my attention, and Kaleb flung it open.

Brent waltzed in—a pretty, tall blonde following him.

"Who is this?" Kaleb asked, crossing his arms over his chest as he studied the girl. "I don't take kindly to strangers in my home."

"This is Kaylee," Brent said, gesturing to her. "She's going to help."

Kaleb huffed, pushing his dark hair back. "You told her everything?" He didn't look impressed.

Kaylee stood smugly next to Brent, appearing proud to be in with a cop, and frankly, if I were in her position, I would have been too. She felt like she knew a secret that she shouldn't, and that, to a woman, was exciting.

Not everything, Brent mouthed when Kaylee wasn't looking.

"We're going to the shooting range. Will should be there," he said, turning to me. "Freya, you're coming too."

"What?" Kaleb grimaced. "No. No way. Brent, are you out of your mind?"

"Kaleb, we're so close to getting enough evidence on this guy to send him to the slammer. He's suspicious of us right now, and that could jeopardise everything."

My eyes narrowed. Where had the bubbly and aloof Brent gone?

"He needs to see us as normal guys, and what's more normal than bringing our girlfriends along with us for some kind of fucked up double date?"

"We aren't getting other people involved in this."

I watched them argue, raising my eyebrows at Kaylee, who shot me a worried look.

"It's two in the afternoon." Brent sighed. "The shooting range will be busy. Will isn't going to try anything in front of anyone, especially when he's not one hundred per cent sure we're lying to him. He's just testing the water right now. Plus, I had these made up last night." He pulled a bunch of business cards from his pocket, and Kaleb snatched one from him, scowling at it.

I joined him, peeking over his shoulder.

B&K Brewery.

Bespoke local beer.

Treat your tastebuds

"B and K brewery?" Kaleb asked with an arched brow. "You couldn't have thought of anything a little more creative?"

Brent snatched the card back. "It's the best I could do at three in the morning. If Will asks, I can give him one of these. I've set up a website, too."

Kaleb nodded towards me. "Freya stays out of this."

"I sure would like some female company," Kaylee chimed in, turning to me with a small smile. "I've heard it's gross in there, and since shooting isn't really my thing, I'd really like it if you could come along, Freya."

Brent had clearly briefed Kaylee on what to say if Kaleb argued against me joining them.

I didn't like the thought of heading back to the shooting range—especially since finding out about the awful things Will had done—but I knew that Kaleb and Brent were desperate to convince him they were just two average guys who enjoyed shooting. If going along with them would help put Will behind bars, then for the greater good, I had to put my worries aside.

A couple of hours. That was all it was.

"I'll go," I said, causing Kaleb to click his teeth shut. "Like Brent said, Will won't do anything with everyone there. If this will convince him that you aren't anything to worry about, then fine, I'll come. But just this once. This will be the last time I step foot in there."

"Freya, you're a lifesaver." Brent beamed a goofy smile, and Kaylee clapped excitedly, snatching Brent's keys from his hands and running out the door, shrieking about how she wanted to drive—something Brent loudly objected to.

Gosh, she was a ball of energy. I kind of loved it.

Kaleb pinched his eyebrows together as he glanced down at me with troubled eyes. "You don't have to do this. This is my problem. Not yours."

I nodded. "I know, but you've wanted to get this guy for years, and you *did* fix my car, so I kind of owe you one."

He laughed, but the humour didn't quite reach his eyes. "I'm serious, Freya. Will can flip at the drop of a hat. We've never seen it personally, but we know what he's involved in. It's not pretty. The responsibility doesn't fall on your shoulders. I want you to be safe."

I shrugged. "I'm using this to avoid doing my project. Procrastination is a new hobby I've taken up."

I was also using it as a way to avoid thinking about how my dad no longer wanted to be part of my life, but I wasn't about to admit that.

I headed for the door, but Kaleb grabbed my wrist, pulling me back, and electricity pulsated through my blood from his touch. It was as if he was a live wire, shocking me into a trance. "Any sign of trouble, and we're out of there. I mean it. I don't care if Will even looks at you in the wrong way. We're gone."

I nodded, gulping at our proximity, hearing the jingle of Kaleb's car keys as he pulled them from his pocket, the sound bringing me back to reality.

"Let's go procrastinate."

Walking back into the shooting range was stressful, but Kaleb comforted me by putting his hand on my back. I appreciated the gesture and could tell he was as apprehensive as I was. Tonight could go one of two ways.

Will could either drop his suspicions of Kaleb and Brent and not say another word about it, or he could laugh in our faces and turn sinister. He'd murdered people before. What was going to stop him from doing it again?

We're okay, Kaleb mouthed to me once he spotted my frown. Brent took his position first and held up his handgun, and Kaylee watched with admiration as he shot three bullets—all but one hitting the target in the centre. I couldn't bring myself to appreciate his efforts, though. My erratic pulse in my throat was distracting me. I needed to remain calm. Will was like a bloodhound, and he'd be able to sniff out any doubt I emitted, only to spur him on more.

"Want a go?" Brent asked Kaylee, and she beamed, taking the gun from him. He began to show her how to hold it, pressing his chest to her back flirtatiously as he whispered in her ear.

"Freya," mumbled Kaleb. "Are you sure you're okay?"

I chewed on my tongue, allowing my gaze to drift over his plump lips and chiselled face, trying to focus on how beautiful he was instead of where we were.

"Kaleb, honestly, I'm okay." *Lie.* "I'm just not with it today." *Truth, but sugar-coated by a lie.*

Humming, he turned his attention away from me after hearing Will's bellowing laughter behind us. He was dressed smartly today—sporting a grey suit and shiny black shoes. I'd never seen him so gussied up.

"Late for a wedding?" Brent teased him, causing Will to smirk and puff on his cigarette.

"Not quite," he responded, his gaze settling on Kaylee for a few seconds before he directed his attention back to the boys. "I've been in meetings all day."

Brent and Kaleb nodded in response. I knew they'd usually try to dig and ask Will what the meetings were about, but today wasn't the day for that. It was all about convincing him they were trustworthy.

"Not going to ask for any more detail?" Will's tone was taunting. "I would have expected you boys to be inclined to ask questions. Like usual." He had a serious chip on his shoulder.

Kaleb shrugged. "You don't look like you're in the mood to be quizzed."

Will pointed at him, clicking his fingers. "Correct, Kaleb, well done. I'm getting another drink. Anybody want one? They're on the house."

I almost shook my head, but Brent spoke up, agreeing eagerly.

Right. We had to look easy-going. Easy-going people accepted drinks from secret drug ring boss murderers.

After Will disappeared to the bar in the room's corner, Kaleb leaned down to whisper in my ear. "Just pretend to sip it," he told me. "Go to the bathroom with Kaylee and throw it down the drain at some point if you want."

I nodded. I didn't fancy being poisoned today.

Will quickly appeared with our drinks, placing them on the small table by our metal wall, flashing his teeth at Kaylee. "You're new," he said, his tone making me want to gag. He was practically undressing her with his eyes.

"Yep," Brent said, taking a swig of his drink—or pretending to. I wasn't sure. "She's my girl."

Kaylee rolled her eyes. "I wouldn't go that far."

"Tell me," Will started, tearing his eyes away from the beautiful blonde in front of him. "How does this alcohol compare to what you make at your brewery?"

Ah, there it was.

Kaleb remained casual, and I mentally applauded him for staying so calm and content—as if Will's question was the most ordinary thing in the world. "It's pretty good," he responded. "Ours is special, though. I'm yet to find a beer that tops it."

Will chuckled, knocking back the rest of his drink, clattering the glass back onto the table a little too harshly for my liking. He was trying to assert his dominance, and it left a bitter taste on my tongue. "I'll have to come and visit you boys one day and try it for myself."

Brent agreed, reaching into his pocket, pulling out one of the cards he'd printed, and passing it to Will. He scrutinised it, flipping it over in his dirty hands more than once before humming, pocketing it.

"I'll be sure to get in contact with one of you and organise picking up a barrel in the near future. It would be interesting to see how it sells here."

"Sounds good to us." Kaleb took a shot at the target, his eyes darkening once he saw Will turn towards me.

"It's good to see you again, Freya." He held his hand out for me to shake, and I did so reluctantly. His skin was rough. He had the hands of a killer, and I was surprised they weren't permanently stained red.

"You too."

Will raised an eyebrow at me, pulling out yet another cigarette from his blazer pocket and lighting it up, the smoke causing me to splutter. "So, do you live around here?"

I stiffened.

"Well, I—"

"Are you trying to make a move, Will?" Kaleb asked casually. However, as calm as he appeared on the outside, I could sense that his teeth were gritted, his jaw muscle flexing.

Will chortled. "Oh, trust me, Kaleb, she's far too young for me."

After hearing his name being called by a few older men in the room's corner, Will smiled at us, again, eye-fucking Kaylee. He clearly had a thing for blondes. "It's been great seeing you again." He reached into his pocket and pulled out the brewery card, holding it up. "I'll keep this handy."

I tried not to stare as he excused himself, and I turned to Kaleb to see him glowering at the back of his head.

We stayed for around an hour before we watched someone walk in and whisper something into Will's ear. The two of them quickly made their way into a backroom, their faces glum and their body language stiff.

Kaleb and Brent didn't want to overstay their welcome, and they took one last shot each before leading us toward the exit.

"Do you think Will bought it?" I questioned as I buckled up my seatbelt in Kaleb's car.

He gripped the wheel tightly as he drove, the metal groaning under the pressure. "It's hard to tell with Will. He's a closed book."

Like my father had been—right before he cut me from his life. I tried thinking back to anything I'd done to warrant this kind of reaction, but I was coming up blank. I didn't reach out to him much when he went away, sure, but only because he always told my mother and me he needed to focus on work. He didn't have much time for us. I'd suggested going for family meals or visiting the movies together a few times, but the idea was always quickly squashed with a bellowing laugh from my father. The prospect of spending time together as a family had become funny to him.

Was it because I wanted to pursue an art-related career? He'd always expressed how creative work was nothing but a hobby and people needed to look at life with a little more common sense. Would he have preferred me to be something more prestigious, like a doctor or a lawyer? Had all of this stemmed from his disappointment in me?

Pressing my head against the window, Kaleb continued to talk, but I wasn't paying attention, and when I heard him calling my name, I turned to him with a spacious look on my face.

"Alright," he muttered, pulling the car over and cutting the engine. "Something's happened. What is it?"

My eyes immediately watered, but I swallowed the tears back down, my throat going dry.

Cursing to himself, Kaleb hooked his finger under my chin as he shuffled closer to me. "Freya, you can tell me."

I ran my hand through my hair, holding up my phone and gesturing to it. There was no point in pretending I was okay in front of Kaleb anymore. He could see right through me. I was the opposite of Will and my father. An open book—the pages displayed for the world to read.

"Come here." He pulled me to him, wrapping his arms around me as a few traitorous tears leaked from my eyes.

"You're killing me here, Freya. Did someone hurt you? Is it Zach again?" His voice was like venom, and I pulled away to see his tongue assaulting the front of his teeth in apprehension.

I shook my head, wiping at my nose. *Attractive*. "No, it's just my dad. He's changed his number. I can't contact him anymore."

Kaleb released a quiet sigh, caressing my cheek before he cleared his throat and dropped his hand. He was silent for a few seconds. "Dads are crappy."

I laughed—little humour in it. "They are."

"Mine left when I was young. He was a gambling addict."

I knitted my eyebrows together. Jackie hadn't mentioned the gambling part. I wanted to ask Kaleb more on the subject, but I didn't want to push him. He had never brought up his dad before, and I doubted he wanted to go through a play-by-play with me.

"Some people are cowards and don't know how to face their demons," he told me. "He'll either come around, or you'll learn to go on without him. Either way, you'll be okay."

I hummed, sniffling.

"You're going to be fine. I promise." His voice held such determination as he wiped away a lingering tear, his thumb travelling down to stop at my lip.

Why did I feel like I was going to pass out? My skin sparked from his touch, and it took everything inside of me not to lean forward and capture Kaleb's lips with my own.

He released a throaty, frustrated groan before he smiled sadly at me, pulling away. "Let's get you home."

Twenty-one: Freya

I opened the front door for Hannah, arching an eyebrow at her as she beamed at me and ushered me aside. She was carrying a giant mood board and gestured to it with pride. "I present to you—our project."

Crouching down to gaze at it, I smiled. Hannah and I had spent the past four days cooped up in her room completing it, and after I'd left hers late last night, she'd called me to let me know she was just applying the finishing touches.

We hadn't got around to sticking everything onto the cardboard, so she had generously volunteered to do that before she called it a night.

I proofread our final essays, and they were pretty good—besides Hannah's awful spelling.

"Now we just need to work on presenting it." I sighed, and Hannah flung her arm over my shoulder as she propped our project against the wall.

"Don't you worry about that. We all know I'm the chatty one in this friendship, and I have no issue taking the reins."

Hannah loved talking to anybody and everybody. If there was an excuse to do so, she was going to find it, and I swore if you were to look up the word *chatterbox* in the dictionary, a giant picture of Hannah's face would take up the entire page.

Kaleb waltzed into the room from the kitchen, glowering as he mumbled into his phone. “We're handling it.” His voice was rough—scratchy. He sounded tense. “He's suspicious, but until we see the situation as too dangerous, we'll keep digging.” A pause. “No, that's fine, Frederick. I'll talk to Brent and keep you updated.”

Hannah was too busy fussing over our project that had fallen over to take notice of Kaleb's conversation, and he watched her carefully for any sign of interest as he spoke. His shoulders were strained, and he glanced at me with a down-turned mouth.

After my confession in the car, he'd cooked me some spaghetti and cream sauce—my favourite dish—and ordered me to get an early night. He hadn't spoken to me much about Will and what was going on with the investigation, and I had a sneaky feeling that my tears had deterred him from involving me further.

Excusing herself to the bathroom, Hannah disappeared.

“Who was that?” I asked Kaleb, testing the water.

“My chief's boss. He's one of the top dogs in the organisation,” he said flatly, avoiding eye contact with me, tapping away on his phone. *Yep, he still didn't want me involved.*

“Sounded tense.” My attempt to lighten the mood fell flat.

He ran his hand down his face, groaning as he took a seat on the couch. Even when he was stressed, he was gorgeous. He'd failed to shave over the past few days, and I couldn't help but notice his accumulated excess stubble.

“What was he saying?”

Kaleb swallowed. "He's pushing. He wants Will arrested within the next week. I don't know if we'll be able to gather the information we need without coming across as brazen, though. It's risky."

I nodded at his admittance.

"What fucking now?" Kaleb glared down at his beeping phone, reading the text that had just come through and turning the screen toward me.

Brent: Kaylee really enjoyed spending time with Freya. She was wondering if you guys wanted to go on a double date tonight?

I smiled, and Kaleb shook his head.

"No." His tone left no room for persuasion.

I scowled, crossing my arms over my chest. "Why not? It's the weekend. It'll be fun." I fancied getting out of the house—having been working hard and in need of something to perk me up.

Watching me with cautious eyes as I leaned up against the wall, my breasts slightly pushed up in my burgundy tank top, Kaleb's frown faltered. "I don't have time."

I laughed. "Really? What are you doing tonight? Sitting at home being grumpy?"

"It's a full-time job," he quickly retorted back.

"See?" I kicked at his foot. "You can be fun when you want to be."

Huffing, Kaleb surveyed my pleading expression, lolling his head back and grumbling to himself. "Jesus, why can't I say no to you? Alright, fine. We'll grab a drink with them."

Hannah re-entered the room, wiggling her phone at me, causing me to arch a brow. "What?"

"You're all set for your date with Ty."

I almost choked on my saliva at her words, and Kaleb's eyebrows flew into his hairline before he quickly composed himself, taking a deep breath.

"What? No," I said, and my best friend glared at me, taking a fleeting look at Kaleb before smiling.

"Yes. He'll be ready to meet you for lunch in thirty minutes. I thought I'd give you some time to freshen up since you look..." She took in my sloppy outfit and hair that was pulled back into a claw clip, humming in disapproval.

Kaleb's hands were clenched, his jaw was taut, and his grey eyes bored into mine—as if daring me to agree. His phone rang, and he frustratingly swiped it up and swiftly exited the room, his pissed-off voice sounding from the kitchen

"Hannah," I whisper-yelled, grabbing her by the shoulders. "What the hell are you doing?"

"We said you were going to go on a date with Ty. I didn't want Kaleb to think that we were bluffing, so I organised it for you."

I pinched the bridge of my nose. "No. I'm not going on a date with Ty."

Not only was Ty just a friend, but I didn't want to be flaunting a date in front of Kaleb. We weren't together. We hadn't even spoken about our feelings for each other, but whatever we had going on, I didn't want to ruin it by 'dating'. The sexy, sweaty jogging plan had been funny, but I didn't like this.

"I mean, I didn't specifically call it a date to Ty, so if you want to just meet him as friends, then fine. Sometimes, guys just need a push, and Kaleb could use a big one. Occasionally, you have to force their hand."

I knew Hannah thought she was doing the right thing, and there were no malicious intentions when it came to her. She was impulsive and reckless, though, and often didn't think things through.

"Trust me," she said. "Just go and meet Ty. Kaleb will rethink all of his priorities. Also, you could use another friend. Ty is a good guy and sounded excited to see you again."

I huffed. I had a shortage of friends right now. Most of them had been real partygoers, and I'd lost contact with them all once I decided I didn't want to spend five nights a week drinking.

Hannah had been one of the only people to stick around, and even though she still loved to indulge in more than enough glasses of wine on a weekday, she had definitely toned it down. In her words, *you could take the girl out of the party, but you could never take the party out of the girl*.

Throwing my hands up in the air in frustration, I agreed. Ty and I had gotten on well in high school, and there was no harm in reconnecting with him. As a friend.

Glancing at the kitchen doorway, I refrained from going in and explaining to Kaleb that meeting up with Ty was going to be nothing but platonic. His seething tone towards the person on the phone was enough to warn me off.

After changing into a pair of jeans and a cardigan and letting my hair down, I grabbed my car keys and headed for the front door. Kaleb had left the house while I was upstairs—most likely to sort some shit out with Brent about the investigation. That, or he wasn't happy about my date with Ty.

Why did I have to get so turned on by Kaleb's apparent jealousy? My abdomen tightened at the blaze in his eyes, my upper lip sweating, my heart pumping a mile a minute.

Hannah had explicitly told me not to feel guilty about having Kaleb think I was going on a date. She claimed he just needed to rot in his own jealousy for a few hours until he started thinking straight, but I wasn't too sure that was going to do anything.

We were wrapped up in our little flirtatious bubble right now, but once he left, there was a fat chance that I was never going to see him again. He'd be moved to a different base to begin new work, and not only could it be states away, but it could be countries away.

Driving to the coffee shop Hannah instructed me to, I parked up and peered through the gleaming glass. Ty was sitting patiently in the corner with a cup of coffee. His dark hair had been cut a little shorter, and he was dressed in navy—his favourite colour from when we were close.

"Hey," I said with a smile as I made my way into the shop. I gave him a hug, his muscular arms wrapping around me, before I ordered myself a decaf mocha.

He beamed. "I have to say, when I received a text from Hannah about meeting you, I was kind of confused." Ty's tone was questioning, and he raised one of his eyebrows as we settled into a booth.

I didn't know what to say. There was no way that I was going to tell him that Hannah had arranged for us to meet because she wanted to make a guy who Ty thought was my boyfriend—even though he wasn't—jealous. I was here because I wanted to see Ty, not because I wanted to piss anyone off.

"My phone's broken," I lied through my teeth, making a mental note to keep my phone in my pocket while here. "We used to be close, too. It's sad that we lost contact." My heart panged. It was so strange how someone could go from being one of your best friends one day, to an acquaintance the next.

He nodded in understanding. “So, working on any new pieces recently?” Ty was nowhere near flirty—which was something I'd always appreciated when it came to him. He truly believed that men and women could just be friends. There were far too many people out there who didn’t have the same view.

I shrugged. “To be honest, I haven't had as much time as I would like to draw. College is a bitch, but I’ve managed to get a few pieces in.”

“I'm glad I didn't take that route.”

“How is hockey going?” I sipped my drink, mentally cursing myself for taking too big of a gulp and almost searing my tongue off.

“I mean, it looks glamorous on the outside, but training is tough. I'm on the second team right now, but the coach says that if I really work this season, I could make it to the first.”

“That’s great, Ty. You always did belong on the ice.”

Time went by quickly, and we slipped right back to how we used to be back in high school. Ty told me about how he was staying with his aunt and uncle while he saved up for his own place since his parents now lived halfway across the country, and I told him about my parents' divorce. He'd laughed, letting me know he'd seen it coming from a mile away. We all had, really, but I’d been in denial at the time.

Bringing up my father pulled hurtful thoughts to the forefront of my mind. I hadn’t expected him to change his number, and when I'd informed my mom, she’d scoffed and rolled her eyes, proceeding to curse his behaviour.

I glanced at the clock on the wall. “We should definitely do this again, but I have to head back. I've got a shit tonne of college work to get on with.”

“Sure. I’ve got work at the restaurant in an hour, anyway.”

Watching Ty make his way to his car, I pulled out my phone, having felt it vibrate in my pocket throughout our conversation.

Kaylee: Hey, Freya. It's Kaylee. Brent gave me your number. Kaleb booked a table at the Dirty Parrot for seven tonight. I just wanted to check what you were wearing. I've never been there before and don't want to overdress.

I'd thought that with Kaleb believing I was going on a date with Ty, he'd be too pissed off to go out tonight, but it seemed that wasn't the case.

Kaleb needs to believe you have other options. He needs to know that you have the attention of other guys. Then he'll drop this cocky act and stop bullshitting about not wanting you.

Hannah's words echoed loudly inside my head.

I hadn't been out in a hell of a long time, and I was actually looking forward to it. However, I couldn't help but feel like the volcano was due to erupt tonight, and I didn't know who was going to end up burned.

Twenty-two: Kaleb

Ty had a punchable face.

The idea of Freya going on a date made my blood boil, and I cursed at whoever was up above looking down on me and giving me the worst luck known to man. Perhaps I had been even more of an asshole in my past life.

The bar was bustling, and I scowled as we stepped into the Dirty Parrot, the lights blinding me and the sound of people laughing and nattering reaching my ears. Fuck this. Brent had assured me this wasn't a place that blasted shitty, overplayed pop music or that was filled with drunken, horny partygoers. He'd lied on both accounts.

I snuck another glance at Freya, my throat tightening at just the sight of her. She was dressed in a brown halter neck top and jeans, her breasts pushed up and the denim of her pants hugging her hips. Even when I was pissed off, I couldn't cease my desire for her.

I yanked out my phone, pretending to message someone in an attempt to distract myself. It was times like these that I wished I had social media. In my opinion, the sites were a waste of megapixels, but aimlessly scrolling on one of them sounded like a saviour from my current situation.

"Do you guys want to tell me how you two entered the bar with guns strapped to your belts?" Kaylee questioned as she gazed over the top of her daiquiri, beaming.

Brent shrugged. "The bouncer is a buddy of mine."

"Of course. So, Freya, what have you been up to? Do anything fun today?"

"Oh, I went to see my friend Ty." Freya's eyes flickered to me for a split second, and I stiffened, dropping my phone down on the table and turning my attention to the girls. I wanted to hear this.

Kaylee wiggled her brows at her words as Brent looked at me awkwardly, and I tapped my fingers impatiently against the table.

"What's he like?" Kaylee gushed. "Is he *really* just a friend? Or something more? Is he hot?"

"Kaylee," warned Brent under his breath, but she only furrowed her eyebrows at him with confusion before waving his concern away. Freya tentatively sipped her strawberry mojito, her naturally long lashes fluttering as she dragged her glossy bottom lip into her mouth.

God dammit. I was a fucking goner.

"I mean, yeah, he's good-looking." Freya shrugged, refusing to look at me. "He's a hockey player."

"Oh, he must have fantastic legs." Kaylee laughed as Brent pulled out his phone, attempting to show me something to do with work to distract me, but I merely held my hand up to my friend to let him know I wasn't interested. My undivided attention was on Freya.

She met my eyes, looking sheepish, offering Kaylee a small smile.

"Would you fuck him?"

That was enough to make me scrape my chair back with a grunt and head over to the bar, settling down on a stool. I laced my hands together, squeezing tightly, grinding my teeth. The waitress eyed me up, leaning forward and smiling at me. "You look like you could use a drink." She placed a small glass of whisky in front of me, and I glared at it, not trusting myself to resist throwing it halfway across the room.

"What's your problem?"

I turned my head to see Freya beside me, a scowl plastered on her beautiful face.

"I don't have a problem." The words came out harshly, and her eyes blazed as she laughed in disbelief, shaking her head.

"Yeah, sure. Until one minute ago, you'd barely looked at me tonight."

Not true. I'd stolen many glances when she hadn't been paying attention.

"You were the one who made it clear that our kiss was crossing the line." She pushed her curled hair away from her face with a huff. "You wanted us to forget it happened."

"You agreed." I deadpanned her.

"Yes, because your reaction made it very obvious where we stood. But now you're acting like this and—" She paused. "Fuck it. I'm going to the bathroom."

I swore under my breath as I watched Freya stalk away, and before I could register what I was doing, I slipped off my bar stool and followed her.

Twenty-three: Freya

I heard footsteps behind me but ignored them, rounding the corner towards the lit-up bathroom sign. Before I could shove the door open, though, my wrist was grabbed, and I was pressed against the cold wall. Kaleb stared back at me with fiery eyes, his touch tentative and soft—yet possessive and dominant.

He gulped as he studied me. "If you think I'm going to sit and listen to you talk about your date with another guy, then you're incredibly mistaken, Freya."

He was so close. His minty breath fanned across my face, and I swallowed harshly as I studied his smooth skin. He'd shaved before coming out, and I resisted the urge to trace my fingertips down his jawline.

"I won't allow someone else to take what I want."

His words rang loud and clear as they entered my ears, bouncing off the inside of my skull and giving me a banging headache. How could a headache feel so good, though?

I won't allow someone else to take what I want.

My core was warm, and my arousal grew, the feeling of Kaleb's sizzling body so close forcing me to release a small whimper. He gazed down at my lips, and before I knew it, they were on mine—desperate and demanding.

He held my wrists above my head as his mouth moved against my own. I'd never felt something so explosive. So incredible and magical. I couldn't think clearly, but I also didn't want to. This was an enchantment that I never wanted to be freed from.

Kaleb's rock-hard cock brushed past my thigh, and I pushed myself further up against him, causing a strained grunt to escape his mouth.

The sound was going to haunt me.

"Did he touch you?" he asked in between kisses, his lips finding my neck.

I tilted my head back to give him better access. "What?"

"Your date. Did he touch you?" I shook my head, but Kaleb gave me a gentle warning squeeze. "Use your words, Freya. Tell me if he touched you."

"No. He didn't touch me."

He hummed huskily, and it seemed he released a pent-up breath, his chest expanding as he relaxed from my response.

I squeezed my legs together to block out the burning sensation between them, but it didn't help, and Kaleb smiled against my skin. I arched my back as he released my hands, his palms travelling down my arms and stopping at my breasts.

"Tell me," he mumbled as he pressed another kiss to my lips, his finger tracing my hardened nipple. "Could he ever make you feel like this?"

No, no, and no.

I clamped my mouth shut as I swallowed because I knew that if I didn't, I was going to beg Kaleb to do things to me that were definitely not appropriate for a bar corridor.

Pinching my nipple between his fingers, he pulled back, shuffling so that one of his legs was in between my own, his thigh against my core. "I'm waiting for an answer, Freya. I'm not a patient man."

"No," I sighed, meeting Kaleb's lust-filled eyes. "He couldn't."

Humming, he studied me. "Remember that the next time you go on a date with him." He dipped his chin at me, watching me intently.

God, I wanted his lips back on mine.

My phone suddenly clattered to the floor—having fallen from my pocket as it vibrated—and Kaleb hooked his finger under my chin to stop me from gazing down.

"Ignore it," he ordered, pressing his lips back to my neck, but when it buzzed again against my shoe, I groaned and quickly snuck a glance at it to see who was hounding me. My breath hitched.

An unknown number.

Instinct took over, and I bent down to answer the call.

My lips parted. I could hear a quiet voice on the other end of the line—his distinctive huskiness was easy to identify. My eyes turned to saucers, and Kaleb glanced down at me with concern before he shoved a fire escape door open, gesturing for me to exit.

The wind whipped around me violently, my hair whirling around my face, and I clutched the phone even tighter in my numb and quivering hand.

"Hello? Dad? Say that again," I shouted, my voice wavering slightly. It didn't feel real—like I was having some out-of-body experience.

Kaleb watched me with a taut jaw, the muscle pulsating at the mention of my father.

"Freya? Freya, can you hear me?"

My heart leapt out of my chest at the unmistakable sound of his voice. I nodded. "Yes, I can hear you. Dad, where are you? What's going on?"

He sighed heavily, and I picked up on some shuffling and muttering before my father spoke again. "Listen to me very carefully. Things are messy right now. I don't know what's going to happen, so—"

He didn't finish his sentence.

Nausea wafted through me at his words, my face blanching, and I suddenly felt as if I was about to pass out. For some pathetic reason, I'd believed he was calling to let me know he was about to board a plane home and would see me tomorrow. Instead, this sounded more like a goodbye.

"What are you talking about?" I muttered, my throat drying up. "Dad? Where are you?"

"I don't know." His voice turned frosty.

"You need to come home."

I could faintly hear my father speaking, but I couldn't make out what he was saying. It appeared as if he had set the phone down.

"Is this about the debt?" My tone took on a frantic inflexion, and my eyes met Kaleb's. His own father had struggled with gambling, and perhaps the risky pastime was also my own father's vice. "If it is, we can sort it out. Just come back, and we can fix this."

Muttering. Multiple people muttering.

My father wasn't alone.

I flinched at the sound of a yell, and I gathered the phone had clattered to the floor, the sound of a struggle reaching my ears.

"Dad? Are you okay?" My body was screaming at me in alarm.

"Freya?" A pained groan escaped his mouth.

"Who are you with? Who's there with you?"

"They're—"

Before my father could respond, the call was cut off, and I stood frozen in the middle of the tiny trash area with Kaleb drifting towards me. I immediately attempted to call the number back, but it failed, indicating I'd been blocked.

"Freya," muttered Kaleb as he cupped my cheeks, my hazy eyes looking straight through him as he crouched down to my level, trying to gain my attention. "Hey, talk to me. What happened?"

I wanted to scream. To yell, but it was as if all my emotions had been sucked from my body, dissipating into the surrounding air. I felt empty. Numb. "My dad..." I muttered, my voice barely above a whisper. I was surprised Kaleb heard it over the pumping of the music.

"What did he say, Freya?" He pried the phone from my hand, studying my call history.

"He wasn't alone, Kaleb. It sounded like someone... was hurting him."

Kaleb cursed under his breath, glaring down at my screen. "It's alright. Come on."

Brent and Kaylee were more than understanding when Kaleb explained to them I needed to leave because of a family emergency. He drove like a drag racer all the way to the police station, shoving past the line of people waiting and placing his hands on the reception desk, still clutching my phone. "We need to speak with someone."

The grey-haired receptionist glared at him, cocking her head as she repositioned her glasses onto the tip of her nose. “Well, I'm afraid you're going to have to—“

Kaleb huffed, yanking out a badge from his jacket, practically shoving it into her face. She gawked at it for a few seconds before she widened her eyes, nodding, gesturing for us to take a seat and letting us know that somebody would be right with us.

I bounced my leg up and down anxiously as we waited on the rock-hard chairs—with Kaleb clicking his tongue as he cracked his knuckles. He still held onto his badge, and I leaned over and tentatively took it from him, swiping my fingers over the cool metal. I couldn’t sit in silence any longer.

“Do you carry this with you everywhere?” I asked, and he nodded.

“Except for when I go to the shooting range.” His eyes were fixated on the wall in front of us. He always seemed to close himself off when I brought up his job.

“Brent told me about the raid you guys did a little while ago, where that guy died.” I wasn’t sure why I was bringing it up, but a small part of me hoped that Brent was exaggerating. Knowing that Kaleb was risking his life every time he disappeared to work caused my stomach to flip.

His eyes faltered, and he turned to me with a stone-cold expression. “He wasn't the first and certainly won't be the last.”

It was the harsh reality of his line of work. Deep down, I knew that, and I cleared my throat, waiting a few seconds before asking my next question. It’d been playing on my mind recently, but I hadn't mustered up the courage to spit it out. I took a deep breath. “Have you ever killed anybody?”

Kaleb froze, greedily inhaling oxygen as he gazed down at the rings wrapped around his fingers, playing with them—yet another nervous habit he seemed to possess. “I have.”

It wasn't the news that I wanted to hear, but I’d been expecting it. He killed criminals—criminals he had to kill before they killed him.

“Does that make you look at me differently?” Kaleb queried, hiking his eyebrows up, the artificial police station lights casting shadows onto his high cheekbones and jawline, making them look even more defined.

“No. You have to do it.”

He chuckled—no humour to it. “That's a nice way of calling me a murderer.”

“You’re not a murderer, Kaleb.”

He hummed. “I've seen more shit in the past five years than most people see in their entire lives. I've had people I’ve worked with die on me, and I've had to watch them bleed out on the floor of old warehouses, too busy trying to stop myself from getting killed to save them.” He cocked his head at me. “I knew what I was signing myself up for, though. I knew the nature of the line of work I was going into when I started, but nothing prepares you for the feeling you experience when you shoot your first live person in the head or when you watch one of your friends die at your feet for the first time. That shit fucks with you, and now I think nothing of it. I’m so accustomed to it that I actually enjoy killing people that deserve it.”

I ground my teeth together, placing my hand on the side of Kaleb's cheek, caressing it gently. “Maybe you need to talk to someone about this.”

“The base has therapists. It's one of the reasons they want us to live close to them—so they can monitor our well-being. A few people within the organisation have taken their own lives.”

I inhaled deeply, the thought of him ever having to deal with those sorts of emotions causing my heart to ache, and I opened my mouth to speak, but he interrupted me with a chuckle.

"Don't worry, sweetheart. I'm not about to jump off the top of a building. Who would rid the world of sex traffickers and mafia lords, then?"

"Mr Evans, it's good to see you."

I dragged my eyes away from Kaleb at the sound of the voice, glancing at the stocky, bald man in uniform peeking out of his office, waving the both of us inside.

"Mr Walliams," Kaleb greeted, closing the door behind him and pulling a chair out for me, placing my phone on the desk.

"What can I do for you today?" he asked as he typed on his computer, a friendly smile plastered on his face.

"This call," Kaleb said as he tapped on my screen. "Trace where it came from."

I sighed. *He really wasn't one for manners, was he?*

Mr Walliams snickered, taking my phone in his hands. "Demanding as always, Mr Evans. I'll just need to take a few details first."

Twenty-four: Freya

Defeated. There was no other word to describe how I felt.

Kaleb and I had waited around at the police station for almost two hours before Mr Walliams came to tell us that the call was untraceable. Kaleb, being Kaleb, had kicked up a fuss and demanded that they try again, but after an uncomfortable stare-off between the two men, I dragged him home.

I fiddled with my phone as I gawked absent-mindedly at the TV in front of me. Kaleb had thrown on some crappy late-night television, and he continuously snuck glances at me with perturbed brows.

I should've been on a high—because Kaleb and I had kissed. Instead, the fact that the police couldn't give a shit about my missing father was filling my head, snatching any joy away from me and directing my train of thought to a more pessimistic place.

I'd never seen him so worked up, though, and I mentally gave Hannah some props for knowing exactly how the grumpy bodyguard would react to my fake date. It was as if she had a microscope into his mind. Perhaps psychology in the male brain was actually her calling.

"Do you think my dad was calling from a burner phone?"

"It's hard to tell. They should have been able to pinpoint which radio tower he was connected to." Kaleb swallowed, his own phone buzzing for what was probably the tenth or eleventh time in the past ten minutes. He was having an intense conversation with someone.

I inhaled deeply, pulling my knees to my chest and focusing back on the wall behind the TV, dragging my bottom lip into my mouth and biting it harshly. The taste of iron filled my mouth, but I revelled in it. The pungent flavour was distracting.

"Hello?" Kaleb said into his phone, his voice gravelly. The call lasted no more than fifteen seconds—with Kaleb not saying much—and I watched as he stood, running his hand through his hair.

"What is it?" I asked, pulling my blanket further up my body.

"It was my chief," he muttered, his eyes hard. "The police need backup for a raid about thirty minutes from here."

My breath hitched. All it would take was one bullet to lodge itself in the wrong part of his body, and he wouldn't make it out of there alive, but I kept my face as neutral as I could. Worrying wasn't going to stop him from getting hurt.

"My mom and Jackie should be back soon," I said, attempting to swallow my anxiety, the feeling thick in my throat.

"Invite over your chirpy friend," Kaleb instructed, nodding to my phone, and I scoffed.

"Hannah?"

"You're not staying here alone, especially not like this." His face softened as he gazed at my deflated form. "I'm texting Brent the login details for the cameras outside. He'll get a notification whenever it picks up movement."

I kind of wanted to be alone, but I also knew that wouldn't help. Sitting by myself and sulking wasn't going to conjure up my dad beside me, and it wasn't going to convince the police to actually give a crap about the case, either.

"I'm not leaving until Hannah's here." Kaleb looked at me expectedly, and I rolled my eyes, sending her a quick message.

"There. Happy?"

"Somewhat." He smiled before disappearing upstairs.

Hannah made it over in record time, barrelling through the door with an armful of snacks, her mouth snapping shut once she noticed Kaleb descending the steps.

I'd never seen him in his raid uniform before—black combat boots like usual, dark cargo pants, and a matching top. Over the top was a bulky vest, the straps velcroed together tightly, his gun hanging from his waistband.

But, as sexy as he looked, he was also menacing.

"Please be careful," I said, wrapping my arms around myself.

"I always am. Keep everything locked. Call Brent if you need anything. I asked him to leave the bar, so he's just around the corner if anything happens. Don't answer the door to anyone, and you have the app on your phone, so you'll get a notification if the cameras detect someone outside."

I resisted the urge to roll my eyes. Zach had been radio silent since Kaleb had broken his nose, and Will had no clue where I lived—not that he would come after me, anyway.

Our goodbye wasn't awkward, but it also wasn't *not* awkward. Hannah was mimicking a statue in the room's corner, trying not to make a noise, but I knew that even if Kaleb and I were alone, we wouldn't know how to leave it.

Mere hours ago, I was moaning against his lips while his hard cock pressed against me, but that ballgame now felt worlds away.

My stomach dropped as I watched him leave. It wasn't going to be the last time I saw him. He was going to come home in one piece. He was a trained shooter—a good one.

"Did you hear about Zach?" Hannah asked me with a mouthful of popcorn, causing me to turn to her with a frown as I stress ate myself through an entire box of red liquorice.

"No?"

"Apparently, he got kicked out of college."

"Really? Why?"

Hannah shrugged. "Some illegal shit he'd done, but that's probably some rumour. I imagine his grades were slipping."

I shook my head. "Surely that's not it? He went to every lecture and always got his work done on time." In fact, one of our lecturers had a soft spot for Zach due to his talent in abstract painting. He was cocky, though, and it ruined a lot of his artwork. He rushed his pieces, fully believing that whatever he created was a stroke of brilliance, and so often wouldn't put the time and effort in. He had potential, but it seemed he hadn't lived up to it.

"Where'd you hear that?"

"Josh. He heard some guys talking about it. Let's hope it's true, so you'll never have to see his lame ass again. He could be a real weirdo when he wanted to be."

I shivered. "Yeah, he could."

The rest of the night ticked by painfully. I couldn't stop worrying about Kaleb, and I found myself glancing at my phone every few minutes to see if he'd texted me.

How long did raids usually take?

Hannah had left shortly after my mother and Jackie had returned home from volunteering at the local care centre. It was Jackie's New Year's resolution—to help others more—and she wanted to get a head start, which, in my opinion, defeated the purpose of a New Year's resolution.

The house was so silent you could hear a pin drop. I was curled up in bed, shivering under the covers, unable to sleep—and not because my toes were so cold I was wondering if I was going to develop frostbite.

Kaleb had been gone too long, and my mind was running rampant, conjuring up gruesome images of him being shot at by conniving criminals, bleeding out on the floor with no one to help him.

I scowled up at the ceiling, counting sheep in my head, willing my body to let go and drift off.

Twenty-three sheep.

Twenty-four sheep.

Twenty-five sheep.

My eyes rounded as I heard the front door open, and I pushed myself out of bed and padded downstairs to see Kaleb's tall form moving through the doorway. It was pitch black, the only light source being the rays from the moon peeking through the sliver between the door and the wooden frame.

His forehead was slick with sweat, and he sighed heavily as he cursed under his breath, having not spotted me.

"Kaleb?" I muttered quietly. He flicked on the lamp beside him, his eyes raking over my red tank top and tartan pyjama bottoms. However, I couldn't avert my gaze from his forehead because it wasn't slick with sweat after all. It was blood.

"Did I wake you up?" he asked with concern, his eyes hazy.

I cupped his cheeks in panic, dragging his head down to me so I could look at the gash, blood still seeping out of it slowly. "What the hell happened?"

"It's fine. A guy got me with a knife."

"A knife?" I questioned, my stomach twisting. "Come here." I dragged him towards the bathroom, forcing him down on the closed toilet seat as he chuckled, pushing his hair away from his face.

"I'm fine, my little artist," he said, folding his arms and leaning back, the sleeves of his top rolled up, revealing his inked arms.

My mouth popped open at the nickname.

My little artist.

Fuck.

"Don't, *I'm fine,* me," I said, scowling, pointing at his head while I rummaged through the bathroom cabinet, yanking out wipes and gauze. "You got slashed in the face with a knife. You're not fine."

Kaleb hummed, taking in my frantic form as I squeezed some antiseptic lotion onto a cotton ball. "I like you all worked up. Maybe I should get hurt more often." He grinned.

"Quit getting on my nerves."

"Why? It seems to be a particular talent of mine."

Rolling my eyes, I dabbed at his wound, wiping away all the blood that was stuck to his forehead. Kaleb watched me the entire time with curious eyes, a chuckle escaping his lips as I forced my brows together in concentration.

I gulped, studying his chiselled jawline and plump lips, his five-o'clock shadow easier to see in the bathroom lighting. How could someone look so good even after being sliced in the face?

"You didn't clean this before you left?" I asked.

"I wiped it with my sleeve if that counts?"

"Not funny." I glared at him for a split second before I pressed on the wound with a gauze, grabbing his hand to replace my own. "Keep pressure on it for a few minutes. Are you hurt anywhere else?"

He shook his head.

I picked at my cuticles. "Did anyone die tonight?"

"Three people. None of ours."

"Who was being raided?" I scrubbed at the basin, Kaleb's droplets of blood staining it.

"A prostitution ring. It's a place the police and my organisation have had their eyes on for a few months now. The criminals were stupid, and they gave a lot away in a very short amount of time."

I hummed. "So not like Will, then?"

"No." Kaleb gritted his teeth. "Nothing like Will."

Swatting his hand away, I nodded with satisfaction to see that his blood had begun to coagulate. "This might scar," I told him, and he shrugged, unbothered by the prospect. He already had a few—not overly noticeable—but his line of work practically came with the promise of accumulating them.

"Thank you," he said, glancing at himself in the mirror before his tired eyes settled on my form. His body towered over me, and he tucked a strand of my dark hair behind my ear, his Adam's apple bobbing up and down as he swallowed. "I need to take a shower, so unless you want to stay and watch, I suggest you take your pretty self up to bed." A smile broke out on his face.

I shivered, my heart beating erratically against my ribcage, pausing for what felt like an eternity. The battle between the angel and devil inside my brain was heinous, and I clamped my eyes shut, trying to quieten the argument. "Don't get soap in your wound," I said, dipping out of the bathroom and exhaling loudly as I quietly padded up the stairs.

You fucking coward.

I groaned at myself, allowing my mind to fantasise about what would have happened if I *had* stayed.

Twenty-five: Kaleb

"What do you mean, you can't trace the call?" I snapped with gritted teeth into my phone, causing my chief to sigh from his end of the line, taking no more than a second to respond.

"We don't deal with personal matters, Kaleb," he said with little to no expression. "Somebody's father doing a runner isn't our problem. It's not a case we're working on. The police are aware of it and will apply their resources without needing our help."

I resisted the urge to berate him, but there was clearly no changing his frigid mind.

"Any more on Will?" he asked me, changing the subject, and I internally groaned.

"No." I scratched the back of my neck as I leaned up against the wall, my eyes travelling to the photos of my sister hanging on the wall. I ran my tongue along the front of my teeth, my jaw aching from having it clenched for so long.

"When will you next be heading over there?"

"Tonight," I responded coldly.

"Let me know how it goes."

I cut off the call, running a hand down my face as I glared out of the condensation-covered window. The weather outside reflected my mood. Shit.

The anniversary of Brie's death was fast approaching, and no matter how much I prepared myself, whenever the date swung around, I found myself battling intensely with my inner demons.

My mother often spiralled around this time of year, but since her good friend had moved in and had been keeping her company, she'd been distracted. It was a good thing, but I was concerned that the grief was going to hit her full force on the day.

Annoyance flowed through my veins, but I pushed it aside to make my way upstairs to knock on Freya's bedroom door.

"Just a second," she called from the other side, and I waited with my arms folded and my shoulder leaning against the wooden doorframe.

She yanked her door open, gazing up at me with surprise, her face slightly flustered.

"Call in sick to college today. I'll be waiting downstairs," I told her, descending the stairs.

"What?" She swung her arms over the landing railing, and I arched my brow at her, my face stern.

"Just call in sick, Freya." My tone left no room for argument.

I was going to take her out. She hadn't been herself all weekend because the police claimed they couldn't trace her father's call. *Couldn't* and *wouldn't* were two very different matters, though, and something wasn't right.

Now that Monday had rolled around, Freya was having to force herself to head to college and plaster her usual contagious smile onto her face in an attempt to fool everyone into thinking that she was okay.

In reality, she was struggling, and I hated it. I'd do anything to take the pain away from her. I didn't care what it was.

I waited three minutes before she came barrelling down the stairs in a rush, her face full of concern. "What's going on?"

I chuckled at her lack of faith in me. "We're going out."

"And I have no say in this?"

"If you'd rather sit in a classroom full of pretentious art students who all believe they possess an ounce of the talent you do, then be my guest, sweetheart, but I doubt your lecturer will be teaching you anything today that you don't already know." She shivered at my words as I took a step closer, and her ears tinged red, making me smile. "Let's go. I'm driving."

We didn't speak much during the ride. I could tell that Freya had a lot on her mind, and whenever she dropped her happy façade, her eyes would glaze over, and she would sink back into her state of overthinking and anguish.

I hated that there was nothing I could do for her regarding her father. The police were doing jack shit, and my chief had declined my request to trace the call—there wasn't anyone in the organisation that worked in the necessary department I could ask that wouldn't report back to him.

"We're here." I opened up Freya's door for her, and her eyes expanded at the sight of the pottery studio in front of us. "I thought this might cheer you up, but if you're not in the mood for it, we can give it a miss."

Art and I weren't the best of friends. I'd never had much interest in it—besides tattoos—but Freya was good. Too good for the people she was surrounded by at college. I'd dug deeper when I'd got Zach kicked out and had done some research on the students in her class.

Their pieces were mediocre at best. They lacked passion, originality and charm.

But there was something about Freya's work that drew people in. Even my mother had spotted her sketch pad that she'd left open on the table the other day and had commented that her drawings looked like something you would see selling for thousands of dollars. My little artist just lacked faith in herself sometimes when it came to her talent.

"Kaleb," she breathed, shaking her head and smiling up at me. "This is perfect."

The lady behind the studio desk got us all set up—the fact that I had to wear a stupid oversized apron made me groan. But I was willing to do it for Freya. I'd do anything she wanted me to do, no matter how ridiculous it made me look. If it would make her smile, it was worth it.

"What are you going to make?" she asked me as she whirled her clay around using the pedal connected to the potter's wheel, her hands effortlessly moulding it into a long tube. I was surprised by how easy she made it look.

"I don't know. Have you ever done this before?" I questioned her, and she shook her head sheepishly.

Of course, she hadn't, but like I'd expected, she took to it like a duck to water.

"What got you into art?" My thigh brushed her own, her body relaxing.

She hummed in response, stealing a glance at me before turning her attention to her perfect-looking vase. "Um, I guess it was the one thing I had control of when I was younger. My mom and dad fought a lot when he wasn't working, and I knew there was nothing I could do to stop them from arguing. But when I drew or painted, everything was my choice. The colour. The shape. The emotion the piece portrayed.

I had control. A lot of my artwork revolved around anger when I was a child. It was the one thing my mom noticed. It was usually red or contained fire."

I bit down on my bottom lip, feeling frustrated by Freya's admittance. Art had been her comfort growing up—it had allowed her to escape from a family that battled one another. She hadn't felt heard in her own home, and that was deathly wrong.

"I don't have any siblings either." She shrugged. "It was hard to find something to do. My mom wanted more kids, but my dad didn't. Apparently, it took him a lot of convincing just to have me."

I nodded in understanding, my head snapping up once Freya released a loud laugh, her eyes focused on my vase. Well, what was supposed to be a vase. It actually looked more like some kind of deflated elephant penis.

"Do you want some help?" she asked, moving off her stool and gesturing for me to shuffle up, perching on the edge of mine. Her body was so close, and I could feel her breath on the side of my neck as she took over the pedal of the potter's wheel.

My jaw was solid as she took hold of my wrists, moving my hands around the clay slowly, shaping it into a model similar to hers. It caused my skin to tingle. She was so soft. Tentative. Delicate. I wondered if she'd be as gentle when touching—

"Kaleb, you need to concentrate," Freya complained, shaking her head and frowning at the collapsed clay.

"You're making it very hard for me to do that, sweetheart."

We called it a day after around thirty minutes of whirling my pottery around—admitting that I just didn't possess the natural talent that Freya did when it came to moulding shapes—and left the pottery studio to head home.

We organised to pick up our masterpieces in a few days once they'd been cooked in the furnace, and I was glad that it gave Freya something to look forward to. She had smiled today. Not her phoney beam that she'd been putting on all weekend whenever someone spoke to her, but a genuine smile that caused the sides of her eyes to crease and her nostrils to flare.

"Thank you," she told me as we made it back into the house. "I really enjoyed that."

"Of course."

Freya clicked her tongue as she rocked back and forth on her feet. "I was working on some potential submissions for my college work. Would I be able to get your opinion on them? I just can't tell what they're missing."

I didn't even hesitate. "Lead the way."

She released a small laugh before nodding at me to follow her upstairs, where she rummaged through her bag and pulled out her sketchpad, handing it to me on the landing.

I hummed in approval as I flicked through the pages.

The drawings lacked colour and energy, looking dreary yet still extraordinary. Freya had something special. She could pour her emotions out onto a page and influence those who viewed them. Despair rocketed right through me just looking at them, the multiple shades of sorrowful blue she'd used leaping off the page and hitting me square in the chest.

"They're incredible," I said, furrowing my eyebrows, handing the pad back to her. "But they're sad."

It caused her to shrug, and her eyes flickered with hopelessness again—the same they'd looked all weekend.

I sighed. "About your father. My chief wants nothing to do with it for the moment, but I'll try again."

Her dark brown eyes rounded, and she plastered a small smile onto her face and nodded.

"You don't need to do that with me, Freya."

"Do what?"

"Pretend you're not hurting. It's not necessary to put on a fake smile for me." I moved towards her, picking up on how her grip tightened around her pad as she gazed up at me.

"I know." She swallowed, and I saw a flash of something behind her eyes.

Need. Want. Desire.

My cock tightened, and I hooked my finger under her chin, allowing myself to lose all train of thought as I pressed my lips to hers greedily, backing her up against the wall. She moaned into my mouth, wrapping her arms around my neck as she pushed her body flush against mine, my hands gripping the sides of her waist.

I lifted her up in my arms, and she gasped, her back arching against me. Her head lolled back, and it gave me perfect access to her neck, allowing me to press hungry kisses to her hot and burning flesh.

"Kaleb," Freya moaned loudly. "Touch me. Please."

My breath hitched in my throat at her request, and I wasted no time kicking the door to my bedroom open and dropping her down on my bed, standing at the foot of it. She was breathless, her chest rising and falling as she took in deep gulps of oxygen as if she were a fish out of water.

I knelt down in front of her, seizing her legs and pulling them closer to the edge, my fingers trailing over the button of her jeans as I tipped my head to the side. "Is this what you want?" I asked huskily, dipping my fingers in to play with the lace of her lilac underwear.

The sexual tension between us was unmatched—I'd felt it the second I first laid eyes on her. But it was more than lust with Freya. I wanted to please her. To make her happy. I despised the idea of her being anything other than content with life, and I wanted to be the person to give that to her.

"Yes. Please, Kaleb."

"If it's what you want, then it's yours." I pulled down her jeans, throwing them to the side and parting her legs, giving me access to her core. My dick twitched at the sight of how wet she was for me, the fabric of her underwear darker from her arousal. She whined as I dipped my fingers into the material, feeling her moisture, causing her to arch her back and moan.

Breathing heavily, I plunged two of my fingers into her, working my way in and out slowly as my thumb circled her clit at a torturous pace. My fierce eyes watched her as she gripped the sheets underneath her. *My* sheets. She was dripping all over *my* sheets. *Mine.*

"Fuck, Freya, you're so tight," I grunted as I pulled her underwear all the way to the side, giving me a view that had me biting down on the inside of my cheek to prevent myself from devouring her.

"Kaleb, faster," she mumbled, and I chuckled, shaking my head, a smirk toying at my lips.

"No can do, my little artist." I continued to work her pussy at a slower pace, moving on top of her and briefly pressing my lips to hers. "I've been wanting to punish you ever since you played out your little teasing operation on me in your tiny shorts and sports bra."

Freya's eyes widened, and she released another moan. "You—you knew?"

I raised my eyebrows like it was obvious. "You don't run, darling."

I'd humoured her by allowing her to think I was completely unaware of the fact that she was trying to get a rise out of me that day. Seeing her dressed in her skimpy gym attire had ignited something inside me, though. She was absolute perfection.

Slowing my pace down even more, the sound of Freya's wetness and gasps filled the room, and she bunched up the front of my T-shirt in her fist. I pushed her cardigan up, my eyes roaming over her lace-covered breasts, and I reached into her bra to roll her nipple between my finger and thumb, squeezing it.

"Kaleb! Are you here?"

Shit.

I groaned under my breath at the sound of my mother's voice outside my door, and I sent Freya a warning look as I continued to pleasure her, leaning down. "Stay quiet." My order was hushed. "Yeah?" I called out so my mom could hear me while Freya wiggled underneath me, clamping a hand over her mouth to silence her sounds of bliss.

"Do you know if Freya is here? Her sketch pad is out here on the floor."

"Fuck, Kaleb," Freya muttered into my chest, shaking underneath me, and I knew she was reaching her peak.

"I know, baby, I know," I whispered huskily. "No, I don't think she's home!" My voice was thick as I addressed my mom.

And I definitely don't have my fingers buried deep inside of her right now.

"Alright, I'll put it in her room." My mom moved away from my door, and I felt Freya's pussy tighten around my fingers as I sped up, her hands scratching at my back as she released underneath me. Curse words fell from her mouth as she cried out into my chest, and I swore along with her, watching her as she came undone. Both the sight and sound were mesmerising.

Her glassy eyes. Her blushed cheeks. Her parted lips. Her scrunched-up eyebrows.

Fuck. The image was going to be etched into my brain for the rest of eternity.

However, Freya and I were now in water waist-deep, and it was going to be a hell of a problem when the waves finally hit.

Twenty-six: Freya

I was floating in heaven—or whatever was considered to be better than heaven. I was unable to concentrate, and I felt like I was walking around the mall like a cloud. My limbs were light and airy, and my mind was primarily empty—filled with the memory of Kaleb hovering above with his fingers arched inside of me, causing me to unravel until I was a mess.

Hannah, Josh and Ty continued to look at me like I was on drugs as I stared off into the distance mid-conversation, having to clamp my eyes shut to rid my mind of Kaleb's perfectly thick fingers that had brought me to an orgasm so strong, it had me seeing stars.

"Someone's a little distracted today." Ty laughed from next to me, and I blinked, realising I'd been looking at the same T-shirt on the rack in front of me for the past two minutes, not having moved an inch.

"I've had enough of shopping," Josh groaned from next to Hannah, and she sighed.

"Yeah, we're going to head home. Ty, I know your car is in the garage. Do you need a ride?"

He shook his head. "My house is pretty far out. I'm fine with catching a cab again, but thanks, Hannah."

We said our goodbyes, and I made my way to my car, shifting in my seat uncomfortably at the sudden burning feeling that spread over the back of my neck. I scratched at it, clearing my suddenly barren throat.

I'd never felt anything like it before, but it was as if someone's eyes were boring into my soul, and I twisted around to peek out my window. The parking lot was full of cars and people milling about, but nobody appeared to be paying attention to me.

Paranoid, much?

Shoving the feeling aside, I turned out of the lot, heading back towards the house, having picked up some art supplies at the mall. It'd been good to get out of the house, and seeing my friends had ceased the intrusive thoughts that my father needed help swirling inside my head. Again, the police weren't fazed.

Kaleb's little pottery date had really perked me up, too, and my heart ached that he'd gone out of his way to take me to a place he knew I'd enjoy, even though it was far from his idea of fun.

I shivered in my seat as the same searing feeling spread across the back of my head, and I clicked my neck from side to side and glared through my rear-view mirror. There was a sleek black sports car behind me, and even though it looked as normal as anything, I quickly developed an uneasy feeling.

The windscreen was tinted, so it was hard to make out the driver, but I could tell that whoever was seated behind the wheel was stocky and muscular. They barely fit in the vehicle—it looked almost comical.

The car was a little too up my ass for my liking, so I sped up as I wound down the narrow road, turning right, only for them to do the same. I turned another right, and so did they. A left. They were still right behind me.

The hairs on the back of my neck spiked up, and I immediately took the next turn, cursing when the car copied my movements. There weren't many houses down this road, and I knew that if they didn't stop and park outside one of them, then I was being tailed.

I held my breath, connecting back up with the main street. The car hadn't stopped.

"What the fuck?" I muttered as I attempted to squint through the darkening early evening to identify the man behind, and I gasped as I almost swerved right into a car barrelling towards me. Their horn blared out and caused my bones to rattle inside my flesh, panic hitting me.

I debated parking up along the side of the road and getting out to demand why this man was copying my every move, but that was the perfect way to get myself killed, and it was probably exactly what he wanted me to do. Nobody was going to stab me and drag me into the woods tonight.

Making a few more turns—with the midnight-black car still tailing me—I signalled to head down a slender road to the left, only to swerve and cut off a car coming my way. It disconnected me from my stalker, and I stepped on the gas toward Kaleb's house.

The car was still stuck at the junction—nobody letting him out—and I breathed a sigh of relief, my blood running cold inside my veins. No longer was the burning feeling pricking the skin at the back of my neck, and I all but sprinted into the house once I parked in the driveway.

Somebody had been following me, but I didn't know why.

Twenty-seven: Kaleb

"You're lacking in the bonding aspect of this job, Kaleb," my chief murmured into the phone, and I gripped it tightly against my ear, huffing. I wanted to strangle it.

"The quicker people realise there isn't much point in us all bonding, the better," I said. "We're all doing our jobs. That's the end of it."

"Frederick is my boss, Kaleb. That's what you need to understand. I answer to him. He believes that everyone having a better connection will help with the jobs. People's communication will improve, which will result in more arrests and fewer casualties on our side. You're great at what you do, Kaleb. You're one of the best, but my boss is noticing your absence when it comes to group activities."

I rolled my eyes, having no interest in this conversation. "I didn't sign up for this job to go to fancy dinners and get wasted at crappy clubs."

"I'm aware of that, and like you, socialising isn't my favourite pastime, but it has to be done. It comes with the job. You have to work with this team, so bring someone along to the party this weekend."

I pinched the bridge of my nose.

The stupid bodyguard party. I 'd almost forgotten about it.

"I'm not—"

"Obligated to bring someone, I know. You've said." My chief's voice became huskier as his frustration flourished. "The other guys need to get to know you, though, besides Brent, and you bringing someone will make that easier. It'll help you loosen up, I'm sure. Nobody knows anything about you."

And that's how I wanted to keep it.

"Who do you expect me to bring?"

"Anyone, Kaleb. Grab a homeless man off the street and claim he's your long-lost brother for all I care. Just bring someone. Show Frederick you're actually trying, or I'll never hear the end of it." My chief ended the call.

This job wasn't about making friends. There was no point in getting close to other workers when you knew they wouldn't all survive. Keeping your distance prepared you for their deaths, and in the long run, that made you much better at your job. Emotions didn't rule your life. They didn't get in the way.

However, when Freya was brought into the mix, emotions very much got in the way. I didn't like getting close to people. I didn't like letting anybody in, but she was able to chip away at the rock-hard wall I'd spent so long constructing. She'd walked right through it, and I didn't stop her. Instead, I'd pretty much invited her in.

The front door burst open, and my heart jumped out of my chest as I honed in on a wide-eyed Freya, her skin flushed.

"What happened?" I asked her, gripping my gun, and she gestured outside, holding up her car keys.

"Someone was following me."

My back stiffened. Rage coursed through me, my fists clenching, guilt hitting me brutally. If Freya was being followed, Will had to be behind it, and that was the fault of Brent and I. We had dragged her into this, and now Will was taking his anger out on her.

I wanted to march down to the shooting range and blast a bullet straight through his skull, but ending up in prison wouldn't help anyone—especially not Freya.

"I lost them but couldn't see who they were." Her hands shook slightly, the jingling of her metal keys filling the silence. I cursed, taking them from her and hanging them up on the hook, pulling her towards the couch.

"Car registration."

Freya relayed the first half to me, but she was unsure of the last few numbers, claiming that her mind was running amuck, fogging her memories.

I tapped my fingers against my thigh, skating my tongue along the front of my teeth. "You didn't get a sighting of the person?"

"They were big. It wasn't Will's stature. It was someone else."

I didn't know who this person was, but I was going to find them, and they weren't going to enjoy it.

Freya sighed, her tongue darting out to lick along her bottom lip, and I inhaled deeply, remembering how my own tongue had been doing just that a couple of days ago.

Her eyes. Her body. Her voice. *Her*

I hadn't thought of anything else.

My mind had been torturing me with her moans and gasps, replaying them over and over again while I lay in the same sheets she'd dripped all over. I craved her. I'd had my taste and was addicted. She was my personal Class A drug, and I had no interest in getting sober.

"Have you got anything else on Will?" she suddenly asked hopefully, looking like she wanted a distraction. I frowned, disliking that I would have to deliver news she didn't want to hear.

"No. Will wasn't there when we last went to visit. We think he's out of town for business."

Freya exhaled, her fingers ripping at the skin around her nails, and I placed my hand on hers, stopping the action.

"You're not staying here alone while Brent and I leave town. Not if someone is following you."

Freya appeared worried, and she took a deep breath. "You're leaving?"

"Only to go to a party." I had to force down my smile at her reaction.

"Oh." She tilted her head at me. "*You're* going to a party? You hate parties."

"It's for work, but I'm not leaving you here without protection. You'll have to come with us for the night. We'll be put up in the hotel."

I watched in anticipation as Freya bit down on her bottom lip before slowly nodding in agreement. My heart rate picked up, and she smiled at me, the action creating a tiny dimple at the corner of her mouth.

My worries and concerns always seemed to melt away when she looked at me like that, but I couldn't help but allow my thoughts of what would happen once I finished my case with Will to invade my mind and ruin the moment.

I was so close.

So close to putting Will behind bars, but also so close to losing her.

The day of the bodyguard party came around quickly, and to say I wasn't looking forward to it was an understatement. I'd rather gouge my own eyes out with blunt forks than attend. However, knowing that Freya was joining me caused my stomach to tumble. I didn't get nervous often. Fuck, anxiety and I were residing on two separate planets, but the foreign feeling of an elevated level of cortisol soaring through my veins made me more than uncomfortable. I wasn't used to feeling so out of control—as if my body didn't belong to me.

I was cautious every second we were on the road, observing every car for suspicious activity and monitoring anyone I believed to have been tailing us too long. Nobody matched Freya's vague description, but that didn't mean I wasn't scrutinising anything and everything.

"So they have these every year?" Freya questioned me, gazing over at the GPS. A look of relief flooded her face when she came to the realisation that we were supposedly only four minutes away from our destination.

"Not that I go every year, but I didn't have a choice this time."

My chief filled my consciousness, his familiar unimpressed scowl at the forefront of my mind. Sometimes, I really hated his face, but I knew deep down we were more alike than I cared to admit. Stern. Short-tempered. Withdrawn. He hated these functions just the same as I did.

I gazed at my phone as it lit up, a text from Brent coming through, letting me know that he and Kaylee were due to arrive in approximately forty minutes. We'd driven separately—much to the girls' objections—because I knew I wouldn't have been able to handle listening to his excited yipping for hours on end. He emitted golden retriever energy. I loved the guy, but he was a pain in my ass.

"You don't think our moms suspected anything, do you?" Freya worried, twiddling her thumbs, the nervous action gaining my attention before I shook my head. She'd told her mom she was staying at Hannah's. We'd left at separate times, and I'd picked Freya up from her friend's house an hour after she had initially left mine.

"We aren't the likeliest of pairs." I chuckled. Freya was an artist. She was creative and had a wild imagination. She liked to see the good in people. Warm and gracious—whereas I was dark. Moody. Saw things in black and white. Good and bad. Yes and no.

We were opposites, and yet, it felt as if we fit perfectly together—like a jigsaw created where the picture was up to interpretation, but was beautiful when you took the time to really look at it.

"That's true." Freya grinned wickedly. "You're rude and obnoxious."

I arched an eyebrow at her teasingly, cocking my head, releasing a throaty laugh. "Oh, you're going to regret saying that, sweetheart."

We pulled into the hotel parking lot. Valet was an option, but I purposely avoided it. I didn't want someone else's grubby hands on my car.

Freya's eyes bugged out of her head as she glanced up at the tall, regal building, almost falling out of the vehicle. I understood why she was so astounded, but having seen this setting more than a few times, I viewed it as nothing more than a too-large building where pretentious snobs wasted their money, boosting their egos and proving to others they had enough cash to throw away on things that didn't matter.

Luckily, my organisation had booked out the entire venue, and no snooty fucks were going to be present.

"How can your work afford this place?" Freya questioned as we stepped into the grand foyer, both of our bags clutched in my hand. The flooring was made of shiny, tanned stone with a huge metal fountain standing in the middle—a koi fish squirting water into the shallow tank below. *How original.*

A red carpet lay across the floor leading towards the reception and the elevators, and people mingled around, carrying luggage and following the hotel staff.

"The hotel gives us a discount since we book up the entire place. Still, I can't imagine it's cheap." Not that it mattered. My organisation had more than enough money and paid us enough, too. It was the least they could do for asking us to continuously put our lives on the line.

We stood in line for the reception, the large granite desk manned by almost ten staff members to get everyone checked in as quickly as possible. An older lady with a neatly slicked-back bun called us forward.

"Kaleb Evans," I said to her, holding up my ID and badge. She nodded and tapped on the keyboard of her computer before grabbing us some keycards.

"So, you've got room two-four-one booked for tonight, which is our king-sized bed suite. Enjoy your stay."

I arched an eyebrow. "A double bed?" I had let my chief know I was bringing someone and had specifically requested either two separate rooms or a room with two beds. Freya and I had been intimate, but that didn't mean she was going to be comfortable sharing a bed with me as if we were a couple.

The lady behind the desk frowned, double-checking the booking. "Yes, Sir. This is the room you were booked into. If this is something that you're not happy with, I'm sure I can try to sort something." She hummed as she pressed a few keys on her keyboard. “No, there are no other rooms available for tonight, I’m afraid.”

Freya cleared her throat from next to me. She looked slightly stiff but leaned forward to take the cards. “That’s fine. Thank you.”

Eyeing her up as we reached the elevator, she stepped inside, studying the keycards between her fingertips.

“Freya,” I breathed out. The last thing I wanted was for her to feel like she had to sleep in a bed with me. “I didn’t book it, and I’ll be speaking to my chief about—“

She cut me off with a small laugh, shaking her head at me. “Kaleb, you literally made me come the other night in your room. I think we can stretch to sleeping in the same bed without it being weird.”

My fists clenched, causing my knuckles to turn white at her words. They came out confidently—her voice not wavering in the slightest like it often did whenever a sexual innuendo was the topic. I liked it. I liked her so sure of herself. She had every right to be.

“You’re going to have to give me a warning if you’re going to mention that in public again,” I told her, my voice husky, and as the elevator door opened to reveal people waiting, I pulled Freya over to me to stand in front of my body. The last thing I needed was for the people I worked with to see my solid rock-on.

She giggled as we made our way out of the elevator and into our room. The enormous bed was coated in a creamy, soft duvet and matching pillows, and the walls were dark—dotted with fancy paintings of people too old to identify or care about.

There was a massive flat-screen TV hooked onto the wall, and the large ceiling-to-floor window gave us the perfect view of the countryside below, where the gardens were decorated with rows of colourful flowers and greenery.

I forced myself to look away from Freya's perfectly sculpted body to give my cock a chance to settle down, and I recited my most recent grocery list in my head until my dick was no longer straining against my jeans.

"You better not snore," she told me, crossing her arms over her chest, rummaging through her bag, and pulling out her clothing options.

I watched in amusement at the sheer number of jeans, summer dresses, and skirts she'd brought, knowing she wouldn't need any of them.

"Did I forget to mention that it's a black-tie event?" I said with a smirk, causing Freya's eyebrows to arch and her mouth to pop open. Frustration took over her usually harmonious features.

"Are you kidding? Kaleb, I have nothing suitable!"

I hummed, taking a step closer to her, picking up one of her slinky dark green skirts and playing with the fabric between my fingers, imagining the material enclosing her curved hips and thick thighs.

She snatched the skirt away, sighing and shoving it back into her bag, heat clear on her face.

"I think I can fix that."

Twenty-eight: Freya

I fiddled with the neckline of my dress, flattening down the sleek, black fabric. My heart had almost fallen out of my ass when Kaleb pulled out a long slinky gown from his bag, handing it to me as if it was nothing and settling down on the bed to flick on the TV.

I noticed the smirk playing on his lips, though, and he pretended not to notice my mouth hanging wide open as I clutched the dress between my fingertips.

It was beautiful. An off-shoulder gown with a slit stopping mid-thigh, soft fibres of material skimming the ground as I walked. I'd tried to look at the tag that was attached to it, but the price had been picked at.

I could only make out the faint markings of four numbers clustered together, and the sight had made me almost topple over. The dress had cost thousands of dollars, and judging by the condition of it, Kaleb hadn't picked it up second-hand.

"I can't afford this dress," I told him for the fifth time as we stood at the entrance to the hotel ballroom, the glorious wooden doors inscribed with meaningless Latin, the ceiling high and glistening as the setting sun beamed through the crystallised stone.

"Well, it's a good thing you didn't buy it then, isn't it?" Kaleb answered.

He looked incredible. My heart was still racing at the sight of him all suited up—but he didn't wear it like the other bodyguards I'd seen lingering around the foyer. He wasn't pristine like them. His shirt wasn't buttoned all the way, and his blazer sleeves were bunched up, revealing his heavily tattooed forearms. He wasn't putting on a show for anyone. He wasn't trying to fool people into thinking that he always dressed so immaculately because, frankly, he didn't care.

"We won't be here long, right?" I said, my voice laced with anxiety. This wasn't the sort of party I was used to, and I didn't know how to trick people into perceiving me as majestic and poised.

"Not with you looking like that," Kaleb whispered into my ear, leading me into the ballroom.

He hadn't been able to take his blazing eyes off me since I slipped into the dress and fastened my heels around my ankles, his grey pools imprisoning me and holding me captive.

There was a buzz in the room. Everybody was sipping wine and mingling—some seated on red leather couches pushed into the corners of the room and others hanging by the bar.

"Freya, you look gorgeous!"

I turned my head at the sound of Kaylee's excited, high-pitched voice, and I smiled, engulfing her in a hug. Her blonde hair was curled to frame her face, and she was dressed in a long, cobalt blue, strapless dress that hugged her body perfectly.

"You look beautiful." I stood back and admired her.

"Well, don't you scrub up nicely?" Brent teased me, raising a brow and turning his attention to Kaleb, nodding over to two older men sitting at a table in the corner of the room. They looked to be in the middle of a pretty deep conversation, their eyebrows caving in as they clasped their hands together in front of their stiff forms. "They want you over there."

"I'll be back," Kaleb told me, but Brent shook his head, gripping his friend's arm.

"Both of you."

I gulped. I knew there wasn't a need to be nervous, but the men looked intimidating, permanent frowns scarred onto their faces as they nodded at one another, taking tentative sips of their drinks.

Kaleb placed his hand on my lower back. "These guys can be obnoxious. Just a warning."

I nodded, plastering a fake smile on my face as we approached the table, and both men turned to us with curious expressions.

"Kaleb," one of them uttered, nodding at him and holding his hand out for him to shake. "You took my advice and brought someone."

"It wasn't so much advice—more a demand."

He'd been asked to bring someone?

"This is my chief, Reggie," Kaleb said as he gestured to the short, stubby man before shifting his attention to the beefier gentleman beside him. "This is his boss, Frederick."

Frederick was a large man—with what appeared to be an even larger ego. He didn't smile. Instead, he leaned back in his chair, tilting his drink towards me as he downed the rest, keeping intense eye contact.

I shivered uncomfortably under his gaze.

"It's a pleasure to meet you, Freya," Frederick finally said, his lip curling as he smiled.

I arched my eyebrow, meeting the man's intense stare.

"She didn't tell you her name." Kaleb's jaw twitched.

Frederick's brows lifted in surprise, and he nodded towards Brent and Kaylee, who were busy dancing to a smooth jazz song. "Your partner over there clued me in."

Kaleb ground his teeth together, releasing a heavy sigh.

"Now, I know we're not here to talk work," Frederick said, leaning forward. "But I have to know. There isn't any new information on the case, is there? Freya, I assume you know all about this since you're Kaleb's other half?"

"Well, if she didn't, she does now," Kaleb huffed, running his hand through his dark, tousled hair.

"Time is running out, Kaleb," pressed Frederick, his greying hair falling out of place and blocking his left eye, dulling his grimace. "We have people's lives hanging in the balance."

"We don't have enough evidence yet."

The chief also agreed. "We won't get a good conviction. Trust us, Frederick, Will and his team will end up behind bars, but we have to be patient."

"Make it happen." Frederick clicked his tongue, looking slightly frustrated, and he gave one sharp nod as he got up from his chair and grabbed his glass, heading for the free bar.

Reggie hummed, shaking his head. "Frederick can be impatient. Enjoy tonight, and we can worry about Will tomorrow."

The chief excused himself, and Kaleb's stature stiffened as he led me back toward Brent and Kaylee.

"Well, Frederick was a character."

"He can be calculating. A few workers have filed complaints against him for the way he handles things, and he often influences my chief, too." Kaleb shot Frederick one more frosty glare over his shoulder before Brent turned to us with a frown, following his friend's gaze.

"Frederick is such a creep, man." He sighed, taking a swig of his whisky. "I try to avoid him at all costs."

"How did you get roped into speaking to him earlier?" I asked, and Brent pulled his eyebrows together in confusion.

"I haven't spoken to him tonight. I'm hoping it'll stay that way."

Kaleb inhaled deeply, his hand still on my lower back as he clenched his free fist, his fingers looking ready to grab his gun that was hidden away in the back of his pants.

I swallowed, watching Frederick as he leaned up against the bar, chatting with a few other workers, his cocky grin ear to ear as he scanned the ballroom. His dark eyes settled on me for a split second before he dragged them away, downing yet another drink while he tried his best to wipe the smug look from his face.

The rest of the party was tense. Although, Frederick didn't talk to us again. Nor did he even look in my direction. I'd tried to finish my glass of wine to aid my relaxation, but my stomach lurched every time I swallowed the sweet liquid, and I had to hand the rest to Kaylee.

Glancing at the clock, I sighed when I noticed we hadn't even been here for three hours, and I picked at a fancy salmon and cream cheese canape as I leaned against the wall next to the buffet.

I'd never seen people eat so much, but it made sense, considering most people in the room were ninety-eight per cent cold, hard muscle, including the women. They could snap me like a twig if they wanted to.

Kaleb hadn't had a drop of alcohol tonight. Instead, he'd been watching Frederick's every move, ensuring he had sight of me the entire time. The man's lie about how he knew my name frustrated him, but as creepy as I found Frederick, I managed to semi-convince Kaleb that he was most likely just nosy and had found out on his own accord.

I wasn't so persuaded by my explanation, though.

"So, you were asked to bring someone?" I questioned, cocking my head and raising my eyebrows at Kaleb playfully, causing him to shrug.

"Yes, but I would have wanted you here with me, Freya, even if I hadn't been. All I want is to keep you safe." He sighed as he led me away from another crowd of people we'd been roped into talking to. "Come on, I'm tired of this party shit."

I let out a small yawn, covering my mouth with embarrassment. It was almost eleven, and I was exhausted. We'd spent most of the day travelling, and I was ready to flop down on our king-sized bed and fall into a restless slumber.

We said our goodbyes to Brent and Kaylee—who were nearing tipsy—and made our way out of the ballroom and to the elevator. I slumped against the mirror, my feet aching from my heels, and Kaleb watched me intensely as we entered our room.

Leaning down to unclasp my shoes, I gasped, his hand on my wrist stopping me. The only light source in the room was the moonlight streaming in from the tall window, casting shadows along the wall, giving the room a sultry appeal.

"I told you that you were going to regret calling me rude and obnoxious earlier," Kaleb said huskily, and I gulped, heat pooling between my legs as I settled down on the bed in front of him.

He began to unbutton his shirt, and my skin prickled with heat as I watched him slide the fabric away from his body, his rock-hard abs inches away from me.

"What have you got on underneath that dress, Freya?" he asked me, and I shivered at the sound of his voice, blood rushing to my ears. He tilted my chin up with his forefinger. "Are you going to make me ask again, my little artist?"

I shook my head. He knew I wasn't wearing underwear. I'd been too paranoid about a panty line. "Nothing," I breathed, my chest rising.

I could see Kaleb's cock straining against his pants, and he swallowed once he spotted my gaze drop to his obvious arousal.

"If you want it, all you have to do is take it, baby."

I almost choked at his words, and he held his hands up defensively, gazing down at me with a smirk as he waited. He knew what I wanted. I'd imagined what his dick looked like a thousand times.

Moving my clammy hands, I pressed my fingers to his pant zip, sliding it down, the sound making my thighs impossibly slicker. I shuffled his pants and boxers down slightly, my eyes bulging as his cock sprung free, the sheer size causing my throat to constrict and my heart to slam into my chest.

"Eyes on me," Kaleb ordered, and I gazed up at him, his thumb running over my bottom lip before I inched forward slightly. A low growl emitted from his chest, and he watched me with a burning stare as I took as much of him into my mouth as I could, gripping his cock at the base and forcing more of him down my throat.

He grunted loudly, cursing under his breath as he pulled his dick out of my mouth, slowly angling his hips to thrust it back in at an agonisingly slow pace.

I was drenched. I could feel my wetness dripping onto the expensive dress he'd bought me, but with my lips wrapped around his cock, I didn't care. I wanted him deeper.

My tongue swirled around the head, teasing him before I dragged him from my mouth and took even more of him in, repeating the action over and over until Kaleb was groaning above me.

I clenched my thighs together to stop the sensation between my legs from flourishing, but Kaleb gripped the back of my neck, gathering my hair and pulling it. He did it just hard enough so it was pleasurable and not painful, causing me to moan with my mouth full, my eyes fluttering closed.

"Don't press those thighs together and pretend you aren't fucking soaking for me, Freya," he said roughly. "Hike that dress up and touch yourself while I fuck this smart mouth of yours."

I immediately adhered, spreading my legs and bunching up my dress on either side of my thighs. All I could think about was the sweet taste of Kaleb's cock in my mouth and the throbbing need emitting from my pussy, and I dipped my fingers down, my wetness soaking them.

I moaned as he thrust into my mouth, twirling my fingers around my clit, my back arching as I widened my throat.

"Am I rude now, Freya?" he grunted as he picked up the pace. "Am." *Thrust*. "I." *Thrust*. "Obnoxious?" *Thrust*.

My muscles tensed as my orgasm approached.

"Let me see those beautiful eyes when you come."

I opened them and gazed up at the god-like man above me. My body was chasing my orgasm, and I tried my best to delay it, wanting to prolong the euphoric feeling for as long as possible. But, the pit in my lower abdomen multiplied in intensity by the second until I couldn't take it anymore, and I reached my peak. The world came crashing down around me—an inferno surrounding my already flaming body, heat encasing me.

Moaning loudly, Kaleb grunted before pulling out and placing his hand on my chest, guiding me down onto the bed. He fisted himself for a few more seconds as I came down from my orgasm, strings of his cum coating my bare thighs as he groaned.

I breathed heavily, pushing my dark hair away from my face, and a bead of sweat trickled down the back of my neck as I watched Kaleb with clouded eyes.

He studied me curiously, breaking out into a wide smile, a throaty laugh escaping his mouth, causing me to do the same.

I was inhaling straight euphoria and breathing out pure exhilaration.

I no longer needed oxygen.

This feeling was what my body survived off.

Twenty-nine: Freya

I'd been paranoid the past week. I felt like everywhere I went, somebody was following me. Watching me. Stalking me. Kaleb kept a close eye on my movements, having Brent watch me when he couldn't—as if I had my own personal bodyguards—but I just couldn't shake the feeling that somebody sinister was keeping tabs on me.

Tonight, Hannah, Josh, Ty and I were heading to a Christmas fair—much to Kaleb's displeasure. He claimed it was risky, but we knew I couldn't remain hidden away inside the house forever. I had to live my life, and we'd agreed he'd come but keep his distance.

"I'll be with Brent," Kaleb told me in the parking lot. "I better not see any wandering hands from your waiter friend tonight."

I rolled my eyes at the teasing. "He has a name."

"And I don't care to use it." He placed his hand on my lower back and pushed me in the direction of the fair entrance, where I had arranged to meet my friends. "Now go and have fun."

I flashed the security guard my wristband, squeezing through a small crowd until I saw my friends huddling under a large glistening Christmas tree—a fake snowy log cabin with plastic elves surrounding it to their right.

Hannah and Ty engulfed me in hugs while Josh nodded in my direction as he stuffed his face with his mustard-covered hot dog. Apparently, he was only here for the food.

We spent the next two hours perusing the Christmas stalls, ordering an obscene amount of curly fries and burgers, and ride-hopping. Although I was having fun, I was continuously watching my back, locking eyes with multiple large, beefy men who only stared back with confusion, their significant others ushering them away while shooting me cold glares.

I hadn't caught sight of Kaleb or Brent, but I knew they were watching us. The fact that I couldn't see them reassured me because I knew it meant that if somebody else were spying on me, they wouldn't have spotted them either. The boys were trained to blend into crowds and go unnoticed when needed, and they were doing just that.

"Anyone want to do the Christmas maze?" Hannah yelled over the booming live music, the musicians tickling their electric guitars and piano keys up on the brightly lit stage.

My eyes rounded. "Yes! Let's go."

Ty and Josh groaned from behind us, and when Hannah and I saw that the line for it was practically non-existent, we smirked at each other.

The maze was huge, and the paths were separated by tall, thick Christmas trees and wooden fences. Its dirt paths had been sprinkled with colourful gravel to make the attraction appear even more festive—it was as if an elf had thrown up all over it.

Hannah and I scurried through, and even though Ty and Josh did their best to keep up with us, after a couple of minutes, we'd lost them.

"This way," Hannah instructed me, pointing toward a narrow path with bright red lights shining down it, lanterns hanging from the trees and arching over the top.

Nope. Dead end.

There were others in the maze, and they appeared just as confused as we were, rushing around like working bees as they pushed past each other in an attempt to find the exit first, causing me to almost topple over.

"Do you know which way we need to go?" a woman asked me, looking frustrated as she called over her shoulder for her children, the little demons scampering off in different directions, screaming in excitement.

I shook my head, holding back a laugh. "No, I'm sorry. We're lost too."

The woman rushed off to follow her kids, and I turned around with an open mouth, ready to ask Hannah what our next move was, but my face fell when I was met with nothing but the swaying baubles on the tree in front of me.

"Hannah?" I called as I glanced around, cursing and hurrying down a path in a direction I was pretty sure we'd already tried.

She'd just disappeared. *What the hell?*

The air was suddenly icy cold, and I wrapped my arms around myself and shivered as I continued advancing across the gravel, meeting more than a few dead ends, forcing me to turn back around.

My heart picked up its pace when the familiar burning sensation accumulated at the back of my head—as if someone was boring into my soul—causing me to whirl around and peer through the darkness. The lanterns and fairy lights were bright, but there were parts of the fence they didn't stretch to, leaving holes of blackness for me to wander through warily.

"Where the hell is the exit?" I muttered to myself, becoming increasingly frustrated and concerned. Hannah wouldn't have just run off without me. "Hannah!"

Snapping my head to the side when I heard footsteps approaching, I quickly made my way down a path, the spines of the trees grazing against me painfully, marking my skin red.

If this was a dead end, I was going to have to become Spider-Man and start climbing.

I breathed a sigh of relief once I reached a split in the path, and after biting down on my lip and praying to whoever was watching me up above to help me decipher the correct direction to choose, I turned left, sprinting down it.

But I screeched to a halt when I spotted a figure in front of me moving slowly in my direction, their appearance tall and stocky. My throat dried, and I gasped, turning on my heel—only to release a loud scream when someone's chilly hand gripped my wrist, yanking me back.

I was face to face with a beast of a man—a creature painted with gnarly scars and eyes so dark they were almost black. A wicked smirk was plastered onto his face, and he tilted his tattooed head at me and chuckled, the glint of a gun in his large hand catching my eye.

I blanched as I attempted to pull myself away from him, but he merely dragged me down the path after clamping a dirty hand over my mouth. I kicked at him, and he released a grunt of pain when my foot collided with his chest, but he was quick to recover, jerking me closer to him.

It looked as if he was going to speak, and I took the opportunity to pull my fist backwards, launching it towards his face. Blood splattered onto my face, and I stared in horror—and also pride—to see that I had broken the man's nose. He growled, grabbing me by the back of the neck.

"Let me go!" My muffled demand seemed to fall upon deaf ears as the man leaned down to whisper in my ear.

"You're going to come with me, or your friend dies." His voice was like venom—sharp and acidic—and I grunted as he shoved me back against the maze wall harshly, his forearm pressing into my throat and constricting my breathing.

"Where's Hannah?!" I managed to gasp.

No, no, no.

My legs felt numb as I was dragged down the path, trying to put as much distance between the man and myself as possible, but when he turned to me with a snarl and clicked his gun, I ceased trying to fight.

If I died, Hannah would too. *What good would that do?*

"When we get to the maze exit, you're going to walk nicely and leave the fair with me," the bleeding man ordered, wiping his nose. "Then and only then will your friend be released by my colleague."

I bit down on my bottom lip, tears brimming my eyes.

He wasn't working alone.

God, I wanted to knock his front teeth out so badly.

This was the man who'd been hunting me. He fit the vague description perfectly. He had tailed me in my car. Watched me at the grocery store. Followed me on my walk back from the dentist. Stalked me after I'd left my teaching session with the kids.

I'd felt him there—his presence eerie—but the sensation would never last more than a minute, meaning Kaleb and Brent could never pinpoint exactly who it was.

I was his prey, and he'd finally pounced.

My brown eyes enlarged when we approached the exit of the maze. Sweat trickled from my hairline, and I snuck a glance at the man to see that he'd hidden his gun from sight. However, I could feel it pressed against me through his thick, blood-stained jacket.

I observed people as we passed them, longing for someone to pick up on my tense posture and the man's meaty snarl and to say something, but no one paid us any mind. It was as if we were invisible.

He had blood smeared across his face, for God's sake.

He roughly guided me over to where we were further away from the crowd, his thick fingers slicing into my flesh as he held onto me tightly, speeding up his steps.

Was this going to be the last time people saw me alive? I didn't know what to do. Scream? Run? Kick him in the balls and attempt to grab his gun and shoot him in the chest? I'd fired a gun before. I knew vaguely how they worked.

I didn't have time to weigh up my options before the man was suddenly yanked back into the open door of a storage warehouse beside us, his tight grasp on my wrist sending me flying with him, landing on the dirt with a harsh *thud*.

A groan escaped my mouth, my ankle pulsating beneath the weight of my body. I peered through the dimly lit room to see Kaleb standing with his gun pointed at my abductor's chest, his eyes full of rage. Brent had his own gun drawn, but it was aimed at a different man, who had dark hair and was also smeared with crimson liquid, looking like he'd been socked in the face a few times.

"Hannah," I breathed out in relief once I spotted her in the corner of the room. She rushed over to me with a wheeze, crumbling to the floor next to me and wrapping her arms around my body. She was fine, besides a tiny gash to her eyebrow, but it wasn't deep.

"Why are you bleeding?" Kaleb questioned my abductor, his eyes flickering to me for a brief second. "Did you do that?"

I nodded, and he hummed, chewing on the inside of his cheek. Was that approval?

"Care to share what you planned to do with them?" Kaleb seethed, taking a step forward and tilting his gun to the side along with his head, keeping it aimed at the man's chest. My abductor huffed, eyeballing the firearm he'd dropped on the muddy ground mid-fall, his fingers twitching. "Don't even fucking think about it," snapped Kaleb. The room was silent besides the sounds of heavy breathing and erratic heartbeats.

"He won't stop." The dark-haired man next to Brent chuckled as he coughed up blood, collapsing into a crouch and groaning, clutching at his side. "You think killing us will stop him from taking her?"

Kaleb's back tensed, and he shot me a firm look before turning his attention to the two men again, his smouldering eyes causing my heart rate to soar. He looked menacing—as if he was ready to lodge ten bullets into the guy's skull for his attempt to snatch me up.

"*We* may have been unsuccessful, but someone else won't be. He'll keep going. He won't give up."

"Who?" demanded Brent, but he was ignored, both of the men sucking on their teeth, the noise grating.

They weren't going to talk beyond what had already been said.

My eyes widened as the man who had stormed me in the maze tilted his shoulder down towards the ground, his arm snaking out to grip his gun, and Brent cursed loudly at him to stop.

I watched in horror as he lifted it, pointing the barrel towards his accomplice, the dark-haired man's forehead slick with sweat as his eyes bugged out of their sockets.

"We're as good as dead anyway," he told his quaking friend, clicking his neck from side to side. "Might as well keep our pride and do it ourselves. Before he does."

I knew the *he* that he was talking about wasn't Kaleb or Brent.

"Don't shoot!"

I released a gasp as the bald, tattooed man pulled the trigger, cutting off his colleague's words, the bullet soaring through the air and hitting his accomplice square in the chest. It caused his bleeding body to tumble to the floor, a loud grunt escaping from between his parted lips as he landed in a heap.

Hannah squeezed my arm tightly, a loud cry falling from her mouth as the killer then turned the gun on himself. But before I could see him blast his brains out, Kaleb moved to stand in front of me, blocking my line of vision.

I flinched as the trigger was pulled, my hands shaking, and Kaleb turned around and quickly scanned my body, crouching down in front of Hannah and me, pulling his car keys from his pocket. "Leave the fair. Go and wait in my car. Do *not* speak to anybody, and keep your hoods up. Lock the car when you're inside. There are two spare guns in the glove compartment. We'll be there in a few minutes."

I stared at him, stunned, adrenaline seeping from my pores, my mind completely blank. I couldn't fathom what we'd just witnessed.

"Freya, for God's sake, will you just listen to me for once and do as you're told?" he growled, his eyes darkening, and I launched to my feet, snatching the keys from him.

Dragging Hannah out of the warehouse along with me, we hurried towards the exit. We tried to remain calm as we weaved in and out of the crowd, my ankle still throbbing and Hannah's body rattling against mine.

"Freya," she whispered breathlessly, yanking her grey hood over her head. "Shit." She took a deep breath. "We almost died."

"It's okay." I covered my own head with my hood, glancing at my friend with unsettled eyes. "Almost."

Thirty: Kaleb

I had wanted to kill them. I'd almost shot those fuckers right in their ugly faces. The only reason I didn't? Freya was behind me, watching my every move. She didn't deserve to witness such a scene. That, and I wanted to get as much information out of them as possible before I ended their miserable lives. But I never got the opportunity.

I'd never felt so much rage in my entire life. It was as if a demon from the pits of hell had melted into my body and taken over, making me land punch after punch to the dark-haired man's hideous face—while Brent ensured Hannah was alright—demanding for him to tell us where his accomplice was.

I would've shot them myself had the coward not turned the gun on himself and his friend.

Luckily, the heavy rock music outside drowned out any sound of yelling or guns going off, and security was none the wiser. I'd called my chief, and he'd sent some more of our men and the police to the scene.

Although I'd expected them to cut the fair short and evacuate everybody, they didn't. They wanted to keep it under wraps since Will could be involved, and Brent and I were told to leave so they could handle the repercussions.

He won't stop.

He'll keep going.

He won't give up.

I clamped my teeth together as the words rang clear in my head, bouncing off my skull and filling my bones with tension. Somebody had a vendetta against Freya, and it had to be Will.

It was my fault. He was doing this because he knew Freya meant something to me. He knew Brent and I were up to something, but I couldn't understand why Kaylee hadn't been targeted either. I'd questioned Brent on whether she'd noticed anything out of the ordinary, and she hadn't. She continued to live life normally and without worry. Why was it only Freya was being hunted? Brent had made it clear that Kaylee was his girl, and I didn't understand why Will wasn't having her stalked, too.

I slammed my car door shut before shoving my hands in my pockets and making my way through the overgrown field. My mood was glum—reflecting the grey cloud-coated sky above me.

Not an ounce of sunshine. *Good. I was in no mood for it.*

My boots trudged through the mud as I weaved around multiple large rocks, chewing on the inside of my cheek. I stopped in front of the bulkiest one, next to a decaying tree, and gazed down at the stone, gnawing on the inside of my cheek.

Here lies Brie Evans.

The sun shines less brightly with you gone.

The stars no longer twinkle.

The moon doesn't glow.
You were the one that gave the world light.
Now, we see nothing but darkness.

My mother's words—she'd written them on a particularly bad day.

Guilt swarmed me, the waves riding higher and higher until it was a tsunami of remorse, hitting me full force and nearly knocking me to my feet.

Five years. Five fucking years without her. A death that I had caused.

Blackness had been consuming me—clouds of ominous turmoil cast over me that followed me wherever I went—but for whatever reason, whenever Freya was near, I forgot I was being rained on.

I'd learned to redirect my intense emotions for the most part. It was why I would slip away and shoot—to refocus my mind on something helpful, like learning how to blast a sleazy drug dealer or child rapist in the face. That was going to make the world a better place. Not wallowing in my self-pity.

"I met someone, Brie," I muttered as I settled down on the small boulder opposite her grave, ensuring it wasn't taken. The last thing I wanted was for a corpse to reach through the mud and grab my ass for perching on their resting spot.

I imagined Brie's teasing look. I knew she'd be laughing—giggling out of control as she gazed up at me with her bold, grey eyes, urging me to continue and tell her about the girl who was slowly thawing my icy heart.

"She keeps me on my toes," I said, casting my eyes down and fiddling with a twig, ripping the small delicate leaves off and throwing them to the ground. "She's fiery."

Just like me, Brie would have said.

I grinned at the thought, but it quickly dropped. “I fucked up, though.” The wind pricked the back of my neck hauntingly as if my little sister was controlling the weather and warning me. “I dragged her into things. She’s mixed up with the wrong people now, and it's put her at risk."

Brent and my chief had to physically restrain me and shove me against the wall at the Christmas fair. Fury had been coursing through me, and I wanted to do nothing more than march down to the shooting range and choke Will until he was a bag of bones.

I couldn’t, though. He wanted this reaction from me, and killing him would do nothing for me but land me in a prison cell—even if he was a seedy criminal. The police and my organisation didn’t want him dead. They wanted him behind bars where they could gather information from him about the trades he was working in.

I ran a hand down my face, groaning as I tilted my head back and glared up at the looming clouds angrily. They were threatening to downpour on me, and I cursed at them in response.

Fuck, history was repeating itself.

This was yet another person who I cared about that I was going to get killed.

I kept my sopping wet hood up as I entered the house, kicking the door shut, my hands shoved into my jean pockets. Everyone was still out, and I settled down on the couch, not caring if I soaked it through.

I braced my elbows on my knees and held my head in my hands, grunting to myself. Droplets of water trickled down my forehead and nose and dripped onto the wooden floorboards, filling the silence with steady *bloops.*

Brent had been watching Freya today while she was at college since it was the anniversary of Brie's death. I'd spent a couple of hours at her burial site—not having visited in a little while. I had a feeling it was the reason precipitation had begun to beat down on my back painfully. Brie was letting me know she wasn't happy about it.

I'll be better, I'd told her.

It was fucking hard living with the fact that the consequences of my own actions caused the death of my innocent little sister. Hindsight was a wonderful thing, though; no amount of wishing it hadn't happened would change the fact that she was no longer alive.

The front door opened, and I raised my head to see Freya entering the house. She smiled at me, and even though I was in a foul mood, it was enough to brighten my thoughts and drag me out of the powerful current that was keeping me under.

"How was college?"

"Same old. How was... Brie?"

I could tell she was hesitant to ask, but as uncomfortable as I felt talking about my sister, for whatever reason, I didn't mind the subject with Freya.

"Probably pissed at me because it was the first time I'd visited in a while." I chuckled.

She hummed. "I got you something, and I know it's stupid, but..." Freya dropped her bag from her shoulder, leaning down to rummage through it.

I watched with curious eyes. "Freya, I don't need—"

"Shh. Close your eyes."

I groaned but adhered to her request, scowling as she took my hands in hers and pulled them toward her, forcing them into a cupping position. Another few seconds passed, but I then felt something soft and plush touch them, and I peeked my eyes open.

A fuzzy brown bear sat in my palms—eyes so wide and brown they mirrored Freya's. A red scarf was wrapped around its neck, and it held its paws out wide—as if inviting me in for a hug.

I furrowed my eyebrows. "Oh... thank you." I attempted to hide the confusion from my voice, and Freya laughed, tapping the cuddly toy's belly.

"You don't have to do it now, but when you want to, squeeze his stomach."

"His stomach?"

Freya dipped her chin. "Yeah, but maybe wait until you're alone before—"

Without thinking, I squeezed the bear, and my throat constricted as the most magical noise sounded.

Brie. Singing.

Freya appeared sheepish as my little sister's vibrato bounced off the walls, and she picked at her cuticles nervously as she gauged my reaction.

I couldn't react, though. I couldn't move. It was as if the bear had been welded into my skin, and we were connected for life. Fuck. I wanted to be. I wanted to carry around this little creature for life—forever able to hear Brie's beautiful tone.

"I got your mom to send me some recordings," Freya said as Brie's voice fizzled out.

I couldn't do anything but stare. My blood was rushing through my veins, and my heart was pounding to keep up with it. *Elation*. It invaded every spare inch of space inside my body.

"Kaleb?" Freya cleared her throat. "Too much?"

I immediately shook my head, a smile breaking out on my face. "No, not at all. Fuck, Freya, this is perfect. Thank you."

Her shoulders sagged in relief. "I wasn't sure."

I studied her gift for another second before placing it on the couch next to me, cupping Freya's cheeks and pressing a soft kiss to her forehead. "I've never been given something so thoughtful. Ever."

"She'd be so proud of you, you know? I know you don't like to talk or think about it, but I know she doesn't blame you for what happened. She'll always love you."

My chest tightened, and I swallowed down the urge to disregard Freya's words—not because they didn't matter to me, but because I didn't agree with her. There was nothing that could convince me I wasn't the sole reason for Brie's death, but it was something I was working through in my head.

I would never rid myself of the guilt. That was something I was going to carry with me for the rest of my life, but having Freya by my side made it a whole lot more bearable.

"Are you sure about this?" Brent questioned as he glanced up at the derelict building before us, spitting rain sprinkling onto our hooded heads. "We're going to be outnumbered in there, and Will could easily kill us."

I shook my head. "He won't. He'd be stupid to do that. The chief knows where we are, and it'd be too easy to pin the murders on him."

Brent hummed in a way that said *I'm not so sure about that,* but Will was clever and calculating. It was the reason it had taken our organisation years to pile up evidence of his crimes. He wasn't an open book, and everything illegal he partook in was very much under the radar. Gaining his trust was the reason he'd let things slip, but now that he didn't believe we were who we said we were, he was going to be hostile.

I wasn't here to gather more information on his crimes, though. I knew we weren't going to get any more of that—despite what my chief believed. The reason I was here was to confront him about stalking Freya. To warn him to back off because if he didn't, there was a fat chance I was going to kill him myself.

Brent and I made our way inside, the aura feeling much more adverse than usual. We were no longer welcome here. Beady eyes lingered on us, following us as we peered around the room casually, cigarette smoke wafting through it and making it a little harder to see.

It wasn't busy, and the few people who were shooting turned away from us after a couple of seconds, minding their own business as they continued with their day.

"You're brave, boys."

I gritted my teeth at the voice, turning on my heel to see Will leaning against the doorway to the hallway in a plain white T-shirt and slacks, his mouth void of a cigarette for once. His hair was messy instead of being gelled back, and the dark circles under his eyes indicated he'd been skipping out on sleep.

His eyes flickered down to my handgun hanging from my waistband, his thick eyebrows raising questionably.

"I'm not here to shoot you," I said calmly, gaining a chuckle from him. "No matter how much I want to."

Will scowled, but it was exaggerated, a glint of cockiness and danger lingering in his dull eyes. "Now, why would you want to do that, Kaleb? You were the ones to infiltrate my business in an attempt to frame me for a variety of heinous crimes."

There was no point in denying it. Will knew what Brent and I were, and I wouldn't insult him by trying to convince him we were here simply because we enjoyed his company. I just couldn't figure out how he'd found us out, though. We'd given little away about ourselves, and although some people *would* see that as suspicious, it was odd that Will immediately jumped to the conclusion that we were here to collect evidence against him after having trusted us for years. Something had changed his mind—I wanted to know what that was.

"There's no need to lie to us, Will," I said. "We both know the shooting range isn't a business. A cover-up is a much more suited word."

Will's expression didn't falter, and he gestured towards the bar where a young blue-haired bartender was working before stepping aside to give us a view of the receptionist tapping away at her old and outdated computer. "I have staff." He cocked his head as if challenging us to deny the fact. "They work for me and get paid. Therefore, I think we can all agree that the shooting range is very much a business."

He was deflecting.

"Whatever helps you sleep at night, Will," Brent spoke with a tight jaw. "Although judging by the dark bags under your eyes, it looks like you haven't been getting much. Why is that? Been busy?"

We already knew he had. More handovers regarding the drug ring had been going on over the past few days, according to my chief. They had enough evidence to arrest him on those charges, but it was the murders they really wanted to get him with, and as of yet, that evidence wasn't strong enough to hold up in court.

"Never heard of insomnia? It's very common. Look it up."

"I'm not here to talk about your sleeping habits." I took a threatening step toward him, my eyes blazing. "I'm here to talk about the guillotine you have hanging over my girl's head."

"Your possessiveness is excessive, Kaleb. It's not a good look."

I didn't care. I didn't care what Will thought of me. All I cared about was him staying the fuck away from Freya.

"Freya has nothing to do with this, Will," snapped Brent, his mouth curling into a snarl as he glared at the seemingly unperturbed man before us.

"You're right. She doesn't, and that's why I have no idea why you're coming to me with this," Will snapped, appearing bored by our intrusion. "I'm a very busy man, boys. You both need to leave and next time you step foot in here, I won't hesitate to fire bullets into your shins."

Displeasure flared inside me at his threat, and I closed the gap between us, keeping my vibe calm yet threatening. "You give your little stalkers a warning for me then, Will." A deadly smile graced my lips. "None of them will get anywhere near Freya, and if they try, they'll end up dead. The last thing they'll see is the barrel of my gun, and I'll be sure to make their deaths as drawn out and as painful as possible. Mercy isn't something I possess."

Will smiled coldly, moving past us and disappearing around the corner, and Brent sighed, following me out of the building with his hand tactically on his gun.

I knew Will was going to take my threat seriously. It was obvious I didn't like people messing with what was mine, but that didn't mean he was about to order Freya's stalkers to step down.

If there was one thing I knew about Will, it was that his pride came before anything else.

Thirty-one: Freya

I swiped through the gallery on my phone, glancing down at the photos of my father and me eight Christmases ago, smiling as we held up our favourite gifts we'd received. My father—a brand new electric razor, and myself—a set of expertly designed coloured pencils encrusted with my initials. It was the last time I'd actually seen my dad smile—even if it was fake for the camera.

Still, the police were idiotic if they believed I was going to allow them to sweep his case under the rug as if it were a pile of trash. He may not have been the greatest father, but he was my flesh and blood and was in trouble.

The police didn't want to listen, but I was going to make them.

Freya: Heading to the police station to file another missing person report for Dad.

Kaleb: Brent is outside, so he'll follow you there. I'm taking over his watch in around twenty minutes anyway, so I'll meet you at the station after you finish.

Kaleb never questioned me when it came to my actions regarding my father, and that was something I liked about him. He knew I needed to do this for my peace of mind, and he was supportive no matter what—even if he knew it wouldn't make much of a difference.

Brent tailed me as I drove. My paranoia was still jostling around inside my head, my eyes darting from side to side whenever a car overtook me or pulled out.

I entered the police station warily. It was significantly less busy than when Kaleb and I had visited, and I marched right up to the desk where a middle-aged man was waiting with a frown.

"Can I help you, Miss?"

"I need to file a report for a missing person," I said, sighing. "Again."

The man behind the desk hummed, and he gestured for me to take a seat.

After a few minutes, the sound of an office door clicking open gained my attention, and I gazed up to see Mr Walliams—Kaleb's supposed work acquaintance—poke his head out of the doorway. He called me in, and I took a seat in the uncomfortable metal chair, the icy material biting into my flesh.

"What can I do for you today, Miss Henderson?"

"My father. He's missing, and something's wrong. Not to mention I'm also being followed. I've already reported it, but nobody is taking any of this seriously." Scowling, I inhaled deeply, causing Mr Walliams to click his tongue.

"I'm more than happy to add some notes onto your already open report," he responded, "but as of right now, that's unfortunately the best I can do until we get any leads."

"No one is even investigating it," I complained, running a hand down my face. "I'm sorry to be rude, but we're talking about somebody's life here. Something needs to be done."

As expected, the police weren't willing to investigate the case any further than they claimed they already were, and I left the police station with frustration bubbling up inside me, threatening to boil over.

"How'd it go?"

I gasped loudly at Kaleb's husky voice, and I spun around to see him smirking at me with raised eyebrows, the setting sun bouncing off his chiselled jawline and causing my heart to flutter. Everyone looked good in golden hour, but Kaleb was on another level.

"I didn't expect them to actually care," I replied, ripping at my nails. "If I keep at it, they'll have to listen to me eventually, though."

"We'll keep trying. Come on, let's head back. I'll follow you."

Pulling out onto the busy road, I turned on the radio to drown out my sorrows, making a mental note to ask my mom to also visit the police station once she returned from her two-day business trip. Jackie had joined her since the hotel was included. She needed a couple of days off work to distract herself from Brie's anniversary.

Suddenly, I gasped, honking my horn in annoyance when somebody swiftly pulled out behind me, almost clipping my bumper. I glowered at them through my rear-view mirror, noticing Kaleb's Jeep a few cars back.

The dark SUV behind sped up, coasting along next to me and forcing me down an exit in the opposite direction of the house. I glared at the ghoulish man sitting behind his wheel, a slimy smirk plastered onto his lips.

Shit.

Kaleb was stuck in traffic behind me, and I had no choice but to press my foot on the gas and rush down the barely used road. Overgrown trees and bushes blocked part of it, causing me to swerve.

My potential kidnapper was right behind me with every turn, copying my manoeuvres and making my body break out into a sweat. My tyres screeched from underneath me as I took a corner too fast, my clammy palms gripping the steering wheel tightly as I narrowly avoided ploughing straight into a tree, sharply turning down a dirt road. The SUV flew past me at high speed.

Answering my ringing phone with shaking hands, I continued down the dirt stretch, having no clue where it led to, pinching my brows together when my car groaned and tilted.

I had blown a fucking tyre.

"I'm about to be right behind you," Kaleb said through my speaker, his voice laced with fury. "Ditch your car and get in."

Killing my engine, I leapt out of my creaking car once Kaleb's Jeep screeched to a halt at the entrance to the road, and I threw myself into the passenger seat.

"Are you okay? Are you hurt?" he questioned me with frantic eyes as he scanned my body while trying to pay attention to the unkept road we were barrelling down.

"I'm fine," I said breathlessly. "Where's he gone?"

"Put your seatbelt on." Kaleb's veiny hands encased the steering wheel as his gun sat between his legs, and his jaw ticked with displeasure. "He'll most likely be doing a loop to come down the road you turned onto."

My gaze remained glued to the car's rear, and I stared at the winding road we were leaving behind, muddy tyre tracks coating it from the Jeep's large wheels.

"I'm going to fucking kill Will," Kaleb growled.

"He was right," I said, shaking my head. "He's never going to stop. He's always going to be after me."

Adrenaline was filling up the car, forcing itself down mine and Kaleb's throats as we breathed heavily, and once I spotted the SUV speeding up behind us, I almost began choking.

"Shit," Kaleb cursed, quickly grabbing his gun from in between his legs, undoing his window. "I'm going to need you to steer for me, baby."

I hadn't even registered what he'd said before he released the wheel and leaned out of the window, firing his gun at the man behind. Yelping, I clutched onto the wheel, swerving us harshly back into the middle of the road, avoiding rolling down into the muddy ditch beside us.

The black SUV veered to the left, and my stalker leaned out of his own car, aiming his gun at us and firing. The back window of Kaleb's car smashed into a million pieces, and I cried out and ducked my head down, keeping my eyeline just above the wheel so I could see the road.

"Kaleb!"

"Just keep your head down and drive," he ordered, firing another couple of shots, the blast of the gun echoing through the cold air, causing my ears to ring.

Luckily, there were no other cars on the road. There was no way I'd be able to live with myself if I was the reason to get an innocent person killed.

I bit down harshly on the inside of my cheek, and my eyes widened once the SUV behind us buckled—Kaleb having hit one of its tyres. The man behind the wheel slammed down on it in fury, taking a few more shots before Kaleb's next bullet hit him in the chest.

He slumped against the wheel, the car flying down into a ditch and smashing against a large tree, the sound of crunching metal being carried by the wind.

Kaleb pushed himself back down into his seat and took the wheel from me casually, offering me a small nod. "Thank you, beautiful."

My mouth popped open, and I exhaled as I took one last glance at the deceased man inside the battered SUV, nausea causing my stomach to twist and turn.

Kaleb had just killed a man. For me. And for some psychotic and fucked up reason, it lit something ablaze inside.

Rain beat down against my window, pounding onto the glass and frustratingly keeping sleep at bay. I usually found it comforting, but every time the noise of a droplet of water hitting the framework sounded from behind me, I couldn't help but convince myself that it was somebody outside attempting to get in.

Sitting up in bed, I peered outside for the tenth time in thirty minutes, only to—yet again—see nothing but the sidewalk and tufts of grass beneath me.

My stalkers could have moved, though. They could be at the front door with their guns ready, about to press them to my forehead and force me out of the house and into an unmarked car.

Sweat accumulated on my upper lip, and I shoved the covers off my clammy body and opened my bedroom door, padding towards Kaleb's room. Lingering outside, I took a deep breath, leaning against the wall next to it and fiddling with the lace of my white pyjama shorts.

I didn't want to be alone.

"Freya, you don't have to hide outside."

My cheeks became flushed at Kaleb's words, and I inhaled deeply as I pushed his door open, taking in the sight of him sitting at his desk on his phone in just a pair of black boxers. The fabric clung to his body tightly, and he stood up with questionable eyes, my own instantly dropping to his defined abdominal muscles.

"Did you come in here to gawk at me or because you also can't sleep?" he asked with a chuckle, and I snapped my gaze back up to his face.

"I couldn't sleep," I admitted. "I feel like... someone is out there."

Kaleb's face softened, and he sighed, shuffling his way over to his bed and patting the space next to him. "Come here."

I crawled in next to him, contentment encasing my soul as he wrapped his arm around me and pulled me to his chest, my leg hooking itself over his waist. He was pure muscle—lean without being too bulky. I'd expected him to be uncomfortable to lie on, but it was like resting on a cloud. A lumpy cloud, but still a cloud.

We hadn't wrapped ourselves around each other like this before, even when we'd slept in the same bed at the hotel. I'd awoken with his arm draped over my waist, but this embrace felt desperate—as if we needed to be in each other's arms after the danger we'd faced earlier.

"You have no idea how much I want to rip Will's heart from his chest." Kaleb's eyes were shut, and his thick fingers danced across the skin of my thigh.

I traced his tattooed chest, eyeing up the intricate ink. "You'll end up getting yourself killed if you do that, and if not dead, at least in a lot of trouble."

"At this current moment, I don't really give a shit."

I rolled over so I was on my stomach facing him, our lips dangerously close. "Don't be reckless, Kaleb."

He opened his eyes, studying me, and he smirked. "Why not? Doesn't that excite you?"

My throat suddenly felt thick. "No."

Yes.

He chuckled, his hand sliding up the curve of my back and resting on the back of my neck, gripping it tightly, knotting his fingers in my hair. "Is that so, my little artist?" A hum sounded from his chest. "You don't like it when I'm reckless? Would you prefer me to let you get away with anything and everything, then? To keep my desire in check?" He moved his lips dangerously close to my ear. "You and I both know you don't want that."

I shivered at his words, arousal pooling between my legs at the feel of his hard cock pressing against my thigh, and I had to muster up all the strength I possessed not to gyrate myself against it.

He arched his hips into me, and I gulped, my eyes hazy as all thoughts that didn't involve Kaleb flew out the window. I crushed my lips to his, and his tongue invaded my mouth, his body pressed impossibly close to mine as I moved to straddle his waist.

Kaleb shuffled upwards so he was sitting up on the bed, his back against the headboard as he cupped my ass, pressing my core against his erection. I wasn't wearing underwear, and my thin cotton pyjama shorts provided little protection from the intense and pleasurable friction.

I rested my forehead on his broad shoulder as he trailed his hands down the front of my shorts, dipping into the waistband. His fingers found my wetness, moving up to my clit, causing a loud moan to sound from my mouth.

“Nobody’s here tonight,” he whispered, slowing his fingers down, teasing me. “Be as loud as you need to be, sweetheart.”

“Fuck,” I breathed, clutching onto his forearm as I ground against his hand, my nails digging into his flesh. My eyes widened as Kaleb gripped the back of my neck and straightened me up, pulling me away from his shoulder. "That feels so good.”

“I want to see your face when I make you come,” he said huskily, lifting my hips off him with his free hand and yanking my shorts off, throwing them to the other side of the room, leaving my bottom half bare. He pushed me in between his legs—so I was resting my hands behind me—and continued to rub my clit, his fingers slipping into me and pumping in and out slowly.

My hands found their way to his thigh, and I gripped at the fabric of his boxers, begging Kaleb to move his fingers faster. My legs shook as he hit my sweet spot, and I kicked my head back and attempted to control my breathing as my orgasm crashed into me, my muscles contracting and jolting. “Kaleb, shit. Holy fuck.”

“Look at me, baby.”

I met his gaze, drawing my bottom lip into my mouth as I cursed and whimpered, the heightened pleasure slowly dimming.

My muscles were tight and achy. However, that didn’t stop me from dropping my eyes to Kaleb’s hard dick, barely hiding beneath his boxer shorts, and I reached forward to toy with the waistband, slowly dragging the fabric down until his cock sprang free.

Fuck. I still wasn't over his size.

Wetness was sticking to my thighs, and I crawled up Kaleb's body so I could press my lips to his, his hands cupping my cheeks as he groaned. Wrapping my hand around his thick cock, I positioned it against my entrance, and Kaleb pulled his lips from mine, arching a brow.

"Are you sure you want to go there, sweetheart?"

"I'm more than sure," I said, fisting his dick a few times, causing him to curse and tilt his head back, kissing his teeth. A sudden gasp escaped my mouth as he flipped us over, pressing his body to mine, his dick dangerously close to my core. I wiggled against him desperately.

"You should know that the second my cock is inside of your sweet little pussy, you're mine. You'll always be mine, and I'm a very selfish person, Freya. I don't share." Kaleb's thumb brushed against my bottom lip, and I nodded.

"Make me yours, Kaleb. Please."

His jaw twitched, and he tucked a strand of my dark hair behind my ear before reaching over to his bedside table to grab a condom, ripping it open with his teeth and rolling it onto his length. A pleasurable whine left my mouth as he slowly pushed into me, the sensation causing my head to kick back. My muscles constricted, accommodating his size, the stretch pleasing.

"You okay?" Kaleb questioned me, raising his thick brows as he stilled, allowing me to adjust to his size.

I nodded, widening my legs for him. "Just fuck me."

His clouded eyes were glued to mine as he thrust in and out a few times, grunts escaping his lips. My walls tightened around him, gripping onto his cock as he fucked me to the perfect rhythm, the sound of our skin connecting filling the room.

"Fuck, baby, you're so tight," Kaleb grunted from above me, pushing my white tank top up and over my head, gripping my thighs in his large hands and widening them even more, allowing him to fuck me deeper and harder. He picked up his pace. The way he stretched me caused my eyes to water.

I'd never felt anything remotely like this, but it was as if my entire being was on fire, and the lapping tongues of flames were burning me to a crisp. I wanted nothing more than to give myself over to the flaming inferno, though. It felt too good being scorched.

"No other man will ever feel this pussy wrapped around his cock," Kaleb said from above me, rolling one of my nipples between his fingertips. "Do you understand?"

"Yes," I moaned between breaths, gripping the back of his neck, pleasurable tears pricking my eyes.

"What was that?" He smirked.

"Yes." I shuddered. "Yes. Oh, my God."

I was blinded with bliss, and I immediately began panting when Kaleb slipped out of me and gripped my hips, twisting me until I was on all fours. My heart slammed against my ribs when I felt his hot breath against my pussy, and he suddenly latched his arms around my legs and hoisted me towards him so his tongue was lapping me up.

"You taste incredible," he told me as he sank two fingers into me, my head twisting to watch him. "Look at you, fucking dripping all over my sheets."

"Kaleb, please," I begged, and he chuckled, pushing his cock into me and pounding into my pussy until stars exploded in my eyes. I shook as grunts and groans sounded from his lips, and he reached around my legs to tease my clit, his fingers skimming over the sensitive spot.

"Let me hear how good it feels, Freya," he said as he gripped my ass, squeezing it almost painfully. "Tell me how much you want to come."

"I want to come, Kaleb," I whined, a sob of pleasure wracking my body as I pushed back onto his dick, meeting his every thrust.

Had I imagined what Kaleb's dick would feel like inside me a thousand times? Yes. But did I have any idea the intense sensation would envelop every one of my senses, filling every fibre of my being with serenity and bliss? No. It was akin to a gentle drizzle of rain after a long drought, each droplet a cool touch on my parched skin.

This man was otherworldly.

"That's. It. Baby," Kaleb grunted, his hips shuddering. "Come for me."

I reached my peak as he instructed, and I released an anthem of deafening moans as my pussy clenched, and I came for the second time, white light taking over my vision.

I collapsed down on the bed as he continued to fuck me through my orgasm, the pleasure so intense my heart felt as if it was about to burst out of my chest, and after a few more seconds, he released, gritting his teeth and muttering my name in a husky tone. Kaleb sighed, and I could feel his smile as he pressed his forehead to my sweaty lower back.

My throat was too dry, and my breathing rate too elevated to speak. Words didn't need to be spoken, though. Kaleb and I had just made a promise to one another. We were in this together.

Thirty-two: Freya

To say I hadn't got much sleep that night would have been an understatement. The only time my eyes were shut was when I was coming around Kaleb's cock, or when my face was being shoved into the pillow as he took me from behind.

He always cleaned me up after, wiping the sweat from my body before kissing every inch of me, his lips scalding my skin blissfully. Even when showering together, we couldn't resist but bring each other to another orgasm, and I was certain we'd racked up a hell of a water bill.

I'd never felt so comfortable with anyone before—despite the fact that Kaleb was one of the most menacing people I'd ever met. His glare could halt wars, and even though he gazed at the rest of the world with harsh eyes, they softened when I was in view.

"Why are you squirming so much?" Hannah asked me with narrowed eyes as I continued to tap on the keys of my laptop, refusing to meet her gaze. I'd been acting strangely all day, and it was because I couldn't think of anything other than having Kaleb on top of me again, our skin flush against each other and the sound of our moans intertwined. It was a beautiful symphony—my new favourite song.

"Freya." Hannah snapped her fingers at me, stalking over to my side of the couch and moving to stand in front of me, forcing my laptop shut.

I sighed, meeting her amused gaze. "Can I help you? I'm really busy trying to look for a job. This was your suggestion, remember?"

She laughed, crossing her arms over her chest after flicking her mousy brown hair over her shoulder, the realisation causing her eyes to transform into saucers. "Oh. My. God. You got fucked."

"You're lucky nobody is here right now," I told her, shaking my head, a small smile threatening to appear.

"So?"

I narrowed my eyes at her before sighing. "Okay, yeah."

My best friend beamed, her hazel eyes glowing as she puffed her chest out proudly. "I take credit for that. My plan made you two inevitable."

"Right." I rolled my eyes. "Can we actually look for some jobs now? It's our final year, and I want something lined up. I don't want to be a floater."

The thought of finishing college without a job placement frightened me, concerned about being stuck in a place of indecisiveness. I loved the kids I taught, but I didn't want to be doing it for the rest of my life. I had other ambitions.

Although the world seemed to be against me, I was actually doing pretty well with my classwork, and Hannah and I had been nominated to graduate early. It freaked me out as much as it flattered me, so she and I immediately cracked down to begin job hunting.

Hannah had already found a few of interest, applying to work in a museum and a company that scouted upcoming artists.

"There's this one," I said, turning my laptop toward her.

Hannah looked as if she wanted to pry about my budding relationship with Kaleb, but she clicked her teeth shut instead and focused on my screen. "We are looking for a talented and unique artist to help design book covers for our clients' novels," she read, her eyes flickering to me. "When's the last time you read a book?"

I snorted. "It's not about that. I'll have a degree, and it's a job I know I'd enjoy. My photoshopping skills aren't bad either."

"Then go for it. The worst they can do is say no."

We spent the next hour applying for art-related jobs, and my mom called me midway through to update me on the house-hunting situation. Since our old home had been repossessed, our debt had been voided. The police weren't taking my father's situation seriously, so my mother had decided to find us a small apartment. We couldn't stay with Jackie forever, and even though I agreed, the thought caused my stomach to lurch.

Not living with Kaleb—I didn't like it.

I hadn't told anyone about the fact that I was being followed. Only Kaleb, Brent and Hannah were aware because there wasn't much I could say to people without giving away information about a secret investigation, which would put innocent people in danger.

That, and I knew that my mother would probably suffer an aneurysm if she found out I was being hunted by a murderous drug ring.

My head snapped up at the sound of the front door clicking open, and I clutched onto my thigh painfully, instantly relaxing when Kaleb appeared. I didn't even need to look into his eyes to know he was up to something, the mischief and excitement radiating off him and crushing me against the back of the couch. The sensation was disabling.

"Do I even want to know what you've been up to?" I asked, taking a sip of my coffee.

"I have a gift for you." He smiled, and I pinched my eyebrows together.

"Why do I have a feeling it's not going to be a bouquet of fifty roses?"

Kaleb hummed. "Sweetheart, if I were to get you flowers, I wouldn't stop at fifty. I'd make sure to get you *five hundred* roses and fill the entire house with them so you couldn't even turn your head without thinking of me."

Hannah almost passed out from behind him, sucking her bottom lip into her mouth as she shoved down an exasperated giggle. Meanwhile, I was doing my best to bury my yearning for him, but judging by Kaleb's throaty laugh, I was failing miserably.

His hand slid behind his broad body, and he yanked out something from the back of his jeans, placing a small glistening handgun into my palms. The sight made me sweat.

"It took my chief a lot of convincing, but he eventually agreed I could give you one to help you protect yourself."

My hands shook as I turned the firearm around in my palms, my eyes narrowing when I spotted the *F* that'd been delicately engraved into the handle. I wasn't much of a shooter, but I couldn't lie and say that having a weapon that I could access if I needed to didn't give me peace of mind.

"Thank you," I said, smiling at him, and Hannah shuffled over to look at the weapon, releasing a whistle in admiration.

"It comes with a strap to hold it in place around your thigh. I know women's clothing lacks pockets. You'll need to practise firing it, too, but I can help you with that."

"You're going to be such a bad bitch," Hannah exclaimed, grinning. "I want one."

Kaleb turned to her with a raised eyebrow. "I think the last thing the world needs is you with a gun in your hands, chirpy."

"Oh, come on! That's not fair!" yelled Josh as Hannah grabbed one of his game pieces. She chuckled as Kaleb, Brent, Kaylee, and I laughed at his pouted lip.

We were having a games night at Brent's house since his parents were out for the evening. Hannah was currently winning, and Josh and Brent were busy arguing, claiming she'd somehow rigged the board before coming over.

Brent chugged down yet another beer, slinging his arm over Kaylee's shoulder, and she leaned toward him to plant a kiss on the side of his cheek.

The sound of the doorbell dragged me from my haunting thoughts, and Brent flung the door open to reveal a sheepish-looking Ty who clutched a crate of beer to his chest.

Kaleb turned to me with raised brows, and I shrugged at him.

"Ty, you made it," Hannah called from next to me, waving him in and patting the space next to her, Josh still playfully seething over losing yet another round.

"Any more surprise guests?" Brent questioned.

"Be nice," I murmured to Kaleb once I spotted his deepened brows.

He grinned at me, shooting me a wink. “I'm always nice.”

Thirty-three: Kaleb

Another ear-splitting scream echoed throughout the room, and I turned my head to glare at Hannah as she wriggled on the couch at the scene playing before us. Kaylee was a lover of horror films, and it'd been her idea to put one on and frighten the crap out of everybody. Even Brent was shaking in his boots, and I rolled my eyes as I threw another piece of popcorn into my mouth.

Ty and I hadn't spoken much. We'd socialised when necessary—like during the board games or when I'd asked him to pass me a can of soda. I didn't actually have anything against the guy. He wasn't making any moves, but I was going to make it clear that Freya was my girl—whether or not she'd told him otherwise on their date.

Hannah jolted again as somebody's neck was torn clean off by some badly CGI'd goblin on screen, and she launched her bottle of soda into the air, the contents of it landing on top of Freya, small droplets splattering my white T-shirt.

"Hannah!" Freya complained loudly as she shot up from the couch, fizzy pop dripping from her hands, her entire top soaked through.

"I'm sorry!" Hannah said with wide eyes, hiding behind her hands. "I didn't mean to!"

"Come on." I stood up and nodded towards the stairs. "I'll get you a spare change of clothes."

Brent hummed, waving us away. His gaze was focused intently on the TV, and I could tell he was trying to impress Kaylee by suppressing his cowering bottom lip and sweaty palms.

Freya groaned in disgust as she peeled her clothing away from her body once in Brent's room, and I cocked my head as I gazed at her from the doorway with folded arms. She was wearing a matching baby pink bra and pantie set, the lace tinged orange from Hannah's chemical-filled drink of choice.

The moonlight shining onto her through the open window sent me wild, her curves accentuated and her skin smooth. My cock strained against my jeans, and I took a step toward her.

"I assume you don't want to spend the rest of the evening wearing sticky lingerie?" I asked, circling her slowly, my boots hitting the wooden floorboards harshly. She bit her lip as she watched me, goosebumps coating her skin as I traced her collarbone, hooking my finger under her bra strap and letting it fall down her shoulder.

I pressed my lips to her flaming skin, doing the same with the other strap, unhooking the entire bra with one hand. Pulling her to my chest, I cupped her cheeks and placed a soft kiss on the top of her head.

"You should shower," I whispered into her ear. "Your skin is all tacky."

"Won't Brent—"

"He won't care, sweetheart." I pulled my T-shirt off in one swift movement. Her eyes watched me with such want and desire that a hurricane of arousal hit me, and I wanted to do nothing more than stand tall and embrace the storm.

God, this woman was going to be the death of me.

Leading her into the en-suite, I turned on the shower and dropped to my knees in front of her, my fingers gripping her sticky underwear, pulling them down. She stepped out of the fabric, and I tapped her legs, signalling I wanted her to part them.

Freya's eyes widened once I pressed my lips to her upper thigh, trailing upwards until my breath was fanning across her clit. I moaned as she gripped my hair, her nails digging into my scalp, pushing me towards her core. My tongue darted out and licked her, and I smiled against her skin as her knees buckled, a whisper of my name escaping her mouth.

"Don't be afraid, baby," I told her, sucking on her clit. "Don't be afraid to show them all downstairs who you belong to."

She was so sweet—like honey, and I lapped at her sensually before my finger found her chin, and I stood. Freya pressed her lips to mine, and I backed her up against the shower wall, the spray beating down on our sides almost painfully.

"Kaleb, I need you."

I hummed. "Show me how much you need me, then. Let me see how wet you are for me."

Freya's eyes flickered before she brought her fingers to her core, dipping them into her wetness, beginning to fuck herself. I stood back and watched in bliss as my beautiful girl pleasured her pussy, soft moans falling from her plump lips.

"Does that feel good?" I asked her, my entire body tingling from the sight.

"Yes, but I want you."

My heart was thumping harshly inside my chest. I never wanted this moment to end. However, I couldn't take not touching her anymore, and I pushed myself up against her as I crushed my lips to hers, my tongue battling with her own.

"Fuck me, Kaleb," Freya moaned against my mouth, and I gripped the back of her neck and fisted her hair before exiting the shower to grab a condom from Brent's bathroom cabinet. She followed my every movement with lust-filled eyes. Twisting her around quickly, I guided her down until she was bent at the waist, my dick hovering just behind her dripping core.

Her hands were flat against the shower wall, and I teased her with my length before pushing it in inch by inch, sighs of pleasure falling from her mouth as she attempted to push back onto me.

I tutted at her, pulling out altogether. "You need to work on your patience, my little artist."

"I can't be patient, Kaleb," she growled, causing me to chuckle.

Freya whimpered as I bottomed out inside of her, the entirety of my cock surrounded by her walls, and I began to pump in and out, clutching onto her waist and watching how her core gripped me. The sight was hypnotic.

There was something about fucking Freya that altered my brain chemistry. This girl had me in a chokehold, and it didn't matter what she asked of me. I would do it. If there were something she wanted, I wouldn't think twice about giving it to her. Her wish was my command.

"You're so good at taking this cock," I praised her. "Tell me who this pussy belongs to, baby."

Freya moaned in response, circling her clit as her back arched, causing me to grip onto her tighter as I ceased movement.

"I'm waiting for an answer."

"You. It belongs to you," she whispered, her voice thick with lust. "Please, don't stop, Kaleb."

I picked up the pace. Whatever she wanted, she got.

I'd never felt anything like it. I was cocooned in the euphoria that was Freya Henderson, time pausing, the world fading away, leaving only the serene connection of our two souls. *Fuck.* This girl was God's gift.

Freya's walls clenched around me, and her free hand scratched at the bathroom wall as warm water cascaded down her. As if sensing my nearing release, she choked out a moan, my name pouring from her mouth as she came undone, her muscles seizing up and her pussy clutching onto me as if it was afraid to let me go. It was enough to drive me toward my own orgasm.

My chest was heaving, and Freya's rapid breathing bounced off the shower tiles as she straightened up and stepped directly into the stream of water, cleansing herself with a smirk. I merely watched as she washed, my eyes roaming across every inch of her body, taking in her beauty.

She really was a masterpiece, and as selfish as it was, she was *my* masterpiece.

The weird looks we received when we came back downstairs were enough to make me chuckle and for Freya to turn an intense shade of red. Ty seemed slightly uncomfortable, and he kept his eyes glued to the TV screen while Hannah filled the silence and laughed about how Brent's hands were shaking.

The guy killed people for a living, but put him in front of an actor in a poorly-made alien costume, and he close to shitting himself out of fear.

My phone began to buzz in my pocket, and I growled, glancing at the screen.

My chief.

Giving Freya a quick squeeze, I exited the living room and made my way into the kitchen, ensuring that nobody could hear me.

"Kaleb," murmured my chief in his usual glum tone.

I swear, you could pelt the guy with cupcakes and stuffed unicorns and he still wouldn't crack a genuine smile. I felt sorry for his wife.

"I have no more updates on Will," I told him, frustrated that he had interrupted my personal time. "I told you everything that happened when Brent and I visited him last. We haven't been since."

"That's not why I'm calling, Kaleb." A pause. "The police have informed me that some additional evidence has come to light, and now that it's solid, they've shared the information with us. It's tedious to explain, so I'll have someone drop the files to you tomorrow so you're in the loop."

I scrunched my eyebrows together, a groan falling from my lips. "Yeah, okay. I'll look at them. I'm being serious, though, when I tell you I don't know if there's anything else Brent and I can get you. Will won't tell us shit."

My chief hummed. "I understand, Kaleb. But I no longer believe that's going to be a problem."

Thirty-four: Freya

Kaleb had been distant over the past week and a half. He wasn't ignoring me by any means, but I could tell something was wrong. Even when I questioned him about it, he insisted he was just tired and stressed about the case.

I had a niggling feeling that he was keeping something from me, though, but there was nothing I could do to get him to open up—especially since I had half convinced myself that I was actually going crazy and reading into things too much.

I hunched over next to a tree, bracing my hands on my knees and inhaling oxygen greedily, filling my lungs. Gazing back to look at the steep hill I'd just climbed, I laughed as Jackie and my mom stopped to catch their breaths, clutching at their chests. It was sunny today, and they'd insisted that we all get out of the house and go on a hike.

Kaleb had tried to get us out of it, but I couldn't decline once Jackie's pleading eyes honed in on me. She'd enjoyed taking Brie hiking, and I didn't want to leave her to do it without company.

Kaleb was already at the top of the hill—showing no sign of fatigue—and he leaned back against a large oak tree and pulled out his phone, tapping away at the device. He'd been glued to it lately, and when I'd made dinner for the both of us while our moms were out, he got up from the table twice to answer calls from his chief.

He hadn't been laughing or smiling as much, and even when I dragged him along with Hannah and me to one of Josh's football games, he sat in the bleachers with a rigid posture and strained jaw. Kaleb enjoyed sports, and it made me uneasy that even a game couldn't pull him from his own thoughts.

"I'm dying," I spluttered as I dropped to the ground next to him, feeling the need to lean my head against his calf.

Gazing down at me, Kaleb smiled, chuckling, pocketing his phone and scanning the area. Forest surrounded us, our bodies perched on the top of a dirt-covered hill, two verdant trees swaying in the brisk wind at the peak. The sun peered over the clouds, shining brightly, and the bustling woodland below us basked in the sun's rays.

"I had no idea this was so near us," I said. I understood why people came to places like this to think and clear their minds. It was beyond relaxing.

"My mom's been coming here for years."

"Is it your first time?" I knitted my eyebrows together. Kaleb looked so troubled, and I hated it.

He shook his head. "No, I took her here a few times right after Brie died. She really enjoys how secluded it is, and it's become her favourite hiking spot." Although a small smile graced Kaleb's lips, it didn't reach his eyes—empty grey spheres of nothingness.

I turned around to see my mom and Jackie sitting on the grass halfway up the hill, taking large gulps from their water bottles.

Knowing we were out of sight, I placed my hand on Kaleb's cheek, his overgrown stubble grating against my fingertips. "I know I've asked you this a thousand times, and you're probably sick of hearing it, but are you sure you're okay? You haven't been yourself since we got back from Brent's."

His eyes turned hard, and he subtly shrugged me off and walked forward a few steps to lean over the wooden fence that circled us, clasping his hands together as he cleared his throat. "I'm just tired. My chief is on my case, and I'm worried about your safety. Until Will is behind bars, I won't be happy."

"I'm sure they'll be arresting him any day now. Sorry for pestering you."

"You're not." Kaleb caught a strand of my hair in the wind and tucked it back into my claw clip for me. "It's just—" His jaw tightened as I looked at him, and his eyebrows collapsed in on one another as he shook his head. "It's just work. It's a lot right now."

I opened my mouth to respond, but once I heard my mother's bellowing laughter behind us, I took a step away from Kaleb. I couldn't help but recognise the small glimmer of guilt that swam within his eyes, though. It was just a flash—a spark—and within seconds, it was gone, but I'd caught it, and it indicated he wasn't being entirely truthful with me.

"I hate to be a negative Nancy, but that's weird, right?" Hannah mumbled with her mouth full of food, clutching her mojito and nodding towards my drink.

I rolled my eyes, sipping on it, the taste of minty alcohol burning my tongue but momentarily distracting me from my dreary thoughts.

"I know." I gazed around the bar, smiling at a grumpy Brent, who sat in his booth in the corner of the room, looking as miserable as ever. Kaleb was busy with something tonight, so Brent was having to watch me while I had a much-needed catch-up with my best friend. "We went from sleeping together and being unable to take our hands off one another to just... nothing."

Hannah's thin eyebrows flew into her hairline. "Nothing?"

"He won't talk to me unless I start the conversation, and when we *are* talking, he's distracted and closed off."

Hannah gazed at me sadly, dropping her fries back down into their bowl, a bitter expression taking over her face. "I swear to God, if he's seeing someone else, I'll kill him."

My chest tightened at the thought, and I swallowed harshly, my throat spasming.

Kaleb with someone else. I felt sick.

We weren't officially together, but I liked to believe that if he wanted to cut things off because he'd met someone else, he would have the decency to speak to me about it first.

"I just don't know what's happened in the past two weeks. Something's going on, and he won't go into detail. He says it's work, but usually, if work *is* bothering him, he tells me about it. When I'm talking to him, it's like he's there, but he's also not, you know?"

Hannah hummed, tapping her finger against her chin.

I turned my head towards Brent, and he averted his gaze, having been watching us intensely. He wasn't close enough to hear our conversation, but I had a feeling he was trying to read our lips over the music. Waving him over, I waited for him to join us, and he settled down into the chair beside me, arching a brow.

"Am I one of the girls now?" he asked teasingly.

I rolled my eyes. "How's work been? Kaleb said there haven't been any updates on Will."

Brent ran his hand through his short, buzz-cut hair, humming. "No, we haven't heard much. Because Will knows what Kaleb and I are, there's not much need to involve us."

That was what Kaleb had said, too.

"I mean, technically, it is actually Christmas break for us now." Brent laughed. "Obviously, that doesn't mean work stops for us, though. We could still get called to do emergency raids, but I think the chief is giving us a bit of slack."

Slack.

Then what was making Kaleb so stressed and distant?

"When will you be heading back to base?" questioned Hannah, pushing her fries over to a starving Brent, and he dug in, shrugging in response.

"Should be the second week of January, but it depends when we get appointed our new locations."

I gulped. I prayed Kaleb would be stationed nearby, but I understood the chances were slim.

"Any news on that?"

"Kaleb hasn't said anything to me regarding a new base. The chief's called me twice to discuss it, and he's given me the names of a few he believes I'll be stationed at, but it's not a guarantee."

"So, you and Kaleb won't be sent to the same one?"

Brent shook his head. "We've been partners for years, but that was only because we were from the same area and could spy on Will easily, so no, I doubt we'll be sent to the same base after he's charged."

Blissful ignorance. It was damaging our relationship. Kaleb and I were both frightened for the future, but sweeping it under the rug wasn't going to benefit us in any way. It wasn't a topic we could put off—not with everything happening so quickly.

"Are you finished?" I asked Hannah.

"Yep, let's go."

Brent drove Hannah and me back to our houses, and I wrapped my arms around myself as I made my way up the stairs and towards Kaleb's room. I wasn't sure what he was doing tonight—yet another thing he'd been vague about.

"Kaleb," I called, rattling on the wood of his bedroom door, waiting a couple of seconds before pushing it open, poking my head in.

His desk lamp was on, the yellow rays beaming down onto piles of paperwork. His bed was unmade, and his clothes were strung all over the floor. He usually kept his room pretty spotless, so it was unusual to find it looking like a bomb had detonated inside.

The scent of his musky cologne hit me, and I breathed it in meanly, stepping into the room further. I'd never really taken too much of a good look around Kaleb's room—always far too distracted—but it wasn't overly inspiring. Heavy weights thrown to the ground. An open wardrobe full of mostly black clothing. A bookcase shoved into the corner, filled with thriller novels that appeared untouched.

Grunting to myself as my hip bumped into the corner of the desk, I cursed as his paperwork and files tumbled to the floor. *God dammit.*

I leaned down to pick them up, my hands swiping up the papers, attempting to keep them in order as I stacked them back up on his desk. But one particular yellow file caught my attention.

Mark Henderson.

My face blanched, and my shaking hands reached for it, bringing it closer to my face as I took a deep breath. My eyes skimmed over the papers, but I struggled to pick up more than a few words, my head spinning.

Involvement.
Drug ring.
Will Sheffield.
Location unknown.
Negotiation is possible.

My heart slammed against my ribcage, my muscles cramping up as I stared at the file Kaleb had on my own fucking father—claiming he was involved with the most dangerous drug ring in the city and was working alongside the notorious Will Sheffield.

Thirty-five: Kaleb

The police had a lot to say about their evidence during the meeting my chief and I had attended earlier.

It turned out that they'd known Mark Henderson—Freya's father—had a connection to Will Sheffield and his drug ring for quite some time, but they didn't want to arrest him and tip off Will that he was coming under fire. They were after the big dog, desperate to have Will behind bars. His little workers were an afterthought.

It was why they hadn't taken Freya's missing person report seriously. Her father was a criminal, and they didn't want to search for him and jeopardise the Will case. They'd have to arrest Mark if they found him.

The only reason they were now interested in getting in contact with Mark Henderson was because the police realised time was running out for them since Will was putting the pieces together.

They wanted to set up a negotiation with Freya's father since he worked so closely with their prime target. They were hoping to offer him a lesser sentence if he spilt all he knew about his boss, incriminating Will for the murders.

When the file containing Freya's father's photos and information was dropped off two weeks ago, I'd had an hour-long conversation with my chief, repeatedly asking if it was some kind of mistake. It wasn't, though. The police now had enough to charge Mark Henderson, and they'd involved us since the evidence was solid.

They'd acquired old photographs and camera footage of him running drugs and attending meetings. He'd also taken business trips with other ring members to discuss potential deals with other crime organisations, which made sense considering Freya told me he travelled a lot.

I'd been informed that when Freya and I had asked the police to trace her father's call, they'd actually located a few radio towers his phone had pinged off. It didn't give his exact location away, but they knew he was actually way closer than they'd believed him to be. He was hiding out somewhere.

Namalix was just a front that Freya's father and many other group members used to excuse their high income—much like Will did with his shooting range.

Guilt. It was choking me alive—like a viper wrapping around me and squeezing my lungs tighter and tighter until they were nothing but dust.

I'd come close to telling Freya a few times but didn't know how to. The police and my chief hadn't forbidden me from informing her about her father and his involvement, but whenever I opened my mouth and looked at her, I couldn't get the future images of her distraught face out of my head.

I was lying to her. It was wrong, but I was working on a case that meant hunting her father down and getting him sentenced.

Brent was also aware, and he'd been keeping the secret from Freya. I could see the indiscretion was slowly eating him alive, too, but he could put their friendship aside for the sake of getting Will arrested.

It wasn't so easy for me, though.

Because I loved her.

I fucking loved that woman.

I was consumed by my yearning for her. Physically and mentally. She lived inside my head all day and night, and as much as I tried to push her aside, I couldn't. This was going to break us, and there was no fixing it. I knew that. I didn't know how to explain to her that even though her father was involved, I couldn't step down from the case. I was expected to help finish this, and how was I supposed to continue a relationship with her when I was poaching her flesh and blood?

Fuck. This.

Slamming my car door shut—having had it fixed since the chase—I entered the house and immediately headed for Freya's room. Brent had informed me he'd dropped her home.

"Freya," I called from the other side of her door, knocking a few times before pushing it open after getting no response.

Empty.

I sighed, my gaze drifting down to her bed, my eyes narrowing, and my heart faltering.

Mark Henderson's file stared back at me.

It felt as if the world was about to swallow me whole—like the earth beneath my feet was crumbling, ready to drop me down into the pits of hell.

Shit.

Freya knew.

Thirty-six: Freya

Kaleb had lied to me. My father was involved in all this, and he hadn't told me. Was it the reason he'd got so close to me? To weasel information out of me about my father? I felt sick. I wasn't sure about the timings of everything and when certain information had been made apparent, but I knew one thing for sure. My father was a criminal, and the man I loved was adamant about putting him behind bars without my knowledge. Did he expect me never to find out? Was he planning on keeping it from me forever?

I couldn't think. I was driving on autopilot over to Hannah's house with a racing heart. I couldn't stay at Kaleb's house any longer, and I immediately muted his number so I didn't receive any calls or texts from him. I wasn't in the frame of mind to talk to him about all of this.

When I reached my best friend's house, she flung the door open and engulfed me in a spine-crushing hug. I wasn't complaining. Even without her lanky arms wrapped around me, breathing was a task, anyway. My body was rejecting the oxygen.

I told her everything, and she remained quiet as she allowed me to vent. I clutched onto the hot cup of coffee she'd made me, relishing in the way the heat stung my palms and took my focus away from the crushing sensation my heart was experiencing.

This wasn't the life I'd envisioned for myself. I was no longer going to have a father. He was a felon, and his work buddies were hunting me for some unknown reason. They were dangerous, and that also meant that so was my dad. Had my father been involved in murdering people, too?

My head spun.

How would I ever look Kaleb in the eyes again without thinking about him helping lock my father away and getting so close to me without admitting it to me? Kissing me. Sleeping with me. What I thought was perhaps loving me. Fuck.

I fiddled with the gun he'd given me in my hands—it had become a habit to bring it everywhere.

"You're going to be fine," Hannah soothed me, offering me a sad smile.

I wiped at my teary eyes. My emotions were running rampant, wreaking havoc on my body and destroying me mentally and physically. It was as if I was being swallowed whole, encased in a dark blanket of heartache and agony.

What had my life turned into?

Hannah and I spent a little while talking about everything, but after an hour, we settled into a comfortable silence and focused on the TV. My throat was hoarse from speaking, and nothing else needed to be said.

My phone vibrated.

Ty: Hey Freya, the party starts at seven tonight. In advance, I'm sorry about the house. It's kind of ridiculous, but my auntie and uncle have far too much money and like to make it known. See you and Hannah soon!

Hannah gazed at me as I read the message aloud, and she cursed under her breath.

"I have work tonight. Damn it, I forgot about Ty's party." She pouted.

"So had I." I sighed, running a hand down my face. Apparently, Ty's auntie and uncle had explicitly asked him to invite some of his friends to their dinner party to keep him occupied. I felt awful leaving him with no one to keep him company—none of his hockey buddies could attend.

"I'm sure he'll understand if you—"

"No." I shook my head. "I'll go. I don't want to let Ty down. He seems excited."

Hannah allowed me to shower and raid her closet, and I slipped into one of her old dresses, dusting my face with a tad of makeup.

The house was forty minutes away, and we spent most of the journey in tortuous silence. I wanted to open my mouth to speak, but I didn't have control of my body. Hopelessness had taken the reins. I was going to need to plaster a phoney smile on for tonight.

"Jesus," Hannah muttered as she slowed the car down and pulled onto a narrow cobbled path leading to a steep hill. "Ty's uncle and auntie are rich as fuck."

The hedges directing us down the path were freshly trimmed and blossoming, and the large manors and estates that we passed were definitely worth millions. Their exteriors were exquisitely decorated, with gargoyle figurines standing guard outside each door, the stone glistening in the setting sun.

"This is it," I said, pointing to a set of open black iron gates. "I'm not sure Ty's uncle and auntie will appreciate me bringing this in." I laughed as I gestured to the gun that sat on my lap, and Hannah shook her head at me.

"You have people wanting to kill you, Freya. Sorry to be blunt, but you need it. What they don't know can't hurt them."

I nodded, hiking my long burgundy dress up and wrapping the gun's strap around my thigh, clicking it in. It felt inappropriate to bring it to a dinner party, but Hannah was right. I needed to make sure I had it handy, just in case.

A suited and grey-haired butler was waiting in the manor's foyer as I stepped in, and he nodded at me and took my coat, hanging it up with the rest of them. I tried my best not to gawk at the beautiful tiled flooring and regal ceiling, but I'd never seen a house so lavish. It oozed elegance.

I was directed into a room to the left, and I pushed open the door to reveal it to be full of guests in expensive dresses and designer shirts and slacks. There was a glossy wooden table in the room's corner—an array of canapes and alcohol placed on it.

I was out of my depth here, but I released a sigh of relief once Ty squeezed his way past a few people and bounded up to me, dressed smartly in a shirt and pants.

"You made it."

"I did." I smiled, the action feeling fake. I was far from happy, but Ty didn't need to know that. The last thing I wanted to do was ruin his good mood. "Hannah had to go to work. She's annoyed she forgot."

He handed me a glass of champagne. "No problem. Thank you so much for coming. This really isn't my scene, and I wanted to head out instead, but my uncle and auntie were adamant about meeting some of my friends."

I smiled, sipping my drink. "No, of course. This place is amazing."

"Making enough money to afford moving out can't come soon enough. This place is way too tacky, and most of these guests are snobs. Between you and me, I can't name one of them I actually like."

Ty introduced me to a few people, and although I tried my best to pay attention, I couldn't shake Kaleb from my thoughts. The only thing I knew I could do was give myself some time to step away from the situation and register it—otherwise, I'd end up doing or saying something hurtful.

I didn't want to associate him with my criminal father, but that was now inevitable. The idea cut me deeply, leaving me with throbbing open wounds.

"Oh, Freya," said Ty as he nodded toward the crowd. "My uncle is over there. Is it okay if I introduce you to him so he doesn't hound me any longer about you being my girlfriend?"

"Sure, let's go."

I apologised to a few people as I weaved around them, keeping my arms and legs close together so as not to scrape against anyone. The sensation of my cold gun grazing against the skin of my thigh came to my attention, and I feared it was going to fall from its strap and clatter to the ground. *That wouldn't be a good look.*

"Freya, this is my uncle." Ty gestured to the back of a lanky man, and at the sound of his nephew's voice, he turned, causing my heart to seize up, my blood running cold as it pumped through my constricted veins.

"It's great to meet you, Freya," he jeered, a small smile on his face, his evil eyes sucking me in, chewing me up, and spitting me out.

My hands shook, and I released a small gasp as my glass of champagne slipped from my clammy fingertips to the tiled flooring, smashing into tiny pieces by my feet. I drew in a sharp breath, nausea wavering through me.

Standing in front of me was the man who I assumed wanted me dead.

Will Sheffield.

I inhaled deeply, my lungs collapsing and my head throbbing. I felt the colour drain from my face, leaving me snow-white.

Ty was quickly ushered away by Will to grab a dustpan and brush to clean up the shattered glass, and I stood glued to the ground in the corner of the room with Will towering over me, his usual cigarette hanging limply from his mouth.

One of his hands clutched his gun strapped to his waistband, most of the firearm concealed by his suit jacket, and he leaned a little closer to me. "You're going to come with me, or I'm going to start shooting innocent people," he growled, his voice hoarse and breath stinking of smoke. "If you try to run, I'll kill you. My butlers all have weapons, and they won't hesitate to shoot you in the head at my command."

My body shook. My dress was wet with champagne and my perspiration as I considered my options. I needed to get out of this alive, and the idea of being shot in the head didn't leave me with a tremendous amount of optimism.

I had my gun, and although I wasn't the most confident when it came to actually using it, I was sure I could take a shot at Will when he wasn't looking to keep him down long enough to run. Then, I could find a back entrance to slip out of, avoiding the butlers.

"Make your decision quickly, Freya," warned Will, a strand of his gelled hair falling in front of his penetrative eyes. "Before my nephew comes back and I have to involve him in all this."

I grimaced, and my lips settled into a frown before I nodded at him, glowering at his cheerful expression.

"Perfect." Will grinned—a smile that could curdle cream. "Come with me."

Thirty-seven: Kaleb

I scratched at my stubble as I turned the steering wheel of my car a little too sharply, causing the car next to me to blare its horn, the driver waving his middle finger at me. I blinked a few times, ridding myself of my daze, quickly overtaking the car and speeding down the road.

Freya hadn't answered my calls or texts, and nobody was home at Hannah's, so I headed to her work to ask her if she knew her whereabouts.

My chief had been trying to talk to me about my new base over the past few days, but I'd been putting it off. I didn't want to hear where I was going to be stationed because, knowing my luck, it would be halfway across the country—or in a different country entirely.

If that was the case, I knew there was no way I was getting my girl back.

My throat tightened at the thought, my knuckles turning white. Pulling to a stop, I parked outside the hardware store where Hannah worked, storming in. “Hannah,” I demanded, and she turned to me with a tight jaw, her eyes dangerous.

“Excuse me,” she apologetically muttered to the customer she was dealing with before stalking over to me with her arms folded. “Yes, Kaleb?”

“Has Freya spoken to you?”

She dipped her chin. “She has.”

I arched my eyebrow, cursing under my breath. Hannah knew what I was asking, but it seemed she wanted to play games today.

“Do you know where she is?”

“I do,” she responded, fiddling with the hem of her work shirt in an attempt to appear unbothered by my invasive tone.

I clenched my fists, grinding my teeth together. “Alright, Hannah. Enough of that. I’m trying to help here. Where's Freya?”

“She’s fine. She’s at Ty’s.”

I froze, the sound of my blood rushing through my veins pounding in my ears. My jealousy spiked. “What?”

Hannah shrugged. “For a party.”

“Address?”

I was met with silence.

“Hannah, Freya has people after her. This isn’t about us as a couple. I’m trying to make sure she’s safe, and parties are a perfect setting to kidnap someone without being noticed.”

“She has her gun.”

“And you think one gun versus multiple men who have been trained to kill is going to cut it? That gun was given to her as a precaution. It’s a last resort.”

Rolling her shoulders uncomfortably, Hannah snuck a glance at her boss, who was eyeing her up suspiciously from across the store.

"Kaleb, I'm working our delivery tonight, so I'm in a bad mood. I really need—"

"All I need is the address, Hannah." My tone was low, causing her to exhale deeply, and she reached into her pocket and scribbled on an old receipt.

"From what I can remember, that was it. But don't even let her know you're there. Check the party out and make sure it's safe. That's it. Don't ruin it for her, Kaleb. She doesn't want to speak to you right now."

I nodded, exiting the store and hopping back into my Jeep, unfolding the receipt and staring at the paper with pinched brows.

A chill ran down my spine.

What the fuck?

There was no fucking way.

This was the address we had on file for Will.

Yanking my phone from my pocket, I dialled my chief's number, his frustrated voice quiet on the other end.

"We need all available workers ready immediately," I demanded as I hastily pulled my car out in front of an unsuspecting driver. "Will has Freya."

Thirty-eight: Freya

The basement was bitter, and goosebumps developed on my bare arms as the frosty air pricked at my skin. Will's grip was firm on my wrist, and although I pulled away from him multiple times, it only caused him to tighten his long fingers around me.

I'd scanned the area around for an escape route while being led away from the party, but multiple butlers stood watch with their guns on show, and Will pressed his own into my back, the barrel poking at my spine painfully.

It wasn't a grimy and vulgar basement as portrayed in movies. Although it was bare, the wooden flooring was sparkling, and the walls were covered in expensive layers of deep maroon wallpaper. The only light source was a small bulb hanging limply above my head, and I peered through the dimly lit room to see if we were alone.

It looked like it, but the sound of someone shuffling reached my ears, alerting me.

I knew I could try to whip out my gun and shoot Will, but there were butlers standing guard at the top of the stairs, and I had no doubt that if I tried to run, they would shoot me in the kneecaps and drag me back down here to finish me off slowly. There would be no escaping if my kneecaps were blown out.

They'd taken my phone and thrown it against the wall in front of me, smashing it into a thousand pieces, the device shattering just like my hope for a somewhat normal future.

"What the fuck do you want with me?" I spat as I spun around, plastering a glare onto my face. I was secretly terrified, but I wasn't going to show Will that. He was the type of person who fed on people's fear. It empowered him, and I intended to bruise his ego by faking my confidence.

"I'll tell you what, Freya," Will muttered, picking at the dirt underneath his nails. "I have impeccable luck."

I scowled. "What does that mean?"

"It's probably easier if I show you," he responded, moving over to the wall and flipping on the main light. My breath hitched as I spotted a man seated in the room's corner, a raggedy length of cloth tied around the back of his head to cover his mouth. His body was limp and eyes droopy, his hands bound behind his back.

My father.

"What the hell?" I whispered, yelping when Will grabbed me again after I tried to step forward. "What have you done to him?"

"Your father lost me a lot of money, Freya. He screwed up."

I scoffed, my fingers twitching. "Let him go."

My demand caused him to release a throaty chuckle, and he nodded his head at somebody behind me, my wrists suddenly being yanked back and tied. I fought against them, kicking my leg out to strike them in the balls, but they dodged my attempts and shoved me to the ground. I gazed at my father pleadingly as he shook his head, wheezing.

"Almost four hundred thousand dollars was lost because of your father's idiocy," Will snarled. He stepped closer to me once I'd been dragged back against the wall, my body having been twisted painfully, my dress ripped up the side. "He was being followed on a drug run, and our entire stash was stolen before it could be delivered."

I shot a haunting look at my father. He wasn't the person I once thought he was. He was a liar. A drug dealer. A criminal.

"I enjoy revenge, Freya," Will muttered, aiming his gun at my father and cocking his head, a wicked smile on his face. It was obvious that my father had already suffered some abuse. He was coated in dry blood and was weak, his head lolling to the side as he tried to keep his gaze steady.

"What is killing us going to achieve?" I tried to reason with Will. "We'll just be more murders under your belt. More years in prison."

Will chuckled, rolling his eyes at me. "I've avoided prison for this long. I think I'll be just fine, Freya." He lowered his gun slightly. "I knew Mark, here, had a daughter, and when you came into the shooting range and had the same surname, I kept tabs on you. Not only that, but then you ended up befriending my useless little nephew. It seemed the odds were siding with me."

"Leave Ty out of this."

"Oh, I intend to. He'd run to the police the first chance he got."

I turned to my father, dread blazing under my skin. "Dad," I said shakily. "Why? Why were you involved in all of this?"

"It's only right he gets to explain to his daughter that he brought all of this upon himself." Will nodded again at the butler standing next to me, and he moved over to my father to yank off the cloth from around his head, leaning in to tell him he would be shot if he started yelling for help. Not that it mattered much. I had no doubt it was soundproof down here.

"Freya," muttered my dad, his eyes bleak. "What the hell were you doing going to a shooting range?"

"What the hell were *you* doing drug dealing?" I snapped back.

He sighed. "Will, let my daughter go. I can get you back the money. Freya has nothing to do with this."

This caused Will to double over in laughter, and he lit up a cigarette as he tried to compose himself. "Who do you think I am? A fairy godmother? You think I'm here to grant wishes?" He chuckled. "You know the rules, Mark. You mess up once, and you're gone. It's just unlucky for you that your first screw-up cost me hundreds of thousands of dollars. You're going to watch me kill your daughter, and only then will I put you out of your misery."

I was going to fucking die tonight. My heart rattled against my ribs, and my sweaty hands quivered behind me, but my eyebrows furrowed when I felt something sharp scrape against my skin.

I stilled, waiting until Will was distracted talking to one of his butlers to turn around. I spotted a pipe attached to the wall—a large crack struck through the middle of it. Some of the metal was sticking out, looking as if it had been kicked in during a struggle of some sort.

I subtly began to scrape the thick rope wrapped around my wrists against it—thankful that it didn't create a shaving sound—moving my wrists only when I was certain that neither Will nor a butler was watching.

It was going to take a little while for the semi-blunt metal to tear through the rope, but if I could release myself when everyone least expected it, there was a chance I could shoot them down and make a run for it before calling the police to come and save my father.

Imagining it was easier than actually doing it, though.

"Kaleb and Brent won't go unscathed," Will continued, sending me a pointed look. "For years, they deceived me, and I don't take that lightly. They and everyone they care about will be disposed of."

Rage bubbled up inside of me. I was angry at Kaleb, but the thought of anyone touching him made me want to throw fists.

"Stop moving," barked the bald butler as he noticed my slight wiggling, and he gripped onto my chin tightly and dragged my face to his, his bloodshot eyes blazing. "Your father didn't just lose that money for Will. We were all due a cut, so this is personal." He then clipped me across the face, and I landed on my side with a *thud*.

Will strode over to my father as he swore at his ex-colleague, grabbing him by his sodden shirt and getting in his face, silencing him with the cloth.

The metallic taste of blood exploded on my tongue, and I blinked, pushing myself back up so I could continue trying to cut my rope.

Note to self: Not when Baldy's looking.

Will spent the next hour nattering on about how much my father had fucked up—as well as answering a few phone calls and leaving the room to rejoin the party for a few minutes at a time so nobody grew suspicious.

My father and I were watched like hawks, and the butlers seemed to enjoy getting a few extra hits in while Will wasn't looking, blood dribbling down both of our chins and forming small puddles on the wooden floorboards.

"Dad," I whispered when one butler left to go upstairs and the other was occupied on the phone. "You called me. Whose phone did you use?"

My father nodded towards the butler, and I sighed in defeat. I'd been hoping he had a secret phone stashed away somewhere, but it appeared he'd got his hands on someone else's before they ended the call and beat him for doing so.

I used this time to continue moving my wrists back and forth against the metal. Not only was it scraping against my restraint, but it was also scratching at my wrists, and I could feel my skin being rubbed raw and warm blood trickling down my fingertips.

My head snapped towards the staircase once I heard the floorboards creak, and my heart skipped a beat. Will was back to finish the job. There was no way out of this.

But my mouth popped open at the sight of Ty gazing at me with frantic eyes.

"Freya? What the hell?" He made a move towards me, but the lone butler had ended his call and had his hand on Ty's chest, forcing him back.

"What are you doing down here, boy?"

Ty scoffed, shoving him off. "Get the fuck off me. What are you doing?"

"Ty," I said breathlessly. "They'll kill you. Quick, get help, please!"

He fumbled around in his pocket, pulling out his phone, but he released a grunt when it was snatched from his hands from behind. Will appeared at the base of the stairs with a menacing scowl.

"Who let him down here?" he rumbled, his furious tone bouncing off the walls. "This is now a thousand times more difficult." He clutched onto his nephew's neck, and another butler made his way down the stairs in a panic and pulled some ropes from his pocket, tying Ty up and throwing him against the wall opposite us. He cursed in pain, yelling at his uncle until they wrapped a cloth around his mouth, ceasing his howling.

"We need to get on with it," Baldy growled impatiently, tapping his foot, causing Will to snarl.

"Don't rush me. I need to figure out what I'm going to do with him now." Will tilted his head towards his nephew.

Ty kicked his legs out frantically, but he was ignored, and I continued to grind my wrists against the metal pipe, glaring at Will as he sauntered over to me. He crouched down and snapped his fingers at my father to get his attention.

"Go to hell," I spat at him, and he chuckled, shaking his head.

"I *do* love your fire, Freya," Will complimented me before the butlers gripped my father's head, forcing him to look in my direction. "You're just collateral damage, though. It's nothing personal."

I forced down a sob as he pressed his gun to my chest, and my wide eyes honed in on a terrified-looking Ty behind him, yanking against his restraints.

This was it.

I was seconds away from death.

I squeezed my eyes shut, hearing nothing but my rapidly beating heart and the rush of blood in my ears.

The sound of a gunshot echoed through the basement, and I jolted, but I felt nothing. No pain. Just emptiness. Was this what death felt like? Was it actually more painless than we'd been led to believe? I hoped so.

After a few seconds, realising I was still alive, I peeked a lid open.

Will was staring at his bald butler, who was on the ground with a bullet wound to his chest, blood spurting from the hole, creating a crimson-coloured fountain.

What the fuck?

My eyes became blurry as a geared-up Kaleb and Brent barrelled down the stairs, their large guns drawn. Kaleb's fierce eyes immediately found mine, and his pupils blew out once he spotted the blood smeared across my face.

"Did you do that to her?" he seethed as he shot at the remaining butler, dodging one of his bullets. The object whizzed past Kaleb's ear as the butler cried out, collapsing onto the ground and shaking his head.

"No, I didn't touch her," he responded, pointing at his deceased co-worker. "It was him."

Kaleb huffed, looking at him with a deadpan expression. "Try the fuck again." The butler did nothing but groan, and Kaleb tutted before firing again, his chest heaving, causing the butler to gargle on his own saliva as he convulsed, stilling after a few seconds.

Will was heavily distracted, and I continued to move my wrists back and forth quickly, praying that the rope was going to fray.

"Drop the gun, Will," Kaleb warned dangerously, turning his weapon to him.

Will still had the barrel of his gun pressed to my chest, and he smiled before releasing a throaty chuckle, repositioning the firearm so it was pointed at my head.

Kaleb's jaw pulsated. Fury didn't even begin to describe the look on his face. It was as if he had ripped his emotion straight from the bottomless pits of hell—stealing all the hatred and rage that was held there, projecting it all onto the man who was threatening to end my life.

"If you shoot, then so do I," Will warned casually—as if the idea of murdering me was nothing but a simple chore. A walk in the park. A day-to-day activity.

"You've already touched her." Kaleb nodded towards my split lip. "So you're already going to die. It's up to you how painful I make it. Drop your fucking weapon, Sheffield."

Brent growled from beside Kaleb, monitoring the stairs while he also aimed his gun at Will's head, spitting threats that seemed to go in one ear and out the other.

"You're not going to kill me, boys." He chuckled. "Your organisation and the police want nothing more than to keep me alive to sentence me. If I die, all your work will have been for nothing."

"Things change when you're holding a gun to my girl's head," Kaleb spat, taking a threatening step forward, causing Will to tut at him, pressing his firearm harder against my skull. I whimpered.

"Here's an idea then," Will said, cocking his head. "I'll give you a choice. I'll be generous and only dispose of one of them." He gestured to me and my father with his free hand. "You get to choose who that is. The only catch is, you have to do the honours."

My eyebrows flew into my hairline, and panic set in as Kaleb's eyes flickered between my father and me. I pressed my wrists harder against the metal pipe.

No, no, no.

"Kaleb, don't—"

"Shut up," Will hissed into my ear. "Come on, Kaleb. Make a decision. I'm giving your girlfriend an out here. I'm willing to let go of my need for revenge. Mark will just spend the rest of his pathetic life locked away if he survives anyway, but she," he tore his eyes away from my father and jostled me, "actually gets to live. All you have to do is kill her father. You know I'm a man of my word."

That was true. If there was one redeeming quality about Will, it was that he always stuck to his promises.

It was obvious what he was doing, though. He wanted to get back at Kaleb just as much as he wanted to get back at my father, and he was willing to put the need for revenge for my father aside if it meant having me loathe Kaleb for the rest of my life.

Killing my flesh and blood... Will knew *that* was going to kill Kaleb. There was no need to end his life—as long as I could never forgive him.

Kaleb's eyebrows furrowed, and he breathed deeply before he slowly changed the angle of his gun, the barrel of it pointed towards my father.

My body tensed. "No, Kaleb, don't!"

He clamped his teeth down on his bottom lip as he glowered, and I could see his tongue running along the front of his teeth under his lips, indicating he was battling with himself tremendously.

I painfully chewed on the inside of my cheek as I angled my wrists against the pipe so that each scrape was also deeply cutting into my flesh. The pain was nothing to me, though, and I pushed the searing sensation aside, watching Kaleb in horror as he glared at Will menacingly.

"Time is running out, Kaleb. Who's going to survive this? The choice is yours. I only have a brief window of opportunity to disappear, so make up your mind before I do it for you."

Snap.

My heart stopped.

Not because a gun had gone off, but because the rope tightly bounding my wrists had been severed in half.

My breathing faltered. I had one shot at this. Otherwise, somebody I cared about was going to die. I didn't know who, but I needed everyone to come out of this alive—besides Will.

I gazed down at the rip in my dress, actually thankful that the stupid butler had torn it, the split giving me easier access to reach down and grasp my firearm. Will's gun was still to my head, but he was focused on a perplexed-looking Kaleb, his aim still on my limp father.

I took a deep breath, suddenly yanking my gun from the strap, holding it up to Will's face and firing. A cry left my mouth as he collapsed backwards, blood splattering all over me. Kaleb and Brent shot at him as he fell, and I allowed my gun to clatter to the floor, crawling away from him, a sob rising out of my mouth.

Oh my God.

I'd just shot somebody.

I'd just killed somebody.

Just as Kaleb took a step toward me, others rushed down the stairs, all strapped up in police gear and sporting heavy-duty weaponry. I pulled my knees to my chest as I cried, my hands shaking, smearing fresh blood from my wrists all over me.

I'd never seen Kaleb look so heartbroken, and he crouched down in front of me, droplets of sweat trickling from his forehead. "Freya, you're fine, baby. You're okay. Just breathe for me."

My entire world was crashing down around me.

"You lied to me," I whispered, a chill wracking my body. "You fucking lied to me."

My lungs were failing me, and I faintly heard one of the police officers call for the paramedics to enter through his radio. Kaleb attempted to reach for me, but I backed away from him, shaking my head and squeezing my eyes shut momentarily.

"I know, baby." Kaleb gulped. "I'll fix it. I promise I'll fix it."

Death. The place reeked of it, and I turned to the side and retched, covering my mouth to stop myself from vomiting. I was no better than Will or my father. I'd taken somebody's life. I was a killer.

"Tell the paramedics to hurry the fuck up," Kaleb demanded, his face etched with anguish, the creasing between his eyebrows accentuated.

Men and women in navy uniforms soon rushed down the stairs to tend to everybody, and two women immediately dropped to my side to ask me questions.

They took hold of my wrists, analysing the wounds and wrapping them up as I cried, fighting against them. Adrenaline was soaring through me. I wasn't thinking straight. All I knew was that I needed to get out of here, but my legs were too shaky to allow me to move.

"Freya, they're trying to help you," Kaleb said from in front of me as I pushed myself further against the wall away from everyone, shaking my head. "Let them help you, sweetheart."

"I don't want to be in here," I said with panic, wheezing. "I—I can't breathe."

My eyes met Kaleb's—his filled with turmoil and distress.

Murderer.

Killer.

I cried as I covered my ears with my hands, willing for the evil thoughts to dissipate and leave me be, and my frantic eyes snapped to Will's lifeless corpse—a hole in his face.

I'd done that.

I'd fucking done that.

I felt warm arms wrap around me, and I wilted against them as I was carried in the direction of the staircase, my vision blotchy and my heart racing so quickly I thought it was about to give out.

Blood.

I was covered in the stuff.

I glared at my palms.

All I could see were the hands of a killer.

Thirty-nine: Kaleb

Sixty days. Sixty fucking days without seeing or talking to Freya.

My heart felt like it was going to explode, and my head throbbed from lack of sleep and dehydration. She'd been taken to the hospital the evening of the incident, but after that, she'd immediately moved in with Hannah. I understood why she felt like she couldn't see me. I hadn't been honest with her, and I'd almost shot her father. Almost.

In that moment, I couldn't think, but the thought of Will killing Freya… terror had torn through me. Would I have actually shot her father? I wasn't sure. I liked to think I wouldn't have and was just trying to stall Will, but it was impossible to place myself back in the situation.

I'd sent Freya a couple of texts, but she hadn't responded. I didn't want to crowd her, though. She'd talk to me when she was ready—if that feeling ever came. Each passing day without her felt like a bulldozer was agonisingly crushing my body to the ground over and over again, rendering me helpless.

Freya's mother had moved out too—to a cute little apartment not far from the house—and after a week away, Freya had joined her.

She was all I could think about; it was eating me from the inside out.

What was worse than dying? Feeling like I was dying, but knowing it was just my mind playing tricks on me and I wasn't going to eventually succumb to the pain. My body was completely healthy—it was my mind that wasn't. Without her, I was lost. Nothing. A shell of a man.

This was fucked.

The beat of the booming music irritated me, and I leaned back against the booth and scanned the crowd, seeing nothing but wildly drunk people singing and dancing.

I wanted to stick forks in my eyes. It'd beat being at a club.

I sipped on my ice-cold water, grinding my teeth and rolling my eyes when a smiling brunette slipped into the seat opposite me, blocking my view. I was here for one reason and for one reason only, and it didn't involve the chipper girl.

"How come you're sitting here all alone?" she questioned, leaning forward, and I glanced at her for a brief second, praying that my irritation was evident in my tired eyes.

I was in uniform. Was she blind? Did the bulky bulletproof vest not give it away?

"Working," I responded, looking past her shoulder at my client, a big smile plastered on her face as she twirled around on the VIP dance floor with her friends.

"Oh." The girl in front of me raised her eyebrows. "Are you a bartender here?"

"No."

She hummed, her hand brushing against mine, and I pulled away before she could continue her unnecessary touching.

"What's your name?"

"Respectfully, I'm going to need you to go away. I have no interest in you or what you're offering."

The brunette's teeth clicked shut, and she swallowed, shooting me a sour look before rushing off.

Some people just couldn't take rejection.

My phone vibrated from my pocket, and I pulled it out at record speed, my face dropping when Brent's name flashed across the screen. I wasn't supposed to take personal calls when on the job, but I hadn't spoken to Brent for just over a week.

"Hey," I said loudly over the music, plugging my other ear with my finger.

"Hi. Man, where the hell are you? It's loud!"

"At some shitty club," I said. "How's base?"

Brent had been moved to a base in Colorado and rarely had time to talk. Apparently, he was swamped with cases.

"It's fine. Kaylee's visiting next weekend, so I'm looking forward to that." He paused. "Still heard nothing from Freya?"

I stiffened at his question. I avoided talking about her, and when my mom would bring her up, I'd cut the conversation short. Even just hearing her name sent my thoughts into a spiral of bleakness and despair.

"Nothing," I said, my tone sharp.

Brent sighed. "Listen, Kaleb, I love the girl. She's great, but is she worth this? I just want to make sure you're making the right decision for you."

My tongue skated across the front of my teeth. There wasn't a doubt in my mind. "She's worth it."

"Okay, that's all I needed to hear."

I hummed in response, scanning the crowd for any sign of danger. Nothing—unless overpriced shooters and confetti were threatening.

Brent and I talked for about five minutes, and we planned to meet sometime soon. I'd been so used to seeing him every day that it felt alien to have him in another state, hours away and not easily accessible.

My chest felt hollow, my gun poking into my ribcage. It wasn't painful—more uncomfortable—but I didn't bother to adjust it. The ache was distracting me from *her*. Somewhat.

Running my hands through my hair, I yanked out my wallet, deciding I was going to torture myself for the hundredth time tonight. Pulling out the crumpled piece of paper, I unfolded it, huffing.

It'd been wrong of me to do so, but I'd stolen the sketch from Freya's pad a while ago. It was my favourite piece she'd ever done.

A striking bluebird—its wings drawn as it soared through the sky, feathering so detailed it looked like it could be a photograph. Each stroke of the pencil was done with passion and love, shading so detailed I noticed something new about the creature every time I looked at it. My stomach lurched whenever I did so, but it also filled me with comfort, remembering what I used to have.

I'd had the honour of meeting Freya Henderson. Not only that, but loving her.

It was something I wanted to remember for the rest of my life, even if she didn't.

Forty: Freya

"Do you want to get out of bed today, honey?" my mom asked me, and I yanked the sheets further up my body, shaking my head. It was the weekend.

So what if it was four in the afternoon and I hadn't left my room yet? Not even to brush my teeth or use the bathroom. It wasn't a huge deal.

My new room wasn't finished yet. I didn't possess the motivation to finish painting it. I'd stopped halfway the other day, looking down to see I was splattered with paint. Only, I didn't see it as paint.

The light cream colour had morphed into a crimson shade of red, and a scream had escaped my mouth as memories of the incident that had occurred two months ago flashed before my eyes.

Murderer.

Killer.

"Please, mom," I sighed, squeezing my eyes shut painfully. "I just want to sleep."

"Freya, don't you think we should talk about—"

"No," I interjected. "I want to sleep."

My mom's eyes grew teary, and guilt slammed into me. She'd been trying to get me to talk to her about what had happened, but I just couldn't bring myself to relive it.

She'd been forcing me to see a therapist regularly. I hated crying in front of people, but my first conversation with the trained professional had caused me to break down. However, she reminded me she was no stranger to traumatised people.

"Alright, I'm going on a hike with Jackie. Call me if you need anything." The name caused my heart to skip a beat. "I'll be gone for a couple of hours. I love you."

"I love you too."

I didn't want to think about Jackie because when I did, I also thought about *him*. That was dangerous. It caused my emotions to whirl around me like a tornado, pricking at me, taunting me.

Most of my happy memories involving *him* felt like they were overpowered by despair, the fear creating a thick film over my mind and altering my way of thinking. A trauma response—something that I was going to have to work through eventually, but the idea of doing so was frightening.

My gloomy bubble was comfortable because the moment I allowed happiness in, I was hit full force with the idea that I didn't deserve it. I'd taken somebody's life, and whether or not they deserved it, matter-of-factly, I was a killer and was struggling to come to terms with it.

"And how does that make you feel?" my therapist questioned me, crossing her legs.

I hummed. "Umm, powerless."

She nodded in response. "It's perfectly normal to feel powerless after going through a traumatic event, but something you need to remember is that nothing that happened to you was your fault. You did nothing to warrant it; self-defence is not a crime."

Murderer.

Killer.

I clamped my eyes shut, inhaling deeply before opening them again.

I knew the way I was thinking wasn't logical. If I hadn't shot Will, then either my father, Kaleb, Brent, or I would have ended up dead. I did what I had to do to survive, but the guilt that consumed me was asthmatic.

I hated Will—with a passion, feeling no sympathy towards him. But it was weird to think of him as dead after everything. He'd been a human being, and I'd drained the soul from his body using a single bullet.

"I'm really pleased with the way you're progressing, Freya." My therapist smiled—proud and joyous. "When we first started having these sessions, you would barely say a word on the subject. I truly believe this is something you are going to get through."

I nodded. "Thank you. Talking about it is less painful, but it's still difficult." I swallowed harshly. I'd reached my limit for today. My mind was frazzled.

"Let's book you in again for next week. In the meantime, I think going out and meeting your friends will really help you. Push yourself. I know it's scary, but just remember, you can do it."

Forty-one: Kaleb

I fiddled with the shoelaces of my boots; my forearms settled over my knees as I adjusted myself on the pointed boulder in front of Brie's grave. The teddy bear Freya had given me sat next to me, and I stole a glance at him, feeling embarrassed that he'd just witnessed me pour my heart out to a gravestone.

I told Brie everything. Every thought I'd ever had, but the silence I received back was deafening, causing my eardrums to ring as if a bomb had just detonated right beside me.

"Well, looks like it's just you and me now, buddy." I huffed, staring at the ball of fluff next to me, grimacing when he did nothing but smile back at me creepily, his bold brown eyes boring into my soul. "Fuck," I hissed to myself, pinching the bridge of my nose and gently swatting the bear off the boulder so he toppled over the edge. "I'm sitting here talking to a fucking stuffed animal."

The force of the fall caused the bear to sing, Brie's voice emitting from his skin and whirling around me with the wind. I stared at her headstone, reading over my mother's morose words again and again, chewing on the inside of my cheek as if it were gum.

My body wanted to break down, but it was as if it didn't know how to. Too many emotions were running wild throughout my mind, and my fists clenched on their own accord as the sun above disappeared behind a cluster of grey clouds, cloaking me in gloominess.

I refused to quit on Freya, though. No matter how long I needed to wait. It didn't matter to me. Time was nothing.

Don't give up on her. Brie's bossy tone bounced off the inside of my skull.

There was no way in hell I was going to. Satan would have to drag me down himself, tie me up and throw me into a lake of blazing fire to cease my efforts. Even then, I wasn't sure I'd surrender.

I picked up the bear from the floor, dusting the dirt off his fluff, resisting the urge to apologise to him for thumping him. He was one of the few ties I had left to my girl—both of my girls, really—and even though I definitely didn't take myself for a soppy person, I found myself squeezing him and falling asleep to the sound of Brie's singing more nights than I cared to admit.

It was hard to look at him sometimes, though. He reminded me of both of them. Both of the people that I loved and had lost.

I cursed, but after hearing Brie's *don't give up* command for the second time poking at my brain, I pulled my phone out of my pocket.

Giving up wasn't on my agenda.

Forty-two: Freya

I glared at my sketchpad with fatigued eyes, my retinas burning due to the lack of sleep. Falling into a restless slumber wasn't easy for me, and my body was feeling the effects.

I ripped at my cuticles—watching as blood rushed to the surface of my skin—and glared down at my artwork, the pieces deepening my already sullen mood. Sketching my emotions onto paper was helping me come to terms with what I was feeling.

After the incident with Will, I'd refused to even look at a pencil, but after some conversations with my mom, she'd managed to convince me to lean on my sketchpad for comfort.

Blue was the distinct colour covering my page, though.

A lonesome man standing in the rain, clutching onto a *blue* umbrella.

Roaring *blue* waves crashing onto a sandy beach, the gloomy moonlight reflecting on the surface.

A woman and her small child—both of them dressed in knitted *blue* scarves and coats as they trudged through a snowstorm.

Every scene was sad, but I couldn't find it in myself to draw anything else.

My therapist was pleased, though. Despite the glum artwork I was producing, she was insistent that the fact that I was drawing again meant I was coming back to myself.

I *was* happier—not by much—but I noticed myself smiling and laughing throughout the day, and even if those moments of happiness only lasted a few seconds, it was a step in the right direction.

Hannah gently pried my sketchpad from my hands, gesturing to the scenic park in front of us. "Take a breath for me," she insisted, smiling. "This is the first sunny day we've had in a while. Allow yourself to be at one with nature."

Hannah had been taking yoga classes recently, and apparently, her instructor was a huge wellness freak. It had clearly rubbed off on her, and she encouraged me to shut my eyes and inhale deeply, allowing the crisp morning air to fill my lungs.

Being outside was more refreshing than I'd thought it would be. Getting me out of bed at the crack of dawn had been a struggle for my friend, but now that I was here, I was glad she'd convinced me to leave the house.

I knew as soon as I was alone, though, my inner demons would take the reins. I was never going to be the same person, and not only because I'd been kidnapped by Will. My heart was still beating, but I wasn't sure how. It had crumbled into a thousand tiny pieces, and there was no fixing it—not after everything that had gone on with Kaleb.

I was now able to think of his name without my stomach lurching painfully. Saying it was another story, though, and the thought of moving my mouth to form it caused my heart to twinge. I missed him. Everything about him. About us.

Was I a coward? I wasn't too sure. All I knew was that I wasn't ready to delve into the details of why things had happened the way they had. Not yet, anyway. Especially since I wasn't even sure which base he'd been stationed at.

I needed to heal first, but that was a hell of a struggle when there was a giant wedge between me and the one person I needed to survive.

Forty-three: Freya

"I can't believe *we* got VIP tickets to see Madison Ainsley!" Hannah squealed from beside me, wrapping her arm around my shoulder.

I laughed as we stopped and stared up at the massive stadium in front of us, crowds of people chattering as they swarmed in.

"I know. I've missed you," I replied.

I hadn't seen Hannah for around three weeks. We'd both been busy since scoring our new jobs after graduating from college early.

My friend was settling in nicely in her role as an artist talent scout, and I'd secured the position I wanted at the indie book cover design company. I hadn't worked on my own project yet. I was still learning the ropes and helping my colleagues with their clients.

So far, I was enjoying it—to the degree that I could.

I couldn't help but feel deflated, though. It was as if I couldn't fully put my heart into my work—because somebody else had taken it.

Tonight wasn't about that, though. It was about Hannah and I—a celebration of our new careers in the art world.

We'd purchased the concert tickets eight months ago, but when I'd received an email from the ticket company last week, claiming that we'd been randomly selected to have our tickets upgraded to meet Madison Ainsley after her concert, I was more than sceptical. I was convinced it was a scam, but after some research and a few emails, Hannah and I were both bewildered to discover it was legit. She saw the gift as a sign that we were on track.

Things didn't feel that way, though. My train was slowly veering off course.

My father had been sentenced to thirty-five years in prison, and the man that I loved had almost shot him to save my life—as well as keeping the fact that he was working to put him behind bars a secret. And to add more to the mix, I'd killed Will Sheffield.

Murderer.

Killer.

I mentally cringed, remembering my therapist's advice, closing my eyes and taking a deep breath, imagining the thoughts dissipating into thin air until my mind went blank.

Noticing the struggle in my eyes once I opened them, Hannah cupped my cheeks. "Hey, we're going to have the best time. I'm proud of us. You've got this."

I smiled, nodding at my best friend before heading into the stadium. Our tickets were scanned, and we entered the pits, squeezing past a few people for a better view. Madison was due to come out any minute, and as excited as I was, I wasn't looking forward to a few of her slower and more emotional songs. If there was one thing that Madison loved to do, it was to sing about heartbreak. That was *not* what I needed.

People surrounded me, and even though it was slightly overwhelming to be stuck in the middle of a large group of people, I reminded myself that we were all here for the same reason. We all wanted to have a good time at a concert. Nobody would be focusing on me.

The crowd went wild as Madison stepped out onto the stage, dressed in a beautiful long white dress, her dirty blonde hair curled to frame her face. It was hard not to be jealous of someone so naturally stunning. Not only that, but she was blessed with the voice of an angel. *God really had his favourites.*

Hannah and I sang along with Madison—as did most of the crowd. I tried my best not to choke up at some of the songs, pushing Kaleb from my mind before the tears threatened to spill over. Her lyrics reminded me of him, and I hated it and loved it at the same time.

You're stuck in my mind.

I want no one else, baby.

You and me, against the world.

A shiver wracked down my spine, and my mouth curved downwards as I attempted to block out Madison's beautiful voice for the remainder of the heart-wrenching ballad.

The rest of the concert was incredible, and my throat burned from singing. Hannah and I followed the sign leading to the meet-and-greet, my hands slick with sweat and my blood pumping through my veins at a rapid speed. We waited in the short line outside the red-curtained room, but I struggled to feel the excitement, my entire body numb.

"What do you think she's like?" asked Hannah as she bounced excitedly.

"I just hope she's nice." Nothing was worse than discovering that your favourite celebrity was actually a raging diva.

"Next." The beefy bouncer eyed us suspiciously before nodding, opening the curtain and gesturing for us to enter the room.

I plastered a smile onto my face, immediately spotting a beaming Madison, who stepped forward to wrap her arms around us in a spine-crushing hug. I released an exasperated laugh. However, my heart skipped a beat, and my blood turned icy when I noticed the tall, muscular man standing behind her.

Grey eyes.

Tousled dark hair.

Tattoo-covered arms.

Oh my God.

There was no way.

Kaleb.

I couldn't take my eyes off him, and his own bored into mine with apprehension, a frown masking his face. I assumed he'd left to continue work at another base, but that clearly wasn't the case.

Madison noticed my staring and turned awkwardly, gesturing to Kaleb. "Um, this is my bodyguard, Mr Evans," she said hesitantly, and Hannah's mouth popped open once she spotted who I was gawking at. "Did you girls enjoy the concert?"

I blinked, yanking my gaze away and returning my attention to Madison, nodding. I couldn't think. My thoughts were whirling around in my head like a tornado. I felt as if I was about to pass out. "Um, yes, it was incredible, thank you."

Kaleb shuffled from behind the celebrity; his intense stare focused on me for the entire three-minute interaction. I was shocked, though, because although memories of Will and my father came rushing back, haunting me, so did the happiness. The joy. The longing. It was intense—almost so intense that I nearly doubled over.

"Next," called the bouncer from outside the curtain, opening it up to reveal more squealing fans as they waited for their turn to meet the star. Madison hugged us again after quickly autographing Hannah's poster, and Kaleb stepped toward us, pulling back the curtain on the other side of the room for us to exit.

I didn't know what to say to him. He didn't seem overly surprised to see me, his eyes remaining the same size and holding the same emotion the entire time.

Enraptured? *Check*. Captivated? *Check*. Surprised? *No. Not one bit.*

My skin sizzled as I felt a warm hand gently grip my bicep, and I gulped, Kaleb, peering down at me with his jaw flexing painfully.

"Freya." He sighed, running his tongue along the front of his teeth. "I finish in fifteen minutes. Please, can you wait for me in the foyer? All I want to do is talk."

I inhaled deeply, my throat constricting. My arm tingled from his touch, dizziness taking over briefly before I blinked a few times to bring myself back to reality.

He was here. He was actually here.

"Okay." I inhaled deeply. "I'll wait."

A modest smile replaced Kaleb's deep frown, and he nodded, taking a small step away from me. I instantly missed the warmth of his touch, feeling chilled without him. "Thank you."

Hannah stared at me wide-eyed as we made our way down the long corridor, tiny droplets of sweat accumulating on my hairline as my clammy hands clutched onto my CD that I'd failed to get signed. I'd been far too distracted to ask.

"What the fuck?" Hannah muttered. "He's her bodyguard."

I nodded, exhaling in disbelief. "I know."

"What are you going to say to him?" she asked once we reached the foyer.

"I don't actually know. Seeing him again felt... weird. Everything came rushing back at once. The bad stuff, but also the good stuff. I wasn't expecting that to happen."

"I guess you just have to decide if the good outweighs the bad." My friend smiled. "I'll wait in the car until you're done."

She scurried off while I sat on the foyer floor against the wall, waiting for Kaleb. I couldn't even begin to think about what I wanted to say to him. I hadn't prepared for this. Tapping my fingers against my thigh impatiently, I stared at the enormous clock on the wall, longing for the hands to tick faster. Every second felt like an eternity. My eyes drooped.

"Freya."

I jumped at the soothing voice, noticing Kaleb standing above me with furrowed eyebrows. He'd changed out of his bodyguard uniform and was sporting a pair of jeans and a tight, long-sleeved black top. *Fuck, did he look good.*

I wiped my hands on my jeans nervously as I stood. "Oh, hi."

"Hi."

"You're still here." I paused. "I thought—I thought you would have been shipped off to another base."

"I was going to be, but I took this job," Kaleb said, grinding his teeth together, "so I could stay."

I arched an eyebrow. "What?"

"They usually give the body guarding jobs to the lower-level workers who get paid a lot less. I wanted to stay assigned to my current base, and this was the only job going, so I took it."

Madison Ainsley was a local singer. Although she was well known around the country, she didn't perform shows or travel often, hence why it was so hard to get hold of tickets. I had heard she lived just a few towns away.

"You took a lower-level job just so that you could stay here?"

"I couldn't leave, Freya. Not after... everything." Kaleb's voice was hoarse.

I clicked my tongue, resisting the urge to pick at my fingers. They were already red raw. "Did you know about my dad the entire time?"

We were going straight for the deep stuff.

"No, Freya. It was fucked that it was all linked so closely, but I only found out about your dad being involved with Will a couple of weeks before he took you. My chief can vouch for that."

It was a relief to hear that Kaleb hadn't known about my father for long, but my trust in him was still damaged, considering he wasn't honest with me.

"Why didn't you tell me? I understand you were in a difficult situation, but I deserved to know."

"You're right." Kaleb nodded. "I was in the wrong for keeping it from you. I just didn't know how to tell you. You were near graduating, and I didn't want it to mess that up for you. I was expected to stay on the case until it was closed, and I didn't know how to explain to you that your father was a wanted man and I was supposed to be helping hunt him down. It was selfish of me, and I'm sorry. Words can't describe how much I regret not admitting it to you right away."

"That night," I clamped my eyes shut, "were you going to shoot my dad?"

Murderer.

Killer.

Kaleb's voice interrupted the slimy one in my head. "I'm not going to lie to you, Freya. I don't know. I'd like to say I wouldn't have, but Will had a gun to your head, and I was willing to do anything to get him to let you go unharmed. I can't truthfully tell you what I would have done if you hadn't—" he stopped, gulping before taking in my stiff form.

Talking about it was causing everything to resurface when all I wanted to do was bury it deep inside of my brain—so far down that I never had to think about it again. My therapist constantly reminded me of how dangerous that was, though. The coping tactic never worked in the long run.

"How *is* your dad?" Kaleb asked, taking the attention away from the subject of me being a murderer.

"In prison. I'm visiting him next week."

"Right."

I narrowed my eyes. "You don't seem surprised to see me."

Kaleb dipped his chin. "I'm not. I knew you were going to be here."

"How? What did you—" Something clicked inside my brain, and my mouth popped open. "Oh, my God. You sent the email."

"Well, technically, the ticketing company sent the email," he replied, the corner of his lip curving upward. "I just paid them to do it."

I glared at him, which caused him to chuckle. Fuck, this was confusing as hell. There was nothing more I could ask Kaleb regarding my father because he truly wasn't sure if he was going to go through with Will's request to kill him or not. I wanted a definite answer, but I understood how illogical that was. It was something I'd never know.

"Tell me about work," I asked, changing the subject.

Kaleb nodded. "The bodyguard job, even though I hate it, has its perks. It doesn't actually require me to be stationed at or near the base, so I can live where I want while watching Madison—as long as it's within a reasonable distance. She's only a thirty-minute drive from me, so it works out. My contract is for a year, and I've moved into my own apartment down here."

I swallowed. "You're staying?"

"I'm staying."

We settled into silence, and my eyes raked over Kaleb's entire form. Not in a sexual way, but because I wanted to take every cell of him in. He didn't feel real, and I was concerned that my trauma had finally caused me to lose my sense of reality. *My mind wouldn't be that cruel, would it?*

"I'm sure you already know this, but I need you, Freya," he said, his fingers twitching beside him. "I miss everything about you. The situation you were forced into—it wasn't right. I'm so sorry that you were dragged into it. The last thing I ever wanted was for you to get hurt, and the guilt is killing me, but being without you is killing me more."

I hesitated before answering. "It wasn't your fault my father was a criminal."

"It was my fault that Will discovered you, though." His eyes flashed with pain. "Seeing you like that." He paused to calm himself. "I felt so helpless."

Kaleb had already gone through losing Brie, and I understood how desperate he'd been to ensure I didn't succumb to the same fate. I couldn't blame him entirely.

"I don't really remember a lot from it," I said, dropping eye contact and shuddering. "I blocked a lot of it out."

Besides the fact that you're a murderer.

Kaleb's tongue skated along the front of his teeth. "Don't do this alone, Freya. If you need to talk to someone, talk to someone. Whether that be with your mom, Hannah, your other friends, or me."

He was speaking from experience, and I didn't take his advice lightly. I knew I was due a mental breakdown soon if I didn't allow myself to fully come to terms with what had happened. I was still in denial, though. I wanted to return to my old life, the longing crushing me. I shivered, inhaling when I felt my phone vibrate from inside my bag. "Hannah is waiting for me. I should go."

Kaleb scratched at his stubble. It looked like he hadn't shaved in a few days, and I wondered how many hours a day he was actually bodyguarding Madison. Judging by how exhausted he looked, it appeared he was working around the clock.

"Freya," he said as I turned to head towards the exit. "I'll wait—as long as it takes."

Forty-four: Freya

I stood back from the computer, cocking my head as Abigail and I studied our final product. We'd been working on a beautiful book cover for the past couple of days, and after hours of effort, we believed it was finally done.

"I think the author is going to love it," Abigail said, tapping away on her computer and beaming at me. "I think you're ready to take on your own clients, Freya. You're good—way better than we would expect you to be at this stage. I know many authors that would be excited to work with you."

Elation bubbled up inside of me. "Really?"

"Most definitely. I'll speak to Roger about it. I'm sure he'll agree with me, and we can set up some meetings with some clients for you." My mentor shut down her computer and grabbed her coat off the hook. I did the same.

We'd hung back at the office late, and my mom had called me to let me know she was heading over to Jackie's for dinner. Apparently, she'd asked if I felt like coming, and before I allowed myself to overthink the situation, I agreed.

Abigail and I made our way into the office reception, and a magazine on the coffee table caught my attention. On the front was a paparazzi photo of Madison Ainsley, and behind her, holding her car door open, was Kaleb. The bags under his eyes were dark, and his mouth was set in a firm frown.

"Freya?" asked Abigail, a small chuckle escaping her mouth. "Are you a massive fan or something?" She nodded toward the magazine that I'd been examining.

"Um, yeah," I stuttered. "I went to see her in concert last week."

Abigail hummed, brushing her blonde bangs out of her eyes. "Her bodyguard is hot." She grinned at me, and I nodded stiffly, rushing out the door.

Although thinking of Kaleb stirred up emotions inside me—some positive and some negative—they reminded me I was alive and breathing, and that was something to be grateful for.

Okay. It seemed today was a positive day. Thank fuck. I needed one.

I stopped off at a bakery on the way to grab a box of brownies and pulled into Kaleb's driveway, taking a few extra seconds to park and put off going inside. I clutched onto the box tightly as I rang the doorbell, a smile forming on my face when Jackie flung the door open.

She and my mother had been made aware of everything that had happened—minus the fact that Kaleb and I had practically been an item.

She engulfed me in a hug. "Oh, Freya! How are you? You look so grown up! Wow!"

"It's only been a few months, Jackie," called my mom from inside, letting out a witchy cackle.

I stepped into the house, my shoulders tense as I gazed around the room.

Was he not here?

"Kaleb is running late," Jackie told me, taking the brownies from my hands and thanking me. "There was an incident with his client, but he's on his way back now."

Incident? Worry engulfed me, but I tried to remain neutral as I settled down on the couch, sipping the glass of wine Jackie had handed over. It helped to calm my nerves, and I resisted the urge to guzzle it down and pour myself another.

After a little while of surface-level conversation, Jackie and my mother disappeared into the kitchen to finish cooking. I found myself bored, unable to resist the temptation to search for more photos of Madison Ainsley, sifting through recent ones and noticing Kaleb in the background of more than half of them. Most of them were dated within the last month, and he looked increasingly drained as time went on. His face was the same in every photo—stone-cold, not even a glint of happiness. He looked ready to sock someone in the face.

I jumped as the doorbell rang, and I opened it hesitantly, my heart faltering at the sight of a shocked Kaleb.

"Hey," I said, stepping aside to let him in. "Your mom said there was an incident at work?"

"I didn't know you'd be coming tonight." A smile graced his lips. "And yeah, some idiot tried to pull Madison's car door open and climb inside. We all had to file a police report."

I couldn't help but admire him in his uniform. If I were some crazed fan of Madison's, I definitely wouldn't go anywhere near her with Kaleb lurking around. Every muscle was visible through his clothing, his impressive height suddenly dawning on me. I'd almost forgotten how tall he was.

Kaleb's eyes travelled down to my own attire, and he smiled. "Have you just come from work?"

I nodded. "Yeah. I work for a—"

"Book cover design company. I know."

"How do you—"

"Just because you weren't speaking to me didn't mean I wasn't keeping up to date with your life events."

I glared at him, shaking my head. "Creep."

"I thought we'd established that by now." He smirked. "I'm going to go shower and get dressed."

My heart skipped a beat, and for some reason, memories of our passionate shower sex forced itself to the forefront of my mind. My ears tinged pink, and I swallowed harshly. *What the hell had got into me?*

Kaleb cocked his head, and it seemed he knew exactly what I was thinking.

"Does that mean something to you, Freya?"

I gulped, his stormy grey eyes captivating. *Fuck, I'd missed this teasing.* Arousal bubbled up inside of me, pooling between my legs.

"Are you going to use your words, sweetheart?"

"Yes," I said breathlessly.

"Which question are you answering?"

I swallowed. "Both of them."

Kaleb hummed before smiling, stepping back and heading up the stairs.

I almost instinctively took a step after him, the electric current between us sparking and causing my skin to tingle in the most delicious way. I craved the feeling, desperate to chase it. *Shit.*

I snuck glances at Kaleb throughout dinner. He looked beyond belief when freshly showered, and it looked like he'd purposely avoided towel-drying his hair so that droplets of water trickled down his neck. He knew it was a weakness of mine.

"So, are there any cute guys at work, Freya?" Jackie asked me as I stabbed at the casserole, my eyes flashing to hers, feeling Kaleb tense next to me. He stopped chewing, arching his brow, waiting for my response.

The truth was… no. Women mostly worked at my company, and the few men we did have were much older than me—with wives and kids. I didn't have a sliver of interest in other men besides Kaleb, though. I hadn't even thought about anyone else over the past three months.

"No, not really," I said, my social battery having depleted. Not only that, but I was exhausted. I hadn't been sleeping. Will had been haunting my dreams.

Murderer.

Killer.

I mentally cringed as if I'd been scalded.

"Kaleb, Jackie tells me you've been assigned a job bodyguarding for Madison Ainsley," announced my mother. "She's an amazing singer, and I heard she's single, too!"

"Not to mention gorgeous," Jackie chimed in, and Kaleb's eyes darkened.

"I stay professional," he said. "There's a strict no fraternising with our clients' rule, and even if I were allowed to pursue something with her, I wouldn't be interested."

My chest loosened at his admittance.

The rest of the dinner went by quickly, and as delicious as Jackie's food was, I couldn't stomach a lot, my anxiety getting to me.

It was always late at night when Will's words would invade my mind, his hideous voice bouncing off the inside of my skull, reminding me of what I'd done and how evil I was. I even found myself talking back occasionally, letting him know that he deserved it and I was only defending myself, but he always chuckled tauntingly in response. The effect trauma had on the brain was frightening.

Kaleb and I hung back in the living room while our moms cleaned in the kitchen. They'd insisted they didn't want any help, but I had a feeling it was just because they wanted to sneak another few glasses of wine in. My eyes travelled to the photograph of Brie on the wall and Kaleb's own gaze followed mine before he sighed.

"Losing her was one of the worst days of my life," he admitted. "We did everything we could to stop the bleeding, but it wasn't enough. I promised myself I'd never let anything happen to the people I care about again." Kaleb's throat bobbed. "I hated who I was before I joined my organisation. I didn't realise how easily someone's life could be taken away."

"We all live with regrets. You can't punish yourself forever. Everybody makes mistakes, Kaleb."

He hummed. "But most people's mistakes don't end in them getting their little sister killed. I refused to let you succumb to the same fate, though. There was no way I was going to allow Will to—"

"I know," I interrupted him, not wanting him to say the words. My heart was battering inside my chest, my throat barren. "You don't need to say it, Kaleb. I know."

My hands shook slightly as I positioned my house key in front of the lock, shoving it in, having beaten my mom back from Jackie's house. But once I pushed the door to the apartment open, my eyes popped out of my head.

Roses. Everywhere. Tied together in large bouquets and positioned all over the living room. My throat ran dry, and I followed the trail of them leading up to my bedroom. More bouquets surrounded me—bright and bold—and I picked up the lilac-coloured note on my bed, scruffy male handwriting having been scribbled onto it.

My little artist,

I told you that if I were going to get you flowers, I wouldn't stop at fifty.

I hope this made you smile. I know breaking into your apartment and gaining worried looks from your neighbours made me do so.

-K

Forty-five: Kaleb

I quickly checked myself in the mirror, glowering at the dark circles hanging under my eyes. *God, I needed to get some fucking sleep.* I could never switch off, though. My mind was always racing, and there wasn't anything I could do to slow it down.

I caught sight of the bear Freya had given me sitting on my desk, and I clicked my tongue, my insides knotting up at the sight of him.

I was meeting her today, and although I claimed that anxiety was something I didn't have the capability of experiencing, it was all I'd been feeling for the past three months—pure, intense anxiety.

The thought of Freya not wanting me anymore... fuck. It was enough to send me to my knees. I'd do anything for her. I'd carry the world's weight on my shoulders if it meant she could live carefree for the rest of her life. I owed that to her—at least.

I reached the restaurant quickly. I'd offered to pick Freya up, but she'd insisted that she wanted to drive herself, and I wasn't going to argue with her.

"Hi," she said with a slightly tense smile once she spotted me, looking me up and down. Fuck, she smelled like vanilla. It made my mouth water. "You're wearing a shirt." She took a deep breath.

I shrugged, smirking. "I've got to look my best for the most important date of my life."

My comment caused her to roll her eyes, and the waiter showed us to our table. I'd specifically requested ahead of time that we be seated in a corner—away from everyone else. Freya struggled to relax in big crowds, and I didn't want her stressing.

"You look beautiful," I told her, releasing a content sigh. She'd pulled her hair back into a fancy-looking bun—a hairstyle I'd never seen her do before—and it caused my heart to falter.

A soft blush coated her cheeks. "Thank you. You look—"

"Like shit, I know." I chuckled. Being without my girl had an extreme effect on me. I was aware I wasn't glowing.

She shook her head. "You could never look like shit."

Our food came quickly, and Freya ordered a glass of wine to help her relax. She'd asked for the cheap stuff, but all it took was a slight nod from me for the waiter to understand that I wanted her to be served the best wine they had. The cost didn't matter.

"What's your favourite colour?" Freya suddenly asked me, and I released a chuckle, causing her to shrug, a smile gracing her gloss-covered lips. "We're on a date—as you called it—so I assume we should ask each other date-like questions."

"Alright, my favourite colour..." I hummed, smirking. "Let me see your eyes quickly."

Freya scowled at me, shaking her head. "Kaleb."

"Okay, it's blue-green. Kind of like a turquoise colour, but less vibrant. Yours?" I already knew it. Purple.

"Lilac. It reminds me of spring, and it's a pretty colour to use in artwork." She popped a piece of calamari into her mouth.

"Okay, favourite holiday?"

"Thanksgiving."

I nodded. "I don't have one."

Freya arched an eyebrow. "There isn't one you like? Not even Christmas?"

"I had to spend Christmas without you, so it left a sour taste in my mouth."

At the mention of my mouth, Freya's eyes flickered down to my lips, and I allowed them to curl up into a slight smile. "What's your biggest dream?"

My question seemed to jolt Freya from her daydream, and she blinked, attempting to bring herself back to reality. She clicked her tongue in thought. "Umm... ever since I was little, I've always wanted to visit the Louvre. There's just something about it. I feel my life won't be complete without visiting it at least once."

A chuckle escaped, remembering how Ty had expressed that Freya's talent would get her artwork in the museum one day. There was no doubt in my mind that he was right. The world needed to see the talent she possessed. It was a crime to live without it.

"What's *your* biggest dream?" Freya questioned me, tilting her head in the most adorable way, and I gazed at her with heavy eyes.

Fuck, I was utterly obsessed with this woman.

"I'm already living it," I told her, and her throat bobbed as she swallowed, nodding once before turning her attention back to her meal. I could tell she was fighting a smile, though.

After our date—which I'd insisted I paid for, much to Freya's distaste—I leaned back against the hood of my Jeep and crossed my arms, watching as she pulled her car keys from her purse.

"Thank you for tonight. I haven't been out for food in months."

"I'm proud of you," I told her, taking a tentative step in her direction. "I could tell how nervous you were beforehand."

"That obvious, huh?"

"It's not a bad thing, Freya. Nerves make you human." I was speaking from first-hand experience. I'd been a robot before I met her—working on autopilot and never allowing myself to truly feel emotions other than guilt. Being with Freya made me feel alive, though—like the world was actually rotating again. Negative emotions were a part of being human, but so were the positive ones, and before my beautiful artist had walked into my life, I'd refused to allow myself even a sliver of happiness.

She inhaled deeply, and I reached my hand forward and hooked my finger under her chin, angling it so she was looking at me. "I mean it. You're doing so well."

At my comment, Freya stepped into my chest, and I wrapped my arms around her and pressed a soft kiss to the top of her head.

The world made little sense unless she was in my arms.

Forty-six: Freya

I awoke with a gasp, my body coated in sweat and my eyes teary. My heart was pounding, causing my ribs to ache, and I glanced at my bedside clock to see that it was almost six in the morning.

Yet another nightmare. This time, I was being dragged into the depths of hell by Satan himself, his raspy laugh echoing around me and bouncing off the tongues of flames that surrounded us.

You belong here, he'd said.

This is where murderers go.

You're going to suffer for all eternity for what you've done.

There was no way I was going to get back to sleep, so I pushed myself out of bed and hopped into the shower. I was visiting my father in prison today. I needed answers. I knew nothing he would say would satisfy me, but I wanted to hear why he'd got involved with such a career in the first place. Gaining clarification was going to help with my healing—something I'd discussed with my therapist.

I stole another glance at the sheer amount of roses I had piled in the corner of my room. They made me smile. Although, my mother had almost suffered a heart attack when she came home to find them—I had stashed the majority of them—and I told her they were from Kaleb's organisation as an apology for getting mixed up in things. She believed me, but scowled and commented about it being a little excessive. She wasn't wrong, but that was one thing I loved about Kaleb. He always surprised me.

I straightened my spine as I strolled into the prison entrance, checking in and receiving a quick body search. The prison officer spent a little too long fiddling with my bra, and I resisted the urge to tell her that there was no way for me to shove anything in there when it was already filled with my tits.

My dad was waiting for me along with other prisoners, and my stomach contorted at the sight of him in his grey joggers and white T-shirt. The attire didn't suit him, used to seeing him in suits and designer shirts.

I nodded as a greeting, immediately picking up on his dark under-eyes and pale skin. It was clear he was having a rough time adjusting, having always enjoyed the lavish things in life—and this was far from it.

"I didn't think you'd show," he told me, and I clasped my hands together as I slid onto the chair opposite him, gulping. I wanted to rip at my cuticles, but I'd been trying my best to stop abusing them for the past few days.

I shrugged. "I need answers."

My father hummed, his expression unreadable. "I didn't intend for you to be dragged into all this. I did my best to keep it private."

I nodded. It didn't matter, though, because he hadn't tried hard enough. "Why would you want that life, Dad? Why not choose a normal career?"

His eyes darkened, and for a second, I feared him. He'd always had a bit of a temper, and I supposed it was why he fit into the criminal world so well. "Do you know how much money I was making, Freya? A lot. More than some crappy business job would have got me."

I scowled. "But yet we were in debt? A debt you were hiding from us. How does that make sense?"

"I didn't say I was great at saving money. I admit, I became cocky, and I spent a lot of it. I also invested it, but that backfired, and I lost most of my earnings. Then I fucked Will off by losing our stock, and I couldn't afford to pay my way out of it."

"You were selfish," I stated, leaning back in my chair, trying to remain as calm as possible. The surrounding prisoners could smell fear, and I was concerned that they'd pounce if they were to get a whiff. "You put both Mom and I in danger, and we almost lost everything because of you."

I had to admit, though, if my father hadn't been such a fuckup, I never would have met Kaleb—the only positive thing to come out of it.

"I don't regret the money I made us," my father said nonchalantly. His demeanour was a vast difference from the panicky man he'd been when Will had a gun to my head, but adrenaline changed people in wonderful ways. This was who my father really was. Cold. Detached. And selfish. "I provided you and your mother with a good home, and we were able to take expensive vacations when you were younger."

"How was that all worth it? You lost all the money, you and Mom got divorced, I almost ended up being killed, and now you're in prison."

"We have different morals, Freya. You value the life of others, and I'm not so bothered. I'm happy that you're content with having such a normal life. It means you won't end up in the same situation I'm in."

Was my father admitting to being part of the murders? He hadn't been charged with them. There wasn't enough evidence, but deep down, I felt like I knew the truth. A chill ran down my spine.

Like father, like daughter.

Taking a deep breath, I grimaced. This wasn't helping at all. If anything, it was making me angrier because I knew there was no saving him—this was who he was.

"I need to go," I said, rising from the chair. "When you learn to actually feel remorse for everything you've done, including fucking up other people's lives besides just your own, take a break from rotting in your cell and give me a call."

Not that I'd answer.

My father's eyes flickered with irritation as he watched me leave the prison.

He hadn't been a good person for most of my life. He'd done nothing but cause me pain and dejection, and I was much better off without him.

Ty gazed at me over his coffee cup, his eyes bleak and his face solemn. I hadn't seen him since the incident, and I didn't know how to feel. I was sitting opposite my friend, and I'd killed his uncle—right in front of him.

"Well shit," he muttered, running his hand through his hair and chuckling in disbelief. "This is completely fucked."

I dragged a hand down my face. "Yeah, I know."

"Freya, I swear. I had no idea what Will was going to do. I didn't know he was some psychotic drug lord. He was always a little strange, but I thought that was just because he needed some medication or something." Guilt pooled in his baby-blue eyes.

"Ty, you know I don't blame you. I'm pretty sure he was going to kill you, too. I'm sorry for—"

"If you apologise again, I'm going to throw hot steaming coffee in your face." He smiled, shaking his head at me. "How are you doing, though? Like seriously?"

It was a question everyone had been asking me lately, but I played it down every time. I wasn't sure what I was supposed to say.

Oh yeah, Will haunts me in my sleep, and I can't get the fact that I killed someone out of my head to where I stay awake all night or throw myself so deep into work that I can't stop for days at a time, but other than that, I'm great, thanks.

"I'm seeing a therapist, and it's slowly helping. I know it's her job, but I can't help but feel awkward opening up about everything to her. I think I'm afraid she'll judge me."

"There's nothing you can say that'll surprise a therapist. They've heard it all, so don't feel you need to hide from them."

"Maybe ice hockey isn't your calling, Ty."

He chuckled. "I think I was a psychiatrist in my past life."

The sun was setting, and my thoughts were becoming just as dark as the sky outside. I wanted to head home and distract myself with some stupid rom-com movie and a pint of ice cream, so I excused myself and began the drive home.

My eyes were drawn to the road leading towards Kaleb's house, and I passed it slowly. We hadn't spoken too much over the past few days besides a few texts. He'd been working long shifts bodyguarding

Madison, and I'd been distracted creating myself a portfolio of projects I'd helped complete at work.

My mother was out tonight, so I had the house to myself, and I buried myself in my bed and wrapped myself up in the covers as I attempted to focus on my laptop screen. But the movie sounded like gibberish. Nausea wavered through my stomach, and I released my grip on my ice cream tub and set it aside.

Murderer.

Killer.

Murderer.

Killer.

"Get the fuck out of my head," I spat with gritted teeth, slamming my laptop shut as Will's face flashed in my line of vision. I clamped my eyes shut, shaking my head and cursing.

My heart hammered, and I bit down harshly on my bottom lip until the taste of iron filled my mouth. It sent me right back into that basement, blood trickling down my chin as one of Will's butlers struck me, my wrists painfully bound behind my back.

The pain.

The heartache.

The way my world had shattered in the space of a few hours.

I released a desperate sob, reaching for my phone and dialling the number of the only person I knew could overpower Will's venomous abuse.

"Freya?" Kaleb muttered through the line.

My breathing was shaky.

"Freya? What's happened?"

"Can you come over?" I asked, my voice wavering and my teeth chattering.

"I'll be there as soon as I can." I heard shuffling and then the purr of a car engine before I hung up the phone, my tingling hands unable to support the device's light weight any longer.

Pulling my knees to my chest, I took deep breaths, trying to calm my racing heart. This wasn't like me. I was usually so calm and easygoing, and I was furious with myself that I had allowed Will to change me. He was haunting me from hell, and I guaranteed he was loving every fucking second of it.

Murderer.

Killer.

Murderer.

Killer.

Murderer.

Kill-

I jumped as my bedroom door was pushed open, and Kaleb appeared in the doorway, a frown taking over his beautiful face. How long had I been sitting in bed shielding myself from Will's cruel words?

"How did you get in here?"

"I know how to pick locks, Freya," Kaleb said, shrugging, making his way over to me slowly, perching himself on the edge of my bed. "What's going on, baby?"

Tears fell from my weary eyes, and I placed my hands on either side of my head. "He won't leave me alone."

Kaleb's brows creased as he reached for me, wrapping his large hands around my wrists and prying them from my head. "Who?"

"Will. He's in my head. I'm going fucking crazy."

He shushed me, pulling my sobbing form into his arms and rocking us back and forth slowly. He stroked my hair, saying nothing. But he didn't have to. His presence alone was calming enough, the smell of his cologne wafting up my nostrils. I buried my face in his neck with clenched fists.

"You're not going crazy, my little artist," he told me, pressing a soft kiss to the top of my head.

"I am. I'm a murderer." Snot dripped from my nose. "I shot him in the face. He couldn't have survived that, Kaleb. He tells me every night. I can't sleep. He's always there in my head, laughing at me because he's going to see me down in hell."

Kaleb shook his head. "You're not going to hell, Freya. I can promise you that." He looked pained, running his tongue along the front of his teeth before nodding towards my laptop. "What were you watching?"

I followed his gaze, sniffling. "Um, just some stupid romance film."

"Great, let's watch it together." He manoeuvred us so that he sat with his head against my bed frame; my body curled into his with my head on his chest. The steady beating of his heart soothed me, and I clutched onto the hem of his black T-shirt tightly and attempted to steady my breathing.

Will's murderous threats all but disappeared as I snuggled into Kaleb's side. One of his hands circled me while the other rested behind his head, the position causing his T-shirt sleeve to roll up, exposing a part of his shoulder.

Colourful ink captured my attention, and I cocked my head. The space on his skin hadn't been tattooed months ago, and the new artwork intrigued me. But, when I caught sight of a bird's blue wing spread out—feathers sticking up as wind swirled around the creature—I narrowed my eyes.

"What is that?" I mumbled, nodding towards his shoulder, and Kaleb clicked his tongue, revealing the entire tattoo.

The tattoo of *my* drawing.

My eyes turned to saucers, and I leaned over him to slide my fingers over the ink. "When did you—"

"I took the sketch out of your pad a while ago."

"And then you got it tattooed?" I questioned, shock rocketing through my body.

Kaleb had a permanent reminder of me on his body.

"It's my favourite piece."

My lips parted as I studied it, gazing up at him with knitted brows. "More than the cobras?"

He laughed, pressing a soft kiss to my forehead. "More than the cobras."

Forty-seven: Kaleb

Freya had fallen asleep around twenty minutes before the film ended. She'd explained that she hadn't been sleeping well lately, and after seeing how soundly she was doing so on my chest, I refused to move.

Her skin was dull, and her eyes had been lifeless, and for every hour she was unconscious, I knew her body and mind were healing. If staying here was going to keep her nightmares at bay, then that was what I was going to do. Every night. Until she no longer needed me. Regardless if I was desperate for a piss or not. I could hold it.

I didn't have work today, but I'd organised something for Freya. Judging by how much she was struggling with the thought that she was a cold-hearted killer, it was much needed, and I hoped this would comfort her.

"Good morning, beautiful," I whispered as she opened her eyes, appearing slightly confused before she dropped her head back down on my chest. "Time to get up. There's someone I want you to meet today."

Freya arched an eyebrow at me but obliged, showering while I waited in the car. The last thing we needed was for her mom to see me and bombard us with questions about what was going on between the two of us. We were going to explain it when the time was right.

"Where are we going?" Freya asked me, and I admired her with a smile. How could someone be so beautiful without even trying?

Her eyes flickered to the gun stuffed into my waistband, and her jaw tensed before she averted her gaze, causing me to move my jacket to cover it quickly. The last thing I wanted to do was trigger her, but my gun was something that I would never leave the house without. Her well-being was my priority. But so was her safety.

"To meet a friend of mine," I said, starting the car and pulling onto the road.

The journey wasn't long—filled with casual conversation—and I parked outside a small bungalow.

"I know you won't," I said, opening Freya's door and helping her out, "but don't stare."

"Stare?" she muttered, and I smiled, knocking on the bungalow's front door.

Pierce opened it with a smile, and Freya's dark eyes widened briefly before she composed herself, plastering a smile onto her face.

"Kaleb," Pierce cheered, holding his hand out for me to shake. "Nice to see you again. Please, both of you, come on in."

We settled onto his leather couch, and Freya shuffled uncomfortably, fiddling with her fingers in her lap.

"My name's Pierce. I used to work with Kaleb." My old colleague grinned. "Let's not beat around the bush. You're probably wondering why I look the way I do."

Pierce's face was disfigured. He'd undergone countless surgeries, but the doctors could only do so much for him. He was blind in one eye, and his skin was lumpy—indents scattered across his face from where the surgeons had attempted to stick the flesh back together.

Freya chewed on the inside of her cheek nervously.

"We were on a raid, and I got shot in the face." Pierce chuckled. It was always something he found funny, and I gathered that humour was his way of coping with what the event.

"How did you survive?" Freya's mouth popped open.

He shrugged. "More people survive from being shot in the face than you think. The recovery wasn't easy, and I'm out of work because of it, but I'm still here."

Freya turned to me, realisation slapping her in the face. She knew what we were doing here. She was adamant that she'd killed Will by shooting him in the face, but Brent and I had also fired at him milliseconds later, and I'd aimed right for his chest.

There was a chance that Freya had killed him, but there was also the possibility that it was actually Brent or I who'd done it. She may not have been the one to deliver the fatal blow. The human body could survive miraculous things, and Pierce was a walking example. I refused to allow my girl to live with the guilt of a death that may not have been at her hands.

"I may have lost my good looks, but at least my wife still stuck by me." Pierce released a loud cackle, taking a sip of his ginger tea.

He babbled on about the raid and his recovery for the next couple of hours, with Freya interjecting to ask a question now and then. I'd already heard the story a thousand times, so I sat in silence and let Freya gather the information she needed to ease her destructive mind.

When it was time to leave, it looked as if some kind of weight had been lifted from her shoulders, and she took a deep breath as she buckled her seatbelt up.

"I know it might not mean a lot, but I wanted you to know that there is a possibility that you weren't the one that killed Will," I told her.

She smiled, her eyes becoming slightly teary. "Thank you. Not just for that, but for everything. I've never had anyone fight for me like this before."

"When you're the only thing grounding me to this Earth, you're more than worth fighting for, Freya. I'm nothing if not with you."

"Kaleb, that's not true."

I chuckled. "You are the only thing that keeps me sane, and *when*, not *if*, but *when* you fully accept me again, I'll be here. Even if I have to wait a lifetime."

I grunted as I pushed the barbell up for yet another rep, sweat trickling down my bare chest before I wracked it. Working out had been the only way to stop me from stalking down to the prison and gripping Mark's neck until he was red in the face. The thought that what he'd got his own daughter involved in had affected her to where she couldn't sleep or even think in peace irked me.

The sound of the doorbell to my apartment ringing pinched me from my thoughts, and I wiped my sweaty hands on my grey sweatpants before opening it. Surprise took over when I spotted a sheepish-looking Freya.

"You're early," I said.

"Sorry," she muttered, stepping in, her gaze fixated on my shirtless form. "I thought the drive would take longer, and frankly, I was excited to see the place."

I smiled. I wasn't complaining about getting to spend more time with her.

My apartment was pretty nice—since I had the money to afford a swanky one. It was around a twenty-minute drive from my old house, which meant I could easily stop by and check on my mother when I needed to.

"Still not subtle with your staring, I see," I teased, chuckling, causing Freya to narrow her eyes at me.

"Still not subtle with your arrogance, I see," she remarked.

God, I wanted to kiss her. So badly. But this was on her terms. I understood there was a boundary, and I would not disrespect her by crossing it when she wasn't ready.

Her mood had improved since our visit to Pierce. It didn't kill off her inner demons in one big swoop by any means, but it helped, and that was all I wanted. Step by step. Little by little.

"You said Brent was on his way?" Freya looked unnerved by the thought. They'd been friends, and he'd also lied to her about her father. It wasn't easy for him to do so, and I knew he felt guilty about it.

"And Kaylee," I responded as I gave her a tour of the apartment. "Their flight landed about thirty minutes ago, so they should be here in the next hour."

Freya nodded, distracted by my large king-sized bed, her eyes skating over the soft fabric covering it before she sighed. I knew what she was thinking, and it caused the flaming pit in my stomach to flourish.

I showered while she waited in my bedroom for me, cuddling under my blankets and tapping away on her phone, looking for inspiration for a new design for a client. She'd received her first project to complete alone and was panicking about not coming up with something good enough.

That thought was laughable, though. The talent she possessed was unmatched.

"Freya," I called from the bathroom.

"Yeah?"

I ground my teeth together. "I left my towel out there. Can you please grab it for me, sweetheart?"

I heard her shuffle around for a few seconds before she opened the bathroom door, my towel clutched in her hands. I hadn't asked her to come in, but her curiosity had clearly got the best of her, and her gaze travelled down the entire length of my body. Her lips parted, her pupils dilating.

"Baby, you're going to need to stop looking at me like that," I took a step toward her, "before something happens that I know you're not ready for."

I would never touch her—not if she didn't want me to. But right now, it looked like lust was clouding her judgement, and I didn't want her to allow something to happen, only for her to regret it later.

Freya sucked on the inside of her cheek, holding her head high. "How do you know what I'm ready for?"

I cocked my head. I could feel the blood rushing to my dick at her words, and she seemed to notice it, too, her eyes growing. "Your body language speaks volumes, my little artist, and you're still tense around me."

Her shoulders immediately dropped, indicating that she'd suddenly realised how strained they were—despite how turned on she was.

"I'm not going to touch you until you show me you're completely and utterly comfortable." Taking the towel from her and tying it around my waist, I moved towards the doorway, lingering behind her. "Until then, don't forget that you're still mine."

Her eyes fluttered closed, and she tilted her head back, a gasp leaving her lips when she realised how close my own were to her skin.

"You were mine the second I laid eyes on you after you opened my front door for me, thinking I was a pizza delivery guy. You were mine after we first kissed at the shooting range. When I first buried my fingers inside of you and made you come for me, and when you became the first woman other than family that I've ever loved."

Her eyes snapped open.

"And if you ever forget that, I'll be right here to remind you—in whatever way you desire. But only when I know you're well and truly ready."

Work had been a killer. Madison was gaining more popularity due to her recent shows, and the paparazzi weren't easing up. I had no problem threatening them, though. All I had to do was flash them my gun, and they took the hint and backed off.

I'd been thinking about Freya all day—my mind filled with memories of last night. My arms wrapped around her as she slept in my bed after a night in with Brent and Kaylee. I'd given them strict orders not to mention anything about the incident unless Freya did first, and although she looked a little nervous around Brent, she enjoyed the evening.

My hands tightened against my steering wheel. I was struggling to let go of my desire for revenge on the people who had actively harmed Freya. Will's crime ring was large, and I was aware there was no way we'd caught everyone who had some kind of involvement. All of Will's finances had been frozen and seized, though, and without his money, his crime ring had nothing.

My eyes narrowed as I gazed down the long, windy road that led to his shooting range, and in a split-second decision, I turned the wheel. The barren and dreary building came into view, a few more windows having been smashed since it'd been abandoned. There were more than likely a few squatters in there.

Lifting weights had become my vice—besides Freya—since a shooting range wasn't so accessible, and although the searing pain that accumulated in my muscles felt good when I pushed my body to its limit, it wasn't quite the same as the sensation of a handgun kicking back in your palm after firing it.

I made my way into the building, ignoring the *permanently closed - do not enter* sign. Shoving the heavy glass door open, I waltzed down the corridor and into the main area. Everything looked the same. The floor was still sticky from spilt beer. Bullets coated the floor. And dust was collecting on top of the tables and chairs.

Nearing a target, I began firing, relishing in the sensation of having a deadly weapon at my fingertips. Bodyguarding involved little gun work. I had it as a precaution, but so far, I hadn't had to use it—which was a damn shame.

I smirked, satisfied when all four of my bullets hit the centre of the target, but when I heard a voice from behind me, I turned with my gun drawn.

"Excuse me, you need to leave the premises."

My eyes widened.

Frederick.

"Kaleb?" he questioned, appearing shocked, but he quickly wiped the disturbance from his face.

I lowered my gun. "What are you doing here?"

"The building is due for demolition in a few days, and I was sent down to scope it out beforehand. I'm just here to take final photographs before getting a crew in to clear everything out in preparation for the building going down."

Everything had been seized from the property—including weapons, drugs and files, but since everything was in Will's name, there weren't many people we could legally lead things back to. They'd also found Mark Henderson's personal cell phone, and it dawned on me that it'd probably been Will who'd answered Freya's call, where she heard nothing but breathing.

"You shouldn't be in here, you know," Frederick reminded me, and I chuckled.

"There wasn't a *no trespassing* sign. Legally, you can't do anything."

That caused him to smile. "I'm going to get to work."

I followed him, narrowing my eyes at his attire. He wasn't in his work uniform. Instead, he was dressed in all black—including gloves and a beanie. Not a good look for an older fellow.

I gazed around the place in boredom as Frederick snapped a few photographs, humming to himself as he manoeuvred through the dirty building. He spluttered, wiping at his nose. "God, Will didn't keep up to date with his cleaning, did he? I've never seen a place so unkept. I'm hoping this is my first and last time visiting. It's fucking up my lungs."

I cleared my throat, studying Frederick as he moved over to a door—a barely noticeable supply closet in the corner. It blended into the wall easily, and even I'd missed it until Frederick brought my attention to it.

There was a pin-pad to the left, and he nonchalantly entered the code and flung the door open, sighing as he snapped more photos of the space filled with unused cleaning supplies.

I froze. "How did you know the code?"

"What do you mean?"

"The code." I nodded towards the pin-pad. "You knew it—off by heart."

Frederick turned to me agitatedly, the creasing between his eyebrows deepening as he ground his teeth together.

"The workers who initially came in here to seize everything would have broken the door down to get inside, and judging by the fact it's still intact, and the supplies are still there, that indicates they missed it and didn't go in. That would mean the initial code that Will set still stands." I stepped closer to Frederick, my fingers twitching beside my gun.

"Kaleb, I don't think—"

"Let's just say they *did* leave the door coded and the supplies still in there for whatever strange reason, wouldn't you be reading it from a note? You punched in that number a little too casually for my liking—almost as if you've done it a hundred times before. It's also worth mentioning that you're not in uniform." I glowered. "Is this really your first time here, Frederick?"

He glared at me, and his long fingers wrapped around the gun hanging from his waistband, causing me to do the same, aiming it at him.

"Drop your weapon, Kaleb. That's an order!"

"Your order means nothing to me," I spat.

"What are you going to do? Bring the evidence to your chief? I could relinquish both of you from your duties at the drop of a hat. Don't be so foolish." His voice was venomous, and it was with that threat that I knew Frederick wasn't who he said he was.

"How long have you been working with Will?"

"You're a good worker, Kaleb, but you know I'm going to have to kill you now, right?" His nostrils flared, and I smacked his arm away just as he pulled the trigger on his gun, the bullet soaring past my head. Shoving him against the wall, I pressed my forearm into his throat as he fought against me, gasping for breath.

He kicked out, and I grunted as his booted foot came into contact with my shin, giving him an opportunity to land a punch to my side, and he raised his firearm again. I ignored the pain, though, gripping him by the throat and slamming him to the ground with a loud *thud.*

"How's Freya coping, Kaleb?" Frederick managed to gasp with a smirk, and I ripped his gun from his grip, causing his bloodshot eyes to widen, panic seeping into his fine lines. Flinging it to the ground behind me, I pressed the barrel of my own weapon into Frederick's chest.

"You fucking traumatised her," I seethed, malice dripping from my tongue.

My fucking boss. He'd been a part of this. He'd played a role in kidnapping my girl and fucking up her life.

"What are you going to do now, then, huh? Kill me?"

I cocked my head at him, angling my gun down and firing a bullet straight through his thigh. He released a deafening scream, the sound piercing my eardrums. "That's exactly what I'm going to do." I crouched down beside him, gazing into his blazing eyes. "Let this be a message to anyone you're working with, Frederick. You touch what's mine, and you fucking burn."

I blasted a bullet through his other thigh, and tears streamed down his face as blood spurted from his wounds. I'd ripped open vital arteries, and Frederick was going to bleed to death in roughly three minutes, but that didn't mean that I couldn't make it the most painful three minutes of his life.

I wasn't usually so sick and sadistic. Murder wasn't something I cherished being part of—unless the person deserved it. Then, I relished in the idea of being the one to rip their soul from their body. When Freya was involved, anyone that even so much as thought about hurting her was going to face an agonising fate.

"Do you want money? I can give you money," cried Frederick, and I clicked my tongue, sighing mockingly.

"You don't have any money, Frederick."

He shook his head. "I will. I'm working with a hacker, and he was going to get all of Will's funds sent to me! The movement was going to be completely untraceable! Let me live; half of the money goes to you, I swear!"

I hummed. "So that's why you wanted him to get caught." It was the reason Will had switched up on Brent and me so quickly—Frederick had come to him and told him what we were when the time suited him. I tutted. "Unfortunately for you, Frederick, your money means nothing to me. I only want one thing from you."

His eyes bulged as he pressed down on his wounds with as much force as he could muster, attempting to stop the relentless bleeding. "What is it? I'll give you anything you want."

"Good." I nodded once, smiling down at him. "I want to hear your screams for mercy."

Moving to the bar in the room's corner, I grabbed the liquor bottles and poured them over the floor, arching my eyebrows as Frederick tried his best to crawl his way to the exit. It made me chuckle. A fucking snail would get there faster.

I saved the last bottle of whisky for him, taking a quick swig of it and dunking it over his body, soaking him head to toe. He screamed in pain as the alcohol seeped its way into his wounds.

Opening a cabinet next to me, I searched through the empty drawers until I found an old lighter.

"Kaleb, don't do this!" Frederick begged. "A promotion? I can give you a promotion! You can take my job. I—"

I tapped my foot impatiently against the sticky wooden flooring before crouching next to him again, shushing him. "Frederick, do me a favour."

He gulped, shaking his head, muttering incoherently.

"Burn bitch." I then set the floor alight, stepping back and watching as the room around me erupted into glowing, hot flames. The fire wrapped itself around Frederick, yells pouring from his mouth as he wriggled, swatting at it pathetically.

I observed him for a few more seconds before exiting, taking one last look at the burning building, and starting my car.

I wasn't going to stop at the shooting range. If Freya was going to burn, everything around her would go up in flames, too. That way, she wouldn't feel so alone.

Forty-eight: Freya

"This is good, Freya," Robert—my boss—said as he looked over my work. "Really good." He pushed his glasses further up onto his face.

"Thank you." My body heated slightly. I'd been so nervous about running my final design for my first solo client by him, and I hadn't expected him to be so complimentary. He wasn't a man of many words.

"I'll get this sent over to the author straight away. They might have some minor tweaks they want to make, but overall, I'm very impressed." He closed the tab on his computer. "You can pack up your things and head home. Good work today."

Thanking Robert, I exited his office, clenching my fists with excitement and resisting the urge to yip with joy. I'd been enjoying work more, and I had a feeling it had something to do with the fact that Kaleb was back in my life.

When he was around, it was like there was a clear path to take. Nothing was blurred. A bright, white light shone above me, leading me in the right direction.

My phone buzzed.

Kaleb: I'm picking you up today. I'll be outside in five minutes.

I smiled, heading over to my desk and packing my things away. Kaleb's sparkling black Jeep was waiting for me.

"Cab for Freya?" He grinned as he flung the door open for me, and I rolled my eyes as he began to drive—in the opposite direction of my apartment.

"Where are we going?"

Kaleb shot me a grin. He'd just come from work, and I salivated at the sight of him in the bodyguard uniform. Tight black clothing that showed off his delicious muscles and tattoos. Including part of *my* tattoo.

"There's a grand opening for a huge new late-night bookstore just outside of town. I thought we could go and take a look at some of the art. Give you some inspiration for your upcoming clients."

"You hate art." I laughed.

Kaleb hummed. "I like *your* art."

He knew how stressed I'd been to receive my own clients, and although Robert had liked my first design, that didn't mean I had an endless vault full of ideas. Artists needed to pluck inspiration from somewhere sometimes, and browsing book covers in all kinds of different genres was going to be a massive help.

The drive didn't take long, and when we pulled up, the bookstore owner was outside, giving a short speech. The small crowd buzzed with excitement, and Kaleb clutched onto my hand tightly as he glanced at everyone suspiciously. Even though I was no longer in danger from Will and his employees, Kaleb still scrutinised everyone that came within ten feet of me, his eyes narrowing at them before he decided they weren't a threat and he could move on to the next person.

"Let's go," I said excitedly after the owner stepped aside with a grin, the small crowd piling in.

Looking around the bookstore was useful, and I took some reference photos of a few book covers that followed a good colour story and had unique sketches on the front, hoping they'd inspire my next creation. We used our computers at work for the final design, but all covers started with a sketch—and that was my favourite part.

Kaleb and I ascended yet another set of stairs leading up to the top level. We were completely alone. So alone you could hear a pin drop.

"This one is nice," I said as I picked up another horror novel, my fingers skating over the smooth cover.

Kaleb leaned back against a bookshelf, crossing his arms over his chest as he watched me, causing me to turn to him, raising an eyebrow.

"What?"

"Nothing." He smirked. "Am I not allowed to admire my girl?"

My girl.

My feet were frozen to the ground as he stepped closer to me, gazing down with curious eyes. They flickered to my lips for a brief second before he dragged them back up, biting on the inside of his cheek. My palms became slick, and the book I was holding dropped to the ground, causing a small gasp to escape my lips. Bending down in front of me slowly, Kaleb picked it up, staying on one knee on the ground. Our eyes were locked in on each other. I couldn't move them, and I didn't want to either. My back was up against a bookshelf, and although it appeared as if I was trapped between it and Kaleb in the corner, he left a small space for me to squeeze out of if I needed to.

"Kaleb." I inhaled deeply. "Kiss me."

Searching my face for any sign of hesitancy, he rose to his feet, hooking his finger under my chin. I allowed my eyes to flutter shut, knocking my head back on the shelf behind me, and the feeling of his lips connecting with the skin of my neck made me seize up.

I'd been without this for months, and now that I was getting another taste, I couldn't fathom how I had gone so long without him.

"You just tell me when to stop, baby," Kaleb breathed onto my collarbone, and a small moan fell from my mouth.

My mind was numb but buzzing at the same time. I was feeling nothing and everything all at once, and before I knew it, Kaleb's lips were on my own. I immediately responded, cupping his stubbly cheeks and grazing my hands upwards until they were tangled in his dark hair. They yanked on his strands, gaining me a pleasurable grunt from him.

I smiled into the kiss. But suddenly, the trajectory of my mind altered, and I found images of Kaleb clutching onto his gun and firing bullets into Will's already blood-covered body flashing before my eyes.

Murderers—the both of you.

I pulled back, placing my hands on his chest and firmly pushing him away. My heart vibrated inside me, and I took a few deep breaths.

Fuck this.

I refused to allow Kaleb to be a trigger for me, and I attempted to pull him back down, but he tilted his head at me, swiping his thumb over my bottom lip.

"There's no rush, baby. Don't push yourself past what feels right. You know I'll wait."

"You won't wait forever," I muttered. If I couldn't get my shit together, Kaleb was going to pack up and leave. He wasn't going to admit it to himself, but unless I could move past what had happened, he wouldn't have any other option. I wouldn't allow him to derail alongside me.

He ran his tongue along the front of his teeth. *Oops.* "That's where you're fucking wrong, Freya. I *will* wait forever, and when forever ends, I'll wait after that. If you aren't ready in eighty years and we're nothing but bones in the soil under people's feet, it doesn't matter because I'll be patient well into the afterlife. One day, you'll fully accept me again, whether in this lifetime or the next, and as long as I get to call you mine, it'll be worth it."

Forty-nine: Freya

A laugh bubbled up my throat as I almost kicked Kaleb in the face, his fingers still skating against my heels. I dragged myself off the couch, my throat burning from my squealing. "Don't tickle my feet, you psycho."

He grinned at me, his shirtless form splayed out on the couch, looking god-like as always. I'd been staying at his apartment the past couple of days, and we both had today off. I'd made us breakfast while he worked out, and he'd showered and thrown on some grey sweatpants—a hell of a contender for my favourite outfit of his.

"Okay, no more tickling." Kaleb held his hands up defensively. "Get the lotion from my room, and I promise I'll actually rub them this time."

I narrowed my eyes into slits and stalked into his bedroom, grabbing my bottle of strawberry-scented body lotion that sat on top of his chest, but before I could turn to exit, a glint of metal in the corner of the room caught my attention.

Handcuffs hung limply over the back of his desk chair.

Kaleb was a cop, so it made sense that he had them, but I'd never seen a pair in person before. I jostled them in my hands, and a mischievous thought popped into my head, causing me to grin. Stuffing them into my back pocket, I waltzed into the living room and stopped in front of Kaleb.

"Why are you smiling like that?" he questioned cautiously, and I shrugged, moving to stand in between his legs. I placed my palms on his shoulders, rubbing softly.

"I want to give *you* a massage," I lied, trying to hold back my smile when Kaleb groaned in bliss as my hands kneaded his muscles. Once I noticed he'd closed his eyes in contentment, I took the handcuffs from my pocket and slapped one around his wrist.

"What are you—" He watched me with furrowed brows as I encased his other wrist in the metal, stepping back and laughing.

"That's for tickling my feet," I said as Kaleb stood, and he huffed at me, wiggling his hands in frustration. "Maybe I'll just go and take a nice warm bath and leave you like this."

My teasing wasn't appreciated, and he pursed his lips, his eyes dangerous. However, I couldn't help but notice the obvious bulge in his sweatpants, and my heart fluttered, my arousal blossoming.

At one point in time, it had been almost impossible for him and me to keep our hands off one another, and I missed that greed we possessed. It was still there but rooted deep within my body, struggling to force its way through the anguish and worry filling my muscles and cartilage.

"I won't be very happy to be left like this, sweetheart," Kaleb warned, his form towering over me, causing me to gulp. My eyes lowered to his hard cock again, and before I knew what I was doing, I dropped down to my knees in front of him. My hands found their way to the waistband of his sweatpants, and I dipped my fingers in, studying Kaleb's facial expression.

He looked uncertain and tilted his head at me, silently asking if this was what I wanted. I didn't even need to answer him, though. My blushed face and hazy eyes were enough to give me away. That, and the fact that I was tightly squeezing my legs together in an attempt to stop the throbbing of my pussy from flourishing. I hadn't been this turned on in a very long time.

Releasing a pent-up breath, Kaleb craned his neck back and cursed under his breath; his hands balled into fists.

I pulled his dick free and shuffled his sweatpants down his legs, leaning forward to stroke the tip of his cock a few times with my tongue. Months of built-up frustration was scratching at me from the inside, desperate to escape, and although my inner demons were lingering at the back of my head, eager to take control, I shooed them away.

They would not ruin this for me. This was my life. My body. My mind. They couldn't control me.

"Freya," Kaleb groaned as I took most of him in my mouth. "Holy fuck, baby." He began to move his hips slowly, gently thrusting into my mouth, his dick hitting the back of my throat.

I gazed up, and I could see the irritation lingering in his eyes as he glared down at the handcuffs, causing me almost to laugh.

"I've missed those lips wrapped around me," he said. "You're so fucking good at taking all of it. That's it, keep fucking taking me."

The praise caused me to moan, and I sucked harder and faster, my free hand gripping the base of his dick to keep it still. Kaleb's thrusts soon became rougher, and I opened my mouth as wide as it could go, the room filled with his moans and grunts.

"Look at me with those gorgeous eyes." Kaleb cursed loudly, his jaw twitching as he dragged his bottom lip into his mouth.

Pleasuring someone had never felt so good, but all I wanted to do was please Kaleb. Fuck, just watching him fend off his orgasm drove me wild.

His thighs shook, and the jangling of the metal handcuffs above my head caused my stomach to tighten in humour. Teasing this man was my favourite pastime.

My mouth was soon filled with hot cum, and I gulped it down, the liquid salty. I dipped my fingers down into my sweatpants, finding my clit. However, Kaleb pulled out of my mouth, tutting, crouching down in front of me.

"Let me see that pretty pussy of yours, Freya." He nodded to the fabric, and I slowly yanked my bottoms off, throwing them behind me. My legs parted on their own accord, and I leaned back on my forearms, giving Kaleb a perfect view. I breathed heavily as he studied me, his gaze settling on my slick thighs. "So fucking beautiful."

His fingers were gentle as they caressed me, swirling over my wetness, his touch so delicate I could barely feel it. It only made me want him more, though.

"I need it Kaleb, please."

He arched a brow. "Hmm? What do you need?"

I growled in frustration. "I need you to make me cum."

"Have we forgotten our manners today?"

"I need you to make me cum. Please," I said between gritted teeth, although, I secretly fucking loved it.

"Good girl." Kaleb wasted no time dipping his head down, licking up my wetness before sucking my throbbing clit into his mouth, his tongue swirling around it menacingly. His teeth scraped against it, and I yelped, feeling him smirk against my skin.

"Fuck, Kaleb, don't stop. I need more."

He sucked me until I was a heaving mess, and I gripped onto his shoulders as if trying to pull him impossibly closer.

"If you let me out of these handcuffs, I'd be able to make you feel even better."

My teeth instinctively dragged my bottom lip into my mouth as I smiled, shaking my head. "No can do, Mr Evans."

The nickname seemed to spark something inside of Kaleb, and he grunted, a low growl emitting from his chest before he licked me like there was no tomorrow. My muscles were so tense they were cramping up, but pain had never felt so good. So warm. So inviting. My tits bounced as I gyrated against Kaleb's face, desperate for more. My body jolted, and a shrill scream of pleasure bounced off the walls of the apartment as I came undone, my toes curling. "Oh my fuck," I moaned, my nails scraping at the carpeted floor as I clamped my eyes shut, euphoria wracking my entire being. I felt as if I'd been hauled to an entirely different planet, my mind cloudy and vision blurry.

But after a few minutes of heavy breathing, my moans having fizzled out, Kaleb peppered kisses down the inside of my sweaty thigh. "Now that you've come back down to Earth, get me out of these damn handcuffs, Freya."

His request caused a hearty laugh to escape my mouth, and I pushed myself up into a sitting position to plant a gentle kiss on his lips.

"It's great to actually see you smile, Freya," my therapist told me, offering me one of her own. She placed her clipboard down in front of her. "Now tell me, what about your old self is it that you miss?"

I twiddled my thumbs. "I was always so sure that I was a decent person, but ever since the incident, I've had doubt. It's slowly disappearing, but I'm worried that I'll never be able to get back to the person I used to be."

She hummed. "Well, what if you could merge the old version of yourself with the new version of yourself? Both the old you and you now possess excellent qualities, and I believe it would be a shame to lose what you've learned since the incident."

I scrunched up my brows. I'd never thought of it that way. Since being kidnapped, I'd noticed I was much more sensitive, but perhaps that wasn't necessarily a bad thing. It had been a habit of mine to pretend I was okay, even when I wasn't, but I was slowly allowing myself to open up to others.

"Maybe you're actually more in touch with your emotions now? The confidence will come with time, but you seem more honest about everything—not only with what happened to you with your kidnapping but also with your parents' divorce and the assault you suffered at the hands of a boy from college."

My therapist and I had dug deeper into my past. In the beginning, I hadn't been overly willing to talk about it, claiming they weren't the reasons for my need for therapy. But now, looking back at it, I realised that I'd allowed everything to build until I was smothered. The situation with Will had been the final straw that had thrown me off the cliff's edge.

"I understand it's hard, but if we can begin looking at the positives regarding the situation, healing will become much easier for you. Even if you still focus on the negatives, just accepting that there *are* some positives will allow you to accept your past."

I left the session with a skip in my step, feeling relatively positive, and when I felt my phone buzz inside my pocket, I pulled it out and beamed down at the text from Kaleb.

No way.

Fifty: Freya

I couldn't believe it. *I* was at a celebrity party. Madison Ainsley's party, to be exact. With Kaleb. He was off the clock, having finished right before it had started, and he'd sent me a text to let me know Madison had asked if I wanted to come too before he picked me up.

"It was really nice of Madison to let you have a plus one," I told him as we made our way through the hall.

"We're a package deal." Kaleb flashed me a smile, taking my hand in his. He looked incredible tonight in his blue shirt and slacks, the sleeves rolled up to reveal his forearms, his hair styled messily on top of his head.

"Remember, we can leave whenever you want."

Therapy had been going well, and although I was still plagued by nightmares some nights, I reminded myself that there was a chance that I hadn't killed Will. I was clinging to that when occasionally teetering on the edge of insanity. But the relief that washed over me whenever I thought back to Pierce's situation stopped me from plummeting over the edge.

"*This* is Madison's house?" I spluttered.

"One of them." Kaleb smiled. "Not only does she make money from her singing, but she also invests in properties, which makes her a lot of money. She's a smart woman."

I felt a flash of envy briefly reach the forefront of my eyes, and Kaleb chuckled before I had the chance to conceal it.

"Relax, my little artist. You're the only one I want."

I shivered at his words, arousal gushing from my pores at the huskiness of Kaleb's voice, and his large hand travelled down to the curve of my hip. Pushing back against him, his chest became flush against my back, and I breathed in a sigh of contentment.

"I don't really want to be getting a hard-on in the middle of Madison Ainsley's foyer, Freya," Kaleb told me, his hot breath fanning against the back of my neck, causing me to stifle a laugh.

There weren't too many people in attendance. Madison preferred to keep her circle small, which only heightened the feeling of honour that I'd been invited. If somebody had told me a few months ago that I was going to be visiting Madison Ainsley's house, I would have laughed in their face and asked what drugs they were on. Life could change so quickly—for the better, but also the worse.

The crowd buzzed with excitement, and Madison rushed over once she spotted us, her eyes a little hazy. It appeared she'd already been on the alcohol.

"You made it!" She beamed, turning to me. "Freya, it's so good to see you again. I still can't believe you came to my meet-and-greet and reconnected with an old lover who just so happened to be my bodyguard!" A cackle rose from her throat. "What are the chances?"

Not like Kaleb had helped put it into play or anything.

"I know. Thank you for letting me come tonight. This place is beautiful," I exclaimed, sneaking a glance over her shoulder to look at the huge dessert table.

Eclairs. Jello. Cake. A fucking chocolate fountain? I was in heaven. If there was one thing I was usually good at, it was eating my feelings.

"Of course, so listen. I've been speaking to your boyfriend a lot about his tattoos since I'm so desperate to get some. He told me you designed the beautiful bird on his shoulder."

My eyes widened.

"I've been searching for someone to draw some designs for me, and it would be amazing if you could be the one to do it. You clearly have talent, and to be honest, that's hard to find around here. Most people are overrated, in my opinion." Madison bounced on her feet hopefully, looking as if she was the fan and I was the acclaimed celebrity.

Designing tattoos? I'd never considered it.

"I don't expect you to do it for free, of course! I'll pay you a good fee for your time."

I released an exasperated laugh. "Of course. I would love to."

"Thank you so much. Let me grab your number, and we can talk about it."

She punched my number into her phone before skipping off happily, and Kaleb laughed from beside me. I turned to him with a cocked eyebrow.

"I swear, I didn't push her to do that at all." He flashed his white teeth. "She made that decision all on her own. Although I can't say I'm not jealous that I'll no longer be the only person with your beautiful artwork tattooed on their body."

"Well, you'll always have the honour of being the first," I teased.

"You have no idea how much I'm going to love telling people that."

Love.

The word replayed repeatedly in my mind. My thoughts raced back to the moment in Kaleb's bathroom when he'd confessed that I was the only woman besides his family that he'd ever loved, and I shivered, having been wanting to bring it up to him but lacking the confidence. I had to leap head first, though. Nobody got anywhere by being safe.

"You said you loved me." My voice was quiet.

Kaleb paused before nodding casually. "Because I do. I'm utterly in love with you, Freya Henderson. Every inch of my mind is filled with your existence. There's no one else I'd rather be obsessed with, and I don't use that term loosely." My gaze travelled to his lips, my eyes desperate, and he cleared his throat. "If you want me, you're going to have to make the first move, sweetheart."

Kaleb grunted as I wrapped my arms around his neck and pressed my lips to his. He tasted like mint and dominance, causing me to melt. All I could think about was the sensation of his fingers digging into my waist and his stubble grazing against my chin as he pulled me impossibly closer. "Kaleb," I whispered as I pulled away, meeting his gaze, his stormy eyes darker than usual, and I smiled to myself as I felt his hard dick graze against my stomach through his pants. "I need you."

There wasn't anything I needed more than him.

My therapist and I had been working on my belief of being deserving of love and pleasure. My mind self-sabotaged itself by conjuring up gruesome images whenever Kaleb and I would get close to reaching another milestone. It was a trauma response to keep myself stationed in the same comfortable position, but I couldn't stay motionless forever. The train was leaving the station, and waiting for the next one was going to do nothing but delay my healing.

Kaleb arched an eyebrow and studied me carefully, tracing his fingers down my neck and across my shoulder, looking for any sign of reluctance. My muscles were free and flexible, though—not an inch of tension invaded them. I'd been working on loosening up my body. It hoarded stress.

I deserved love.

I deserved pleasure.

"I need you to understand what you're saying to me, Freya." Kaleb's voice was slightly strained.

I nodded. "I do."

He dipped his chin, gripped my hand, and led me through the small crowd and down a narrow hallway. It led to a cute study—a mahogany desk placed in the room's corner and bookshelves surrounding us, filled with classic literature.

"On the desk," he ordered me after closing the door. I adhered, hiking my dress up so I could lift my legs. My thighs were slick with arousal, and I leaned back against the wall, watching as Kaleb trailed his fingers up and down the skin of them, dangerously close to my core. "I love seeing how wet this pussy gets for me." He smirked.

My underwear was already soaked, and I muffled a moan as he dragged the fabric aside and sunk two fingers into me, his thumb swiping against my clit teasingly.

"Oh, fuck." My nipples hardened against the fabric of my forest-green dress, rising into stiff peaks, and a shiver wracked through me as Kaleb teased them.

"Have you missed me, my little artist? Have you missed the feeling of me inside of you?"

I nodded, gulping, feeling my walls tighten around his fingers, a pit growing deep in my abdomen as I pushed myself further against him, encouraging him to thrust his digits faster. My heart felt like it was going to explode, and I clamped my eyes shut and took a deep breath when Will's voice threatened to appear inside of my head. But

I barricaded him well before he had the chance to speak, opening my eyes again and focusing on the man working my pussy in front of me.

He quickly pushed me over the edge, and I gripped the front of his shirt as I reached my peak, moaning loudly and kicking my head back, bright white stars flashing in my line of vision. My orgasm was so intense that it left me dazed, and as I composed myself, I leaned forward and unbuttoned Kaleb's pants. Mischief pulsated through me as I pulled his cock free. Studying it, I licked my lips, placing my sparkly heel on his muscular chest when he tried to take a step toward me.

I shook my head.

"What do you want me to do, Freya?" Kaleb swallowed, and I cocked my head at him, raising my eyebrows.

"Beg," I muttered. It was my time to smirk. I wanted him in the palm of my hand. I wanted to call the shots. I wasn't in control of most things in life, but this? This was something I was, and fuck, did it feel great.

Kaleb looked like he wanted to object, but he slowly dropped to the ground in front of me, his eyes blazing. "Please let me fuck you, baby."

I moved my hands from the desk to my pussy, playing with myself, smiling at the way he shivered, his fingers twitching. "You want to fuck me?" I asked, tilting my head.

"Yes, baby," Kaleb said, his Adam's apple bobbing up and down. The sound of my wetness filled the room, and he closed his eyes, leaning his head back until it was pointed towards the high ceiling. "Jesus Christ, Freya. You're killing me here, sweetheart."

"Tell me why."

His eyes shifted to a dark smoky colour. "Because I want to do nothing more than throw your legs over my shoulders and fuck you until you're screaming my name—so loud that everyone on the other side of this wall knows who you belong to."

I hummed in approval. "Then do it."

Kaleb needed no more encouragement before he got to his feet, pulled out his wallet and slipped a condom on, pushing into me. His size stretched me out, but the slight sting only turned me on more, and I yelped as he grabbed my legs and placed them over his shoulders as he fucked me senseless, my fingers finding their way to my clit.

"You look so good with my cock inside you," he grunted, the sound of our skin slapping filling the room.

I clawed at his chest, my nails scraping at his tattooed skin. I'd never willingly taken drugs before, but I imagined that this was the kind of ecstasy users eagerly chased—the type of elation that filled every pore on your body and sunk into your bones, rooting itself so deep that it became a part of your soul.

"Be a good fucking girl for me and take every inch."

My whole being was on fire—as if I was drowning in a pit of lava. The heat was indescribable, though. The dictionary didn't possess the words to express how good it felt.

"Don't stop. I need it harder," I whimpered.

Kaleb grunted. "Your pussy is so fucking greedy, Freya. Look at it, taking all of me."

"Kaleb, fuck," I moaned, my insides tightening again. "Holy shit. I love you."

Silence filled the room, and Kaleb abruptly ceased his movements before he leaned down to gaze at me dead in the eyes, his face stunned. "What did you just fucking say?"

I dragged my bottom lip into my mouth, sucking on it for a few seconds. "I said I love you."

My confession seemed to ignite something deep inside of him, and he gripped onto my thighs tightly as he fucked me harder, pushing my dress up higher so that my tits were accessible to him. He pinched my peaked nipple, harsh groans falling from his lips. "Say it again."

"I love you. Fuck, I love you." Heat erupted through me, and I released again, my pulsing walls causing Kaleb to pump into me a few more times before he finished too. Our heavy breathing mingled—filling the air and making it impossible to breathe, and Kaleb leaned down to press his clammy forehead to mine, planting a loving kiss on my lips.

"Come on," he said. "Let's get you cleaned up and go and enjoy the party."

Madison flinched again as the tattoo artist pressed down on her skin, his pierced bottom lip jutting out with concentration. He narrowed his eyes at her, demanding she keep still.

"I won't get ink poisoning, right?" Madison asked for the third time.

"No, but I *do* have to commend you for getting such a sizeable piece for your first tattoo." The tattoo artist smirked. "It's brave."

Kaleb was on the clock, but Madison had wanted me here to watch her get my design tattooed on her skin. The studio had been booked out completely, and her other bodyguards stood watch at the door, ensuring no crazed fans tried to barge their way in.

"Look at you," Kaleb said to me with a smile. "A tattoo designer to the stars."

I rolled my eyes, swatting his arm. "It's a one-off."

Madison snickered. "That's what you think. Once I show my friends, they're all going to want *the* Freya Henderson to design their pieces!"

The cash was tempting. Madison had forked out way more than I'd thought necessary when I sent her my sketches, but money was no issue to her. She probably made more in a week than I did in an entire year.

I glanced over at the piercer, who sat patiently at her station, picking at her nails with boredom.

"Want to get matching nipple piercings?" I joked, glancing up at Kaleb, and he glared at me, fighting a smile.

"Baby, if you want a nipple piercing, I'm more than happy to do it for you when we get home," he offered, and the bodyguard beside us reddened, shuffling awkwardly from side to side as he attempted to block out our conversation. It caused me to laugh, and Kaleb checked his watch, clicking his tongue. "Alright, I'm done for the day. We need to get going."

Taking one last look at Madison's almost-finished tattoo, I requested she send me a photo when the artist was done before we exited the studio. My eyes honed in on Kaleb's body as we climbed into his Jeep, spotting his shiny gun that poked out from the waistband of his jeans, his shirt having ridden up slightly. He immediately pulled it back down when he saw me staring, his jaw clenching as he cleared his throat.

"You don't have to hide it from me, Kaleb," I said, even though the sight made me shiver. "I understand that it's part of your job. You're not you without your gun."

Silence.

I sighed.

"Do you think you'll ever be able to look at one and not think about what happened?" Kaleb asked me, and I shrugged. My gun had been seized by the police after the incident, and although they had offered it back to me, I'd told them to keep it. I didn't want nor need it.

"I don't know. I'd like to think that one day I'd be able to be around one and not feel uneasy, but my body seems to go into panic mode whenever I even think about them." I pinched my eyebrows together. "Have you found a new shooting range to go to?"

"I have. It's just outside of town." Kaleb appeared on edge talking about it, and he quickly glanced at me, analysing my facial expression and body language with furrowed brows.

It made me scowl. I didn't want to be seen as breakable. Flimsy. Frail. My triggers would not control me. This was fight-or-flight, and I didn't want to surrender.

"Show me," I said, and Kaleb gripped his steering wheel tightly, running his tongue along the front of his teeth at an agonisingly slow speed.

"Baby, I don't think—"

"I want to go, Kaleb." My tone was low. "I'm serious. If I freak out, we can leave, but the only way I'm going to get past my issues is to work on them. Ignoring them won't benefit me."

He hummed, tapping his fingers against the steering wheel as we stopped at a red light. His biceps were tense. "If that's what you want."

It looked as if he wanted to put up a fight, but he clicked his teeth shut, turning the radio on and setting the volume to high. Loud music interrupted intense thoughts, and I gathered it was some psychological trick to get me to remain calm. Kaleb had done his research on trauma, and it warmed my soul.

The journey wasn't too long, and the new shooting range was nothing like Will's shady, run-down building. This one was clean and professional-looking, and we'd received the necessary checks before we were allowed in.

Anxiety was riddling my body, the sound of guns being fired causing my muscles to cramp and my head to spin, but I elbowed it aside. Kaleb comfortingly placed his hand on my lower back, leaning down to whisper, "if you need a distraction, all I need is the word," in my ear.

I smiled to myself. I hadn't immediately legged it for the exit after hearing gunfire and smelling the muskiness of hot metal, and that was a win in itself.

Murderer.

Kill—

I forced the voice from my head, imagining the words disappearing into nothingness, taking Kaleb's hand and pulling him towards an open spot. The target hung from the far wall in the shape of a person, and Kaleb furrowed his eyebrows, gazing around the room.

"Let's pick a different spot. There are circular targets over there." He pointed to the far corner of the room.

I took a deep breath. "No. This one is fine." I gestured for him to begin, and he moved past me slowly, his hand grazing my ass, causing me to stiffen. It made him chuckle, and he sent the bullets flying straight into the centre of the target with ease.

Watching him do something so easily—it was a massive turn-on. This was something Kaleb could do blindfolded. Or in his sleep. Or even blindfolded while asleep.

I placed my sweat-covered hand on his gun when he was done, and he moved behind me, pressing his torso to my back. Images of our first encounter at Will's shooting range flashed before my eyes, remembering how distracted by him I'd been when he'd been manoeuvring my fingers with his own.

We had come full circle.

My instincts were screaming at me. They wanted me to throw the weapon across the room and pelt out of the building, but I remained grounded, imagining that my shoes were glued to the floor and there was nothing I could do but face the music.

"Ready?" Kaleb muttered huskily into my ear. "All you have to do is fire when you're ready."

I nodded, attempting to steady my shaking digits, and I took a deep breath. My eyes closed for a few seconds before I fired the gun, realising that Kaleb had released me and was standing back with a small smile.

The bullet hadn't gone remotely near the target, but it wasn't about that. I'd actually managed to fire a gun after not even being able to even think about one for months without spiralling.

"That's my girl," Kaleb said with a grin, spinning me around and planting a soft kiss on my lips, lowering my hand and prying the gun from my fingers. "You did it."

I nodded. My throat was dry, and my body was shaky, but I *had* done it. Was I going to pick up shooting as a new hobby? Not a chance. But knowing that the last bullet I'd fired hadn't been one to lodge itself into someone's skull—it felt like I was moving on.

Moving on from the girl who loathed herself because of what she'd done.

Moving on from the girl who constantly wondered why her father cared about his job more than her.

Moving on from the girl who was floating through life without much of a purpose—whose future was uncertain.

Kaleb Evans was my new future, and I was a much better and braver person because of it.

“What if she hates me for it?” I asked with concern as we hovered in front of the door to Kaleb’s house.

My comment caused him to chuckle. “Hate you for making her son happy? Freya, that’s not going to happen.”

This was what I’d been dreading—admitting to Jackie and my mother that Kaleb and I were in a relationship and that it'd been going on for a while. They were going to have a million and one questions, and I couldn’t get the image of their shocked and confused faces out of my mind. I loved this man, though, and I was hoping they wouldn't be offended that we hadn't told them sooner.

Jackie and my mother were seated on the couch, and Kaleb clutched my palm in his as he cleared his throat to gain their attention, causing their eyes to dart to our linked hands.

“Can we talk to you two for a second?” I asked.

“Am I correct in guessing that it has something to do with the fact that you two are holding onto each other like your lives depend on it?” my mother said, arching an eyebrow.

“Yes.” Kaleb's voice was calm and collected.

Jackie laughed, slapping her hands down on her knees before standing up. “Well, it’s about time. Sarah and I were getting tired of pretending we didn’t know something was going on between you two.”

My mouth popped open, and I stared dumbfounded as my mother released her own throaty laugh.

"What? How did you—"

My mouth ceased its movement as Jackie held up her phone, a photo of Kaleb and I kissing on the front porch flashing up on her screen.

The porch cameras. *Shit.* I'd completely forgotten about them.

"I wasn't sure if you actually used the login I gave you," Kaleb said, fighting a smile.

"Well, I did. Once, and this was what I saw."

My eyes narrowed up at Kaleb. "It doesn't seem like you to forget about the cameras."

He shrugged, a smile creeping up onto his face. "I didn't. I just didn't care if they saw. Nothing was going to make me hide the fact that I love you."

Jackie and my mother gazed at us with adoration, and my shoulders sagged with relief, a small laugh bubbling up my throat.

"Does anyone fancy a celebratory drink?" suggested Jackie, pulling out a bottle of wine from the cabinet. "It was hard work playing the naïve moms who didn't suspect a thing."

Fifty-one: Freya

Abigail placed her hands on my shoulders as we stood backstage, forcing me to look into her enthusiastic eyes. "Freya, you've got this. All you need to do is head onto the stage and collect your award. There's no need to make a big speech or anything."

"I'm going to say something," I told her, nervously twirling my hair around my finger. "Being given this award is a big deal, and I don't want to disrespect Robert by acting like it's not."

Abigail shrugged, smirking at me before she leaned over to swipe a bottle of tequila from the table next to us, pouring me a shot. "For the nerves."

I gulped the battery acid-like liquid down, holding back a gag. "Well, if I didn't feel like I was going to throw up before, I do now."

She shushed me, pointing out onto the stage, where Robert continued his speech about the company before he clicked a button on the controller in his hands. The slideshow behind him switched to the next slide, where a large photo of me beamed out at everyone.

Oh, fuck.

"Now, it's time to move on to our coveted Designer of the Year award!" Robert beamed. It was one of the first times I'd seen him smile properly, and I wondered if it was because Abigail had also forced *him* to take a tequila shot with her earlier. "I'm sure it comes as no surprise to anyone who it's going to. Freya Henderson has been with us for just over eight months, and she's received the most positive feedback from clients to date! Not only that, but the traffic she's gained for the company is admirable. We're busier than ever because of her designs. Freya, come on out!"

Abigail squealed from next to me, and I straightened my cream-coloured blouse before striding out on stage, grasping Robert's hand in a firm handshake.

The spotlight beaming down on me was blinding, but Kaleb's grin caught my attention as I squinted out at the crowd below. He cheered loudly, and I blushed.

Beside him were Hannah, Josh, Brent, Kaylee and Ty—who all whooped loudly, embarrassing me further. Madison had also been invited since she and I had become friends—I'd designed tattoos for a few of her celebrity friends, and my waitlist was now in the months—but her manager had decided against her attending. He claimed my company wouldn't appreciate dozens of paparazzi trying to force their way into the hotel building to get a snapshot of her at an event, and as disappointed as I was that she hadn't made it, I knew her manager had a point.

Kaleb had signed another year-long contract to remain her bodyguard. He'd learned to enjoy the role, and it was a major plus that Madison had offered him a shit tonne more money to stay.

Although, his chief had been on his back about rejoining his team, letting him know he could pull a few strings and get Kaleb a job on the frontline again for next year—since he had been promoted due to Frederick's... disappearance.

Kaleb wasn't keen to take him up on the offer, though. He missed the work but claimed nothing was worth being away from me for. He was settling into the low-risk life of being a bodyguard, and I could tell he was a lot less stressed since he wasn't worried about being killed every time he left the house—the house we now shared.

I'd also taken up public speaking, and I visited different trauma recovery groups every other month to share my story. It was liberating knowing I was helping others who had fresh trauma. It meant I hadn't gone through it all for nothing.

Robert thrust a shiny gold trophy into my hands, gesturing for me to approach the microphone.

"Thanks, everyone." I cleared my throat. "This year has been crazy. I didn't expect so many people to love my work, but I definitely didn't do it alone. Abigail." I gestured towards backstage, where she looked at me with wide eyes, her face turning red before she hesitantly made her way out. "Abigail was the best mentor I could have asked for, and even to date, I still look up to her. If there's anyone that deserves this award, it's her."

She wrapped her arm around my side and gave me a squeeze, and we made our way off stage and lingered at the back of the crowd before Robert announced the bar was open, causing everyone to cheer, the music starting up again. After Abigail engulfed me in a spine-crushing hug , she excused herself to grab a drink, and I beamed as Kaleb and the others approached me.

"No cash prize?" Brent teased, making me roll my eyes as Hannah squished my face.

"I'm so proud of you!"

Kaylee linked her arms through Brent's, nodding towards the bar. "I say we go and celebrate with shots."

Kaleb nodded. "We'll be right there." He took a few steps towards me as everyone rushed off, and I gulped as his finger found my chin. "I can think of a much better way to celebrate than shots."

I hummed teasingly. "Oh really? Is that so?"

"I can show you if you'd like?"

"What kind of person would I be to turn down a celebration?"

That was all it took for Kaleb to grip my hand and lead me away from the crowd. We moved through a few double doors until we reached a spiral staircase leading to a small booth right above the stage. A thin layer of glass separated us and the crowd, and I peered through to see our friends cheering as they downed shots, bouncing to the music.

Kaleb trailed his fingers down my cheek, smiling at me and pressing his lips to mine—the kiss desperate and dominant but full of love and passion. Wetness pooled between my legs, and I moaned into his mouth as he began to unbutton my blouse, throwing it to the floor at the same time I dropped my trophy.

His hard cock strained against his jeans as he pushed up against me, and my breath hitched when I felt him grip my hips and spin me around, his hand moving up my back so he could gently push me down, leaving me bent over for him.

"Look at all of them down there," Kaleb said. "Unknowing that their most prestigious designer is up here about to get fucked until she's seeing stars."

I gulped, gasping as he slowly peeled my skirt off me, leaving me in nothing but my lilac lingerie set.

"What would Robert think if he knew about this?" Kaleb bent down and latched his mouth onto my pussy from behind, having moved the fabric of my underwear to the side.

"Shit." I gripped the metal of the windowpane, my fingernails feeling as if they were about to snap from the force.

"Good girl. Let me hear how good I make you feel." Kaleb's voice was husky, and I quivered at the tone. He lapped at me, and I pushed myself further against him, indicating I wanted more, causing him to chuckle. "So impatient."

"Please, Kaleb."

"Fuck, I love it when you beg."

The sound of a condom wrapper being ripped open caused my insides to tense in excitement, and a small yelp escaped my mouth when I felt the tip of his cock press against my entrance. Before I could beg him to hurry, he slammed into me, gripping my hips harshly.

"Getting fucked at a work party—it's very unprofessional of you." Kaleb scolded. "But the fact that you wore this skimpy little set underneath your clothes makes me think this is precisely what you wanted."

He was right.

"Fuck, harder, Kaleb." My eyes rolled back. "Oh, shit."

He pounded into me, his cock hitting my sweet spot with each thrust, and I met every one of them, angling my head to look back at my god-like man. But Kaleb tutted, reaching forward to grip my chin and turn it back towards the window.

"Keep your eyes on them. Watch how oblivious they all are to you taking my cock up here."

Knowing how wrong of a setting this was to fuck in—it made it all the better. Moisture dripped down my thighs, and with the symphony of our moans and grunts filling the room, Kaleb circled my clit with his fingers, causing me to pant.

He continued to pound into me until I came loudly, my pussy clenching around his cock, and he grunted, pulling out, gripping my ass and manoeuvring me so my back was pressed up against the window, my legs wide. He slid in with ease.

"If any of them down there were to look up, they'd see you with your legs wide open for me." Kaleb groaned and smacked his hand down harshly on the window next to my head, experimenting to see if anyone could hear us. My mouth hung open as I came again, and he kept eye contact with me as he finished, too, my name leaving his lips over and over again.

"Shit." I clung onto his neck, my body shaking and my chest heaving. "I love you."

He smiled, pressing a lingering kiss to my forehead. "I love you too, my little artist."

Epilogue: Freya

"This is incredible!" I exclaimed in a hushed tone, tightly gripping Kaleb's hand as we strolled through the wide hall inside The Louvre. It was my twenty-third birthday, and as a surprise, Kaleb had organised a trip to Paris.

My mouth had practically dropped to the Earth's crust when he'd pulled out the plane tickets and ordered me to pack a bag. I was surprised I hadn't combusted with excitement.

This place was like nothing I'd ever seen before. Windows lined the ceiling, giving us a magnificent view of the shining sun, and reflections of light glistened along the lined walls. Everything inside was so regal—from the benches to the skirting boards. Nothing lacked finesse. Pillars towered above me; cylinders of white granite helping to hold the building together, the stone cool to the touch.

The artwork was stunning, and I gaped at the pieces, turning around to scowl at Kaleb whenever I noticed him trying to snap a candid photo of me.

"How's Ted liking it?" I asked with a laugh, and Kaleb grumbled, glancing over his shoulder to take a look at the fluffy bear poking out of the top of his backpack.

"Ted? You're still calling him that?" he teased me, rolling his eyes.

"Well, you refused to name him."

I'd told Kaleb to bring Ted along, and it didn't take much to convince him to stuff the bear into his bag before we left for the airport. In a way, Ted symbolised Brie, and although Kaleb and I both knew that, it wasn't something we said aloud.

It was our way of involving her without actively saying her name—despite the fact that Kaleb was getting so much better at talking about his sister. I was proud of him. So proud it almost made my heart burst.

"See that empty space there?" He pointed at an area on the wall that was void of artwork. "Right there is where your art is going to be hanging. I guarantee it."

His comment caused me to roll my eyes, and I folded my arms over my chest. "A girl can dream."

Wrapping his arms around me from behind, Kaleb placed his chin in the crook of my neck. "There's no need to dream when it's going to be reality."

"The faith you have in me is frightening."

Kaleb glanced over his shoulder, nodding at the bear. "What do you think, Ted? Don't you think Freya will make it as a successful artist one day?" He hummed as if listening to Ted's response, turning to me with a smile. "Yep, she agrees."

I froze.

She.

Kaleb knew Ted was a boy, but the slip-up caused me to grin, and my heart swelled.

"Well, tell *her* I really appreciate it." Glee swarmed me.

Both of us were fully aware we weren't talking about Ted.

I'd done a lot of healing over the past year, but I hadn't been the only one. Kaleb and I needed each other. We'd saved one another from ourselves, and there was nobody I'd rather be than the person I was when I was with Kaleb.

I was grateful for it all.

The hurt.

The pain.

The joy.

The love.

It had shaped me into the person I was always meant to be.

Acknowledgements

Thank you to Nick and my parents, who have been my biggest supporters.

About the author

Lottie Moore is an author from the United Kingdom whose love for romance led her down the path of writing her own spicy, action-packed novels. When she's not writing, she can be found hanging out with her cocker spaniel or going to pub quizzes with her friends.

Follow her on Instagram for exclusive content and sneak peeks: @lottiemooreaauthor

Printed in Great Britain
by Amazon

46739824R00216